Praise for Hank Schwaeble and *Damnable*

"Flat-out fabulous. Hank Schwaeble's distinct voice is like a seasoned pro's. *Damnable* kept me breathlessly glued to the pages from start to finish. Fast-paced, edgy, and gripping."
—Cherry Adair, *New York Times* bestselling author

"Hank Schwaeble is a new, talented voice on the scene. He writes with a confidence that could be called swagger if he wasn't so good. *Damnable* is a powerful tale that employs the best elements of many genres to create something fresh and irresistible." —Thomas F. Monteleone, award-winning author of *The Blood of the Lamb*

"With his debut novel, *Damnable*, Hank Schwaeble steps into territory usually dominated by Dean Koontz or the Preston and Child duo, and solidly holds his ground. This is one of the most suspenseful, inventive, and consistently surprising first novels I've read in years, and is certain to put Schwaeble on the map in a big way."
—Gary A. Braunbeck, Bram Stoker and International Horror Guild–award winner

"Fast-paced and tension ratcheting, Hank Schwaeble's *Damnable* is a page-turner sure to satisfy the most fickle supernatural-thriller junkie. This one definitely won't be collecting dust on your nightstand." —Deborah LeBlanc, author of *Morbid Curiosity* and *Water Witch*

"Hank Schwaeble's *Damnable* is a first-rate fusion of horror, suspense, and noir. There are plenty of creeping chills and chilling creeps here for every fan of the dark. Schwaeble takes the horror-action novel to the max." —Tom Piccirilli, award-winning author of *The Cold Spot*

"*Damnable* is chock-full of deeply flawed but intensely intriguing characters, simultaneously unconventional, disturbing, and remarkable. Its flare for the macabre makes the suspense tingle, and the story ling[...] [...]esome kickoff." [...] *Times*
be[...] *Pursuit*

...long after the final page. One of ...

—Steve Berry, *New York Times*
bestselling author of *The Charlemagne Pursuit*

DAMNABLE

HANK SCHWAEBLE

JOVE BOOKS, NEW YORK

THE BERKLEY PUBLISHING GROUP
Published by the Penguin Group
Penguin Group (USA) Inc.
375 Hudson Street, New York, New York 10014, USA
Penguin Group (Canada), 90 Eglinton Avenue East, Suite 700, Toronto, Ontario M4P 2Y3, Canada
(a division of Pearson Penguin Canada Inc.)
Penguin Books Ltd., 80 Strand, London WC2R 0RL, England
Penguin Group Ireland, 25 St. Stephen's Green, Dublin 2, Ireland (a division of Penguin Books Ltd.)
Penguin Group (Australia), 250 Camberwell Road, Camberwell, Victoria 3124, Australia
(a division of Pearson Australia Group Pty. Ltd.)
Penguin Books India Pvt. Ltd., 11 Community Centre, Panchsheel Park, New Delhi—110 017, India
Penguin Group (NZ), 67 Apollo Drive, Rosedale, North Shore 0632, New Zealand
(a division of Pearson New Zealand Ltd.)
Penguin Books (South Africa) (Pty.) Ltd., 24 Sturdee Avenue, Rosebank, Johannesburg 2196,
South Africa

Penguin Books Ltd., Registered Offices: 80 Strand, London WC2R 0RL, England

This is a work of fiction. Names, characters, places, and incidents either are the product of the author's imagination or are used fictitiously, and any resemblance to actual persons, living or dead, business establishments, events, or locales is entirely coincidental. The publisher does not have any control over and does not assume any responsibility for author or third-party websites or their content.

DAMNABLE

A Jove Book / published by arrangement with the author

PRINTING HISTORY
Jove mass-market edition / September 2009

Copyright © 2009 by Hank Schwaeble.
Cover art by S. Miroque.
Cover design by Rita Frangie.
Text design by Kristin del Rosario.

All rights reserved.
No part of this book may be reproduced, scanned, or distributed in any printed or electronic form without permission. Please do not participate in or encourage piracy of copyrighted materials in violation of the author's rights. Purchase only authorized editions.
For information, address: The Berkley Publishing Group,
a division of Penguin Group (USA) Inc.,
375 Hudson Street, New York, New York 10014.

ISBN: 978-0-515-14691-2

JOVE®
Jove Books are published by The Berkley Publishing Group,
a division of Penguin Group (USA) Inc.,
375 Hudson Street, New York, New York 10014.
JOVE® is a registered trademark of Penguin Group (USA) Inc.
The "J" design is a trademark of Penguin Group (USA) Inc.

PRINTED IN THE UNITED STATES OF AMERICA

10 9 8 7 6 5 4 3 2 1

If you purchased this book without a cover, you should be aware that this book is stolen property. It was reported as "unsold and destroyed" to the publisher, and neither the author nor the publisher has received any payment for this "stripped book."

DAMNABLE

PROLOGUE

❖

THE BRUNETTE AT THE COUNTER WITH LOOKS TO DIE FOR, the homeless-looking guy staring through the window, and the man sitting across from him who called himself Benny were all vying for Garrett's attention, but it was doughy, balding, and surprisingly calm Benny who was still getting most of it, since he was the one negotiating the murder of his wife.

"So, when would you, uh, do it? How long before, you know . . . ?"

Garrett took another sip of his coffee. Lots of sugar, lots of cream. It tasted like crap. Sweet, creamy crap.

He lowered the cup, deciding it was too hard to screw up a pot of coffee that badly. Coffee was like pizza and sex—no matter how bad it was, it was usually still pretty good. The taste must have been caused by something else. Present company, most likely.

"That depends," he said.

The man nodded rapidly, as if Garrett's response made perfect sense. Garrett signaled for the waitress, held up his cup, and dipped his head toward it. She came by with a shiny metal pot and gave him a refill as Benny fidgeted and stared at the half-eaten croissant in front of him. Maybe not so calm, after all. Garrett thanked the woman and watched her walk away, deciding she was too skinny. Nothing compared to the babe at the counter. Not even the same sport, let alone league. It was all mental masturbation anyway— he was spoken for, and in a big way. *And getting bigger by the day*. That thought, coupled with a reminder of why he was there, threatened to make him laugh, so he coughed instead, clearing his throat. He dumped two plastic tubs of cream, followed by two packets of sugar, into the ceramic mug and picked up his spoon.

The coffee shop was busy for a weekday afternoon, but not full. Benny had picked the area, but Garrett had picked the spot, based on a recommendation that it was unlikely to be a place he'd bump into anyone he knew. It was like every other coffee shop he'd ever been in. The old-fashioned ones, at least; not the yuppie chains offering expensive blends in foreign sizes. People came for the chance to talk, read, or grab a bite. They sure as hell didn't come for the coffee.

"I suppose you have to be flexible, huh?" Benny picked up his croissant, set it back down. "I haven't exactly done anything like this before."

"What makes you so sure that I have?"

The comment hung out there for a few beats before Benny dropped his head and laughed. Garrett laughed along with him. Benny pointed his finger across the booth, bouncing it, and shook his head.

"You're too funny," he said.

The laughter faded. Garrett watched Benny pull a handkerchief from his pocket and blow his chubby nose. How long had it been since he'd actually seen someone use a handkerchief to blow his nose? Quite some time. The reason for that was obvious as Benny leaned to the side and stuffed the bundle of mucus back into his pocket.

Garrett took the opportunity to snatch another few glimpses of the place, still wondering if this fat piece of shit had brought someone with him as security. That's what Garrett would do, but he wasn't sure that logic applied to a guy who carried snot around in his pockets. The crowd hadn't changed in the past few minutes. A young guy and a girl were sitting at a tiny table near the window, almost mirroring each other with greasy spiked hair over tattoos and face metal. They looked to be around fifteen but were probably twentysomething, their best years almost certainly behind them. An old man sporting a fedora sat in the far corner, reading a copy of the *Times* and working his lower jaw in circles while his pale tongue darted out over his lips. A guy in a sport coat one table over clicked the keys on a laptop and adjusted his glasses every few seconds, his back to Garrett.

At the counter nearby, the babe, a sultry minx with milky skin, sat sidesaddle on one of the stools, smartly arrayed in a taupe linen skirt and vest, sipping her coffee like a lounging starlet nursing a gin and tonic. She was the first he crossed off. Way too hot to be playing back door for this ass-clown, and no human being could feign disinterest quite that well. Two guys in ball caps were a few stools away, talking about the Yankees. Like the schmo on the laptop and the old guy with the paper, and even the kid with the metal when his girl wasn't paying attention, they kept sneaking peeks at the brunette. Even the homeless guy who'd been loitering around the front for two or three minutes seemed to be fixated on her. He didn't blame them. He'd been doing the same thing. There was something gravitational about her, something that screamed *wild in bed*. Just as the thought crossed his mind, she glanced up and caught his eye, gave him the kind of non-smile smile only a knockout was capable of before looking away a split second later. It seemed to Garrett like he could smell her fragrance across the room, a sweet, feral, fleshy scent beneath the aroma of coffee grounds and pastries. The same scent that sent his pulse racing when he brushed against her on his way to the booth.

He remembered a magazine article that said physical contact by a woman was almost never accidental. The thought buoyed him.

Trying to bite back a smirk, he wiped at his mouth. Women and imagination. A dangerous combination. His presence at the coffee shop was proof of that.

Benny tossed a quick glance over his back. The bout of nervous laughter seemed to have stripped his demeanor of pretense and left him jumpy. He cleared his throat and checked his watch. It was large and silver and would have been classy, if not for the *Star Wars* logo boldly printed on it face. The minute and second hands were miniature lightsabers.

Garrett pressed his lips to his cup, pulled back as he felt the heat. *What kind of a fucking dork wears a* Star Wars *watch?*

As often as Benny's eyes let him, Garrett continued to discreetly monitor the other patrons, maintaining a peripheral awareness. Except for that homeless guy, none of them gave off a vibe. But a bum like that seemed a bit conspicuous for a confederate, hovering at the window the way he was. He doubted this schmuck was that careful anyhow, but you could never be sure. Not that it mattered. He dipped his spoon into his coffee, thinking about that. It definitely didn't matter. Not for what he had in store. He was just curious about the way this ass-wipe's mind worked.

"How do you want it to go down?" Garrett asked, making circles, watching the white spirals cloud the liquid, lighten it to a shade of beige, and then disappear before he raised his eyes.

Benny blinked several times. "What do you mean?"

"I mean, do you want it to look like an accident?"

"I figured I'd leave that kind of thing up to you."

Over Benny's shoulder, Garrett saw the homeless guy press his face against the front window again, backlit by the early afternoon sun. Doubts started creeping into his mind about whether this was really a homeless person, but the guy had that weird look. He was wearing a black button-down raincoat, even though there wasn't a cloud in the sky. His thinning hair was a bit disheveled, plastered to his head in places, and he was weaving back and forth like he might fall down at any moment. Something about him made him seem like he wasn't all there. Garrett wondered if maybe he was eyeing the counter rather than the brunette. Longing for some pound cake, perhaps.

The raincoat. Garrett glanced down at the sleeve of his windbreaker, wondering how suspicious it looked in this kind of weather. Murphy's Law dictated that today just had to be the sunniest day of the year. A trained eye would probably make the observation, question why he was wearing it, just as he did with the bum, but after a few seconds he realized it was just paranoia. Benny the fat-ass hadn't seemed to notice anything, and Garrett knew it was unlikely he would. The mope was simply in way over his head.

Garrett tapped his spoon over the rim and set it down on the saucer. "It doesn't work that way. We've got to be on the same page."

Benny mopped his face, mulling over the words. His eyes moved from side to side with a pensive distance to them, like he was sampling a wine. "Right. I guess an accident sounds good. Don't you always want it to look that way? Like an accident?"

"Unless you want me to make it look like a break-in. That's got its advantages."

"What advantages?"

"Well, you'd be able to set up an alibi, for one. And that way there'd also be no need to worry about them figuring out that maybe it wasn't an accident, after all." Garrett brought the cup to his lips, gingerly took a sip. Still a bit too hot. He could feel a numb spot set in near the tip of his tongue. "I could even rape her, if you'd like. Make it look convincing so no one would suspect you."

Benny's eyebrows jumped. "You could do that?"

A prince among men. Where the hell did she find this guy? "Sure. It would cost a little more, that's all."

"There is one thing. She's a few months pregnant. Does that make a difference?"

Garrett tried to maintain a neutral expression. What an absolute creep. "Not if you're okay with it."

Benny squeezed one hand with the other, digging his thumb into his palm and rubbing at the backs of his knuckles. "I suppose you're wondering why, huh?"

"It's not any of my business." *But you're going to tell me anyway, you predictable fuck.*

"She wants a divorce. Even with the baby coming. I've worked and slaved to build a little business. I've got a ton of debt, a *ton* of debt. She'll take half of my interest, and probably the house. I've got partners, investors. I can't let her walk away with half, can't let her take fifty percent of my voting rights. I'd lose control; I might lose everything."

"Like I said, none of my business. So long as I get paid. I told you my price."

"Right. About that—it strikes me as kind of high."

The sound of the door, the intrusion of ambient outside noises drew Garrett's attention. He shifted his gaze over Benny's shoulder again to see the man in the black raincoat enter. Garrett had a much better view of him now, his features no longer in shadow. The man's face was drawn and drooping, his skin a pale gray, like he was sick. There was something about his eyes that caused Garrett to tense up. They were set and focused, fixed in a way he knew meant one thing. Trouble.

"What's wrong?" Benny asked.

Garrett didn't respond as he watched the homeless-looking man walk toward the counter. The guy wasted no time in getting down to it, and Garrett could tell before he got there it wasn't pound cake he was after. He grabbed the good-looking woman by her hair with one hand and swung his other arm beneath her armpit and around her torso in one swift motion. Without any hesitation, he picked her up off the stool and dragged her back toward the door.

A silence fell over the place, accented by a few gasps and a couple of unintelligible exclamations. The baseball guys who'd been talking salary caps and free agency were up off their stools, but then merely stood there, frozen and gaping like everyone else. The waitress dropped her coffeepot and screamed. The man dragging the woman let go of her hair long enough to pull open the door and force her through it. By then, she was kicking and punching and twisting violently.

Garrett was already out of the booth and lunging after them when they reached the sidewalk. The scents and sounds of the city, car exhaust and machinery, the honks and beeps of traffic, the aroma of cooking and the stench of trash, the din of footfalls, all swarmed him. Pedestrians scrambled out of the way. A human semicircle formed, clearing a space, people pointing fingers and covering their mouths as they tried to figure out what they were witnessing. Garrett's first thought was that the man was boxed in, but he didn't try to veer right or left, didn't even seem to notice. He simply kept dragging in the same direction, yanking the woman along with each stiff stride as she struggled and shouted, a parent carting off an unruly child. Step, drag, step, drag. Over the curb, between the bumpers of two parked cars, and into the busy avenue.

"Hey!" Garrett yelled, bolting forward and grabbing the woman by one of her wrists. He tried to set his feet, tripping and staggering as the man continued to move into the street. A car swerved to avoid them, the driver laying into the horn. Garrett felt the soles of his shoes slip across the asphalt, shot a hand out onto the hood of one of the parked cars, clawed at it, then decided to change tacks. He tugged on the woman's arm instead and threw his body forward, launching himself over her, slamming his fist into the side of the man's face. It was a good punch, a lot of propelled weight behind it, a lot of snap at the end of it. He felt the

crack of bones, knew he'd broken his hand the moment it connected. He also knew he'd broken the guy's jaw. He had to have.

The three of them stumbled into the middle of the lane. Tires screeched and a taxi skidded to a stop just short of them. The man turned his head back. His mouth hung with a crooked slackness. He looked at Garrett as if it was the first time he'd noticed he was there.

"Let her go!"

There was no reaction to his words, as far as Garrett could tell; no indication the man had even heard him. Taking a hold of both her arms, Garrett leaned all his weight back and churned with his legs, ignoring the increasingly painful throb in his right hand, but the man's grip remained fast and he didn't seem to budge. Garrett felt the woman's hands lock on his wrists and his gaze jumped to her eyes. Her head was tilted back, a fistful of her hair still in the man's hands. Her eyes were wide but otherwise composed as her body strained against her attacker, her feet kicking back against his legs whenever she could find the footing. And she was able to maintain eye contact. That was good, Garrett thought. Not panicking. Not yet, at least.

"I said, *let her go!*"

Garrett thought this time he may have gotten through. He sensed a subtle difference in the man's stance, felt the woman's body shift. He took a step forward and saw the man's arm slide out from around her waist. He took a breath, slowly adjusting his grip. It was a move in the right direction, at least. Garrett started to pull her closer, staring the man down, willing him to let go of her hair.

But instead the man yanked her head back and thrust his hand at Garrett's face. Garrett gagged as fingers penetrated his mouth, jamming his tongue back into his throat and curling over his teeth. A thumb pressed up from beneath his jaw, digging into his flesh, making it impossible to breath. The man's hand squeezed and Garrett let go of the woman, instinctively taking hold of the man's arm, leaning back, like he was winding a gigantic horn.

There was a rotten, sour taste in his mouth, bitter and foul, and a putrid odor filled his nostrils as he struggled to take a breath. It took him a second to think of biting down. He clamped his mouth shut with all the force he could muster, clenching his jaws. Something sticky and gelatinous oozed over his gums and beneath his tongue as he felt the hard resistance of bone. His teeth sank deep, but the man's grip didn't change. Garrett tried to bite down again, even harder this time, but couldn't.

He realized his eyes were closed. He opened them and began frantically to punch at the man's arm, hoping to weaken his grip. He slammed his palm against the man's elbow, brought a hammer strike down on his bicep, dug his fingernails into the nerve clusters near the end of his forearm. All it seemed to accomplish was to set his injured hand on fire, the hot pain shooting through his arm while homeless guy didn't so much as flinch. The woman was doing similar things, swinging her elbows, stomping back against the man's shin, her eyes on Garrett the whole time. No reaction from the guy, no visible response. Nothing. A second passed, and Garrett found he was able to take tiny breaths through his nose if he inclined his head and relaxed his throat. His immediate fear receded enough for him to think about the possible ways this might play out, whether he might somehow avoid being killed or seriously injured. He heard a siren approaching and hoped the police didn't bother leaning over the hood of the cruiser with a bullhorn and just went ahead and tackled the guy with their nightsticks swinging. He also hoped this woman appreciated what he went through to help her, hoped that she would remember more than simply how pathetic his rescue attempt had been.

As the siren grew louder those thoughts were replaced with a sudden feeling of dread. He shot his gaze over to the woman, then back to the man, and realized he knew exactly what was coming. He wasn't sure how, but he did. He knew the woman did, too, and he briefly wondered whether it was something in her eyes that told him. He did not have time to follow the path of that thought very long before the man flung himself into the next lane, pulling Garrett and the woman with him, the three of them ending up dead center to the oncoming ambulance with the deafening siren that obliterated Garrett's thoughts almost as thoroughly as did the shards of bone shattering through his brain, the driver caught so off guard he didn't even take his foot off the gas until after the vehicle had cleared the bodies, the oversized van thumping over them as skulls and limbs bounced off the pavement and ricocheted against its undercarriage.

Garrett's last thought, the one violently ripped apart, was that it certainly hadn't been anything in the man's eyes that gave it away. There'd been nothing there to see.

CHAPTER 1

✦

JAKE HATCHER KNEW HE WOULD SPEND THE REST OF HIS life right where he was, or somewhere just like it, if he rolled off his bunk, applied a rear choke hold, and snapped his cellmate's neck. But he wouldn't have to listen to the man's babbling anymore, so at the moment it didn't seem all that unfair a trade. He wondered what it took to wear out a set of vocal cords. Less than his sanity could stand, he was sure of that.

"And them Chinese, those are some strange fuckers, let me tell you. You know?"

Hatcher held a breath in his chest, felt the pressure grow, blew it out toward the ceiling a few feet above him. He had serious doubts as to whether Tyler Culp had ever shut up for one goddamn minute his entire life.

"You want to know what I read about 'em? Wanna hear something strange?"

Sleep tugged and teased, drawing his heavy lids closed. He saw Tyler emerging from the womb, pictured the swollen head of a redneck on a baby's body, a flow of annoying goo-goos and ga-gas tumbling incessantly out of his mouth. The last half hour had been a stream-of-consciousness diatribe that started with Tyler recalling all the Korean "free corn" he'd seen, how he'd learned it popped up everywhere over there because farmers ate a lot of corn and shit in the rice fields. That annoying, forceful whisper of his scratched relentlessly at Hatcher's ears as he'd gone on to explain in a variety of ways, illustrated by a variety of anecdotes, how he never, ever ate Korean vegetables after that. Would not eat them when in Seoul, would not eat them in a bowl. Wouldn't eat the vegetables over there, or the tomatoes, which he pointed out was a fruit. Or pussy. Especially not the pussy. Figured any culture where shitting on crops was okay, you couldn't trust the feminine hygiene. Japanese, that was different. He compared that to good sushi.

A monologue would have been bad enough, but Tyler didn't seem to think of it that way. He expected his audience to pay attention, to listen. Listen and acknowledge. Constantly.

"I said, do you want to hear something strange?"

Hatcher tensed the muscles in his jaw, felt something pop near his ear. "It's what I live for."

"I read about these guys got arrested over there for killing these women, prostitutes mostly, but some poor village slopes, too. Gave the parents some yuan, or whatever the fuck they use over there, and ended up snuffing 'em. You know why?"

Tyler's neck was pretty thick, Hatcher thought. It might take a lot of effort. "Can't say I do."

"To sell their bodies to marry dead guys. Ghost brides, they call 'em. You ever heard of such a thing? I mean, ain't that the damnedest thing you ever heard?"

Hardly, Hatcher thought. He'd heard worse. Way worse. Heard worse, seen worse. In the eyes of some, probably done worse.

"Sure is."

"These families would, like, buy them, so they could

bury them with their sons. So they'd have a wife. In the *afterlife*."

He'd said it like it was three words. Af. Ter. Life. Hatcher smiled at that, in spite of himself. That's exactly what kept him in check, and the thing that kept this ass-hat from puking blood and looking for his ribs. The hope of an afterlife. Fifty-eight days, and counting.

"That's why they called 'em 'ghost brides.' Get it?"

"Yeah. I get it."

It was no accident he'd been celled with Tyler; that much he knew. He had less than two months to go, and Gillis wanted him to fuck up. Wanted it badly. Tyler had showed up eight days ago, six foot three and about 285, with a short fuse and thin skin. Fifty-eight days. Hatcher knew he had to put up with him, had to find a way. The alternative was exactly what Gillis had in mind.

"How do you think those people came up with that shit? I mean, who's the first one who plants his kid and says, 'Hey, we gotta find some gal to bury with him, so he'll have a wife over there'?"

The sun was coming up. Hatcher could see the light seeping in from the corridor through the bars, bathing everything it touched in a blue gray glow. They'd be forming for PT soon, then showering before the breakfast formation and work detail. Formations were good. A few minutes of standing in silence where he could sneak some shut-eye. A minute or two of it in the shower, another couple at breakfast. Sleep was a weapon. He was good with weapons.

He heard the first stirrings of the jailhouse, the faint clanging of metal, the creaking of heavy hinges. Since the run-in with Captain Gillis, Hatcher's days had been designed to make him crack. He appreciated the irony of it, of being on the receiving end of sleep deprivation. Probably Gillis's idea of a joke, or would be, if the guy actually knew. Gillis was big on jokes, had lots of them, none of them funny. Thanks to Gillis, Tyler shadowed him everywhere except for his afternoon motivational training, his daily penance for the run-in that started this whole thing. He assumed that's when Gillis allowed the moron to catch up on his own sleep, because at night Tyler seemed to need an hour or two at the most. The rest of the time he talked. And talked. And kept talking. Tyler was beefy, thickly slabbed through the chest and in the arms. Not a chiseled, health-club body, but not just a mass of fat, either. It was the kind of size that would make the guy carrying it think he could take anyone. Make him think he could talk wherever, to whomever, and for however long he wanted.

Hatcher felt a thump through the thin, flimsy mattress. It was a hard enough poke to make him suck in a breath. "Are you listening? I said, who's the first one who plants his kid and looks for some gal to bury with him?"

Fifty-eight days. Shutting him up meant hurting him, hurting him meant additional time. There was no way around it. Hatcher wiped a hand down his face, squeezing his eyes closed and inhaling deeply. He caught a whiff of something pungent in the air, realized it was the asshole's breath.

"Couldn't tell you."

"I think it just goes to show you how scared everyone is. Scared of that big dirt nap. So they start acting like it's not the end, hoping they can believe, believing they can make it not the end. You know?"

"Yeah," Hatcher said. "I know."

"It's like all these people who assume there's a Heaven, but they don't believe in Hell. I mean, what's up with that? You know? Hey!" A couple more thumps into Hatcher's ribs. "You there? *Hello*, I'm *talking* to you."

Hatcher had decided early on that Tyler was just a useful idiot, a pugnacious talker put there to bait him. Guys like Gillis didn't have the balls to actually cut a deal, and certainly didn't have enough sack to sanction the infliction of grievous bodily harm by one prisoner on another. At least, Hatcher didn't think Gillis had the balls. His type would be too scared the guy would talk, too worried about an inquiry if someone got hurt. No, Gillis would have just dropped clues about what he wanted, mentioned in passing how he would be happy if Hatcher didn't get much sleep. Hinted he'd like some trouble to come Hatcher's way without actually suggesting it, and never at the same time he discussed Tyler's upcoming prisoner review board. He probably figured Tyler would catch on, and the rest would take care of itself. Plausible deniability. If Hatcher got curb-stomped, great, but what Gillis really wanted was for Hatcher to buy himself another few years. Showed what a cocksucker Gillis was. All Hatcher had done was dislocate the fucker's shoulder.

"I don't know."

"I'm just saying, you can't have one without the other. Like when people say, 'Oh, he's in Heaven now, sweetie.' How the hell do they know? Does anyone say, 'Oh, so and so's died and gone to Hell?' Do they?"

They sure do, Hatcher thought. Sometimes. "Guess not."

"So, who's going to Hell, right? I mean, somebody's got to be. What d'ya think?"

The recording of morning reveille crackled through the facility speaker system. Hatcher swung his bare legs over the side of the bunk. He felt cool in his T-shirt and boxers, but not cold. It was going to be a mild day, and he hoped they'd be on golf course duty, same as last Tuesday. Gillis always assigned the two of them to the same detail, and mowing the golf course meant separate mowers and loud engines. He could sneak some sleep behind a mower as he enjoyed its innocuous drone and not have to listen to Tyler's incessant prattle. With any luck, the dickhead hadn't realized that.

"You gonna answer me, or what?"

Hatcher pushed himself off, felt his feet slap against the concrete floor. "Somebody's in Hell. No doubt about that."

"You making fun of me?"

Tyler was being particularly belligerent this morning. The more Hatcher thought about it, the more it seemed Tyler had been escalating things for days. He wondered if Gillis had been applying more pressure, dangling something special in front of this lunk to make sure he was properly motivated.

"No," Hatcher said. "None of this has been fun."

Tyler stood, using his three-plus inches of extra height to look down at Hatcher as he pressed in close. "I think you're making fun of me."

So, this was it then. Either Gillis finally decided to force the issue, or Tyler Culp decided he needed the brownie points right away, that he couldn't wait any longer. Review boards meet on Wednesday. Hatcher was willing to bet Tyler's just got moved up to tomorrow.

As Hatcher saw it, the problem was his cellmate's size. Joint locks or nerve strikes were risky with a guy that big. A choke could work, but the cell was small and getting behind him would be tricky. And also risky. Hatcher didn't want to be hanging over him, arm constricting his neck, waiting for the lack of blood flow to knock him out while Tyler tried to buck him off. Big guy like that would spin and thrash, slamming him against the bunk or the bars or the wall. No, to subdue him, he was going to have to injure him. And he knew that was what Gillis was counting on. Whether Tyler realized it or not.

On the other hand, he could always just take a beating, possibly a serious one. The problem with that was there were no guarantees the story wouldn't still be that he was at fault, his own injuries evidence of the fight, giving Gillis the ammunition he needed to get one of the JAGs to prosecute. If he was going to do time for it anyway, he sure as hell wasn't going to be this jerk-off's pinata. He stood there as Tyler's blunt gaze hung over him, the man's hot, rank breaths invading his nostrils, and decided to stop kidding himself. He was rationalizing, big time. No JAG in his right mind would prosecute a guy for getting his ass kicked, and no panel of officers would ever convict. But there was just no way he was going to let it happen. Turning the other cheek wasn't in his nature, which was why he was in this situation to begin with. If anyone was going to get the shit kicked out of him, it was Tyler. But that would be giving Gillis exactly what he wanted.

Of course, another option was to kill the man, make it look like an accident. Have him crack his skull off the side of the bunk. Wouldn't fool Gillis, but that wouldn't matter because he wouldn't have any witness to coach. He wouldn't have any witness at all. And given that kind of situation, he'd probably want to distance himself from the whole ordeal as much as possible. From a purely practical standpoint, Hatcher knew that was the option that afforded him the most control over things. But he really didn't want to send the guy packing for oblivion, as much as he had entertained himself with that very thought over the past few days.

Tyler poked a stiff finger into Hatcher's pec. "I don't like being made fun of."

Hatcher glanced down at his chest and watched the hand hovering in front of it, thinking, sometimes you got to play the cards you're dealt.

"Don't do that again," Hatcher said.

"What? This?"

Tyler stabbed his finger into Hatcher once more, harder this time. Hatcher grabbed hold before Tyler could pull it away, wedging his palm up against it, wrapping his thumb and forefingers around it. The man's hand was large and sweaty, digits like greasy pistons.

For a big ugly, Hatcher realized that Tyler was fairly quick. He felt the man shift his weight, saw him coming over the top with a left. But Hatcher had already set his grip and started to curl his wrist forward and down, bending the man's finger back. Tyler's punch dropped like a dead bird and he fell to one knee, letting out a surprised noise somewhere between a dog's yelp and a moan.

It wasn't something he had planned on, but it occurred to Hatcher that breaking a finger wasn't a bad idea. Clean and inconspicuous. Painful, but not disfiguring. It would swell and bruise, but not leave any real marks. In an inquiry, it would smack of defense, not offense. And most important, it probably lacked any sex appeal to a JAG. Courts-martial were boring enough when a real crime was involved. Gillis would look like a moron pressing the issue beyond the walls of the facility. Or more of a moron, at least.

And Hatcher also knew if he didn't end the class with a bang, this guy just wouldn't learn the right lesson.

"I'm afraid this is going to hurt," he said.

The deep buzzing of the door to the corridor penetrated the cell block, causing Hatcher to stop and listen. Steel bars sliding. Multiple footfalls on the concrete. This was unusual. Procedure was for the cell doors to unlock and for the prisoners to form on the red line five minutes after reveille. Something was up and something being up was rarely good.

Gillis and two military police guards stopped in front of the cell. One of the guards was carrying a clutch of silver chains with cuffs. Hatcher waited a few seconds before letting go of Tyler's finger, making sure Gillis was able to grasp what had taken place. Tyler shook his hand out and seized it with his other, rolling back onto the lower bunk and muttering curses. Gillis glared at Hatcher, then gestured back down the hall toward the closed-circuit camera. A mechanical sound echoed around them, followed by the clunk of the cell's lock disengaging.

"Put your goddamn jumper on," Gillis said. "Now."

Hatcher glanced at Tyler and smiled as he pulled the dark blue coveralls from the end of his bunk, took his time stepping into them and buttoning up. He could feel Gillis's eyes burning into him, so he took even longer putting on his socks and shoes.

"Shackle him."

Both guards stepped forward. Hatcher knew the drill. He

turned and raised his hands to his head while one of them looped the waist chain and the other fettered his ankles. When they were done with those, they spun him around and he lowered his hands to be cuffed, one at a time.

They pulled him forward a few steps until he was face-to-face with Gillis. "Don't I get one of those hockey masks, too?"

"Shut up."

Gillis looked at one of the guards and jerked his head. He started back up the corridor as the guards led Hatcher out of the cell.

Behind him, Hatcher heard the bunk creak. Tyler's voice tried to recapture some its bravado, but failed.

"I'll be here when you get back, punk."

Hatcher slowed and looked over his shoulder, the MPs pulling on his arms. "For chrissakes, open your eyes," he said. He resumed his shuffle, sensing the looks peering out from the cells on either side, watching Gillis open the fortified metal door to the block. Under his breath he added, "They've already gone to Plan B."

GILLIS LED THEM THROUGH THE INTERIOR AND EXTERIOR checkpoints of the confinement unit, past the glass cubicle housing the gatekeepers, and into the adjacent administrative building. They paused in a small reception area as Gillis keyed a coded lock to open a heavy door, then filed in behind him.

Hatcher hadn't been in this building before, but in a sense he had. Virtually all army offices looked the same. Government-issue furniture, plain black safes and beige filing cabinets, drab, tan, utilitarian paint jobs over cracking, sagging wood. Three admins sat behind desks in a bullpen just inside the entrance, two men and a woman, staring at computer screens and pecking on keyboards. The two that bothered to look up as Hatcher passed didn't register any interest.

Gillis cleared the bullpen and entered a corridor lined with doors. One of the doors was marked as a restroom, and Hatcher suddenly wished he'd had a few more seconds to break Tyler's finger and then take a leak before Gillis had come for him. The hall cornered and Gillis stopped near the back of the building. Gillis tugged on the key ring attached to his belt and stretched it out on a reel, unlocking a door to the interior side of the corridor. That meant no windows, Hatcher thought.

They entered a large room with a holding cell in the corner, sturdy round bars bolted to the walls and forming the other half of a large square. At the opposite end was an empty desk with a computer on it. Stacks of plastic chairs with chrome legs stood along the wall opposite the cell. The middle of the room was empty. There were no windows.

There was a man in the holding cell. Early twenties, medium-sized, and lean. He was beefy in the arms and shoulders, sporting the crooked nose of a pug and wearing the same standard prison jumper as Hatcher. He sat on a narrow metal bench affixed to the back wall, leaning forward on his elbows, his hands hidden between his knees. Hatcher spotted the chain around the man's waist, thinking it was probably the only half-comfortable way to sit in these things.

Gillis retrieved another key from his ring and unlocked the door to the cell. He held the door open and gestured for the MPs to put Hatcher inside. The door closed behind Hatcher with a clang and the loud clunk of a solid latch catching snugly.

Hatcher turned, almost losing his balance in the leg shackles, and looked through the bars at Gillis.

"No talking. No lying down. If you need to go to the bathroom, it will have to wait. You'll be escorted to the colonel's office when he's ready for you."

Hatcher said nothing. Gillis was staring at him, but there was an edginess to it, a desire to break eye contact the man was trying to hide. Hatcher made a point of holding his gaze, waiting for Gillis to be the one. Gillis finally gave up, turned to leave after a few seconds, but before he did, Hatcher caught it. A snapped glance over to the prisoner on the bench. No swivel of the head. Just a shift of the eyes. Guarded. Self-conscious.

"A guard will be standing right outside this room until the man who occupies that desk gets in. He's running a little late this morning. We have eyes on you. So don't try anything funny."

The MPs followed Gillis out of the room, shutting the door behind them.

Hatcher looked over to the empty desk, then back to the door. Not much noise was going to make it through there. He glanced over to the far corner where a security camera was aimed at the holding cell. He waited for a blink of red above the lens. Nothing. He suspected the feed had not been activated. He heard the man behind him shift on the bench. He angled his body against the wall. The prisoner was eyeballing him.

"So." Hatcher looked at the name stenciled on the man's jumper. "Cromartie. What did Gillis promise you?"

Cromartie's eyebrows jumped and he pulled the ends of his mouth into a confused moue. Hatcher held his gaze, bored his eyes into the man's pupils. After a few seconds Cromartie smiled and dropped his head low, almost between his legs, nodding.

"Conjugal," Cromartie said. "Need one bad, man. I was only married a couple of months before I got sent here. Got six months left."

So Gillis suddenly had grown a set of balls, after all. Of sorts. "How rough is this supposed to get?"

Cromartie pressed his lips together, someone about to confess some bad news. "Rough."

Hatcher dipped his chin, looked over to the camera, and pictured Gillis feigning outrage, demanding to get to the bottom of things.

"Nothing to send you to the infirmary," Cromartie added,

his voice more upbeat. "And not too much blood. But, yeah. Rough. Couple of teeth on the floor, some gut shots that'll stay with you a while. Oh, and your shoulder. He wants you to feel it in your shoulder, he said."

Hatcher nodded. "Why you?"

"Took a silver at the Armed Forces Boxing Championship two years ago," Cromartie said, shrugging. "Guess he figured I knew how to cause some damage."

"And the cuffs?"

The man raised his arms, twisted his hands back and forth to show his unfettered wrists. With Cromartie's hands up, Hatcher could see the cuffs dangling between his legs, hanging from the waist chain.

"You a boxer, me like this," Hatcher said. "Not exactly a fair fight now, is it?"

"Sorry, bro. Nothing personal."

Cromartie stood. He was a couple of inches shorter than Hatcher, but with a boxer's compact ranginess. He stepped forward, and Hatcher noticed only one leg was shackled, the chain and manacle for the other dragging behind it.

"Afterward, you cuff yourself up and Gillis takes care of the story, is that the idea?"

"That's the idea."

Cromartie looked like a boxer, carried himself like one. Balanced, light on his feet. Good boxers knew how to punch, and punch hard. Hatcher assumed Cromartie would be no exception.

"If you close your eyes and just stand there, I'll try to make it go quick. Can't promise it won't hurt like a fucker, but you might save yourself some punishment."

Punishment, Hatcher thought, repeating it silently to himself. He liked the word. Made the whole thing sound so orderly, so corrective. He tilted his head forward a bit and hooded his eyes, not quite closing them. Through the narrow slit of his lids he could see Cromartie's shoes. He took a breath and exhaled as he watched the man set his feet.

Punching was all about timing and leverage, getting

the most power out of the strike. Hatcher could detect the weight shift to Cromartie's right foot, saw it roll and turn ever so slightly as he drew back. He visualized the rest of the man in a relaxed pugilist's stance, twisting his hips, winding up. The hips were everything. You throw a punch with your ass, not your arm. He watched for the forward shift, tried to sense it happen, sense the timing, that fraction of a second where the body would uncoil, the commitment to the motion.

Now.

Hatcher jerked his head to his right, felt the fist brush by his ear, the bump of the thumb knuckle grazing the back of his skull. Just as he'd hoped, the man hadn't considered the possibility of missing, didn't snap his punch back as he would in the ring but let his weight follow it. Cromartie lost his balance for an instant, bounced forward on the balls of his feet to regain it. Less than a foot closer, but close enough. Hatcher reached out with both hands as far as his cuffs would allow and grabbed hold of the chain around Cromartie's waist. Without any wasted motion, he arched his spine, drew his shoulders back, then snapped forward, slamming his forehead into the bridge of Cromartie's nose.

Hatcher knew the blow dazed him. He saw the man's eyes unfocus and flutter, his hands shoot to cover his face, felt the sudden jerk as Cromartie tried to stumble back. But Hatcher held on, waited the necessary second for the boxer's instinct to take over, for him to ball his fists and move his hands out, keeping them high to block any punches to the sides of the head. Hatcher cocked his head back and butted him again, smashing the hard bone of his forehead one more time against the softer bones of the man's face.

He could tell from the tug against his arms, the sudden droop of weight, that Cromartie was out on his feet. Using the waist chain, Hatcher guided him to fall back onto the wall bench, twisting around to veer him against the corner bars so he'd be propped into a sitting position.

Cromartie's nose was pulpy and bent to one side. A triangle of red draped downward from it over his mouth and chin.

Hatcher sat next to him on the bench, used his weight to slide the man even closer to the bars. He watched for signs of him regaining consciousness, saw none.

"Boxing has rules," he said, shaking his head. "I told you it wasn't a fair fight."

WHEN HE HEARD THE BOLT TO THE DOOR BEING THROWN, Hatcher was standing in a forward corner of the cell, holding on to a light sleep. He opened his eyes to see Gillis entering the room with two MPs. Not the same ones, he noted. One of them was a stocky black guy, the other was tall and wiry.

Gillis paused after a few steps. The surprise registered in his eyes and face. It quickly dissolved to make way for anger as he marched to the front of the cell.

"What the hell?"

The two MPs looked at each other behind him, uncertain what to do.

"He had an accident," Hatcher said.

"You!" Gillis stabbed a finger between the bars. "You did this!"

Hatcher pulled his hands up as high as they would go, about even with his belly, and showed his palms. "How could I do anything?"

Gillis glared, frowning, his lips tight and thin. His hands were shaking. He jumbled the keys attached to his belt until he found the right one and opened the door to the cell.

"Stand against the bars over there and *don't you move*." He glanced back at his men and gestured toward Cromartie. The two MPs dashed into the cell and inspected the unconscious prisoner. Cromartie groaned as they moved his head and checked his eyes.

"Uh, sir," the wiry one said. "You need to look at this."

"Damnedest thing, too," Hatcher said as Gillis moved along the outside of the cell to get a better look. "The guy managed to get his cuffs all tangled in the bars when he fell."

Gillis watched as the other MP shifted Cromartie's body to show that each of his handcuffs were locked around one of the bars instead of his wrists. Both ankles were cuffed normally, but the chain to his leg shackles was looped around one of the bars near the floor.

Hatcher tried to suppress the smile he felt spreading across his lips. Gillis had no choice but to bury this now. He'd outsmarted himself, spreading it out over two sets of guards to make sure no one had the whole picture. As a bonus, it was supposed to give him four credible witnesses to swear he'd done everything by the book. Credible witnesses were now his problem.

He wondered what Gillis was thinking as thirty seconds stretched into a minute and the man did nothing but stare at the floor, then at Cromartie, then at Hatcher, then at the floor again.

The stocky black guard broke the silence. "Sir?"

Gillis straightened his back and puffed out his chest. "Undo his cuffs, clean his face, and get him to the infirmary. Get some rubber gloves and damp towels first. And see if some smelling salts will wake him up so you can walk him over there quietly and not give him the attention he wants. It's obvious what happened. Someone violated procedure and unfastened his cuffs when they put him in here, and he saw an opportunity to do this to himself."

A sigh, a shake of the head, the hint of a clucking tongue.

"I actually spoke to this man earlier," Gillis continued. "He was upset about his wife. This was a protest, against his incarceration. Probably wanted to stage a beating, knocked himself out by mistake."

He's good, Hatcher thought. Must have lots of practice. He could practically see the machinations as Gillis crafted the spin on the spot, thinking out loud. Gillis put just enough phony sincerity into it, countered it with just enough apathy. The worldly, jaded leader who'd seen it all before. The two MPs were buying it. By the time they related the story at the NCO club, it would be just as Gillis had described it.

The tall MP nodded, looking at the stocky one. "I'll go."

"I'll take this one," Gillis said. He pointed his finger at Hatcher. "You. Come with me."

Hatcher exited the cell, taking six-inch steps. Gillis started to grab at his waist chain, then seemed to think better of it, opting to walk an arm's length ahead of him as he led him out of the room. He motioned to the first MP he saw in the hall, snapping his fingers and ordering him to accompany them.

They walked back to the bathroom and Gillis opened the door. He gestured for the MP to wait and told Hatcher to sit on one of the toilets. He wet a paper towel in the sink and tossed it at Hatcher's lap with a contemptuous look.

"Clean your face off. It's got blood on it."

Hatcher picked up the dripping paper towel and bent over low to allow his hands to reach his face. He wiped at his forehead and his nose. The brown paper showed spots of pink.

"I need to piss."

Gillis looked at his watch. "Pissing is all guys like you ever do, other than moaning. You'll live."

"When I leave a yellow trail from here to wherever you're taking me, don't say I didn't warn you."

Sneering, Gillis jerked his head in disgust and turned away. Hatcher stood, fumbled for several seconds with the button fly of his jumper, and urinated into the toilet. When he was done, Gillis growled at him to get moving and stood behind him until they were out in the hallway.

"Where are we going?" Hatcher asked.

Gillis ignored him. He headed up the hall, back the way

they had come, tossing his chin in the same direction. The MP grabbed Hatcher by the back of the arm and they followed.

Hatcher's abbreviated steps caused Gillis to pull ahead as he walked.

"What's up this way?" Hatcher asked in low voice after they passed the room with the holding cell.

"CO's office," the MP said.

Gillis shot a look over his shoulder, then stopped a few steps later and waited for Hatcher to reach him.

"I'll take him from here," Gillis said.

The MP stepped aside obediently as Gillis took Hatcher by the arm. He walked him a few more feet to where the wall opened, revealing a reception area for a corner office. A woman in her fifties sat at a desk behind a computer. Gillis greeted her perfunctorily and led Hatcher past her workstation. The door to the office was open. The nameplate on the wall indicated a Lt. Col. Richard Owens, Commanding Officer. Gillis knocked once on the door frame, then led Hatcher inside.

"I've brought Hatcher, Colonel."

The office was spacious and spartan. A large desk dominated the center of it, a deep brown wood with ornate engraving. Along the wall next to the desk, an oversized set of flags, the Stars and Stripes and a green one bearing the insignia of the army, leaned against each other like crossed swords. The opposite wall was a love-me space, crowded with framed diplomas and certificates.

Owens sat behind the desk in a high-tech-looking black mesh chair with a wide back. He had a gray buzz cut and leathery skin that looked creased and ravaged by the sun. He signed a document with one of his large-knuckled hands and slipped it into an out-box, then leaned back and placed his elbows on the armrests of his chair. There was a large window behind him. Hatcher saw a breeze shaking its way through a tree. Spring would be starting any day.

"Was this really necessary?" Owens asked, holding out

his hand, palm up, looking at Gillis. Hatcher realized he was talking about the restraints.

"Procedure, sir. He's got a history. In fact, we just had an incident with him."

"Unlock him."

"Yes, sir." Gillis glared at Hatcher as he applied a key to the cuffs. Hatcher held his hands out, rubbing his wrists and flexing them.

"Leg irons, too," Owens said.

Gillis bent down and uncuffed Hatcher's ankles, staring up, spilling as much venom out of his eyes as he could.

"I'd like to speak to the prisoner alone, Captain."

"Sir, I don't think that's a good idea. As I've told you before, the prisoner is unstable. Prone to violence."

"Thank you for your concern. I'll call for you if I need you."

Gillis hesitated briefly, then strode out of the room. Hatcher heard the door close. Owens waited a few seconds before speaking.

The colonel swept a hand toward one of the chairs. "Please, take a seat."

Hatcher took the chair closest to Owens's desk. The give of the soft cushion as it received his weight reminded him it had been a long time since he'd sat on a real piece of furniture.

"How did you get that red mark on your forehead?"

Hatcher thought about how to answer that, couldn't come up with anything. "I'm not sure you want to know, Colonel."

"I figured as much," Owens said. "Look, Gillis is an asshole. But he's our asshole, so I have to make do. The harsh truth is, this kind of job needs assholes. By the way, do you know why you piss him off? Why he's got such a hard-on for you?"

"You mean, besides the shoulder?"

Owens waved his hand dismissively. "Yeah, besides that. I know all about what happened there. I've got plenty of people who'll give me the scoop on things. The fact that he had it coming is the only reason you didn't tack on a few years. I was talking about before that."

Hatcher had asked himself the same questions. "I don't know."

"Well, I have an idea."

Hatcher said nothing, waiting for Owens to continue. He was actually starting to like the man. He couldn't imagine that lasting long.

"You scare him," Owens said, picking up a file from his desk. "Evidently, you scare a lot of people. He's just the latest one. SF, insertion teams. Quite a résumé. You were a Kitten, weren't you?"

Hatcher held the man's gaze, trying not to show any reaction. That information could not have been in his file.

"Relax. I have an old ROTC buddy who's at Langley now. I had him do some digging. I know a dummy personnel record when I see one. Just like I know a bullshit charge."

"Why am I here, Colonel?"

Owens slid his chair closer to the desk, clasped his hands, and rested them on his blotter. His pleasant expression dissolved into an austere frown of concern. "Yesterday we received a priority message from the Red Cross. I had to have CID look into it before I told you. I'm sorry to say, it all checked out. Son, there's no easy way to say this. Your brother Garrett is dead. Killed in a traffic accident in New York a few days ago. I'm sorry."

"My brother?"

"Yes. I'm afraid so." Owens picked up a sheet of paper from his desk and held it out. Hatcher leaned forward out of his chair and took it. "Your mother contacted the Red Cross. From what I've been told, she didn't know you were in here."

Hatcher looked at the message. It was a humanitarian application for an emergency hardship release. It requested that Jacob R. Hatcher, Prisoner, be granted leave from custody to attend the funeral of his brother Garrett E. Hatcher, aka Garrett E. Nolan, Deceased, at the behest of his mother, Karen P. Woodard, fka Karen P. Hatcher, Applicant, and to be given additional time to assist with related family matters. It included contact information for his mother, the funeral home, and the Red Cross.

"Since you're only eight weeks or so from finishing your sentence, I ran it by the provost. On my recommendation, he decided to grant the request."

"But, I don't understand. This can't be . . ."

"I know it's hard. It always is. I don't grant these things often. I'm approving you for thirty days. You'll still be considered in custody, but you'll be free to travel to tend to your family. At the end of thirty days, I expect you to report back in. If you do, and you've kept your nose clean, I'm inclined to out-process you for an additional release. It will take a couple of days, but I have the authority to approve it. That would be terminal."

"Colonel, I really don't . . . Are you saying you're letting me go?"

"You'll still be considered a prisoner, but yes. A thirty-day hardship release. And like I said, if things go well, I'm willing to allow you to out-process upon your return."

"Forgive me, Colonel, but this . . . Why are you doing this?"

"Part of it is because I know what happened to you over there. Maybe not the whole story, but I know the forces that put you here. Normally, it's not my concern. But when there's been a tragedy like this, well, let's just say this is a chance to do something right. Lord knows, we don't get many."

"You said that was part of it."

"Frankly, the other part is Gillis. I'm not sure he knows what he's messing with in a guy like you. Turns out your psych evals were missing from your Pentagon file. Can't prove it, of course, but I'm pretty sure that was his doing. It's obvious he's become obsessed with you, as much as he tries to hide it. I don't want any scandals on my watch. If either of you turns up dead or crippled, well, it wouldn't help my bid for full bird, now, would it?"

Something weird was going on, but Hatcher was too confused to figure out what and his head hurt from even trying. Owens had called him a *Kitten*. Coercive Interrogation Tactician. Very few people knew about that, that such a thing even existed. It was both the reason he was prosecuted, and the reason he only got twelve months confinement rather than life. His initial thought was the army was setting him up. But Hatcher trusted his ability to read people, honed through years of experience in extracting information, and Owens seemed to be putting his cards on the table. He appeared genuinely sympathetic and was likely telling the truth about his contact with the spooks. Probably was one of the guys who thought torturing the enemy was acceptable and that prosecuting GIs for trying to win the damn war wasn't. Whatever this was about, Hatcher was confident it didn't involve Owens. Somewhat confident.

Which was good, because he was the one apparently about to let Hatcher go.

"My secretary is preparing the necessary forms, and you'll have to out-process through admin, but it shouldn't take too long. Photo, exit prints, and lots of signatures. A couple of hours at the most. A driver will take you to the local Red Cross office. They'll help arrange for a set of civilian clothes and a plane ticket."

"I'm not sure what to say."

"You don't have to say anything. Again, I'm sorry."

Hatcher stared at Owens for several seconds before dropping his eyes and rereading the message. "Would it be possible for me to make a phone call? In private, that is."

The colonel considered it, then nodded. "Yes. You can use my phone." He slid a large phone with a bank of buttons running down the length of it toward Hatcher. "Use line two. Dial nine for an outside line. I'll be back in five minutes. I'm bending the rules here. Don't make me regret it."

Hatcher picked up the handset and waited for Owens to leave the room. Phone calls from the RCF were expensive and monitored, so the colonel really was doing him a favor. He waited for a standard dial tone before keying in the number contained in the message. Someone picked up on the fourth ring.

"Hello?"

He took in a breath, tilted his head back. "Mom. It's Jake."

"Jacob? Jacob, is that really you? It's so good to hear your voice! Are you okay?"

The tinny voice on the line had an alien familiarity to it. It was the voice in his memory, but not the one he remembered. Twelve years was a long time.

"I'm fine," he said. "All things considered."

"I couldn't believe it when they told me. I thought I was getting in touch with your unit. I almost cried when they said you were in jail."

"Look, Mom—"

"Are they . . . letting you out? I mean, the Red Cross said they were going to request that. Are they going to let you out for the funeral?"

"Yes. But listen—"

"I feel horrible you had to find out this way. Jake, your father is very ill. Garrett dying . . . I don't think he's handling it well. I know this must all come as a shock. I didn't know what else to do. I'm sorry, I'm rambling, aren't I?"

Hatcher sighed. "Yes, Mom, you are."

"I'm sorry, I just get a little excited, that's all. You must have a lot of questions."

"You got that right. Like, for starters"—he looked down at the message, scanned the text about Garrett Hatcher's death—"since when do I have a brother?"

CHAPTER 2

❖

LINDSAY WAS THINKING SHE HAD NEVER SEEN AN APART-
ment so mansionlike or a view of Central Park so sprawling
when it occurred to her she had never set foot in a penthouse before. Maybe they were all this way.

She was starting to sense this gig had serious potential.
She'd just been offered a brandy. Not a beer or a joint or—
God help her—a Spanish fly. A brandy. It was practically
something out of a movie. And to top it off, the guy wasn't
even bad-looking. Reasonably tall, lean, and clean-shaven.
Maybe an old thirty or a young forty, maybe somewhere
in between. Nice head of hair, brown and wavy. And those
eyes. Intense didn't begin to describe them. Like a pair of
emerald lasers. Guy like that who wasn't gay was probably
married, but she figured that wasn't necessarily a bad thing.
She'd always heard married guys made the best regulars.

He held out a large glass with a wide, bulbous bottom.
She felt obliged to hold it the same way he did, fingers
curled beneath it, stem slid between her middle fingers. The
small amount of liquor swishing around the bottom had a

strong aroma. She took a sip. It sent a tingle through her tongue. The taste was unusual. Unusual and expensive.

"It's sweet," she said, letting out a giggle that was half genuine. "It's warming my belly already."

"Please, have a seat."

She settled onto a leather sofa. It was a deep chocolate brown with a hint of red, almost a burgundy. The cushion gave and she felt the smooth material compress around her.

"So," she said. "With a name like Valentine, you must steal all the girls' hearts."

"Is it that obvious?"

She wanted badly to use his first name, to set that familiar tone. What the hell was it again? Christ, he had just told her, not five minutes ago. She was always doing that, letting names drop from her head. Why couldn't she just have them stick? Something-something Valentine. Artemis? *Artemis Valentine?* Could be.

Valentine took a seat across from her in a chair with dark wooden legs shaped like paws and a broad oval back. She thought he looked quite distinguished in his navy blazer against the lavender of the crushed velvet.

"Do you live here alone?"

"Lucas has a room."

She raised an eyebrow, cocked her head slightly. The guy who had picked her up was big, muscular. Bald, with a mustache that curved down and swooped up into sideburns. She'd been scared to go with him at first, but he was driving that limo, and had pulled out that wad. Besides, that voice of his, squeaky for such a giant, convinced her he was harmless.

Valentine gave a dismissive wag of his chin. "Servant's quarters."

"Servant's quarters? Is he, like, your chauffeur? Or butler? I didn't know people actually had servants. Not anymore, I mean. Does that make you his master?"

"More like an assistant, but yes, technically he's my servant. He has his own apartment, but stays here when convenient. Other than that, it's just me. Unless you count pets."

"Oh, I *love* animals," she said. She watched him watch her over the edge of his glass as he took a sip. She could tell he wanted to check her out, so she gave him the chance, letting her eyes wander the room. It was a spacious study, paneled in deep walnut with bookshelves running from the floor to the vaulted ceiling, a huge glass desk set atop the curved tips of scrimshawed elephant tusks, and a walk-in fireplace with an enormous mantel of green marble. But it was that stunning penthouse view she kept going back to. All those leafy treetops, round and lush like rows of broccoli, a vast body of rough green water shimmering in the breeze. The skyline of the east side formed the opposite bank, steel and glass and cement in all its metropolitan glory. She could only imagine what it looked like at night.

"I'm sure they love you, too."

She spread her lips into a thin, mischievous smile. "And what about you? Do I bring out the animal in you?"

"You might say that."

"Well, Artemis—"

"Demetrius."

Damn. "Demetrius." She settled back, inclining a bit. She ran a French-manicured finger around the rim of her glass. "In that case, I take it you like what you see?"

Valentine hitched his shoulders, spread his hands. The jigger of brandy sloshed in his snifter. "What's not to like?"

He was right about that, she thought. She had it going on, no doubt. The mirror didn't lie if you wanted the truth out of it. All the pieces were in place; she'd spent a good deal of time seeing to it. Blonde hair in a Cleopatra cut. Creamy tan from hours stretched out between fluorescent bulbs. Curvy in the breasts and ass, but not too loose in the abs. Nice calves. She was proud of her calves.

She shifted in her seat, hiking up a bit of her skirt. Proud of those thighs, too. No cottage cheese. That was what iPods and treadmills were for.

"It will cost you six hundred. Animal-style included. That doesn't count the two hundred your man-slave paid me to come."

He frowned, swirling his brandy in a tight circle, obviously contemplating her words. "He's not a man-slave. And that's a lot of money."

"Not to the guy who chills out in this room it isn't," she said, swiveling her head and indicating their surroundings with her eyes.

Valentine nodded, then raised his glass before taking a sip. "Touché."

Lindsay worried she may have been too flip. Perhaps *man-slave* wasn't the smartest thing to say. She had to learn to be more careful with her jokes. People could be so sensitive. Never knew who you might offend, or why.

"What do you do?" she asked.

"I created a search engine."

"Is that, like, Internet stuff?"

"Yes," Valentine said, smiling wryly. "I sold it to a large dot-com for a lot of money."

"Neat. Well, what do you think, Demetrius?" She ran the tip of her tongue across her upper lip, still caressing the rim of her glass, careful not to overdo it. "Would you like me to get friendly with you?"

"I have to warn you. My tastes are a bit unorthodox."

Lindsay allowed herself a grin. What was it with rich guys? Get some money in the bank, and a fuck and a blow job suddenly wasn't as interesting as getting pissed on or lashed with a cat-o'-nine-tails.

"It might cost a bit more, depending on what you had in mind." She had already decided she'd go without a condom if he asked. Swallow, too. Rich guys didn't have AIDS or herpes. Hollywood types, maybe, but not guys like this. She was bucking for the repeat business.

"How do you feel about . . . bondage?" he asked.

"Kinky fellow, huh? Sorry, I'm not really into S and M. Not my thing."

"I take that to mean it's a matter of price."

She shook her head, thinking, *You can tie me up and shove a gag ball in my mouth twice a week for six hundred bucks a go.* "I'm really not interested."

Valentine reached behind the lapel of his navy blazer and produced a long, flat leather breast secretary. He removed a series of bills from it and set them on the edge of the coffee table, one at a time.

"That's a thousand."

Lindsay uncrossed her legs and tilted forward, inclining her head and examining the money. Her knees were touching and her ankles were splayed, heels turned out. Guys always seemed to like that kind of pose, vulnerable and sexy. Schoolgirl sexy. Made them think she was letting her guard down, looking hot without trying.

She held the glass across her lap, tapped a finger against her chin. Easy money was the stuff dreams were made of, and this guy was a dream come true.

"The more you lay out there, the more interested I might become."

"I think that's enough," Valentine said. "Wouldn't want you to lose respect for me."

"A thousand, huh?" She did a mental count again, making sure there were ten, looking forward to that new Coach purse. This would be more than she had ever made for one time. A lot more. "I suppose I could do it for that. Consider it an introductory price. If you like it, maybe we can do this again sometime."

Valentine leaned forward. "Who knows, maybe I'll steal your heart and not have to pay you anything."

Lindsay crinkled her nose, laughing with him, and then reached across the table to gather the money. She was still laughing when she put it in her clutch. He didn't stop her. She decided this Demetrius guy was all right. If by some miracle he was the one John in a thousand who wasn't lousy in bed, hell, the mood she was in she might not even have to fake one.

She set the clutch down on the cushion and circled the coffee table. She took his brandy and placed it next to hers, then eased herself onto his lap and laid her arms over his shoulders.

"Are you ready to show me your bedroom?" She slid a hand down his tie, lifting it out away from his shirt. It was a deep scarlet, soft but so thick it felt stiff. "Or are you going to tie me up right here?"

He didn't move as she brushed her lips against his and rested her forehead against his brow, bringing a finger up to touch his mouth.

"I had something more specialized in mind," he said.

She felt his weight shift forward and she pushed herself off his lap as he stood. He held out his hand and led her to the wall of shelving behind his desk. So many books, with titles she didn't recognize or couldn't read, a lot of them almost falling apart, cracked and flaking. More books than she could imagine a person reading. And not a paperback among them.

He gestured for her to stay where she was as he stepped forward and pulled on one of the spines. A section of books popped open on a hinge, a solid façade, revealing a small black plate. Valentine pressed his thumb against the plate, causing a glowing light to glide down from inside it. A click, then the sound of gears engaging, and the wall of shelving split down the middle and opened outward, divided into two equal sections.

Behind the wall was a room about twenty feet wide. A queen-size bed sat in the middle, a metal bar with angled ends suspended above it, hanging by two heavy-duty chains. A pair of leather cuffs was attached to the bar, and an assortment of straps hung limply from the center. Just behind the bed a curtain of red velvet draped in folds and puddled in sections along the tiled floor, a pelmet with theatrical ruffles and golden fringes running along the length of it near the ceiling.

Lindsay guessed there was a giant screen behind the

curtain. Pretty obvious it was something to watch porn on, since there was little doubt this was a sex room. She hoped he wasn't going to make her watch anything disgusting. Guys had tried to show her some sick things before, seemed to get off on watching her watch. But she didn't think Valentine was the type to be interested in that kind of stuff. Too classy for anything gross. It would probably be just some girl-on-girl junk. Wide-screen. The good kind, with attractive models, not butchy dykes. The more she thought about it, the more that seemed like something she wouldn't mind.

"You really are a naughty boy, aren't you?" She stepped forward and stroked a finger down his cheek as she passed by, looking around the room. "Nice guy, but a naughty boy."

Valentine cleared his throat. "I wouldn't say that."

Lindsay stopped at the edge of the bed, pressed down on it as she surveyed the surroundings. The bed had a white fitted sheet and a red dust ruffle along the bottom that reached down to the white-and-black checkered floor. But that was it. No pillows, no comforter. All business, she thought.

A few prints adorned the opposing walls, scenes with winged babies carrying bows and naked people with long hair and laurel wreaths dancing. Artificial candlelight glowed from sconces staggered on each side, barely adding to the wash of natural light from the other room. Below one of the prints was a tall wooden armoire. A plain wooden chair stood next to it. Along the opposite wall was a thin wooden table, bare and empty. She imagined it as a place to set an ice bucket and glasses, a spot to chill some expensive champagne and whatever went with it. Maybe next time. Something to look forward to.

She sat on the bed and leaned back onto her elbows, bounced her weight a bit. Not a very comfortable mattress, but it would do. She tilted her head back and pondered the contraption overhead.

"So, how does this thing work? You strap me in, then have your way with me?"

"More or less," Valentine said, watching from the threshold.

"I hope you're not thinking about breaking out a whip or anything. I don't do pain. Seriously." She regarded him with a smile, hung a finger on the edge of her teeth. "But for you . . . for you a spanking'd be okay. You can even make it sting a bit, if you want."

"No whips." He made an X across his chest with his finger. "Stick a needle in my eye."

Valentine stepped into the room and took off his blazer. He folded it in half and laid it across the back of the chair next to the armoire. Lindsay smiled and pulled the back straps off her heels and let her shoes drop to the floor. She tugged the top of her dress below her breasts, pushed it down to her waist, and wriggled it past her hips. She slid one leg out of it and held out her other foot, letting the garment hang from her ankle.

An amused expression floated over Valentine's face as he took the dress from her foot and tossed it onto the seat of the chair. Lindsay rolled onto her knees, leaned forward on her palms. She looked back over her shoulder at him and pouted her lips, swaying her ass. Just to encourage him, she reached back and slid a thumb beneath the waistband of her thong and worked it down a bit. She hoped the tattoo across the small of her back, the green design spreading out like Indian wings, didn't turn him off, rich guy that he was. The managers at the club hated it when she'd showed them.

Taking the cue, Valentine removed her thong, slowly rolling it down her legs and past her knees. She pressed her ass against him as he did, moving it from side to side, purring her breaths. He pitched the thong onto the chair.

Lindsay pushed herself up to a kneeling position; turned to let him take a look at the goods, let him know he was getting his money's worth. She'd never met a guy who didn't appreciate a real blonde. If he wasn't already harder than a rock, she figured that should do it.

"Let me help you into this," he said, placing a hand on

the bar suspended next to her. He lifted the black nylon strips of the shoulder harness and positioned it for her to put her arms through.

Lindsay looked at the apparatus before she let him set the harness over her shoulders, feeling a vague discomfort set in. She had initially pictured him tying her up with a silk scarf, maybe a rope. This was different.

The bar was round and sturdy. Valentine held it in place while she slid a hand into one of the leather cuffs and buckled the straps. With the bar across the back of her shoulders, she lifted her other hand and started to fit it into the remaining cuff, then stopped. The feel of the metal across her upper back and the grip of the leather around her wrist sent a mild shock of reality through her. The inside of her head seemed to ring, silent alarm bells going off.

Use your head, girl. This is incredibly stupid. It's not worth it.

"I'm having second thoughts," she said. "About this thing, I mean."

"Oh," Valentine said. She waited for him to say something else, but he didn't.

"I'm sorry, I just . . . this is . . . I don't really *know* you? Understand what I'm saying?"

"Yes. I understand. Really I do. It's okay."

"We could still have a really good time, you know." She reached for his crotch and gently rubbed her palm against him. "I mean, you can still spank me and everything."

He took her hand and lifted it, pressed it between his. Then he backed away, letting her hand slip out, and gestured toward her clothes.

"I'll have Lucas drop you off wherever you want. Just leave the money on the table out there."

"Wait," she said. "You mean, that's it?"

He stopped halfway out of the room. "Yes."

She slumped down, one arm hanging from the leather cuff on the bar, the unsecured harness lifting off her shoulders. She had done those furry cuffs before, hitched to the rails of a headboard. A few times when she'd been with one of the other girls at the club, more than once with a guy she dated. Never with a John, but was it that big a deal? A thousand bucks was a lot of money. Not to mention the gravy train she might enjoy if this guy became a regular.

"You aren't psycho, are you?"

"I'm sane according to every legal standard I know. But I understand your concern. No hard feelings. A girl like you can't be too careful."

Lindsay let out a breath, then straightened herself up and pushed her free hand through the other cuff.

"I'll need you to buckle this for me," she said.

Valentine came back to the bed and secured the second leather cuff. The straps of the harness pulled snug beneath her armpits when he tugged out the slack. He clasped the straps behind her back, then checked the other cuff and tightened the buckles on it a notch.

He lay across the bed in front of her, propping himself up on an elbow.

She smiled down at him. "Hey, no fair. Here I am, naked and helpless, and you don't even have your shirt off yet."

"How does it feel?" he asked.

"Weird," she said, shifting her shoulders and swinging slightly as she leaned forward a bit, taking some of the weight off her knees. "But I could probably get used to it."

Valentine inhaled deeply and reached up, placing a hand above her left breast. She shook herself, causing both breasts to jiggle. He cupped one of them and she hummed approvingly. He continued to stare at her chest, moving her breast one way, then the other, saying nothing. His hand was firm and still.

"Is something wrong?"

"No. Everything is just right."

Valentine got off the bed and walked to the end near the table. He stuck his foot beneath the dust ruffle and pressed down. Lindsay heard a popping sound, the slap of a latch being thrown. He circled to the opposite corner, behind her. She strained to see over her shoulder, saw him do the same kind of thing again with his foot, heard the same kind of sound.

"What are you doing?" she asked.

He put his hands on the corner of the mattress and pushed. "Nothing you're going to like, I'm afraid."

"Hey!"

Lindsay felt the bed shift sideways beneath her knees and feet, sliding on a track. It pulled her legs with it as it revealed a rectangular opening in the floor beneath. The perimeter was a few inches smaller than the dimensions of the bed, a square-edged space dropping off into a shallow pit of some kind. She tried to keep her feet on the bed as it rolled to an abrupt stop, stretching and pointing her foot, pressing down with clenched toes, but the sheet didn't offer much traction. Gravity tugged and kept tugging until her feet slipped off and her legs swung back to the center, dangling over the shadowy space, her body twisting back and forth with the bar as she kicked.

"Okay, I don't like this! I don't want to do this anymore! You can have your money back! Just get me down! *Hey!* Do you hear me?"

Valentine didn't respond. She could hear activity behind her, movement, bumping, the sound of cabinet doors.

She looked down at the pit, which she realized wasn't a pit at all. It was about four feet deep, with bare concrete walls. A vertical utility ladder, short, with just a few rungs, descended down the one she was facing. Mounted to the wall to her left was a swinging arm of metal tubing on a swivel, a hinged section of iron grating hanging flat from it. She could see the bottom, four converging slopes submerged in shadow, meeting at a drain in the middle. It looked like the base of an empty pool, an oddly shaped one with squared-off corners.

"What's going on? *Oh, Christ! Talk to me!*" She was starting to feel light-headed, realized her breathing was out of control. Adrenaline surges were causing a jackhammer to go off in her chest, icy hands to clench her lungs.

She tried to spin her body, to look back at what Valentine

was doing. She caught glimpses, brief shots of him snapping in and out of view, facing away from her, standing at the cabinet. She was able to discern a collection of things arrayed inside it, tools of some kind.

"Please say something!"

She sensed Valentine move, swung her head around as he walked the narrow space between the side of the pit and the bed. He was carrying several items, including a large drill and some kind of cylindrical wheel with teeth.

"Do you know how much money it cost to build this thing?" he said, nodding toward the space below her.

"Oh, God, what are you doing? Please! *Please* just let me down, let me out of here!"

Valentine set out the drill, the round metal cylinder, and a couple of smaller items she couldn't make out on the table adjacent to the wall. The drill was yellow with a large square block at the base of its pistol-like handle, allowing it to stand upright. It had another straight black handle sticking out from its side.

"I had to buy both floors. Submitted custom plans for a water exercise tank. Couldn't call it a pool, or a hot tub. Those aren't allowed. But tell them you need swim therapy for your back, make sure the right people find skybox tickets and sideline passes for the Jets, or front row to see *Three Days of Rain*, and you can have yourself your very own one of these. For a modest six figures, that is."

Lindsay tried to speak, but was sobbing too hard to get any words out.

A pneumatic hum coupled with the mechanical groan of bearings and hinges caused her eyes to pop open. Valentine was crouching at the edge near the grate, reaching down, his hand on a lever. The grate was rotating away from the wall, creeping closer.

It stopped with a clang less than a yard in front of her, forming a platform just out of the reach of her foot. Valentine disappeared behind her again. She heard him rummaging, shifting and sliding things.

"Please don't hurt me. God, oh God, oh God, please."

Valentine stepped around and onto the platform, carrying a bundle of multicolored rope and a small laundry basket. He put the basket down and unwound the rope. He made a loop, tied it off, pulled another loop of slack through it.

"Good thing about owning boats," he said. "You learn how to tie all sorts of useful knots."

Lindsay started crying again. She kicked out, bicycling her legs and screaming at him as he moved closer.

"Stay the fuck away from me!"

He caught one of her legs by the ankle, pulled it at an angle so she couldn't reach him with the other foot. He slipped the loop over her foot, then let her go, still holding on to the rope. He picked up the other end of the rope and fed it through a ring on the edge of the platform, pulling it tight, then binding it with a practiced series of quick motions.

"Now, I can lower this platform, thereby ripping your leg off, or you can allow me to tie the other foot. It's your choice."

Lindsay screamed as loud as she could, breaking down into more sobs.

"Shhh! Someone might hear!" The concerned expression on his face melted away quickly. "I'm kidding, if you didn't know. Not only is the floor below empty, but these walls are quite soundproof. Your foot?"

She kicked with her free foot as he took a step, baring her teeth and yelling. Valentine shrugged and backtracked to the wall, reaching for a lever and pressing down on it. The platform bucked slightly then started to descend.

"Okay!" She was crying uncontrollably now, breathing in convulsions, her body trembling.

He untied the rope from the ring. She hung limp as he looped it over her other ankle. Once it was taut, he pulled the rope through a ring in the center of the platform and tied it off. It stretched her body rigid, her toes inches from the grate.

"Excellent."

"Please, please, please don't hurt me. I'll do anything you want."

Valentine said nothing. He climbed off the platform onto the floor and circled behind her. When he returned, he was carrying a syringe filled with a clear liquid, the needle pointed up.

"I want you to remember this. Hey!" He grabbed her by the jaw, cupping her chin in his palm, and forced her to look at him. "I want you remember that when I had the power of God over you, I was merciful. I didn't make you ask, I didn't make you worship me, I didn't make you repent or forsake all others for that mercy. You think about that while you're suffering eternal torment, burning and agonizing as He would have you do for the rest of forever. I'm merciful. God isn't."

"You're crazy," she said, fighting through the sobs.

He felt around the front of her shoulder with his thumb, then stabbed the syringe into the spot he settled on. She felt a burning sensation spread out as he pressed the plunger. She tried to scream again, but couldn't gather enough breath and whimpered instead.

"This is a local," he said, removing the needle and rubbing the spot vigorously. "It will minimize the pain."

Valentine made his way off the platform and over to the table. Eyes blurred, she watched him assemble something on the drill. He hopped back onto the walkway holding the drill with the metal cylinder attached to it.

"This is a six-inch hole saw," he said. "It's primarily used to cut holes in doors. This is the largest they make. And it's the best way I've found."

He squeezed the trigger. The drill let out a whine, spinning the cylinder rapidly. The cylinder kept spinning after he took his finger off, quietly rotating to a stop.

Lindsay swallowed, fighting back her sobs. "Wh-what are you planning to do to me?"

"I thought you already knew. I'm going to cut a hole in your chest and remove your heart."

Lindsay screamed, sucked in a breath, screamed again. Her screams dissolved into sobs of *no* and *please*. Valentine waited for her to finish, a patient look on his face. She dropped her head and cried silently, still mouthing the same words.

"You've asked me several times to tell you why I'm doing this. Do you still want to know?"

Lindsay lifted her eyes, dipped her chin in an uncertain nod. She didn't really want to know. But the only thing she could think of that would be worse was not knowing.

Valentine's mouth stretched into a cold smile and he moved along the platform a few feet toward the curtain. He took hold of a piece of it near the bottom and shook, tilting his head and leaning a bit to the side.

An arm shot out through the part, impossibly long, greenish gray with quills of black hair spiking out of it. Lindsay's scream died in her throat and she gasped, twisting away from a clasping, snapping hand that was barely inches from her as it slashed the air. She let out short, loud groans instead, tiny breathless bleats, her eyes bulging.

Valentine raised his voice. "Back. *Back!*"

The arm withdrew behind the curtain. Valentine waited a moment, then yanked on the curtain's edge, pulling it until the part was a few feet wide.

"This," Valentine said, "is the Get of Damnation."

The black, vertical bars of a cage were visible now. Behind them, illuminated in a spill of wan light, something was squatting. It was facing her, arms looped along the floor in front of it, palms up, spidery fingers curled over, eyes peering out from behind a mop of dark, matted hair. A sheathed penis drooped out of its crotch, almost grazing the floor. Its face was too long, as were its arms, and it had the coiled aggression of an animal. But a feeling worming its way through Lindsay's gut told her it wasn't an animal at all.

Not entirely.

Valentine crossed back to the laundry basket, pulled out

a roll of duct tape. "Unfortunately, you have to be alive while I do this. I would use a paralytic, but believe me, it would be far worse for you, because you would be unable to breathe while your pulse was racing and you'd know everything that was happening. I don't want you going into cardiac arrest, either. So I'm going use this on you. If you resist, things will become painful. Do you understand?"

Lindsay wept. She was looking away, unable to speak, barely able to breathe, sobbing uncontrollably.

"Trust me, you don't want to watch. Now if you try to bite or anything, I will make you regret it. Do you hear me?"

When she didn't respond, Valentine slapped her. "I said, *do you hear me?*"

Lindsay nodded feebly, tears streaming. She didn't resist as Valentine noisily unrolled the tape around the bar, then around her head a few times above her brow, then around the bar on the other side of her, pinning her head back and securing it in place.

She saw nothing but the ceiling when she looked straight, could sometimes make out the top of his head if she pushed her eyes down. There were noises of movement, steps ringing on the metal, things being picked up and set down. Then the whine of the drill.

Oh, God, this is really happening. She shut her eyes, squeezing out tears. Why hadn't she lived a better life? Why hadn't she done more? She remembered so many things she hadn't thought of in years. A boy she loved in high school, that summer with her friends in Florida, those years with her grandmother while her father was drunk and her mother was running around catching up on her own unfinished childhood, too busy for anyone but herself. But what she thought of most of all, much to her surprise, was her grandmother, the woman who practically raised her, the one who dragged her to church all those Sundays, who always preached to her about the wages of sin. Constantly lecturing her on what was important. The old fuddy-duddy she resented so much—no fun, no excitement, nothing to offer but a dreary life of boredom. The one person, she realized, who ever cared about her. The one who tried to teach her. The one she let die alone and forgotten somewhere a few years ago.

Lindsay wondered if any of those things her grandmother told her could still be true. If it wasn't too late to make it a little bit right.

The whine of the drill wound down as Valentine took his finger off the trigger.

"What did you say?"

Lindsay swallowed. Her voice was a stuttery whisper. *"I forgive you."*

Valentine hesitated. Then he started laughing. His laughter grew louder and he shook his head, sighing, catching his breath, before erupting with more laughs. He was still laughing when he started the drill again and pressed the cylinder over the X he'd drawn on her chest. The teeth of the round saw ripped through her flesh, spraying a circle of blood. The whirring of the motor deepened as the blade met the chest plate. Valentine pressed against the side handle, steadying the drill, until he felt the bone give. Her body shuddered and shook. He pushed a bit further, let the teeth clear a groove, then pulled the circular blade out. The whir of the drill died out just before his final few chuckles did.

When he removed the chest plate the heart was still beating. He was quick to cut it out with a long scalpel. He proceeded carefully, dropping the scalpel to grip it with both hands as blood poured from the opening and her body twitched in spasms. He held it out, throbbing, and moved closer to the cage. The long, corded arm of the occupant snatched it and withdrew.

"Hey, Boss. Guess I'm early. I thought you'd be done by now."

Valentine looked over his shoulder. His servant was

standing at the entry to the room, a sleeveless shirt stretched tight across his chest, muscles subtly flexing with each movement.

"Hello, Lucas. I'm just finishing up."

"You okay, Boss?" Lucas asked, shifting his swollen frame. He scratched at the top of his bare, pale head.

"Yes." Valentine blinked several times, took a breath. "I'm fine. I was just thinking of something funny."

"Do you want me to come back later? Give you some, you know, privacy with her, like usual?"

"No. I'm done here. Take her to the incinerator."

Lucas spread his finger and thumb down over his mustache a few times. "The guard has been making noise about wanting more money."

"I trust he doesn't know anything."

"No, Boss. Still thinks we're a lab, disposing of animal carcasses. He's never around to see any different."

"Give him half of whatever he wants, because he'll be asking for twice as much as he's willing to take. We are close, Lucas. He's almost ready. It won't be long now."

"Whatever you say, Boss. Just glad I'll have a front-row seat."

They stood there watching as the thing in the cage finished the heart. It ate it like a piece of fruit, crouched over, shifting its weight on its haunches, hiding partially behind its shoulder, looking sideways at them every few seconds. Between bites.

"What do you think that tastes like to him?"

"Bitter," Valentine said. He glanced over at Lindsay's body. "That's why he likes them. Nothing healthy tastes good."

Lucas let out a chuckle.

"Tell me something," Valentine said. "Do I treat you like a slave?"

"Me? No, Boss. You pay me well. I ain't got any complaints."

Valentine said nothing. He removed his safety glasses. They were splattered with blood. So was his smock.

"This sure was a pretty one, huh, Boss? Not so pretty now, though."

"No," Valentine said. He regarded the girl's body, eyes settling on the ragged hole in her chest. Gristly strips of red and purple hung along the edges of it, dark matter still dripping from the void. "Not so pretty now."

CHAPTER 3

❖

HATCHER DIDN'T NEED TO CHECK THE ADDRESS. IT WAS the right street, and the pink flamingos told the rest. He'd almost forgotten about her thing for those creatures, the mild obsession she'd ceaselessly indulged, taking it with her from place to place, year to year. It was bad enough growing up with the stupid birds always nearby, on the refrigerator, hanging from the rearview mirror, perched on shelves, pinned to her clothes. But having them flocking on the front lawn—gaggles of them stuck in the ground, proudly displayed for everyone in the neighborhood to see—that had been awful. He remembered being enchanted by them as a small child, puzzled by them in elementary school. By fifteen, the whole thing was positively mortifying. New neighborhoods, new neighbors, but always those same damn cheap, gaudy, embarrassing plastic birds.

The half dozen flamingos leaned at odd angles in front of a small split-level, eyeing him warily from atop their thin metal rods as he made his way up the walk. The house was set back a few yards from the sidewalk in the middle of the block on a sloping street in Queens. Dark siding over painted cinder block, covered with some kind of textured mortar. An older neighborhood, probably built in the '50s, with large maples and oaks buckling the concrete paths and curbs in various places, the broken canopy above depositing nuts and branches and leaves on to the small lawns and the narrow roadway. Nicer than anything he could remember having lived in as a kid, but that wasn't saying much.

He climbed the two cement steps onto the stoop and rang the doorbell. Some faint footfalls, then he heard a latch and the door opened behind the screen.

Hatcher's mother stood in the doorway, beaming.

"Jacob! I can't believe it's really you."

He had to step back as she flung the screen door open, narrowly avoiding a smack in the head. She bounced onto the stoop and threw her arms around him. He wasn't sure what to do with his hands as she squeezed his midsection and rocked from side to side. Leaving them hanging at his sides seemed too consciously aloof. Hugging her in return would have been disingenuous. He settled on patting the backs of her shoulders. But not for long, and without much enthusiasm.

She pulled away, sniffling, smiling at him with teary eyes. "You're so big and strong now."

"I eat a lot."

The years didn't melt or peel away as he'd half expected; he didn't feel dragged into the past. It was more like something he had left behind and hadn't paid much thought had just leaped a chasm, caught up to him in the here and now. Heavier, older, but still the person he remembered, time now dragging at her skin, pulling at her curves. She must have given up that fight for eternal youth.

She looked surprisingly domesticated, wearing dark polyester slacks and a light blue knit blouse, a small white apron around her waist. Her hands felt cool and damp as she ran them down his cheeks, like she had hastily wiped them dry. He forced a mild smile, gently took her arms by the wrists, and lowered them. The silence quickly became awkward.

"Did you have any trouble finding the place?" she said, finally.

"No. I took the bus to Queens; it dropped me off a few blocks away."

"Where's my mind gone? Please, come inside."

She stepped back, gesturing Hatcher into her home.

The air was thick with the trapped odor of food. The precise smell was hard to pin down, generations of aromas worked into the walls over years, probably the furniture, too, competing with something more immediate coming from the kitchen. It was a little too much, but not altogether unpleasant.

"I just put some coffee on. It should be ready in a minute."

Hatcher nodded, treading behind her into a small living room.

Karen Woodard kept a tidy house these days, or at least had tidied up in anticipation of Hatcher's visit, he couldn't be sure which. The décor was simple. A bit cluttered, but livable. The stuff of discount stores and consignment sales, early American furniture with wood frames and quilted blankets, wooden tables with gilded lamps and fringed bell shades. A scarred, darkened hardwood floor with small oval rugs stitched in concentric rings. And, of course, flamingos. Pink ones, white ones, tall ones, squat ones, porcelain ones, sewn ones. On the walls, the tables. Flamingos were everywhere, even more so than when he was a kid. She led him to a sofa with a pink flamingo throw pillow and sat. He took a few extra steps and lowered himself into a neighboring chair.

"There's so much I want to know about you," she said, sliding over to be closer to him. "About where you've been and what you've done."

"You mean, why I was in prison."

She shook her head, a pained expression washing over

her face. "No, no. Just about you in general. Unless, that's something you want to tell me."

"All I really want is to know what's going on."

She stood, brushing her hands down her apron. "Coffee should be ready. Would you like some?"

Hatcher rubbed his eyes and blinked a few times. He could already sense this was going to be more difficult than he had thought. It had been nine hours since he'd spoken with his mother on the phone from the confinement facility. She had avoided the subject then, she was avoiding it now.

"Sure. Coffee sounds good."

He watched her head into the kitchen, past a small dining area with a table set for three, then leaned forward, forearms on his knees, and swept the room. On the far wall, above a table of framed photos, was a picture of him from high school in his football pads, holding his helmet. Next to it was a photo of a man he didn't recognize, dark hair and light brown eyes, square-jawed, a controlled smile spreading his lips thin. The teenaged Hatcher wasn't smiling at all in his.

His mother returned carrying a tray with cups and a small matching pitcher and sugar bowl. The warm scent of food cooking, meaty and moist, stronger than the odor of the house, followed her. It tickled his nostrils, made a tangy taste juice the sides of his tongue.

"Cream and sugar?"

"Fine."

He gestured toward the wall of photos. "You still married to Carl?"

"Yes. He'll be home soon."

Hatcher nodded. He would have bet a significant amount of money that they were long divorced. He remembered his mother going from a woman in her twenties fishing for love and romance to one in her thirties looking for a meal ticket. He supposed that should have made him feel some sympathy for Carl Woodard, but it didn't. Then or now.

She dropped a sugar cube into one of the cups using a

tiny pair of tongs, carefully adding some cream. Holding it by the saucer, she offered it to him. It rattled slightly in her hands as he reached for it.

"Mom," he said, coughing slightly. The word felt foreign in his mouth, like a hair that had been stuck in the back of his throat, pushed out with his tongue. "It's time you tell me what's going on."

Karen ran a thumb along the inside of a gold chain around her neck, gently pulling it out. Her throat moved behind it as she swallowed. "It's been so long, Jacob. I've missed you so. You were just a boy, last time."

Hatcher said nothing. There was nothing to say.

"You don't know how long I've been looking forward to this day. I just wish—"

"Look, it's nice you're glad to see me. Really, it is. But right now I just need you to explain things. Starting with what I'm doing here."

Karen looked down at the coffee tray, still fondling her necklace. "Garrett was killed."

"Yeah, I got that much. Who the hell is Garrett?"

"Your brother."

"And I'll ask again, just like I did this morning. Are you saying I had a brother I didn't know about?"

"Yes." She raised her eyes, then lowered them. Her body seemed to sag under the crush of what she was thinking. "You did."

"I'm waiting."

She paused, twisting her head to look out the front window. Her eyes were fixed on some faraway spot. "I had a child before . . ." She paused, took a breath. "Before your father and I got married," she said.

Hatcher leaned back into the chair, ran a hand over his hair. He wasn't shocked by what she said, had even considered the possibility. But he was genuinely confused. Given how she had lived after his father left, he had no reason to think she hadn't slept with other men before the two of them had met. But it still didn't make any sense.

"You said something about my father not taking this well."

"Yes." She took her eyes from the window and peered into her coffee. "I'm worried about how this will affect him."

"Okay, this is where you're losing me. If you had a child before you met my father, how would he even know him?"

"I didn't say it was before I met your father. I said it was before I married him. He had left for Vietnam not long after we started dating. I was only in high school and I found out I was pregnant."

"And he didn't want you to have it?"

She glanced at him with a pained expression. "No, it wasn't like that. He didn't know. He'd already shipped out. It was my parents. I put the baby up for adoption."

"But you ended up getting married."

"He came back a year later. We dated a few times and I felt like I had to tell him. How could I *not*. I was shocked that he asked me to marry him, right then, right after I explained what had happened, while I was still crying and asking him to forgive me. We talked about trying to get the baby back, and I know he tried very hard to find a way, but it just wasn't something you did back then."

"So, this wasn't a half sibling we're talking about?"

"No," she said. A little too quickly, Hatcher noted. Insulted, perhaps. "I can show you the birth certificate, if you don't believe me. I kept a copy. It shows he was your full-blooded brother."

He adjusted himself in his seat, leaning forward. "And now he's dead."

"Yes," she said softly. She let the word to hang out there like it was the first time she had actually considered the possibility.

"How come I didn't know about him?"

"It was complicated. I was going to tell you when you were old enough to understand, but then your father and I split and I was scared. I know I should have. I'm sorry. I just didn't know how, or if it was even the right thing to do. You were always such an angry child. Always acting out, getting into fights. I didn't want to confuse you. I guess I didn't want to give you another reason to hate me."

Now it was Hatcher's turn to stare at his coffee. *Angry child.* He stifled the urge to say something about that, something he knew she wouldn't like. A different school almost every year, a different house every few months, a mother who was living with a different guy every time he turned around, meaning he was living with a different guy every time he turned around. And through all of this, a father who was nowhere to be found. What the hell did she expect?

"You know, when I first saw him, I thought he was you. He's not quite as big as you, but he has your features." Her gaze slipped down to her hands, interlaced in her lap. "Had your features."

"When was this? That you first saw him?"

"Garrett showed up at my door about ten months ago. He was some kind of security consultant, was good at finding information. Said he found out he'd been adopted and decided to research his birth parents, dug through hospital records. He seemed pleased to learn he had a brother."

Hatcher scratched the side of his nose. "Are you sure he was who he said he was?"

"I think I'd know my own son."

Hatcher thought of something he could say to that, but didn't. "How could you know someone you hadn't seen in over thirty years? Since he was a newborn baby?"

"I'd know! I mean, I *knew*. It was Garrett. I'm not completely dumb. Of course I had a hard time believing him at first. But his eyes. They were so familiar. Your eyes, Jacob."

She glanced away, wiped the back of her hand against the corner of her lid, blinking, then started fondling her necklace again. "You always had the greatest eyes."

"Did he want anything?"

"What do you mean?"

"I mean, when he showed up. Did he ask for anything? Money? A place to live?"

"Of course not! He wasn't some bum. He never asked me for a thing. He just wanted to get to know his parents. Is that so hard for you to understand?"

Hatcher ignored the question, thinking, *Yes, very hard.* "I saw the name 'Garrett Hatcher' on the message."

"He started using the name Hatcher after he found your father and me. He said he was going to legally change it back."

"Why?"

"Why not? Your father was very happy about it."

"Speaking of that, what's the deal with you and my father? You sound as if you've been talking to him."

"Yes. It's not like it used to be, Jacob. Your father and I have been cordial since Garrett came back. We've talked on the phone."

"Cordial."

"People change, Jacob."

He took a sip of his coffee. "They sure do."

"I know you're mad at me. You've always been mad at me for something. I wish you could please stop, just for a little while."

"Do I look mad?"

"I always did the best I could, Jacob."

Hatcher finished off his cup, set it on the tray. "What does Carl think of all this?"

"Carl? You know how he is. But he understands. He never spoke much to Garrett, but he was sorry to hear what happened."

Yeah, sure he was, Hatcher thought. What a humanitarian.

Some things change, and some things don't. She was acting like she didn't know why he'd simply up and left after high school, but there was no way, he thought. Just no way. He didn't really remember saying good-bye as much as merely leaving, taking a bus and a suitcase to a tiny college in another state, an undersized and relatively slow linebacker on a Division II scholarship. Her marrying Carl Woodard had been the final straw. Having that clown come in and "lay down the law" had disgusted him to the point of wanting to puke. Or make Carl puke. Blood. All those staredowns and arbitrary rules, those conversations Hatcher could hear where that fucking loser would talk about the "kid" needing to be put in his place. Carl had a stepson from a previous marriage, older than Hatcher, who'd been in and out of rehab and constantly doing time. Carl had cut ties with him after his divorce, but he was always telling Hatcher's mother how Hatcher would turn out the same way if someone didn't get tough with him, teach him to respect authority. Hatcher wondered if the asshole ever knew how close he'd come to getting the shit stomped out of him back then.

"What do you want from me, Mom?"

"What do you mean?"

"What am I doing here?"

"I thought you would want to come, because of your brother."

Hatcher glanced over to the photos on the wall, nodded toward them. "A brother I didn't know I had, that I never met. I haven't spoken to you in a dozen years, and suddenly I'm summoned for a funeral. I'm sorry, it doesn't add up."

"I know. It's all just so horrible."

"That's not what I mean. What I'm talking about is, what made you track me down? Go to the Red Cross? Why was it so important to have me here?"

"I . . . thought I might need some help with all the arrangements. Help dealing with things. The funeral's the day after tomorrow. It's all so overwhelming."

Hatcher tilted a finger in her direction. "You're lying."

"What kind of thing is that to say?"

"If the funeral is the day after tomorrow, you've already taken care of the arrangements. Now just tell me the truth."

"I'm not lying."

"You're trying not to, but you're not being candid. Picking and choosing your words. You're hiding something. Believe me, I can tell."

She poured some more coffee into her cup, steadying the back of her pouring hand with the fingers of her other. "Please, Jacob. This is difficult enough."

"Okay, let me spell it out for you, and make it simple. I can tell by your nonverbals that you're not telling me everything. I can tell by the way you move your eyes, the way you look up and away before you say certain things. I can tell by the way you're holding that cup in front of you right now, like a shield. By the way you use your necklace as an excuse to hold your hand near your mouth. Don't bother trying to convince me I'm wrong, because I'm not. Just tell me."

"I don't want you to think I don't want you here, Jacob. I do. I've always thought of you. You've always been in my thoughts."

Hatcher shot a glance at the ceiling as he took a breath. "What is it?"

"I wasn't sure I'd ever see you again. I'm so glad you're here. I can't tell you how much my heart jumped when I heard the door. When I talked to you on the phone."

"Tell me."

"It was something your brother said."

He nodded impatiently, rolling his hand for her to keep going. "What?"

"A few days before he died, on the phone. He told me, almost like he was joking . . . He said if anything should happen to him, I should find you."

"Me?"

"Yes."

Hatcher's eyes drifted over to the framed photo of the man on the wall, that measured smile. "He probably just meant that you should find me because I'm your son, thinking it would be a good thing. Or maybe you misunderstood him."

"No. We were talking on the phone, and I asked him how things were going, and he said fine, and then he grew quiet, and then he said if anything out of the ordinary should happen to him, that I should find you. I told him he was making me nervous, and he changed the subject, told me to forget about it, laughed a bit, like he wished he hadn't said it."

"Why would he say something like that?"

"I'm not sure. Not long after he contacted me, just after he started talking to me and your father, he became interested in you. Said he never had a real brother, just like you've been saying. A few weeks ago, he said he had located you, that you were on an assignment for the military, and wouldn't be back until the summer. He told me you were in the army and had your unit information. He said in a few months, he'd get in touch with you, had me hoping maybe you'd want to come back and see me."

Hatcher's eyes roamed the room, skipping from flamingo to flamingo as he digested the information.

"That doesn't make any sense. Why would he tell you to find me if something happened to him? He didn't know anything about me."

"Jacob, I think he knew he was in danger, or might be. The police are saying it was some crazy person Garrett got tangled up with in the street, trying to help some woman who was being mugged, but I don't think I believe them. When I remembered what he said . . . it was frightening. I think he knew someone might try to hurt him."

"Even if that's true, I don't see where I fit in to any of this."

"Garrett knew about you, Jacob. He was in the military, too, for a while. The air force. He said you were some kind of elite soldier. He spoke admiringly of you, said men like you made things better for everyone else. With your bravery."

"What could he possibly know about me?"

"I don't know. Maybe enough to trust that his brother would figure out what happened."

Before he could respond, Hatcher heard the sound of a car door shutting from somewhere in front of the house.

"That's Carl now. Please listen to me, Jacob," Karen said, scooting forward to the edge of the cushion. "Your father isn't well. Garrett told me he's been suffering from diabetes for years. He could hardly walk. Garrett forced him into a hospital, insisted he go. In fact, I think Garrett may have been going to visit him when he was . . . when he died. He had just found a special diabetes center for him at a hospital in the city. It's very bad. They may have to amputate."

"I'm sorry to hear that," Hatcher said, though he actually found it hard to feel anything specific.

"It would be nice if you could go see him. I think he and Garrett had grown close. I spoke to him on the phone right after I found out, then again yesterday. He's not taking it well."

"I haven't seen him since I was eleven years old."

"But it would mean so much to him."

"Him? Or you?"

The door opened and Carl entered, pausing to wipe his shoes on the welcome mat. He was still short, with slicked down strands of thinning hair and a gut that hung out over his belt like he was trying to sneak a bowling ball in somewhere. He wore a tan shirt and tan slacks. A state highway department patch was sewn onto one of the sleeves. Some kind of civil service uniform.

"Dear, Jacob's here! Isn't it so nice to see him again?"

Carl grunted a greeting, shooting Hatcher an expression that was part smile, part snarl. Hatcher stood, realized he'd actually been looking forward to this. A little bit, at least. It also gave him an excuse to cut things short and get out of there.

"Don't you look all growed up," Carl said, running his gaze from toe to crown. "Must be nice, sitting around all day, lifting weights, doing nothing."

"Kind of like working for the state," Hatcher said. "Except for the lifting weights part."

"Still got a mouth on you, huh?"

"Oh, Carl," Karen said, slapping his shoulder, an unconvincing look of scorn pinching her face. "Quit being such a grouch."

"I'm just saying, is all."

"That's okay," Hatcher said. "I was just about to leave anyway."

"No!" Karen said, putting a hand on Hatcher's arm. "I've been making dinner all afternoon. A pot roast. Please say you'll stay."

"The boy wants to go, Karen. Let 'im go."

Hatcher held his stare, peering down into those eyes, remembering just how much he couldn't stand living under the same roof with the man, how he marked the time until he would be able to leave and never come back. "On second thought, I think I will stay."

"Oh, good," Karen said. "And I hope not just for dinner. We have a second bedroom with a foldout bed."

Hatcher smiled at Carl. "What do you think?"

"I think you're going to do what you want, no matter what I think."

"Oh, don't mind him. We're happy to have you." Karen hugged him one more time, giving an extra squeeze at the end, then gave Carl a peck before heading to the kitchen. "You just relax. I'm going to check on dinner."

Carl watched her leave the room. "I never thought I'd see you again," he said.

"I guess thinking isn't your strong suit."

"Don't you go making things tougher on her than they already are, convict."

"I don't plan on making anything tough for anyone. Except for you, if you talk to me like that one more time."

"This is my house. I can say anything I want."

"You absolutely can. I'm just letting you know there'll be consequences this time around."

Carl glared fiercely into Hatcher's eyes for a few seconds, then backed off a step. He reached into his pocket and removed a small flamingo figurine, a white one and a pink one sharing the same space, necks intertwined, and placed it on a table next to a few others, glancing over toward the kitchen as he did.

"Unlike you, I wouldn't want to do anything to upset your mother," he said.

Hatcher rolled his eyes. Puh-leeze. "In case you hadn't noticed, being here wasn't exactly my idea."

"Well, it wasn't my idea, either. All the fault of that Garrett, went and got himself killed."

Hatcher shot a look over his shoulder, lowered his voice a notch. "Since you brought it up, maybe you could quit being a jerk for a few seconds and tell me what you knew about him."

"Why?"

"I'm curious."

"Not much. Only that I didn't like him. Didn't trust him."

"Why was that?"

Carl ran his eyes down Hatcher's shirt and then back up, a disgusted grimace contorting his mouth and brow. "Because he reminded me too much of you."

Hatcher's mother came out of the kitchen and announced that dinner was ready. She was only a few steps past the dining area when she paused and tilted her head, lips quavering, hands on her hips, eyes on her new figurine.

"It's beautiful!" she said, rushing to give Carl a hug. "Where would I be without you?"

CHAPTER 4

❖

THE AIR INSIDE THE THIRTEENTH PRECINCT WAS LIKE A
body of stagnant water, smelly and unmoving. There was
something institutional about the odor, the subtle, faded
layers of collected fumes, the chemical scent of paints
and cleaning solvents that combined with the stale reek
of accumulated perspiration and the captured breaths of
the taxed and the governed. It almost made Hatcher feel
at home.

A clock on the wall in a painted wire cage showed just
shy of twenty past ten. Mid-morning, and the station house
was active but languid, a steady current of people coming
and going, announcing their presence for appointments,
holding up citations and asking questions through bulletproof glass. Uniformed and plainclothed escorts periodi-
cally emerged to lead individuals past security doors with
metal detectors. A few minutes earlier, a man with wild,
matted hair and a long beard in a camouflage military
jacket was marched through the waiting area in cuffs and
vomited near the wall as they reached one of the doors.

The rank stink of bile was soon masked by another layer of chemical smell, this one perfumed with pine.

Hatcher had been waiting for over thirty minutes in a cracked plastic chair that dug into his back when he slouched. The chair was attached to a metal frame bolted to a concrete wall. There was an identical row across from him, plastic over tubular chrome set in concrete with seats on both sides. There was another set of seats beyond it, both populated with a similar assortment of the beleaguered. It was hard not to look at the people in front of him, a tired black man scanning the floor, occasionally nodding in response to his girlfriend or wife, a woman who was twice his size giving the guy a shrill ass-chewing in a mercifully low voice. Two seats over, a Latino with tattooed knuckles in an oily wife-beater and baggy jeans bounced his knees and rubbed the top of his thighs. An older couple, the man short and the woman pear-shaped, huddled at the end of the row with the quiet demeanor of the foreign-born. Hatcher was accustomed to being made to wait, but this was different. After more than a week of Tyler Culp, it seemed strange to sit somewhere for so long without craving sleep, alone in a crowd with his thoughts and nothing to do with his hands. But he'd already slept more than he had in longer than he could remember, and his brain was humming with the buzz of morning coffee. He was starting to feel antsy.

The discomfort in his back finally made him stand, and he debated whether to come back later. He told himself he was merely stalling anyway, using the police as an excuse to delay going to the hospital, but he realized he really did want some answers. His conversation with his mother had only raised more questions, questions that had followed him into his dreams, burrowing around his mind while he slept. He couldn't remember what he dreamt, but that didn't stop whatever it was from shadowing him into the waking world, nagging and tugging at his thoughts.

A woman in a charcoal gray business skirt and ivory blouse with a badge hanging by a lanyard around her neck caught his eye as he stretched. Slender but shapely, blonde, leaning into the room from behind a sturdy door near the bulletproof windows. Her scan of the area quickly narrowed as she seemed to home in on him, singling him out among the two black youths, a Latina woman, and a guy with multitoned hair that shared his row of seats. She was looking right at him when she called out his name, loud enough for everyone to hear.

Hatcher crossed the room toward her. "I'm Jacob Hatcher, yes."

She held out a hand for him to take, fingers straight, like a karate chop, and gave him a firm, terse shake. "I'm Detective Wright. This way please."

Hatcher followed her back into the station where a uniformed officer behind the glass buzzed the door open for them. On the other side of it she stopped at a counter where another cop in uniform asked him for his driver's license through a hole in a window.

Hatcher pulled out his wallet, removed his license.

"This is expired," the cop said.

"That's all I have. I haven't driven in a while."

"Then I'll need some other form of ID."

"I don't have any on me." It was a lie, but the way he saw it, the truth didn't exactly work for him. He doubted he'd get much cooperation if he pulled out what they'd given him at the RCF. "It's not like I turned into someone else."

The cop glanced at the detective. She squeezed her lips tight, gave a sideways look at Hatcher. "It's okay. He's related to a homicide victim. I'm taking him back."

The officer squirmed a bit, then slid a clipboard over. The detective filled out a few of the blocks, passed it to Hatcher for his signature. The cop behind the counter typed out his name into a keyboard, then printed out a visitor's sticker with the NYPD logo and a blank for his name and the date on it to wear on his shirt.

"Thanks," Hatcher said as she escorted him away from the counter.

"That's okay. I know you had to wait a long time. Things are kinda crazy right now."

"Why's that?"

She gave a quick shake to her head. "Nothing I can really comment about."

Hatcher noted she had a distinctive voice. Raspy and melodic. A bit breathy. The kind of voice that could make the most innocent comment sound suggestive. He'd noticed it on the phone, but assumed it was the ten months he'd just spent in prison that made it sound so sexy. Now he was starting to think he could have spent ten months in a brothel and it would still sound good.

"This way," she said.

Hatcher followed her across an artificial hall created by six-foot partitions of more bulletproof Plexiglas, uniformed officers manning stations and radio equipment in fortified see-through cubicles. The glass ended where the hall intersected another corridor, and as they crossed it they stopped to allow a threesome to pass. Two were obviously plainclothes cops in rolled-up shirtsleeves. Bulky builds, thinning locks, loosened ties. They were shadowing a short, bookish man in a dark suit with limp hair combed flat and gold-rimmed glasses. All three had just emerged from behind a closed door. The cops did not look happy. Hatcher could hear the man with the glasses explaining how he had no choice regarding some matter, managing to sound both apologetic and irritated at the same time. Another man stepped out of the room a few steps behind them. He was tall with meticulously coiffed salt-and-pepper hair and wore a much more expensive suit than the man with the glasses. It hung perfectly off his shoulders, ventless and smooth, the cuffs of his pants resting gently on the tassels of his cordovan loafers. Custom-made, Hatcher supposed. He was carrying a chocolate brown briefcase that looked like it cost more than the two cops probably made in a week. The man's presence seemed disruptive in the hall, his appearance causing a few other cops to stop or slow down, everyone paying sudden attention to the goings-on. Hatcher figured there had to be more to it than the man's flash.

"Excuse me one moment," Detective Wright said. She doubled back after one of the pissed-off looking cops who had passed them. The cop exchanged a few words with her over his shoulder that Hatcher couldn't hear. Her body language indicated that whatever he told her, she wasn't happy about it.

She stood in the middle of the hall, stuck to the spot for a few seconds, acting like her feet were caught in mud. The trio moved on. She watched for another moment, then started back toward Hatcher, wearing a look of extreme displeasure.

"Sorry about that," she said.

"Something bad?"

The detective's eyes were on the tall man in the sharp suit, drilling him as they passed. He stood his ground, ignoring her. Waiting for something, like he owned the place.

"Yes," she said, still watching the man, the man still ignoring her.

At the far end of the hall Hatcher saw a pair of uniformed cops exit an elevator, escorting a man in cuffs. This one was unnaturally large in the upper body, the product of three-hour workouts, maybe longer ones, five or six days a week. His unflexed arms looked like a pair of thick pythons that had each swallowed a football. He caught Hatcher's eye and fixed him with a cold stare. A prison stare. He was bald, his head shiny and waxed. A mustache curved down around his mouth and up to his ears, forming sideburns to nowhere. Hatcher didn't look away, held the man's gaze even as the tough passed a few inches to his left and looked like he might lean over to take a bite out of Hatcher's face. Each held eye contact until the prisoner eventually turned his attention to the tall man. His guards stopped and lifted his hands so one of the cops could uncuff him. The tall man in the suit placed a friendly hand on the big man's shoulder. The guy glanced back over that hand at Hatcher one more time and stretched his mouth into a humorless smile. He winked before being led the opposite way.

Hatcher turned back in the direction he and the detective were heading just in time to see Wright cross over into the path of another man. This one's suit wasn't so nice. The coat didn't hang so well, the material flat and stiff. The guy wearing it was medium height, on the stocky side, with broad shoulders but a waist that didn't give him any taper. He had a dense head of black hair, pomped straight back. A lot of body on top. Too much, in Hatcher's estimation. Most likely a weave. He'd seen a similar one before, on a CIA agent who debriefed him. You could tell when they sweat. The sides would get wet and flat, but the rug would stay the same. There'd been a lot of laughs when that guy'd left the room.

Detective Wright stepped forward into the man's space, looking almost straight up, her hands in the air.

"You're letting him go?"

The man shrugged. His hands were large, but delicate-looking, almost feminine, with slender fingers. He carried himself with the dismissive demeanor of someone in authority, an air of it about him. Hatcher figured he would have had even more of that air without the weave. A gold shield was clipped to the front of his belt.

"It's not my call, Amy."

"Doesn't anybody in the DA's office have a set of balls? For Christ's sake, Dan!"

The guy thrust his chin in the direction of the big man and the others as they disappeared down the other end of the corridor. "Did you see his counsel? Stephen Solomon. Need I say more? That's heavy-duty representation right there. We knew it was shaky."

She shook her head. "Gutless wonders."

"DA says the search won't hold up and that we're going to be nailed for harassment if we're not careful. I don't like it any more than you do. But the captain agreed. We had nothing to hold him on."

Wright shook her head one more time, twisting her upper lip, then continued walking. Dan watched her, sliding his eyes to Hatcher, obviously not caring whether Hatcher noticed.

She led Hatcher up a flight of stairs to a room packed with desks. Most had computer monitors, but several along the wall had old and faded Selectric typewriters the color of the wild man's vomit before the Pine-Sol. That made them almost the same color as the flecked linoleum flooring that stuck to his rubber soles and made an adhesive peeling sound with each step.

"Forms," she said, noticing where his eyes were as she took a seat behind one of the desks. The desk had a wood veneer top with metal sides painted to approximate a walnut grain. Government furniture, through and through. She held her palm out in the direction of a chair next to it. Also the obvious product of a government contract.

"I'm sorry?"

"We use lots of forms. The computer system is not that reliable, goes down a bunch. We have to file everything on paper. Those dinosaurs are the quickest way to fill them in. The department's too cheap to bring us into the twentieth century. Guess we're not far enough into the twenty-first yet."

"I take it you didn't join the force for the paperwork."

She sighed, contorted the side of her mouth into something that created a dimple, and began sifting through a stack of folders. "You said on the phone you had some questions."

As if hearing its cue, the telephone on her desk buzzed. She gave him an apologetic look, and he nodded for her to go ahead and answer it. She was gruff to the person on the other end, tersely repeating that she was busy, but apparently to no avail. Her body seemed to deflate slightly as she listened. A sag of surrender.

She cupped the bottom of the handset and gestured over

her shoulder. "I'm going to be a minute. Help yourself to some coffee."

Not much for pleasantries, but he decided the rough, sultry sound of her voice more than made up for it.

Taking the hint, he made his way to the coffeepot on a small table near the wall. The squad room had a lot in common with a good number of military offices he'd seen. Bleak, utilitarian. Personalized here and there in a way that only seemed to make it more oppressive. Reminders that some people spent a good deal of their lives in this space, hours they'd never get to live again.

He poured himself a cup and stared at a nearby desk where a splash of color caught his eye. A chalk-white face with big orange wisps of hair sticking out from the sides, a single smaller one on top. Sinister, drooping eye holes shaped like large eggs. A grin that looked predatory. A clown mask. Halloween type. It was displayed prominently on the desktop, pulled over something to hold its shape, like a severed head.

"The Bozo Killer," Wright said as she hung up the phone.

Hatcher looked over to her, tilted his head. "Huh?"

"Some kook went around cutting people up dressed as a clown." She jutted her chin toward the desk. "Reynolds caught him, walking a beat. Homeless guy sleeping in box. Had the murder weapon on him. The bust got him his detective shield."

Hatcher nodded, giving the mask one final glance as he returned to her desk and took a seat.

"Okay." She let out a long breath, rubbed a finger over one eye. "You had some questions."

"I can come back later if this isn't a good time."

"No. No, it's not that. I'm just a bit agitated right now."

"I can see that. Something to do with that guy out in the hall, if I had to guess."

She looked straight into Hatcher's eyes, exploring them.

"I caught you playing staredown with him. I almost said something. Not a good idea."

"And why is that?"

"That's Lucas Sherman. Name ring a bell?"

Hatcher shrugged, shaking his head. "Should it?"

"He made the news a few years back. Serial rapist. Given a . . . *controversial* option in exchange for a lighter sentence."

"What kind of option?"

"A chemical castration."

Hatcher watched her eyes appraising him. He was familiar with the term but knew it had a totally different meaning among people he'd worked with, one involving acids and guys in countries not known for their friendly attitude. He wondered what she'd think about that.

"Doesn't sound fun."

"It's never been authorized in New York. It was part of a plea agreement by some ADA who thought he had a better alternative to incarceration. Well, Sherman was caught cheating. He got picked up with a prostitute during a narc sweep and it turned out he was giving himself testosterone injections to counter the drugs. The DA went to court to invalidate the deal, and his lawyer pointed out the agreement didn't say anything about him not being able to inject anything he wanted. The scumbag ended up laughing at us. He even beat the indecency charge. This was years ago."

"What did he do this time?"

Detective Wright inclined her head, studying him with the look of a jeweler romancing a stone. Her lips bunched together as she seemed to weigh her options. She shot another glance over to the door, then leaned forward and lowered her voice to a gravelly whisper. "One of our patrolmen responded to a tip, spotted a limo in the parking lot after hours at an industrial facility, doing some random drive-by. Apparently it was parked sideways, across a loading zone, with an interior light on. He gets curious, checks it out. Sees the trunk isn't all the way closed and lifts it. Inside, there are plastic sheets laid out with what looks like blood on them." She jutted her chin toward the hall. "He calls it in and arrests our friend there."

"Problem with the search, I take it."

"No PC, according to the DA. Probable cause, that is. Trunk may have not been closed all the way, but he had no right to pop it open and look inside. Rookie mistake. A more experienced cop would have got it to stick."

"By finding probable cause?"

"By lying about whether the contents of the trunk were in plain view."

Hatcher waited for her to laugh, giving away the joke, but she barely grinned. "Blood on plastic in a trunk probably isn't good."

"He says he was burning laboratory waste. RMW. That's a felony. Problem is, even his confession to that is considered fruit of the poisonous tree."

"I'm going to go out on a limb and say you're not upset because he beat a dumping charge."

"His name has popped up in connection with some missing call girls," she said after a pause. "Nothing too solid. No bodies, even. So much manpower is taken up by anti-terrorism activities since nine-eleven, it's hard to devote attention to things like missing persons, especially when they happen to be hookers. But a pattern has started to emerge." She pursed her lips, grunting. "And you heard about the nun who disappeared, I'm sure."

Hatcher leaned his head, gave it another little shake. "I haven't paid attention to the news in a while."

"Wow. I thought everyone in the country knew about it. A couple of months ago. She was young, relatively new to the convent. Vanished without a trace."

"You suspect this guy Sherman?"

"We placed him in the general vicinity. But that's about it. A lot of work has gone into the hunt for her, but it's turned up nothing and we've had to scale back. We've been hoping for a break. I thought this was it." She huffed. "But his lawyer, the one you saw downstairs, he managed to quash our attempts to get an emergency search warrant for the furnace. I don't know how, but he convinced a judge it would be a backdoor way to use the illegal search of the limo. That's a lot of legal firepower for one count of illegal waste disposal."

"Don't lawyers like that cost money?"

"Lots. The whole thing smells. And that guy is bad news. I don't think you want to go messing with him. Even if you do look like you could take care of yourself. I'm assuming you're not a killer. I certainly can't say the same about him."

"I'll watch my step."

"And by the way, you didn't hear any of that stuff from me, okay?"

"What stuff?"

Wright smiled, reserved, but genuine, then reached over and pulled a case file from a short stack. "Let's get to your questions. The reason I may have sounded a little confused on the phone was we had the deceased IDed as Garrett Nolan." She opened the file and set it on the desk. "You were his brother?"

"I . . . yes."

"Well, I'm sorry for your loss, Mr. Hatcher."

"Thank you."

"What would you like to know?"

"Pretty much whatever you can tell me."

The detective thought about that for a moment. "I assume you know that your brother was killed when he was struck by a vehicle."

"That's about all I know."

She lifted the file, propping it open in front of her as she skimmed through it. "It appears he was coming to the aid of a woman who was being assaulted. Witnesses said a man grabbed her out of Bean's coffee shop. You know it?"

Hatcher shook his head.

"It's over on Third Avenue near Twentieth. Your brother was inside, tried to intercede. The tussle spilled into the street, and they ended up in front of an emergency vehicle heading to a call."

"Are you sure that's what happened?"

She nodded. "There was no shortage of witnesses. It sounds like your brother was a brave man."

"I guess it does."

"If it makes you feel any better, according to the coroner it's more than likely he was killed instantly. The EV was moving with a full party hat on, as they say."

Hatcher nodded. That part was probably bullshit, even if she wanted to believe it. Everyone was always killed instantly. No grieving mother was ever told that her son died a horrible, painful death, screaming in agony, pissing and shitting himself on the battlefield, limbs blown off, holding parts of his guts in, choking on his own puke. It was always painless. Nobody ever felt a thing.

Then again, you never can know for sure. Maybe Garrett lucked out. If you could call something like instant death "luck."

The silence became awkward as he tried to think of something to ask and realized he didn't know enough about his brother to come up with anything.

"I have a question for you, Mr. Hatcher, if you don't mind. Do you know who your brother was meeting that day? At the coffee shop?"

"No. Why?"

"No particular reason. The waitress indicated he was there with someone else. We weren't able to locate him. Would be nice just to fill in that blank."

Hatcher considered that for a moment. "Do you think this person may have had something to do with what happened?"

"No. Just thought you might know who it was."

"I didn't really know my brother, Detective."

"That's a shame."

"In fact, I was hoping maybe you could tell me something about him."

The words seemed to catch her by surprise. She skimmed through a few of the pages in the file. It was the kind that secured documents to it via bendable fasteners poked through a pair of holes at the top, and Hatcher thought what he could see of the stack looked to be twenty pages thick. She rubbed a spot at her hairline as she thought.

"I'm sorry, there's not much information here."

Hatcher nodded. "Have you determined why she was attacked?"

"No."

"Who was he? The attacker?"

She shrugged. "We have yet to establish a positive ID."

Hatcher said nothing. He nodded again, watching her closely. The silence expanded for several seconds until she shifted in her seat and continued.

"He seems to have had a psychotic break, picked this woman out more or less at random. Possibly because of the way she looked. We haven't been able to find any connection."

"So you're saying you have no idea who this guy was?"

She swung her chin back and forth slowly, glancing down at the file, scratching the tip of her nose with an elegant, manicured finger. "He's listed as a John Doe. Probably just some street person. I doubt we'll ever know."

"How about the woman's family? They had no idea who he was? He wasn't a former boyfriend? An ex, stalking her?"

"We haven't been able to find any family for the woman."

"Seriously?"

"It happens. Look, Mr. Hatcher, this is a cut-and-dried case. By all accounts, it seems that whatever this man's motive, it didn't have anything to do with your brother. Wrong place, wrong time. It's a shame."

"So that's it, then? Nothing else?"

"For now, yes. We hope to find out more when we talk to her."

Hatcher focused on her eyes. They were an interesting

shade of light brown, almost a mustard yellow. She looked straight at him as he contemplated what she had just said. He was unable to square it with anything he knew. "Talk to who?"

"The woman your brother tried to save."

"I thought they were all hit by the fire truck?"

"Ambulance. All three were. But only two of them died."

"Where is she now?"

"In the hospital, just being released from ICU. In a body cast, I imagine. That's really all I can say. Privacy issues, you understand."

Hatcher noticed her eyes jump beyond him and she nodded. He glanced back over his shoulder. It was Dan, with the hair, leaning against the doorjamb, a look of mild curiosity on his face.

"Mr. Hatcher, I hate to cut this short, but Lieutenant Maloney and I have an appointment."

Hatcher nodded, thanking her as she stood, and walked with her back out into the hall. She told the lieutenant she was finishing up and led Hatcher down the stairs and to the counter he'd started at. A different cop there passed him a sign-out sheet beneath the glass and asked for the name tag back.

"If you leave me your number, I can call you if I get any more information," she said, as she pushed open the doors to the main waiting area.

"It might be easier if I just check back with you."

"Okay. Feel free to call, but don't expect me to have anything to add. This isn't the kind of case that can be solved, if you know what I mean."

"I will. And won't."

He followed her out the way they had come and left the precinct, stepping through the tinted-glass doors into the sun. The concrete and asphalt were starting to warm up, sounds and smells of the city surrounding him, but it still felt cool and damp in the shadow of the building. He set out walking to find Bean's coffee shop, thinking Detective Wright was plenty smart, very attractive in a no-nonsense kind of way, a woman he normally wouldn't mind getting to know. Probably a good cop and maybe even a decent person.

But mostly he was thinking about what it was she was trying to hide, surprised that a veteran New York detective, not the type to be lacking in practice, could be such an absolutely pitiful liar.

CHAPTER 5

✦

VALENTINE UNLOCKED THE GLASS CASE AND CAREFULLY removed the book. It was an oversized tome, bulky and heavy, requiring two hands to hold. He carried it across the room and set it down on a velvet jeweler's cloth laid out across his desk atop a thin rectangle of foam. When he lifted the cover, the sound it made gave him chills. It was a reminder of the enormity of his undertaking: the crackle of antiquity, an echo of eternity. He allowed the ends to spread naturally, easing a roughly equal number of pages to each side. Laying it open had always been a matter of extreme delicacy.

Its parched natural binding, constructed of tanned human flesh, was brittle and flaking, the pages between them desiccated. Each time he handled it, he donned specially made calf-suede gloves, used felt-tipped tweezers with exaggerated square ends to turn the pages. The slightest twitch of any significance, the barest flinch at the wrong moment, and a piece of the vellum would surely break off. But recently he'd grown far more confident opening it, far less paranoid about its condition. He only needed it to last another week or so. Maybe less.

The script was in Ge'ez. It had taken him three years to learn it, the last six months of them in Ethiopia. He'd poured himself into the task, studying the obscure language for the sole purpose of being able to understand the text's meaning directly, without any filtering gloss or interpretation, to be able to read the passages as they were intended to be read. As far as he knew, the book contained the first words ever written by a human being, anywhere. It was not an original, but undoubtedly a copy made directly from the original. The only one in existence. That it was taken directly from the original was crucial. Copies made from other copies were useless.

He scanned the pages, turning them slowly, gently. The words and passages instantly became familiar as he saw them, but with one lone exception, they could not be memorized. He had tried, had spent countless hours staring at the archaic print, reciting wording over and over and lifting his head to repeat sentences as soon as he'd finished them, only to find that they refused to be learned. The text wouldn't allow it. Only the meaning could be retained.

And yet still he knew that passages had changed. He could recall subtle differences each time he read, able to remember prior phrasing while he was reading, but only then. At times he had tried to copy passages as he read them, writing blindly while staring at the pages, but the original would always read differently by the time he was finished, even moments later. Even if he transcribed just two or three words at a time. That was the reason modern translations from copies were worthless. He had to read from the source document. That was the way it was meant to be done. The way Enoch had tried to prevent it from being done.

He found the passage he was looking for, translated it in his head.

Belial shall be let loose by the hand of the Brother, fertile with seed. Ye shall know once his three nets are cast and he has arisen through That Not Meant To Be. And the wages of sin shall prevail. But for corruption thou hast made Belial, an angel of hostility. All his dominions are in darkness, and his purpose is to bring about wickedness and guilt. The Blood of the Host shall be washed in the storm. The blood of the Innocent shall close the Gates.

This passage was the first to have changed, and he was certain it was the only one to change every time he read it, provided he didn't read it until he felt the book call to him, heard the fluttering of its pages like wings in his mind. Unlike the others, this one he could recite verbatim, this one he could repeat to himself often.

The Blood of the Host shall be washed in the storm . . .

That part was new. The passage was nearing completion, reconstituting itself. It would not be long now before the changes would cease, before the book let him know the time was right. He could sense it, like energy in the air. Soon.

Then the whole of the text would reveal itself, and he will have accomplished the unthinkable, something no other man would have dared consider. It was dizzying to even contemplate.

"Hey, Boss."

Valentine looked up from his desk. He was not easily startled but hadn't realized Lucas had entered the room, his attention to the book so rapt. He appraised his employee for a brief moment, then dropped his eyes again, setting down the tweezers.

"I trust you didn't say anything stupid," Valentine said. "Having a friend on the inside only accomplishes so much."

"No, Boss. I'm real sorry. Cop was just snooping around. Your name didn't even come up. Honest."

Valentine carefully closed the book, carried it back to its case. The padded enclosure for it was form-fitted, with one movable edge to allow easy removal and replacement. It slid snugly into place.

"I know it didn't. Just don't let it happen again." He placed a gloved hand on the cover, giving it a tender caress. "There's another matter you need to tend to."

"What's that?"

"Deborah St. James is in a hospital bed this very moment. I have her room number. Those Carnates I warned you about came close this time, but failed. She's vulnerable right now. I want you to personally see to her."

"What about the cops?"

"My information is, she is not being guarded. That's why I'm sending you. I don't want anything to go wrong."

"How, you know, *discreet* do you want me to be?"

He closed the glass top to the case and stripped off his gloves. "Do what you need to. Just don't get arrested."

"But, Boss, it might not be that easy. I mean, I might not be able to help it, you know? There're cops out there that'll bust me if they so much as recognize me, just for the hell of it. Stuff goes down in a hospital, no guarantee I won't get nabbed just for being there."

"If you do," Valentine said, locking the case and withdrawing the ornate brass key to it, "the next person I send to get you won't be my lawyer."

Valentine placed the key in his pocket and lightly slapped his hand against Lucas's cheek, holding it there. He smiled warmly, rubbing his thumb against the man's face. "In fact, he won't even be human."

"YOU KNOW, COME TO THINK OF IT, YOU LOOK JUST LIKE him. Doesn't he, Fred?"

Hatcher smiled politely as she refilled his cup. The man at the end of the counter wearing a tie-dyed shirt and suspenders stared at his laptop and shrugged. He had to be pushing sixty, with long white hair pulled back into a ponytail and a white beard. A hippie Santa Claus, Hatcher mused.

"Oh, yeah," she said. "I forgot. Fred wasn't here. Picked a hell of a day to miss out. But you do look like him. You two must get that all the time."

She blushed. Hatcher could sense her discomfort almost immediately, her realization she was referencing a dead man in the present tense. He took a sip of his coffee and nodded ambiguously, certain there was no more than a passing resemblance, if any. He wasn't even convinced yet he and Garrett had actually been brothers.

"Sorry," she said.

The name tag above her left breast read *Cheryl*. She was a fairly pretty girl, maybe twenty-two or twenty-three, thin-limbed, with honey-colored hair. A faint smattering of freckles was visible over her nose and under her eyes despite a layer of makeup, and a small gap between her teeth gave her smile a hint of down-to-earth sensuousness. He'd been listening to her version of events for around ten minutes, about how the woman was yanked off her stool, how stunned patrons watched as she was dragged away, how Garrett ran after them. What she had described was a lot of confusion, a lot of chaos. A senseless, random act of violence. A man who tried to do the right thing and got killed for it. Hatcher had known his share of those.

"Where was he sitting?" Hatcher asked.

She raised her arm, extended a finger. "Right behind you, in that booth."

Hatcher spun on his cushioned counter stool. The booth she pointed to was empty, like most of the rest of the coffee shop. A pair of disposable napkins wrapped around silverware sat on the Formica tabletop, waiting for the next customer. The place had that traditional coffeehouse look—plastic and vinyl and chrome. It occurred to him this kind of joint, and the thousands of others across the country just like it, had probably looked this way since the forties. It also occurred to him that the flat red piece of vinyl on the bench seat was the last place his brother had sat before he died. If this Garrett fellow really had been his brother, that was.

"What about the guy he was sitting with? Had you ever seen him before?"

"Nope. Can't tell you much about him. Kind of chubby, maybe. Not exactly fat. Kind of scraggly blond hair. Maybe light brown. Real thin on top."

"Do you know what they were talking about?"

"No. I don't think I heard a word of what they were saying. I don't pay attention to that, anyway. You learn to tune that stuff out."

"What'd he do when Garrett ran out?"

"You know, I have no idea. I think he was up with us near the window, trying to see what was going on, but I don't really remember. What I do know is, when the dust settled, he was gone. Never saw him before, haven't seen him since."

"So he just paid and left? Didn't wait around for the police?"

She frowned, her lips bunching into a sort of pout. "No."

"No?"

"He just left. He didn't bother to pay. In fact, I think he was gone by the time I got off the phone with nine-one-one. Don't get me wrong, I wouldn't expect someone to pay after that kind of thing. I wouldn't even think twice about it. But this guy . . . this was different. I realized afterward he'd gone back to grab the rest of his croissant and walked out with his cup and spoon."

"You're kidding."

"Messed up, huh? But you learn to keep counts on those things when you wait tables. His were gone. And he had barely touched his croissant. Funny thing was, that detective that came by with the others, she actually asked if I had his cup or his silverware. Weird, huh?"

It was hard to argue with that. Weird was as good a word as any. "And you had never seen him or my brother before?"

"No. Not that I can remember. And I think I'd remember your brother."

He was about to ask her why that was, until he realized how she meant it. Her smile gave it away. "How about the woman?"

"No. And her I'd definitely remember."

"Why is that?"

"She was drop-dead gorgeous." She seemed to catch herself a moment too late, pausing before glancing down as she wiped some imaginary spot on the counter. "I mean, every guy was checking her out. I'm not into that kind of thing, but if I were, I'd have been checking her out, too."

"The police told me she's not dead."

Her eyes widened as she raised her head. "Really? Wow. That cop who interviewed me, she didn't say anything about that. Then again, I guess I didn't ask. The way that ambulance slammed—I have to say I'm surprised. Didn't expect to hear she lived."

"About the cop . . ." Hatcher described Detective Wright to her, mentioned her voice.

"That's her. I hadn't thought about how she sounded until now, but you're right. She and some other guy came by a day or two after it happened. She's the one I talked to."

"What did she ask you about?"

"The lady cop? Same kind of stuff you are, just a lot more of it. Mostly if I had seen the guy who grabbed her before. Said she was following up on my original statement."

"And you're sure he just came in here and grabbed the woman? Didn't say anything? Didn't have any words with anyone?"

"Not that I heard. I'd seen him staring through the window right before he came in. I was going to have the owner chase him off if he didn't move it along. But we get homeless coming by occasionally, panhandling, you know, so I didn't think much about."

"Why do you think he was homeless?"

"Because he looked like the kind of psycho who goes

around talking to himself. And he looked sick, too. No color in his face. Unless you think kitty litter has a color."

"Do you know what hospital they'd have taken the woman to?"

"No. There's a bunch nearby. What's the one right around the corner? Hey, Fred?" She turned to the old guy at the end of the counter. He was still glued to his laptop, occasionally tapping keys. "What's the hospital right around the corner?"

"Eastside Memorial," Fred said, without looking up.

"Eastside Memorial," Cheryl repeated. "They may have gone there. I'd bet that's where that ambulance was heading. Too bad Fred wasn't here when it happened. Nothing gets by him." She tilted her head in Fred's direction. "Isn't that right, Fred?"

Hatcher glanced over at the man. As far as he could tell, Fred hadn't taken his eyes off his computer screen since Hatcher had taken a seat at the counter. Not even for a moment.

She lowered her voice. "Fred's a conspiracy theorist. Comes in here in the mornings to use our wireless, chatting on message boards about government cover-ups." She made little circles next to her head with her finger.

"I saw that," Fred said, without looking up.

Hatcher blew on his coffee and took a sip, thinking some conspiracy theories weren't quite as nutty as others. "I don't suppose my brother left anything behind. A business card or something."

"No. Sorry."

"He didn't happen to give you his phone number or address, I guess?"

"No, but I would have sure given him mine if he'd asked. So would that woman he tried to save."

"What makes you say that?"

"Because she was checking him out. On the sly, but definitely watching him whenever he wasn't looking. He was a good-looking guy."

Hatcher nodded, unsure what to make out of that last bit of information. "Do you have a pay phone here I can use?"

"A pay phone? We haven't had a pay phone around in years. My boss says people only use those for drug deals or to call Mexico on stolen credit cards."

"Where can I find a phone to use then?"

Cheryl stared at him incredulously for a second, then reached into one of the pouches in her apron and produced a thin phone. "Just don't call China, okay?"

Hatcher thanked her and took the phone. It was flat, much thinner than the cell phones he had seen in the past. He realized he hadn't seen one in almost two years, probably not the latest models even then, and he wondered how much else had changed. Checking the number from the folded paper he'd kept in his pocket, he opened the flip top and hoped he could figure out how to use it.

His mother answered on the third ring. She told him she didn't have an address for Garrett. Just a PO box and a phone number. He took down the number. She asked him if he had seen his father yet. He told her he hadn't, but that he would.

Hatcher flipped the phone shut and started to hand it back to Cheryl, then stopped. "Do you mind if I make another call?"

"Go right ahead." She smiled, leaning forward over the counter. "You know, my number is right there on the screen, when you open it. If you need someone to call you back, I mean."

She slid along the counter, wiping desultorily, glancing over a few times as he watched her move away. He heard Fred grunt from behind his laptop.

Hatcher punched in the number his mother had given him, put the phone to his ear. For some reason, he really wanted to hear his brother's voice, hoped Garrett had recorded a voice mail, wondered what the odds were his phone hadn't been shut off yet.

The call connected after four rings, and a woman's voice said hello. It took him a second to realize it wasn't a recording.

"Oh, hi," Hatcher said.

"If you're trying to reach Garrett, I'm taking messages for him," the voice said.

"Sorry," he said. "Wrong number." He disconnected before the voice could respond. He stared at the phone for a few seconds before placing it on the counter next to his empty cup. He swiveled his stool to look out the window.

People were passing by intermittently on the sidewalk, some going one way, some the other, some in pairs, most by themselves. The majority of them had their heads down, not paying much attention to anything but their immediate paths as they crossed between the shop and the street, between Hatcher and where the man others were telling him had been his brother met his death a few days earlier. He watched the cars rolling over the road, all heading in the same direction, one after the other, some faster than others. Imagined a man who resembled him getting hit by one, the life crushed out of him in an instant. A man who may have come from the same womb, shared the same blood. For the first time, for no particular reason that made sense, it felt likely Garrett was his brother.

"All finished with it?" Cheryl asked, dipping her head toward the phone as she refilled his cup.

Hatcher glanced over to her and nodded, in his mind still hearing that breathy, raspy voice that answered his brother's phone, the same voice he had just listened to less than an hour ago. Detective Wright's voice. He was sure of it.

"Be nice to him, Cheryl," Fred said, his eyes still locked on his computer screen, seeming never to have left it. His tone was subdued, almost muted. "I think the poor boy just saw a ghost."

CHAPTER 6

❖

MANHATTAN EASTSIDE MEMORIAL MEDICAL CENTER stuck out among the green awnings and brick storefronts of First Avenue like some cylindrical 1960s apartment complex, its name in block lettering curving atop a rounded tower almost twenty stories high. Odd pairs of hopper light windows and soft-edged panels of glossy black composite siding adorned a semicircular façade that faced the street. The architecture looked like an aging glimpse into the future, one that was discovered years ago to have been just a wrong guess.

The lobby was considerably cooler than the outside. Despite the vaguely medicinal smell, it reminded Hatcher of a bank, with hard, waxed floors and security guards near the door. He wondered what he was supposed to be feeling as he lingered, pacing in slow circles. Tried to decide what mix of emotions would be normal, thinking that whatever it was, it didn't seem to be there. He scratched the crown of his head and drew an extended breath. Perhaps the feelings not being there meant he shouldn't be, either.

The last time he'd seen his father, he was eleven years old. He'd showed up for Hatcher's birthday, bearing a football. A Wilson "Duke" model, displayed in a box with a top, bottom, and back but no front or sides, allowing him to grip the ball as it was handed to him. It was an awkward encounter. He hadn't known how to respond, wondered whether his father's presence was good or bad and remembered quickly having his doubts validated. Moments later, Hatcher's mother threw a fit when she saw his father at the door, started screaming about child support. His father laughed, told her to take him to court, that he already had a lawyer and snorted something about her having some nerve even bringing that up. Then he told her with all the guys she was sleeping with, he assumed she was making good money, so he wasn't sure what the big deal was. She called him a bastard, threw an object at him—Hatcher had always thought of it as a tumbler containing a sip of Coke and some melted ice, but it really could have been any number of things—and he left. He gave a tousle to Hatcher's hair as he turned to go and told him not to use the ball in the street. It would wear out the laces.

Hatcher's final memory of him was his father stopping briefly, turning to look back after taking a few steps, and saying, "I don't blame you, kiddo. I'm sorry I stopped being your father. I tried, but it's just not who I am, and I can't change that."

Then he was gone.

More than twenty years had passed, and that same ambivalence he felt then, or something close to it, was giving him pause now. He hadn't planned on ever seeing the man again and wasn't sure he wanted to, seriously ill or not. His reasoning was simple. He didn't hold anything against his father and wouldn't mind keeping it that way.

"Excuse me!"

Hatcher turned around when he realized the words were directed at him. A big-bellied security guard with pinkish skin and a vascular nose was approaching.

"*Sir*, can I help you?"

Hatcher looked the man over. The I'm-in-charge-here tone sounded anything but helpful. "What do you mean?"

"You're just standing in the middle of the floor," the guard said. He was built like a cannonball, round and solid, with bushy eyebrows. "Do you have business here?"

"I haven't decided yet."

"*Sir*, you can't just loiter in the lobby."

Hatcher noted his tendency to emphasize the word *sir*. In the military, guys had a way of using it like an epithet, a bulletproof euphemism for *asshole*. Hatcher knew the connotation, since he'd used it that way plenty of times himself.

"I'm here to visit someone."

The guard's cherubic face was slack with contempt, his voice dripping with it. Hatcher told himself it wasn't anything personal. The guy was just doing his job, probably a thankless one at that. A security guard at fifty, he was a good candidate for hating everything.

"In that case," the guard pointed and gave a nod. "The woman at the information desk can help you."

The woman eyed Hatcher as he approached. She was older, extremely overweight, and had orange hair stacked up in a nest on the top of her head. Orange hair, orange rouge, and what looked like dark orange crayon on her lips. She was wedged behind a crescent-shaped counter in the rear of the lobby. Hatcher asked her for directions to Phillip Hatcher's room. She tapped on a keyboard, then peered over the flat rims of cat's-eye reading glasses and told him he would need to check in with the unit nurse at the diabetes treatment center. The woman gave him a floor and dismissed him by pointing to a corridor containing a bank of elevators

Hatcher managed only a few steps before his eyes suddenly fixed on Lucas Sherman. The big man was near the elevators, waiting for one of the doors to open, wearing different clothes than he had been earlier. He was carry-

ing a bouquet of wildflowers, pressing the call button multiple times with his other hand. Hatcher veered to his left
and kept walking, angling himself away from Sherman's
field of vision. Using the corner of a wall for concealment,
Hatcher put a foot on a padded bench and bent as if to tie
his shoelace. He watched as Sherman entered one of the
elevators and disappeared.

"Hey, *sir*, please keep your shoes off the furniture."

It was the security guard again, hands hooked in his thick
belt.

The guard watched him put his foot back on the floor,
holding Hatcher's eyes an extra beat before returning
slowly to his position against the wall near the front of a
small gift shop. Hatcher turned and started back toward
the front desk. Halfway there he noticed Detective Wright
and Lieutenant Maloney entering the lobby through one
of the large glass doors facing the street. He pivoted and
pretended to read a floor directory on the wall, shooting
discreet glances over his shoulder. A few seconds later he
saw the detectives enter the corridor toward the elevators.
He flashed an innocent smile in the direction of the guard,
who had been watching him the whole time, and curled
back to the information desk.

"Did you just see a man and a woman who came through
here?" Hatcher asked. "Dressed in suits?"

The woman pulled down her reading glasses, letting
them hang by the chain around her neck and settle on her
bosom. "Lots of people come through here, sir."

"I mean just now. The woman in the gray jacket and
skirt, hair up in a ponytail?"

"You're talking about the two that just walked by," she
said, eyes narrowing in advance disapproval of whatever he
was going to ask next. "Yes, I saw them."

Hatcher realized they likely didn't need to request information, probably knew their way around the place. Besides, they didn't seem to have stopped on the way to the

elevators. He glanced back toward the corridor. There had to be a way to figure out where they were headed.

"Is there something I can help you with?" she asked, glancing past him at an angle. Hatcher turned his head and followed her gaze. The security guard was at the end of it, his stare still fixed like a bird dog's.

"No. I mean, *yes*. There was a woman admitted here a few days ago. I was told no one's been able to identify her yet."

"And?"

"Can you tell me what room she's in?"

"I'm sorry, sir, I can't give out that kind of information, I can only direct you to the appropriate nurse's station." She seemed to consider his question further, and let out a short *phhhpf.* "And without a name, I can't even do that."

"Do you have any Jane Does listed?"

"That's not a patient designation we use. If you'd like, I can direct you to admitting. Perhaps they can help you." She pulled her lips into an orange Crayola smile. "Or I can call for security and you can discuss the matter with them."

Hatcher locked his jaws, forcing a return smile, then lowered his head. He let himself think for several seconds. "How about this. Where would seriously injured trauma patients be treated? People who'd been hit by a car, for example?"

She looked at him like he was an idiot. "The ER."

"After that."

"It depends on whether they needed surgery. ICU probably, over in Critical Care."

"How about after ICU? Where would they go then?"

"That would depend on their injuries. We have almost seven hundred beds in this building alone."

Hatcher took in a breath, blew it out through his nose. This was going nowhere. "Did you see a big guy, bald, with a wraparound mustache come by right before I did? Maybe heard him mention who he was here to see?"

"No. And I'm really not comfortable answering these questions."

Her eyes jumped over to the security guard again. Hatcher closed his and thought for a moment.

"Which way to ICU?"

She huffed out a sigh and told him. Hatcher listened to the directions and headed back to the elevators, picking up his pace for the last few yards as he saw one open and eject a pair of doctors. A woman entered the same cab just as the doors started to close, pressing one floor above his. She was a redhead, very attractive. Almost too attractive. Lips like strawberries, eyes the blue of a robin's egg. In the tiny confines of the elevator, her scent was intoxicating. He caught himself staring at her breasts, mentally undressing her, imagining what her skin tasted like.

The doors opened and he exited, partly wishing he could have stayed on. He'd been missing women even more than he realized. *What do you expect? You just got out of prison.*

The nurse at the ICU station was much friendlier than the woman at the information desk, but not much more forthcoming. Yes, the woman from the auto accident had been there. Yes, she was transferred earlier out of ICU. No, she couldn't tell him where the woman was now.

"Why not?" Hatcher asked.

"Because her record's been flagged. They usually do that when they don't want the press sneaking into the patient's room."

"Why would the press want to talk to her?"

The nurse shrugged. "You'd have to ask them."

"Look," Hatcher said, resting his forearms on the counter. "I'm not a reporter."

The woman lifted her hands, then let them drop. "Sorry, I'm just not allowed. I can give you the number for patient information, if you like."

"All I want to know is where to send flowers."

He watched her eyes search his. She was a black woman, probably in her forties, and wore an expression that said she had seen and heard pretty much everything, but would play along anyway. "Just send them to General Recovery."

"But I don't know her name."

Pursing her lips, she glanced down at some papers next to a keyboard and ran a finger down one of them. "You can mark them for Patient 097457."

Hatcher thanked her and left. It wasn't much of a plan, he realized, but it was better than nothing. He took an elevator back to the lobby. He smiled at the security guard as he headed into the gift shop.

The cheapest arrangement of flowers they had was twenty-five dollars. He had forty-two in his wallet. He bought them anyway.

Bouquet in hand, he decided to start with the third floor. After a bit of wandering, he learned from an orderly that General Recovery comprised floors seven through nine. He took another elevator to the eighth floor and roamed until he found the nurse's station.

One woman was seated behind a computer in flower-print scrubs that looked like pajamas, another was clad in white, including hose and shoes, leaning over a counter at the other side of the station. Hatcher decided the nurse at the computer would be the one guarding the info. He bypassed her and approached the one in white. She was writing something on a clipboard. Her name tag read Lori Sanford, RN.

"Hi. I've got some flowers for a patient, but I'm not sure if I have the right floor."

The woman gestured absently toward the other nurse. "Give her the name and she can tell you."

"All I have is the patient number: 097457."

She looked at him quizzically. "You don't have a name?"

"She was in an accident." He held up the bouquet. "The guy who hit her wanted me to bring her some flowers."

She glanced over to the woman in scrubs. "Denise, could you look up 097457?"

The woman at the keyboard punched in the number, hit a few more keys. "The records are flagged. Can't give out the room number."

Hatcher nodded, saying nothing. He let the silence hang and expand, a void demanding to be filled. Questions weren't the only way to get people to talk.

The nurse in white eventually stepped over behind Denise and looked at the screen. "You can leave them with me," she said a moment later. "I'll be heading down on my break in about forty minutes and I can drop them off on the way."

Down, Hatcher thought. *Thank you very much.*

"Thanks, Lori," he said. He weighed his options. Leaving the flowers would mean walking around empty-handed. He decided that wouldn't work. "I'm surprised she's not on this floor. This is seven, right?"

"No, you're on eight."

"No wonder. How stupid of me. I'll just bring them down there myself."

He thanked them both and took the elevator to seven.

The nurse's station on seven was almost identical to the one on eight, situated in the same place on the floor. It had the same design to it, a countered space cut out of the interior of the middle of the floor, accessible from parallel halls on each side, and what looked like the same notices on the walls. The main difference he noticed was this one had four nurses behind the counter, huddled together, discussing some matter of importance that seemed to be of too much interest to them to be anything but gossip. Hatcher walked past, eyes ahead. The plan was to act lost if challenged. Nobody challenged him, and he found himself strolling the corridor, glancing into rooms.

He slowed as he saw the woman from the elevator, the stunning redhead. She was wearing a white lab coat, heading his way. She offered a tight-lipped smile before she passed, and he caught her scent again. He closed his eyes, savoring it, then stopped, looking back over his shoulder.

She was wearing high heels and back-seamed hose. Hatcher watched her click away, something about her making him uneasy. Uneasy and aroused, simultaneously. She cut to her right and pushed the door open to a bathroom. He continued walking.

At the far end, an exit stairwell with an emergency push bar loomed, and the hall took a sharp turn. Detective Wright was in the first room after he rounded the corner. She was standing next to a bed, visible through a framework of metal traction railing, nodding. A man in a white coat with a stethoscope around his neck was next to her, gesturing toward the bed as he spoke. The patient was obscured by the narrow angle of his shifting line of sight. Hatcher's view panned as he passed, allowing him to see Lieutenant Maloney at the foot of the bed, staring contemplatively at its occupant.

Hatcher kept walking. The door to the next room was closed, but the room after that seemed empty. The next corner was only a dozen or so yards away, and he stopped after he rounded it and leaned against the wall on the other side. His plan suddenly seemed pointless. What was he trying to accomplish? To see the woman? Talk to her? Find out what Wright was lying about? See if that Sherman lowlife had some connection to all this? All of the above? He wasn't exactly sure. There was something about the woman that Wright didn't want him to know, of that much he was certain. But whatever it was, skulking around the halls of the hospital wasn't going to help him find out.

A bit further up the hall, halfway between him and the nurse's station that bisected the floor, a woman in a white coat wheeled a hospital gurney to a stop. She parked it next to the wall and engaged a wheel brake. Hatcher was worried she was going to call him out, ask him what he was doing just standing there, but she didn't say anything, barely glancing his way. His gaze fastened onto her as she turned and headed in the opposite direction, a brunette with straight, shoulder-length hair and long legs. She was like the redhead, a centerfold-quality bombshell. He watched her do the runway walk up the hall in a pair of bright red heels and no hose, feeling both stirred and wary. Either the medical profession had taken to hiring swimsuit models, or things in the civilian world were a heck of a lot different than he remembered.

Voices echoed down the hall from behind him. Hatcher stuck his head back and peeked. Wright, Maloney, and the doctor were outside the room now, acting like they were about to part company. They milled around near the doorway for several seconds, Wright handing the doctor her card, mumbling something about vital information. The doctor promised to call as soon as the patient was up to speaking. Hatcher heard him say something about the effects of trauma and shock.

"Excuse me."

Hatcher spun at the sound of a voice close by. A nurse in scrubs was standing near the gurney, a clipboard tucked under her arm, pinching the patient's wrist. She was Asian, rather short and a bit plump in the hips. Hatcher realized she couldn't have walked from the station that quickly, so she must have come from one of the closer patient rooms. She was looking directly at him, wearing the same expression he'd been worried about getting from the brunette.

"Have you checked in?" she asked. "Are you visiting someone?"

"More like waiting for someone," Hatcher said, holding up the flowers. "The visit's supposed to be a surprise."

"Well, I'm sorry, but you're going to have to—" She stopped and looked down at the man on the gurney, moving her hand to his throat. "*Oh my God*. Did you see how this patient got here?"

"A woman wheeled him up a couple of minute ago."

There was a jumpiness in her eyes, a glint of urgency. "A doctor? A nurse?"

"I have no idea. She was wearing a hospital coat. Dark hair, on the tall side."

The woman studied the man on the gurney for another moment before double-timing it back up the hall.

Hatcher glanced around the corner again. Wright, Maloney, and the doctor were gone. The nurse would be coming back, so this might be his only chance. He was about to step toward the room when the door next to it opened and Lucas Sherman emerged, leering cautiously in the direction where Wright and the others had been standing. Hatcher pulled his head back behind the edge of the wall as Lucas shot a glance in his direction. He waited for a count of five, then eased his eyes around again. A glimpse of Lucas's back, then the man disappeared into the room where Detective Wright and the others had been. The door shut slowly behind him.

There wasn't much time to think it through. If what Wright had told him about Lucas Sherman was true, the man was a sociopath, a stone killer. And whatever she was hiding, there was no reason to think she had lied about that. That left few options. He could run after Wright and Maloney, tell them what he saw, but by the time they listened to him, something could already have happened. He decided he had to act.

He sprinted toward the door and surged into the room. The space was quiet, peaceful. Empty, but for the patient. The early afternoon light made it bright, gave it an almost cheerful yellow tint. The person in the bed was obviously a woman, feminine even in awkward repose, with a spill of long dark hair pooled next to her gauze-wrapped head. The bed was surrounded by a roll cage of traction rails, looking like a dune buggy, with a trapeze handle hanging down from a crossbar. Hatcher swept from corner to corner, stooped to check beneath the bed. No one else, just a chair, an IV bag on a stand, a tall monitor of some kind. And the woman. Her arms were in casts and one side of her face was bandaged, the other side bruised. He shifted his attention to the bathroom, where the door was partially closed. The door was sturdy, industrial-grade, with a scratched metal kick plate and a push handle instead of a knob. He stepped toward it, listened, then gave it a hard shove. The door slammed against something with a thud, producing a grunt from behind it, then swung back hard into him. Sherman leapt out from behind it and flung the door all the way open, clearing a path and lunging at Hatcher in a single, fluid motion. He wrapped his hands around Hatcher's neck and charged forward, driving Hatcher back.

The grip on his throat meant he didn't have time for anything fancy, so he immediately focused on finding vulnerable points in the attack. This type of bull rush was crude but effective. Sherman's hands were strong, his arms like chiseled pieces of granite forcing him backward. Hatcher could feel the blood to his brain being cut off, felt his airways being shut down. He dropped the flowers, reached up, and grabbed hold of Sherman's shirt with both hands as he backpedaled rapidly. The calculation was almost an unconscious one. A few feet of space to his rear. Two steps, and on the third he dropped. Straight down, all his weight, pulling one knee to his chest and kicking the other leg out between Sherman's ankles.

Sherman's own momentum did most of the work. Hatcher's deadweight yank on his shirt catapulted the man forward, over Hatcher's falling body, slamming Sherman's head into the solid wall. The impact made a helmet-to-helmet sound, a hard pop with no echo. Sherman snapped back, like a ricochet, hands shooting to his head, and dropped to the floor. He crawled aimlessly toward the far corner of the room, moaning in obvious pain. Hatcher rolled away onto a knee, hunched over, coughing.

"What the hell?"

Hatcher raised his head, still coughing and cradling his throat. Detective Wright was in the doorway. Her brow was wrinkled, her eyes like reflective disks. Her right hand pulled back her jacket, finding the handle of her pistol as she scanned the room. At the sight of Sherman on the floor, curled like a fetus and rocking, she drew the gun and brought it forward into a two-hand grip with a slap of knuckles against her palm.

A solid Weaver-ready position, Hatcher noted. He swallowed, trying to clear his throat so he could communicate.

She leaned back out the doorway, twisting her head a bit to her right. But never taking her eyes off of Sherman. *"Dan!"*

Hatcher started to speak, then saw a man appear in the hallway behind her, coming into view from her left. He was large, a full head taller than she was, bald, except for short-cropped fuzz on the sides, wearing a hospital robe that was flapping open. His stare seemed fixed as he closed in. His left arm was raised in front of him.

"Behind you!" Hatcher said, pointing and yelling as loudly as his throat would let him.

Wright started to turn her head, but the man grabbed a hold of it by her ponytail and threw her backward. She tumbled across the hall, bouncing off the opposite wall, dropping her gun and landing on the side of her face.

The man didn't bother to look back at her. He walked into the room, a stilted, rocking gait, and toward the woman in the bed, ignoring Hatcher. His skin was pale, almost a shade of gray. Hatcher saw he was holding a scalpel in his right hand.

Hatcher jumped to his feet and drove his shoulder into the man's ribs, tackling him and knocking him back against a wooden chair that slid out of the way as they crashed to the ground. The scalpel slid across the floor and rattled against the wall. Once off their feet, Hatcher pumped two hard, driving punches into the man's solar plexus. He followed them with a palm-heel strike to the forehead that bounced the man's skull off the hard floor and added a reverse knife hand to the side of his throat.

Satisfied the threat had been neutralized, Hatcher rolled off, leaning back against the wall to catch his breath, his throat still sore. Wright, he thought. He had to check on her. He pushed himself off the ground and was almost standing when he realized the man was getting up.

Getting up and not even breathing hard. Hatcher stared, waiting for the man to collapse. He'd seen it before. Guys who'd been seriously injured or battered not seeming to feel the effects for a few seconds. Only this man didn't collapse or double over. He used the chair to lift himself to his feet and stood erect, clumsy and unbalanced, his robe obscenely twisted, exposing his flabby abdomen and dark, flaccid genitals. Hatcher realized the man not only wasn't breathing hard, he didn't seem to be breathing at all.

The man picked up the chair by its backing with both hands and stepped forward, swinging it at Hatcher. Hatcher ducked, hearing and feeling parts of the wood frame splinter a foot above him. He took aim and threw a roundhouse hook, spinning into it, zeroing in on the floating rib beneath the man's arm. He felt his knuckles connect through the flabby padding over the man's rib cage, thought he could feel it give, maybe even hear the muffled snap of the bone beneath.

Then the inside of his head seemed to explode as the man slammed what was left of the chair down against the top of his skull. He stumbled back against the wall, his eyes clenched, his jaw locked, weathering the pain. The man had already turned his back to him by the time Hatcher opened his eyes. Hatcher saw him pick up the scalpel and stand. He was facing the woman.

His head screaming, Hatcher's eyes locked on the traction bars framing the bed. He jumped up and grabbed hold of the near-side traction railing above it. He swung himself up, flung his legs over the man's shoulders, crossed his ankles, and locked them.

He gave himself a combat reminder, disengaged the natural safety mechanisms in his brain as he committed. *This isn't training. This isn't a potential friendly. Don't hold back.*

In a quick series of moves blended into one rapid sequence, he let go of the rod and twisted his body violently at the hips, slapping the floor with his palms as he landed, the side of his face barely missing a broken piece of chair. He unhooked his ankles and pulled his legs out. There was no doubt this time. He'd felt the pop. Heard the crack.

He took a breath and slowly pushed himself to his feet. The man was lying on the floor, facedown. At first it was exactly what Hatcher expected to see. Heap of a body, misshapen neck. But then the man lifted his elbows and pushed himself up, getting to one knee. His hand found the side bed rail and he pulled himself the rest of the way.

Hatcher hesitated, uncertain what to do. This was all wrong. The man was standing again. His head was horribly offset, his neck crooked and bulging on one side. He wasn't huffing, wasn't groaning, wasn't bleeding, wasn't doing anything, except getting up again. Getting up and still holding the scalpel.

As if sensing Hatcher's confusion, the man turned toward the woman, sliding along the bed rail toward her head and upper body. Hatcher's eyes ricocheted around the room. If he was going to stop this, he needed a weapon. His gaze bounced to his feet, where a leg of the chair lay, the end of it still connected to a shard of the seat frame. Hatcher grabbed it and lunged, swinging it like a hatchet.

The end struck the man in the back of the head, near the base of his skull. The sharp, sharded edge tomahawked deeply, burying a few inches of wood through the bone.

The man stiffened. He turned until he was facing Hatcher's direction, eyes rolled up and out of sight, mouth agape. A pointy piece of wood, its sharp blond tip streaked with red and hung with chunks of gristle, was visible in his mouth like an extra tongue. He stood motionless for a few seconds, then fell forward onto his face.

Hatcher watched the body for movement, waiting several seconds longer than he normally would, then leaned back against the wall. His chest and lungs ached from the adrenaline surge, his muscles suddenly heavy and deflated. He bent forward and placed his hands on his knees.

"Police! Don't move!"

Wearily, Hatcher raised his eyes. Lieutenant Maloney was holding a stainless-steel revolver, the barrel leveled at Hatcher's face. Somewhere in the cacophony of thoughts competing with the pulse in his head, he decided the lieutenant's form wasn't as good as Wright's.

Maloney barked at him to turn around, spread his legs, and place his hands on his head and his chest against the wall. Hatcher mustered the energy to shoot a glance over to the far corner of the room as he did.

The cuffs dug into his wrists, but he didn't make a sound. This was going to be complicated. He hoped that Wright had seen enough to back him up. And, more important, that she'd be willing to, that she was one of those rare cops that cared about the truth more than the collar. He wasn't sure what was going on, but he did know there was only going to be one arrest today. At least for now.

Lucas Sherman was gone.

CHAPTER 7

❖

VALENTINE STOOD IN FRONT OF THE GRACE CHURCH
altar and studied the scenes; saints with fishbowl halos de-
picted in mosaic, receiving instructions from their Savior.
The morning sun blazed through the traceried stained glass
above him, igniting the panels into glowing arrays of color,
a molten rainbow of pigments reaching down through the
triangles of ornate ivory atop the iconography. Fingers of
light stretching from Heaven.

"Have you ever taken the time to appreciate biblical art,
Lucas? It's all around us, you know."

"No, Boss," Lucas said. He was standing next to Valentine, holding his head. "Never was much for that stuff."

"You really should. Society, for all its trappings of faith,
has become biblically illiterate, especially over the past few
decades. That's made representations such as these almost
meaningless to the average person. But there is so much to
be learned from them. It is only through understanding the
Bible that we see man in his true context, that we can hope
to understand the eschatological underpinning of society."

Valentine moved along the chancel. His footsteps echoed in the open expanse of vaulted nave. Lucas trailed him reluctantly, wincing with each step.

"Take the reredos," Valentine said, pointing. "French and Italian marble. *Pierre de Caen*. Such exquisite craftsmanship. Such attention to detail. And the depictions of the Gospel writers, Matthew, Mark, Luke, and John, surrounding the Risen Christ as he gave his Great Commission. Inspired. Truly inspired."

He lifted his gaze to the stained glass. "Or pieces like these. Jacob's Dream, depicting Jacob having stumbled upon one of the gates to Heaven, his discovery of an elusive pathway to the ultimate, most cherished of places. Windows, in the true, metaphorical sense of the word."

Valentine paused, his eyes roaming over the tints and tinges, the bursts of opaque white surrounding candy-glaze reds, chrysanthemum blues, and liquid greens.

"Do you know why I like it here, Lucas?"

"No, Boss."

"Because you can feel the sense of eternity. In the architecture, in the art, in the stone and the marble. Even the plaster. The Gothic spires, the cruciform designs. So much effort, so much energy. The craftsmanship of the engravings, the simple allure of the stained glass. Representations of devotion, of passion, commitment to an idea on the grandest of scales. I come here because of all those things, all the things you see around us right now. To use them. To remind myself of the immensity, the sheer vastness, of what I intend to accomplish. The men who designed the great houses of worship, like this one, they understood. It is all based on one thing, one driving concept, a paramount force in history. The whole of western civilization rests upon the single most powerful idea ever. Do you know what that idea is?"

Lucas hitched a shoulder. "No, Boss. Can't say I do."

"Everything, all of it, Lucas, is informed by the notion of salvation. Everything."

"It's real pretty, Boss."

"I'm not talking about eye-pleasing aesthetics. Ever notice how similar grand churches like these are to mausoleums? The sober, dim atmosphere, the hard, cold surfaces, the echoing quiet that demands whispers, designs and ornamentation harkening back centuries, millennia, in some cases?"

"Never really noticed that."

"It's not merely a shared sense of reverence. What they have in common is far more profound. These are places where some primal part of us has realized we are connecting, however indirectly, with something more vast than we can conceive, points where our tiny estuaries of existence come in contact with the raging current of time, flowing off to infinity."

"Sounds deep."

Valentine huffed a short laugh. "You don't believe in any of this, do you?"

"Sure I do, Boss. Whatever it is, this thing you're planning—" Lucas flinched, clenching his eyes shut and twisting the heel of his palm against his brow. "If anyone can pull it off, I'm sure you can."

"It's all right, Lucas. You don't need to humor me. I'm not offended. In fact, it's why I hired you. Because you think it's all bullshit. That, and your penchant for violence."

Lucas nodded, holding his head. "Boss, I, uh, really think I need to go somewhere and lie down."

"Yes, of course. But you do want to know why I had you meet me here, don't you?"

"Well, yeah, I guess so."

"I've picked this place for the Malediction. They've relocated the congregation for two weeks. I'm going to need you to make some preparations. I did not want there to be any miscommunication about where or what I was talking about."

"Okay, Boss," Lucas said, nodding like a man balancing something on his crown.

Valentine placed a hand on his shoulder. "You understand how important this is, don't you, Lucas? How imperative it is that I succeed, regardless of what you believe?"

"Real important, Boss. I know. I'm just hurting right now. I'll be okay, though."

Valentine patted his arm gently. "Leave through the front. The police will eventually be keeping tabs on you, but they aren't at the moment."

"So, you're not mad at me, are you?"

"No. I'm not mad. You know I don't get mad. At least, not that easily. Have you ever seen me mad, Lucas?"

Lucas considered the question, then shook his head, sucking air into his lungs suddenly and grimacing.

"Thanks for letting me go, Boss." He let out a long breath and turned to leave. After a step, he hesitated. "What about the gal? You want me to go back?" He squeezed his eyes shut. "When my head's better, I mean?"

"She'll be leaving the hospital soon," Valentine said, wagging his jaw. "Until then, the authorities will be keeping an eye on her, undoubtedly plan to keep doing so after she's discharged. Of course, they can only do so much. But the answer is no. I've got something else in mind. She'll be taken care of."

"Whatever you say, Boss." Lucas dipped his chin down as if to nod, but ended up not lifting it, cradling his head in one hand.

"Go. Get some rest. We're only days away. I need you fit."

Lucas tilted his head back after a moment, squinting against the brilliance of the stained glass stretching high above them, keeping his hand above his eyes in a cupped salute. "Boss, I never really asked, but what *do* you have planned? The end of the world or some shit like that?"

"No, Lucas, not the end of the world." He swept his gaze across the altar, took in the mosaics, the towering windows of colored glass. "I'm thinking more long term than that."

CHAPTER 8

❖

"LOOK AT IT FROM MY PERSPECTIVE," MALONEY SAID.

Hatcher rocked the chair back, trying to keep his weight to the rear. One of the front legs was shorter than the others, and that caused it to wobble at an angle if he tried to sit straight. The more he thought about it, the more he decided it wasn't a bad touch, though he doubted it was intentional.

"I mean, we've got you in the would-be victim's room . . ." He extended his left index finger and bent it back with his right one, ticking off a count. "An assaulted cop with a concussion . . ." Another finger. "And a dead body . . ." He pressed a third one down, then held all three up, his thumb across his little finger to keep it pinned. "*Which*, by your own admission, was in that dead condition courtesy of *you*. You're already on the books for twelve months—twelve months you haven't even finished—in a military prison for something arguably similar. What do you expect us to think?"

The small room was more or less square and smelled of

mildew and Lysol. White, sound-dampening tiles made of material that looked like dirty Styrofoam paneled the walls and ceiling, even covered the door, interrupted only by a large rectangular mirror along the wall to his left. Hatcher was cuffed to a sturdy gray metal table, which made him suspect they had already been in touch with Fort Sill. Gillis was probably more than happy to talk to them when they called, to tell them what a menace he was.

"If I were you," Maloney said. "I'd start cooperating." He checked his watch, made a point of adjusting the face with those incongruently slender fingers he had. "You know, your brother's funeral is in a couple of hours. If you just tell us the truth, we might be able to arrange for you to attend."

Hatcher said nothing. All he'd done was cooperate, from the moment he was apprehended until well into the morning, when it became clear Maloney was less interested in hearing what actually happened than he was in pushing his clumsy themes. It was around three a.m. when Hatcher realized nothing was going to get through, no matter how many times he repeated it. He simply stopped talking then. Six hours later, he was back for another round. He figured he had about as much of a chance of attending his brother's funeral as Maloney did getting him to confess.

"You ready to tell me what you were doing there?"

Another cop, a young guy with strawberry hair and bad skin, coughed from the corner of the room. He sat there quietly, freckled forearms showing from under his rolled-up sleeves, pad on his knee, ready to take notes and looking just as uncomfortable this time around as he did the last. So that made two detectives, plus Wright, whom he hadn't seen since the hospital. Hatcher wondered how many were on the other side of the mirror, how many came and went behind the glass just to get a look at him.

The thought caused Hatcher to glance at his reflection. The question he'd asked himself a moment earlier suddenly seemed significant. Why *were* they going through this again? He'd sat sphinxlike for almost an hour the last time without saying a word. Why would they let him sleep, then try again? They couldn't be that dense. He could only think of one reason.

"I already told you," Hatcher said, staring at the mirror. "A number of times."

"Ah, cat's given you back your tongue. Good. Yeah, I remember what you said. But, come on, let's cut the bullshit. What were you *really* doing there?"

It was a matter of broken clocks being right twice a day, as far as Hatcher was concerned. So he hadn't been completely forthcoming about his reasons. Maloney didn't have a clue about that and probably wouldn't even believe him if he explained all his thoughts in detail. Hatcher knew he was clueless because the man had dismissed every true thing Hatcher had told him in favor of strained theories that made absolutely no sense. From his fake hair to his fake manner, Maloney struck him as the type who wouldn't know the truth if it reared back and kicked him in the crotch. At the heart of it, being a cop was still a government job, so Hatcher figured Maloney had earned his rank the old-fashioned way, by kissing ass and playing politics. It certainly wasn't because of his skills as an interrogator, that was for sure. Maloney hadn't shown any interest in verifying anything Hatcher had said, and he was about as subtle with his wording as a crack whore on a street corner. Good enough for petty criminals, probably. Cunning, perhaps. But not an expert. Not a tactician.

"Why don't you tell me what *you* were doing there?" Hatcher asked, shifting his gaze from the glass.

Maloney sucked in his cheeks, like he had just tasted something sour. "I was investigating the death of your brother. Not that you're in any position to ask questions."

Hatcher pretended to hold the man's stare, barely seeing him. Thinking. He wasn't certain what had prompted him to ask the question, but he supposed it had something to do with the way Maloney had looked back at the hospital, standing at the foot of the bed, the glimpse of expression Hatcher had caught beneath that artificial pompadour, half concerned, half anxious. Maloney's reaction was amusing. Of course, no interrogator—no skilled one—really minded a subject asking questions. Questions revealed what the subject was worried about, conveyed information about what he or she didn't know. But an experienced interrogator would rarely give a straight answer to one. You never actually answered a subject's question unless it was one you baited—you turned it around instead, made it into another question. *What do* you *think I was doing there?* The ineptitude on display by New York's Finest was disillusioning. Disappointing, even. Their interrogation procedures were so amateurish they were almost offensive, and several times he felt tempted to demand they get their act together and quit disgracing the badge. Sitting him at a table? Did they use TV shows as training videos?

But presently Hatcher found himself ruminating less about that than about what Maloney had actually said, and how he had said it. *I was investigating the death of your brother.* Not, *I was looking into your brother's death,* not even some fuck-you response to put Hatcher in his place. No, Maloney had given a calculated answer, one that was a bit too formal. Every word enunciated. No contractions. Like he wanted Hatcher or whomever was behind the glass to hear every word clearly.

"My father," Hatcher said. "He's a patient. Look him up."

"I don't mean at the hospital," Maloney said, shaking his head. "I'm talking about her room. Why were you there in her room?"

Hatcher ran his eyes over the mirror, caught his own gaze near the bottom. "I saw Lucas Sherman go in."

"And how did you manage that? Considering no one else remembers seeing him?"

"He'd been hiding in the next room. He didn't see me."

"Oh, right. And you just happened to be there to save the day by driving a broken piece of furniture through the back of someone else's head. Makes perfect sense to me."

"What do you want from me, Lieutenant? A confession? There's nothing to confess. I've already told you everything. Sherman attacked me; I used a leverage move to drive him into the wall. The other guy showed up a minute later."

"And that was the first time you saw him? The other guy?"

"Yes," Hatcher said. It was a lie, since he'd seen the man on the gurney, but surely Maloney knew that, had talked to the nurses. But he hadn't mentioned it, so Hatcher wasn't going to, either. "He came up behind Detective Wright, then went after the woman."

"So you say. But I'd like to know why you jumped through so many hoops to find her room in the first place. We have statements. A security guard saying you were acting suspicious. A woman manning the front desk who says you were in an agitated state, hostile and threatening."

Hatcher rolled his eyes, his gaze ending up toward the mirror again. "And I'm sure those were her own words, too. That's not the way it was, and you damn well know it. I just wanted to see her. The woman my brother saved. That's it."

Maloney leaned forward, resting his forearms on the table and clasping his hands. "But you see how this looks, don't you? Like I said, I'm on your side here. Really, I am. It's just getting a bit frustrating that you won't let me help you. We talked to your CO; we know you're not a bad guy." He inched closer, lowering his voice a notch. "We know that whole military rap you got was a screw job. I'm just trying to figure out how this happened, so we can work on straightening it all out. That's all you want, isn't it? To help us straighten things out?"

Hatcher bent his head down to his cuffs to scratch his nose. Did people actually fall for this crap?

"You want to know what I think?" Maloney asked, pulling back. "I think you went to that room innocently enough. Just to get a look, like you said. When you got inside, you saw this beautiful woman, one your brother had died trying to rescue. She opened her eyes, maybe smiled. And you told her who you were. She tells you how grateful she is for what your brother did, and you move closer, maybe give her hug, a peck on the cheek. All innocent. Then this other guy, this patient, he walks in and accuses you of something nasty, tells you to get away from her. Was probably walking by and got the wrong impression. You tell him he's got it all wrong, but he starts getting all in your face, telling you you're a pervert, when you didn't even do anything. Not really. So you tell him to step off, but he doesn't and you get in a fight. I mean, it's not like you started it even. Right?"

"Do you have any idea how ridiculous this sounds?"

Maloney patted the air with his palms. "Hear me out. Maybe the fight started some other way, but it wasn't your fault. Things just got out of hand. All you meant to do was knock him out, you know, end the fight."

"Why do I think this has something to do with the difference between justifiable homicide and manslaughter?" Hatcher said.

"So you try to hit him with the chair." Maloney mimicked a guy swinging something, hands apart, gripping some imaginary piece of furniture. "But it ends up breaking, and you pick up a leg, try to ring his chimes, only he turns away, and you don't realize it's got that sharp end."

Hatcher swiveled his head until he was facing the mirror as directly as the chair would allow, fixing his eyes on a point in the middle, just above the center. When he spoke, it was to the person behind it. "He was trying to do something to the woman."

"Do what? What was he trying to do?"

"He had a scalpel. He was determined to reach her with it." Hatcher hitched a shoulder. "Do the math."

"You're saying he was planning to kill her?"

Hatcher dropped his head, tossing it from side to side. "I realize it's a big leap, given that all I saw was a psycho with a weapon who took everything I could dish out. But yes. That's what I'm saying."

"Would you mind explaining why, then?"

"You know, he stopped to tell me before he died, but in all this excitement I guess I forgot. That's a stupid question, Lieutenant. You'd have to ask him."

"Well, thanks to you, we can't do that now, can we?"

Hatcher bounced his gaze off the mirror again. "What about Detective Wright?"

"What about her?" Maloney settled back into his chair, interlocking his fingers and resting his hands across his stomach.

"The guy threw her across the hall. She saw me in the room right before it happened. Me and Sherman. She can clear most of this up."

"Yeah, well, her memory about exactly what happened isn't all that clear. You might say that knock on her head scrambled her recollection a bit. Maybe that's what you were counting on. Her not being able to remember."

"This is absurd."

"Look, I don't think you meant to hurt anyone, but once you saw what happened, what kind of trouble you might be in, you went to get out of there. But Detective Wright, she startled you. Then she started pulling a gun, and you're like, *Shit! A gun!* And you realized she'd jumped to the wrong conclusion. So you distracted her, pushed her out of the way. You didn't mean to have her hit her head. It was an accident, right?"

"You're crazy. And you're lying about what you believe. Lying badly, I might add."

The corner of Maloney's lip twitched, flicking upward. "And what makes you say that?"

"I could tell you, but that would take all the fun out of it."

"I don't think you realize the gravity of the situation, sport."

Hatcher took in a breath, deep enough that the weight of his chest huffed it out as soon as he let it go. "And I don't think you realize what a monumental waste of time this is. It's just like I told you. I saw Lucas Sherman go into the room after you and Detective Wright left. I went in after him."

"Why didn't you just come and tell us?"

"Are you kidding me? Run down the hall, go through God-knows-how-many questions about what I was doing there, all while someone you guys like for killing prostitutes is in the room with her?"

"What makes you think we like Sherman for killing prostitutes? Who told you that?"

Hatcher watched Maloney's eyes. They were a yellowish brown, with dark spots circling the iris. They were also narrowed, more interested in the answer to this question, he realized, than they had been to others. "I overheard two cops in the hallway talking about it when he was being released."

"Is that so?"

"Yes."

"But you didn't kill Sherman. He wasn't anywhere to be found. We're talking about *another* guy you just happened to go wild on. He was a jeweler, by the way. Owned a little store over near Thirty-second."

"It wasn't like I had a choice. I just couldn't stop him. Nothing I tried hurt him. And I tried pretty much everything."

"So you just decided to kill him."

Yes, Hatcher thought, *actually, I did.* Regardless of how accurate it was, he knew it wouldn't be a wise answer. Maybe because of how accurate it was. "If I really wanted to kill him, I could have run out into the hallway, grabbed Detective Wright's Glock, and put some rounds into his brain. I just wanted to stop him."

"Look, Hatcher, you're a soldier, I'm a cop; we're both in it to fight the bad guys. I don't think you're one of the bad guys. But you've got to work with me."

"I didn't do anything wrong."

"I know that. That's why I'm talking to you right now.

Because I'm trying to figure out how something like this could happen. I'm trying to give you a chance to help me make sense of it, so I can get this whole matter resolved and help you out. Now, tell me, did you get in an argument with him? Kill him in anger? Or was it just an accident?"

Hatcher paused, deciding he was sick of this. Fed up. "There are nine steps to the structured interrogation technique, Lieutenant."

"What?"

"That is what you're using, or trying to. The Reid Technique. Nine steps. Of course, you've had to modify it for this interrogation, because the fact I was involved in what happened was never in dispute. But still, that just means skipping some of them."

"And if that were true, what's your point?"

"My point is, there are nine steps, and you don't seem to understand any of them. It's really starting to piss me off. What you said after I told you I didn't do anything wrong—do you realize that was the first time you turned an objection around on me? And you didn't even do it correctly. You should have told me you *believed* me, not that you *knew*. If you already knew, you wouldn't need the information. If you believed me, though, in that case you'd need my help to convince others."

"Is that a fact?"

"That's a fact. And another thing. If you understood the first thing about what you were doing, I wouldn't be sitting behind a table. A table is a psychological barrier. A shield. You never allow a subject to have the protection of something like that in front of him, blocking you, providing separation, distance, a way to conceal body language. And shackling me? It keeps the subject from fiddling, aids him in quieting his body language and muting the nonverbals."

"So you're an expert on this now, are you?"

"Compared to you, a kid in a playground trying to find out who stole his marbles would be an expert. I've given you verifiable facts that you ignore. When I started getting bored, I even threw out a few objections like that last one just to see if you knew how to use them against me, and you didn't. And through it all, you don't even seem the least bit curious as to how an overweight, middle-aged man with enough of a medical condition to be hospitalized could weather a rather intense physical altercation with someone twenty years younger, forcing me to have to use a weapon to stop him."

"Oh, I was curious, all right. It's one of the reasons I don't buy your story."

"You just don't get it. The guy had to be on something *strong*. PCP, maybe. Something that'll induce psychosis, increase the pain threshold. A lot. You should be trying to figure out what."

"Well, smart guy, that's where you're wrong."

Hatcher said nothing, watching the lieutenant's face as it rearranged itself into a satisfied smirk.

"Tox screens were negative. He had nothing in his bloodstream except some blood thinners."

"In that case, he must've escaped from the psych ward. Because he shouldn't have been able to keep going the way he did."

"Then why were you so intent on tangling with him instead of going to get help?" Maloney asked, pulling an elbow over the back of his chair and slouching casually.

"Because that woman was completely vulnerable. There was no way I was going to just let her be killed."

The detective gave a sidelong glance to the mirror. "Knock if you've heard enough."

Hatcher heard a rap on the glass. Maloney nodded, then gestured to the redheaded cop with the pad and gave his hand a flick toward Hatcher. "Uncuff him."

The younger detective with the apple-pie face and bad skin produced a set of keys and unlocked Hatcher's handcuffs. The cuffs hadn't been that tight, but Hatcher had to fight the impulse to flex his hands and rub his wrists anyway.

"Mr. Hatcher, you're being released from custody."

Hatcher said nothing.

"Detective Reynolds here will walk you down to sign out, get you your belongings."

Hatcher mulled it over, knew there had to be a play in what was happening here somewhere. "Turning me over to the marshals?"

"No."

"MPs?"

"No. We're cutting you loose."

"I'm guessing this isn't because you suddenly realized the folly of your ways."

Maloney snorted a laugh. "You'd be right about that."

"Mind if I ask why, then?"

"Because a person who would know finally started talking. She told us she saw the whole thing, and that it seemed the person you killed was trying to hurt her. And that you weren't."

The person you killed. The emphasis on those words seemed intentional, like Maloney was trying to establish a fact in dispute. "I thought she was unconscious."

"She'd been sedated. But she said the commotion roused her, got her to open her eyes enough to tell what was going on."

Hatcher let his gaze drift, studied his reflection, focused on what was behind it. "So, I'm free to go. Just like that."

"Just like that."

"And this whole second go-round was because . . . ?"

Maloney shrugged. "Just making double sure of a few things."

Hatcher tossed his chin toward the mirror. "In other words, whoever was behind the glass wanted to see what I had to say. Hear it for themselves."

Maloney curved his lower lip up like a fish, disguising a smile, and raised his eyebrows. "Reynolds, why don't you go on ahead and get Mr. Hatcher's personals together."

Reynolds glanced at Hatcher, then back at Maloney, who

urged him on his way with a curt nod. He left the room, closing the door behind him. That name suddenly registered. The desk near Wright's in the squad room, the one with the clown mask on it. The cop who caught the Clown Killer. Maloney hadn't shown any signs, but Hatcher realized there was some kind of one-way tension between the two of them. Maloney acted all but oblivious to it. But him acting that way meant he obviously wasn't.

"There's someone I'd like you to meet."

Hatcher stood as the door to the room opened partially. Detective Wright stepped in from behind it, holding it halfway.

"I had a feeling it was you back there," Hatcher said. "So this was all for your sake?"

"No," Wright said, moving out of the way. Behind her, a brunette in a gray NYPD sweatshirt and matching sweatpants stepped forward. She was holding something that looked like a cross between a metal cane and a walker. It had a bicycle grip handle on one end and a square bottom on the other above four short legs with rubber caps. The woman's face was a bit bruised, her hair combed flat. One of her arms was in a sling, a cast visible over her wrist, covering half her hand. But there was no denying her looks. Cane or not, bruised or not, Hatcher couldn't help but stare. Any hotter, her clothes would be on fire.

"It was for mine," she said.

Hatcher stared at her for several seconds. "You're the one from the hospital."

"Yes. Deborah St. James. It is nice to finally meet you, Mr. Hatcher."

Her scent found its way to his nostrils. An earthy, intimate fragrance, musky and sweet. Perfume that smelled of lacy undergarments after sex.

"Okay," Hatcher said, lifting his hands and giving a light shrug. "I give up. What's going on?"

"Like I told you, I had a long talk with your CO," Maloney said. "Had to get through a guy named Gifford or something first—"

"Gillis."

"That's it. Talked to him yesterday. That man definitely doesn't think much of you. Your CO, though, was more accommodating. I explained to him that our initial impressions were . . . misinformed. That you were considered more of a witness than a suspect at this time."

Hatcher said nothing. His eyes skipped from Maloney, to Deborah, to Wright.

"In light of that, he's agreed to keep you on your current status, provided we have your cooperation."

"What kind of cooperation?"

"I want to hire you," Deborah said.

Hatcher waited a few beats, hoping what she meant would become clear. It didn't. "Hire me."

"Yes."

"To do what?"

Detective Wright leaned back against the door. "We have reason to believe Ms. St. James may be a target," she said. "Of what, we're not sure. But we don't have the resources to provide her round-the-clock protection."

"How can the New York Police Department not have the resources?"

Wright and Maloney exchanged subdued glances.

"It's not just that," Deborah said. "I know what you did in that hospital, what you went through. And your brother died trying to save me. I'm the one who asked for you."

Her face seemed controlled, not expressionless, but almost blank nonetheless. It didn't matter, a blind man could see that he was being fed a line.

"I have a novel idea. Why doesn't somebody try telling me the truth? For a change."

Wright looked over to Maloney, who didn't look back this time, keeping his eyes instead on Hatcher. A few seconds passed before Maloney abruptly spoke up. "Somebody tipped off Sherman's counsel about . . . certain circumstances that forced us to let him go. According to you, Sherman was at the hospital, in her room.

Detective Wright thinks you may be right. Her location may not have been a state secret, but we weren't letting anyone know about it."

"I found out," Hatcher said.

"But he didn't snoop around and follow a trail like you did," Maloney said. "We checked. He must have gone straight to her floor, because no one remembered talking to him."

Hatcher studied his shoes for a moment. When he raised his eyes, Deborah and Detective Wright were staring at him. The blonde detective appeared uncertain. Deborah was completely inscrutable, her expression neutral.

"Lieutenant Maloney thinks we have a leak in the department," Wright said, breaking the silence.

"And you want me to be her bodyguard while you figure out who it is."

Maloney scratched the flesh beneath his jaw. "Pretty much."

So that's why he had me cuffed, Hatcher thought. Not because he thought I was guilty of anything, but because he knew I wasn't. He remembered something a CIA operative once mentioned, almost in passing, during a training session. *Ask any FBI agent and they'll tell you, if you call a guy a liar in an interview and he takes a swing at you, you can bank on him being innocent.* Hatcher had never actually experienced that, but then he'd never interrogated anyone who was innocent. There were no innocents in his line of work. Only enemies with knowledge and enemies without.

"And if I say no?"

"You won't," Deborah said.

Hatcher took in her eyes. They were a light silvery blue. Round, with thick lashes. "How can you be so sure?"

"Because your brother died saving me. You fought a brutal fight to keep someone from harming me. Protecting others is in your blood."

"Not to mention, you'd have the gratitude of the NYPD," Maloney said, smiling.

"Speaking of my brother, I need to get to his funeral."

"We need your answer," Maloney said.

"Let me think about it."

Maloney made a grunting sound and gestured toward Wright. "As long as you don't take too long. Detective Wright will take you to the funeral home and wait for your answer. Ms. St. James can ride along."

Detective Wright nodded. "I'll get an SPV from the motor pool and meet you out front. Ms. St. James, you should come with me. We don't want anyone to see the two of you together at the station."

Deborah dipped her chin in a quiet gesture of assent. Wright opened the door and let her step into the hallway first. Before closing the door behind her, Wright turned, leaning back into the room. "You seem like a good guy, Hatcher. I'm sorry about your brother, and I'm sorry you've been dragged into this." She gave him a wan smile, then left.

Hatcher and Maloney said nothing for an awkward moment.

"What now?" Hatcher asked, finally.

"We wait another minute, then I walk you down to the custodian and check you out."

"You know, you could have just asked."

"Amy wanted to," Maloney said, shrugging. "I thought you might need a little prodding. And it looks like you're proving me right."

The lieutenant shot a glance at his watch and stood. He held out his hand and gestured to Hatcher with a flick of his fingertips, then made his way to the door and waited. Just as Hatcher started to step through it, Maloney stopped him, grabbing Hatcher's arm, wrapping his long grip tightly around as much of it as he could. His voice was a low, growling whisper.

"One more thing, tough guy. *She's mine.* You make a move on her, I'll put a round in the back of your head and dump you in the East River."

CHAPTER 9

❖

THE MANHATTAN TRAFFIC MOVED LIKE BLOOD FORGING a sclerotic artery, squeezing in fits and starts through bottlenecked passages of double-parked cars and road repair crews. Hatcher sat in the backseat of the Ford sedan, watching the city move around him, pedestrians and taxis and bicycle messengers. They had traveled several blocks before a question that had been floating around his mind found a foothold and flashed into his thoughts.

"Didn't they just release you from intensive care yesterday?" he asked.

Deborah peered back at him between the seats. In the backlit shade of the car's interior, her eyes were a magnetic shade of bluish gray. Alluring, haunting. They seemed to reach out, wrapping themselves around his field of vision until he could see nothing else. "Yes."

"So how are you up and around already?"

"They didn't want to let me go, but I wasn't about to stay there. Not after what happened."

Hatcher glanced over to the back of Wright's head, where

her hair poked through a scrunchie. "I was led to believe you'd broken almost every bone in your body."

"That's pretty much what I was told," Wright said, giving him a half look back over her shoulder. "I suppose it's safe to say the doctors were exaggerating."

Hatcher considered that, remembered Deborah in the hospital bed. He gestured toward her with his chin. "Yesterday you were bandaged up."

"The other wrappings were a precaution, I guess. I'm tougher than I look." Deborah raised her cast, a blue fiberglass wrap, patterned like webbing. She tapped her finger against it. "The X-rays showed this arm only had a hairline fracture, not a compound fracture."

In the confines of the car, her scent was almost unbearably arousing. She ran her cast-free hand back over her ear, tucking her hair behind it. A simple movement that sent a mild current through his testicles. He knew it couldn't be even close to the sexiest thing he'd ever seen, but she definitely made it seem that way. Whatever "it" was, this woman had bushels to spare.

"You're a lucky woman."

"The truth is, I think your brother shielded me with his body. I don't really remember it, though. One of the doctors told me that might explain it. That I was thrown clear without being hit as hard. He saved my life."

Hatcher felt a twinge of something unfamiliar, realized it was pride. Family pride. His brother sounded like a real hero. If, he reminded himself, this Garrett fellow really had been his brother. He shifted his view out the window.

"What time is it?" Hatcher asked.

Wright glanced at the dashboard clock. "A little after eleven thirty."

Hatcher twisted to look over his shoulder. A black sedan was two cars back. He was almost certain it had been there when they left the station, same number of cars behind them.

"I need to stop and get some clothes."

"Do you have a place nearby?"

"No. I mean at the store. Any store will do."

"I'm not sure that's a good idea."

"Look, I've worn this outfit for three days, washed it once. I slept in it last night, thanks to Lieutenant Hair Club's crack detective work. I haven't showered since yesterday morning. I can show up without a shave. I can show up without a suit. But I'm not showing up without a new shirt and some clean underwear. That's where I draw the line."

"And I said I don't like the idea. I'm not a taxi service. I'm giving you a ride to the funeral home. That's all."

"I thought I was released from custody."

"You were."

"Fine." Hatcher leaned forward between the front seats and pointed. "You can drop me off at the next corner then. Have a nice life."

Wright rolled her eyes. "All right. You win. One stop. Just be quick."

"I need you to come in with me," Hatcher said.

"Why?"

Hatcher sat back and stared out the passenger window, watching the reflections for the sedan. "I'll tell you when we're inside."

Wright looked back. Narrowed eyes studied him. Hatcher ignored her.

"In that case, Mr. Mysterious, we all have to go." She glanced at Deborah. "I'm not leaving you by yourself."

The car slowed. Wright ducked her head slightly, taking in the storefronts. After a minute, she pulled over and parked against the curb directly beneath a no-parking sign, then placed a police-business sign on the dashboard.

Hatcher stepped out onto the sidewalk. Deborah was already out of the car, pushing herself up on her cane. She was moving away from the street before he had a chance to help her.

The sedan passed by. The windows were tinted. It didn't

slow down. That didn't mean anything, he knew. But he also reminded himself he wasn't in a red zone.

"Stacy's Men's Shop," Wright said, gesturing toward a store twenty or so yards back. "Let's make it quick."

The door buzzed when Hatcher pulled it open, the noise dissolving into the hip-hop music playing through a speaker system. He took in the styles pinned to the wall and dressed on headless mannequins for a moment, then headed for a rack of shirts. The store was cramped and dark, geared toward a younger, more urban look than he was used to, but he managed to find a short-sleeve khaki button-down with epaulets that looked relatively conservative and a plain tan T-shirt to go underneath. The closest thing to normal underwear they carried was an assortment of silk boxers. He found a pair of dark gray ones in his size, then took everything to a dressing room in the back and changed.

"Looks good," Wright said, watching him as he approached a counter along the wall in the new shirt. Her lips curled into a faint smile. "Guy with a build like yours can probably wear anything."

A thin kid in a jacket with rolled-up sleeves and a skinny leather tie asked him if he was ready to checkout. Hatcher handed him the tags, asked him for a bag to put his old clothes in.

"With tax, that will be fifty-eight ninety."

Hatcher gestured to Wright. "Don't look at me. It's on her. Courtesy of the NYPD."

Wright's mouth parted into a semi-gape and stayed that way. A crease ripped down her forehead as she bore her eyes into him. The only sound she made was a short grunt that seemed to have a question mark at the end of it. Hatcher almost felt bad for doing it to her. Almost.

"I'll pay for it," Deborah said.

"No." Hatcher waved her off. "They owe me. Don't worry, Detective." He patted Wright on the shoulder, gave it a gentle shake. "I'm sure Maloney will approve your chit and reimburse you. Besides, I'm broke."

Shaking her head, Wright removed a wallet from her purse and pulled out a credit card. She was making some more noise now, little puffs of disgust under her breath.

"This better mean you're going to say yes," she said.

Hatcher was already heading toward the door with the bag. "I'm still thinking about it."

The drive to the funeral home took a little over thirty minutes in moderate traffic. It was a brick building, low and long, with a wide green awning reaching out from an oversized set of front doors. Wright was able to park close, since the lot was almost empty. It was painted with continuous white lanes instead of spaces, designed to allow cars to file out in rows.

"Do you want us to wait here?"

"It's up to you."

Wright and Deborah stayed. Hatcher went in through the front. A small placard on an easel indicated the home was holding services for Garrett E. Hatcher, Beloved Son and Brother, with dates and times for the viewing and burial.

There were two sets of doors, one on each side. The doors to his left were spread open to form a wide entryway. He wandered through them into a large reception area. It was daintily furnished with formal, ornate furniture, like the tearoom of someone very old and very wealthy. And very boring, he noted. Wood chairs with rounded backs and lion's-paw feet. Gold velveteen upholstery. Pairs of matching prints in gilded frames depicting floral arrangements adorned the walls.

Another set of doors opened near the far end of the room. Hatcher's mother passed through, holding a Kleenex to her nose. Carl had a supporting arm around her waist. Hatcher watched her face. She wasn't exactly weeping as much as exhaling sad, labored breaths like sighs.

Karen Hatcher noticed her son and tilted her head. She was forcing a smile, but the edges of her lips sagged, tugged by some unseen weight. The lines roughing her brow seemed to be deeper than those caused by crying, and

Hatcher sensed what she was feeling was different than the simple heartache of burying a son. More solitary. The kind of sorrow she could probably never share. The anguish of burying her chance to reclaim something lost, perhaps.

"Jacob. I didn't think you'd make it."

"Sorry. There was a bit of a misunderstanding."

Carl made a short humming noise, but didn't say anything. His upper lip twitched into a sneer. The man sneered a lot, Hatcher recalled.

"They're about to take him to the cemetery," his mother said. "We're supposed to follow. If you go in, they may still let you see him."

Hatcher nodded and headed in the direction she indicated, not particularly wanting to see his brother's body, but knowing she would take it the wrong way if he declined.

The viewing room was much smaller than the waiting area. It did double duty as a generic chapel, with pictures of doves and clouds and a few framed prayers in Victorian script. A man in a black suit was securing latches on the casket as Hatcher walked up the aisle between the rows of chairs. A mortician, Hatcher presumed. The man glanced back and stopped what he was doing, smiling politely. The smile of someone trained, either by himself or others, to appear pleasant but not happy. Hatcher wondered if people called him Mort. He looked like a Mort.

"I'm Jake Hatcher."

Mort's eyebrows rose in understanding and he nodded. Without introducing himself, he turned back to the casket and undid the latches on one side. The casket lining was a shiny white satin that glowed brightly as Mort propped open half of the lid. Hatcher wondered whether funeral directors were also trained not to shake hands or volunteer their names. It seemed possible. Grieving people were probably not in the mood to make new acquaintances.

"I'll give you some time to pay respects," Mort said, before leaving through a side door.

This is probably how I'll end up, Hatcher thought,

pausing before he approached the casket. Alone in a box, mourned by a mother, maybe a father, but likely no one else. Hatcher stepped closer, stared at the body.

So this was the man who everyone was saying was my brother, he thought. What was left of him, at least. Was it still a person? Like a car was still a car, even after the engine failed? Or had what made it a person already left? It was a question he'd pondered in the past, but not one he'd thought about recently. It had been a while since he cared.

He realized that Garrett looked different, less real than in his photos. His skin was a coppery shade of peach, thick and textured with makeup. It seemed to hang a bit loose around the low points of his jaw. The face reminded Hatcher of silly putty, like it could be molded and stretched, maybe pick up a cartoon image from a newspaper if he pressed one against it. Even so, Hatcher saw more of a resemblance now than he had before. Slight similarities in the cheeks and across the nose, in the shape of the eyes and brows. Not a lot, but enough. Maybe, he thought. Maybe.

An awkward feeling started to seep in. Faking it, going through the motions for his mother's sake, suddenly played wrong in a way he couldn't quite pin down. There were moments where it seemed like the kind of person you were was being decided, recorded somewhere, not in spite of no one else being around, but because of it. There had to be a right way to do this. But how were you supposed to say good-bye to someone you never met, someone who may not even be there anymore?

Hatcher thought about saying he was sorry for what had happened, then considered something like, *Wish we'd had the chance to meet*. Neither seemed appropriate. He placed a hand gently on Garrett's chest, trying to conjure up some words.

That last story Tyler Culp had been blabbering on about, the one about Chinese ghost brides, popped into his thoughts. The motivation for those people was now rather easy to follow. He'd never met this man in life, didn't even know if he really was his brother, but still felt an odd sense of obligation pulling at him as he stood there, like wherever the owner of this body was now, he was helpless. Helpless and alone. And he would never be this close again. No wonder grieving family members imagined ways they could help.

"Hope there's something else," Hatcher finally said in a quiet voice.

As Hatcher started to lift his hand, he thought he noticed movement around Garrett's eyes. He leaned closer, studying them, and saw them part to narrow slits. Something cold clamped down on his wrist, holding him in place. Garrett's head lolled in Hatcher's direction. The subdued radiance of a gaze penetrated from the thin space between the lids. The eyes on the other side were lifeless, milky, like they were covered by some thick plastic film. But they managed to bore into Hatcher anyway. A thousand-mile stare, straight at him.

Garrett's mouth opened about an inch. A low, hissing sound came out. Two words reached Hatcher's ears, garbled, barely audible, but somehow unmistakable.

The hand maintained its grip as Hatcher belatedly sprang back. He raked at his arm, managed to pry the hand loose. Garrett's eyes stayed the same, but something that was there a moment ago seemed to have left. The arm stayed up, fingers curved into a claw. It leaned out motionless over the edge of the casket.

Hatcher gasped for a breath, feeling his heart rioting against the walls of his chest. *"Holy shit."*

"Sir!"

Urgent footfalls broke the icy silence. Hatcher looked up just as a very upset-looking Mort moved past him.

"Sir, please! You mustn't disturb the remains! I know how difficult this is. But you must show some respect for the deceased."

Hatcher said nothing, still trying to catch his breath. The man repositioned Garrett's arm so that his hands were folded across his chest. Then he adjusted the head. He pressed the eyes closed with great care, one at a time, using both hands on each.

"See there, you could have torn through the eyelids doing that. We use eye caps to keep them closed. They are not meant to be opened again."

"Eye caps," Hatcher said, absently. He rubbed his wrist, still able to feel where the steely fingers had latched on to him. He kept imagining that it tingled, though he knew that wasn't true.

"This can be a very emotional experience for some people. You're not the first to want one last look into a loved one's eyes, one last embrace."

Taking his time, Mort finished his adjustments and closed the casket lid. He turned to Hatcher, regarded him briefly, then put a hand on his shoulder. Hatcher stared past him at the casket, trying to find a load-bearing spot once again in reality, unsure of where it was he'd just visited.

"You must remember, while you're here to say your final farewells, he has already departed. That is no longer your loved one. Merely his earthly remains."

Earthly remains. Hatcher continued to stare at the casket until Mort nudged him gently by the shoulder, encouraging him to exit. His legs wouldn't move at first, or didn't seem to be moving, but after a few moments he realized he was being led away. He found himself looking back over his shoulder, keeping his eyes on the obsidian wood, half expecting it to open, trying not to doubt his sanity as he wondered how and why those earthly remains managed to voice two words to him. Two words he shouldn't have even understood. Words that shouldn't have made sense, but did.

Protect her.

IN THE WAITING AREA, HATCHER'S MOTHER WAS SITTING in one of the chairs. She was propped on the edge, her legs

tucked to the side and her hands lying palms up on her lap.
Carl was standing near her, looking out a window.

She looked up as her son appeared. "Jacob? Are you
okay?"

It took a few beats for the words to register. Hatcher
pulled a palm down his face.

"Yeah. Yeah, I'm fine."

"Seeing him really affected you, didn't it?" She stood
and moved toward him with her arms out, reaching for his
hands. "You poor dear."

His legs felt numb. There was a bubbly-popping sensation lingering in his head. His stomach had dropped to
somewhere around his knees. Nothing in the room had the
solid look or feel it was supposed to.

"I'm okay," he said. He let go of her hands to touch his
wrist again. "Really."

Movement in the hall, visible through the doorway,
caught his eye. It was Wright. She was drifting in a small
circle, apparently reading the screen of her cell phone,
punching in numbers. He excused himself and headed her
way.

Wright looked up as Hatcher approached. "Is something
wrong?"

"Where's Deborah?"

"She didn't feel well." Wright flipped her cell phone shut
and pocketed it. "She went to use the bathroom."

"Where?"

Wright pointed toward the far end of the entry hall. "In
the back. Why? What's wrong?"

Hatcher brushed past her without responding, cutting toward the back of the building. Wright fell in behind him
and almost broke into a trot trying to keep up.

"Hatcher, what's the matter?"

A door marked *Restroom* stood near a rear wall. Hatcher
knocked on it. No response. He knocked again, harder.
This time he heard something. Could have been a woman's
voice, but it was muffled.

He grabbed the knob, tried to twist it. Locked.

Protect her.

He took a step back and kicked the door as close to the latch as possible, stomping it with the bottom of his shoe. The wood gave off a crunching, splintering sound, but didn't budge.

"Jesus, Hatcher! What the hell are you doing?"

Another kick, a bit harder this time, and the door broke through the latch plate, a crack splitting the molding toward the ceiling and floor. The door swung inward, dented.

The bathroom was open and relatively spacious. Deborah was bent over a sink to the left, holding a wad of toilet paper to her nose, her reflection in the mirror in front of her. The basin was filled with bloody water. She looked at Hatcher over her shoulder.

"Nosebleed," she said.

Hatcher tossed a few glances around the confined space. There was nowhere for anyone to hide. There wasn't even a stall, just a toilet.

"Are you okay?" he asked. "Anything happen to you?"

"I'm fine. I get these all the time. I appreciate your concern, though." She eyed the door, then the cracked frame. "I'm not sure the funeral parlor is going to feel the same way."

As if on cue, Mort came hurrying up.

"What's going on?"

"False alarm," Hatcher said.

"Good Lord, look at this!"

Hatcher glared at Wright. "Don't worry, the NYPD will reimburse you."

"Hey!" Wright yelled. Her face had slackened in some places, hardened correspondingly in others. She looked at the funeral home rep, then at Hatcher, obviously fighting to maintain her composure. She stabbed a finger toward him. "I need to have a word with you. Right now."

Wright nodded politely at Mort and gestured for Hatcher to follow her.

Hatcher turned to Deborah. "Wait right there. Don't move." He pointed at the man in the black suit. "You, keep your eye on her, Mort."

"What did you call me? My name is Peter. And what do you mean? Where are you going?"

Ignoring him, Hatcher spun and walked off.

The hallway was perpendicular to the one that led to the front of the funeral home, bisecting the building with exits in each direction. Wright was walking toward one of the sets of glass doors. She paused a few yards out, waiting for Hatcher to catch up, eyes flashing, one of her heels impatiently digging into the carpet. When he came within a few steps, she started to say something, but he grabbed her arm before she could, stopping her words in her throat, and began walking even faster, pushing her along until they reached the doors. He pushed one of them open and propelled her through.

"Get your goddamn hands off me!"

Hatcher yanked her close, pressing her arm against her side and lifting her by it enough to force her onto her toes. "You tell me what the hell is going on. Right now. Right this minute."

"I said, get your hands off of me! Are you crazy? You want to be put away for real?"

When he didn't let go, she punched at his face with her free hand and twisted, shaking and yanking until she was able to rip herself out of his grasp. Her breathing was suddenly heavy, her face flushed. She whipped her suit coat back and slapped her hand against her holster. Her eyes immediately shot down to her hip.

"Looking for this?" Hatcher asked, holding up her Glock.

Wright's expression froze. She jumped forward, tried to snatch the pistol out of his hand, but wasn't fast enough. He held it above his head, baiting her with it.

"I'm placing you under arrest," she said, stepping back. "Don't be stupid. You give me that gun right now, or I'll add resisting and assault with a deadly weapon. And it *will* stick."

"You tell me what's going on *right now*, or you'll wish I just assaulted you."

She placed her hands on her hips. Her breaths were starting to come under control. "Are you saying you're going to shoot me? That's the kind of guy you are? I can't believe I was so wrong about you." She shook her head, catching her bottom lip between her teeth, all but trembling with rage. "I'm not kidding. You are under arrest, and now you are officially resisting and threatening a law enforcement officer."

"Fine. Take me into custody, if you can. But when I finish quaking in my boots, I'm going to forcibly take your keys off your person, as your type would say, drive your car to a very bad neighborhood, and see that this fine piece of Austrian craftsmanship winds up in the right hands. Or wrong hands, depending on how you look at it. By dawn, I'll lay money it'll be linked to at least three robberies and two homicides."

"And you'll be put away for a long, long time. What is wrong with you, Hatcher? You can't be this stupid."

"I may be stupid, but I've spent the last twelve years working for the government, so I know a little about how things work when you have a chain of command and a bureaucracy. And I'm betting I can guess the rest. So try this for stupid. First, I'll be telling my story about you blackmailing me to join your little extracurricular operation to whoever will listen. Newspapers, IAD, my public defender. Then, I'll tell them how you gave me your gun as part of it, the one that shot its way through Harlem the night before. How many Internal Affairs reviews will you have to endure, do you think? Four? Five? You think Lieutenant Fake Hair likes the look of your ass enough to take all the blame himself? You think your career will ever recover?"

"What kind of a threat is that? What the hell has gotten

into you? Have you lost your mind? First busting down that door? Now assaulting a cop? You think you can just do whatever you want?"

"Funny, I've been wanting to ask the same thing about you and the NYPD. I want to know what the hell is going on. And I want you to stop lying to me. Now."

She stared at him for a stretch, seething. "I don't know what you're talking about."

"You can start with the lies, and what I'm talking about will become remarkably clear right away. You've been feeding them to me since we first met."

"This is ridiculous. If you just give me back the gun, this will go a lot easier on you."

"I'm about to lose my patience." He rolled his shoulders back until his something popped. "It never ends well when I lose my patience."

"Hatcher, you're making a big mistake."

He tucked the gun into his waistband. "Fine. When the family of the person or persons killed by your gun takes your deposition as part of their lawsuit, you can tell them how it was all my fault. Now, are you going to hand me the keys? Or are you going to break your hands punching me while I take them and rough you up in the process?"

She didn't respond. Hatcher nodded grimly and took a step toward her.

"Wait," she said, holding out her palms. "I'll make you a deal. You give me back the gun, I'll tell you."

Hatcher pulled the Glock from his waistband, held it up. "And if you don't?"

"Don't what?"

"If I give it to you and you don't tell me, what then? Are you going to try to arrest me again? Then whine when I take it away? Again?"

"Just give it to me, damn it."

Without breaking eye contact, Hatcher pressed a button on the side of the handle, ejecting the clip. He ratcheted the slide back, popping the live round out of the chamber. He caught the bullet in midair with the same hand that held the clip.

He handed her the gun. The slide was locked back, exposing the empty chamber. "Here."

"I have another clip, you know."

"And I'd have the gun back in my hands before you even touch it. You might even break a nail. Now talk. Tell me what's going on. The truth."

Her lower jaw shoved forward, her bottom lip stuck between her teeth. "I don't know what you expect me to say."

"Why have you been lying to me?"

"What makes you—"

Hatcher shot forward, grabbed hold of the gun by the top of its exposed barrel.

"Okay! Okay. Jesus! Calm down. It's not what you think."

"And just what do I think?"

"That we're out to get you somehow. Damn you, Hatcher—it has nothing to do with you. Not like that."

"I'm waiting."

Wright's shoulders sagged a bit. She hesitated as she started to speak. "Your brother may have been involved in something bad."

"Keep going."

"We have reason to believe he was hired to kill someone."

"Hired? Like a hit man?"

"Yes."

Hatcher glanced back through the side door to the funeral home. "You think he was hired to kill Deborah?"

"We don't know."

"But that makes no sense. She said he saved her. Witnesses saw it."

"Yes. But she may have misinterpreted his actions, along with everyone else. We just don't know."

Protect her. "I think you're wrong, but what else."

"What do you mean? That's it."

"You're lying."

"Quit saying that!"

"Look, something weird is going on here, and I'm really getting sick of being jerked around. If you want me to help you, it stops now."

The muscles circling Wright's eyes bunched together. She appraised him, her tongue visible through her cheeks as she worked it around her mouth. "The man your brother fought with."

"What about him?"

"His name was Walter Sorrenson."

"Okay."

She stared at the ground for a few seconds. "The ME concluded he died of a coronary. That he was dead before the ambulance struck him. Him, or your brother, for that matter."

"Okay."

"A little less than an hour before that happened, Walter Sorrenson keeled over at a deli. A doctor happened to be there, tried CPR. He gave up after a few minutes, pronounced him dead. No pulse. Pupils fixed and dilated."

"You're saying this was the same guy?"

Wright shrugged. "Witnesses said he got up a moment later, looking dazed. From what we could tell, his shirt was unbuttoned from the CPR. Somebody tried to guide him to a chair and grabbed the shirt as he stumbled. The guy said he simply shrugged it off and kept walking. He paused briefly at a mirror near the entrance, then snatched a raincoat from a rack by the door. The owner had worn it the day before and left it there. It was the same coat we found on the body. It had the owner's name in it."

"So the doctor made a mistake," Hatcher said, cradling his wrist and twisting it slowly. It felt cold. "The heart attack didn't kill him, but maybe it damaged his brain, turned him into a psycho."

"That's what we thought. Except the ME confirmed the heart attack did kill him. It was a massive one. He was dead before he fell off his chair."

Hatcher took a few seconds to process the information. "Why do I think that's not all?"

Wright's gaze dropped back to the ground, focusing on a spot near Hatcher's shoes. She took a long time before responding. "That guy whose neck you broke in the hospital? He'd just been sent down to the morgue before that. Died of an embolism."

"You're saying he was already dead, too? That's impossible." He glanced back through the glass into the funeral home. The reflection wouldn't let him see far inside. "Dead people don't walk around."

"See why we weren't anxious to tell you? Or anyone? They must not have been dead. Da—Lieutenant Maloney's been keeping this under wraps, personally trying to run the traps, consulting the feds. We're not even letting the info out among the department. We think somebody may have slipped them something, some kind of toxin that made them seem dead."

"But you found nothing in their blood," Hatcher said, guessing.

Wright shook her head. "No, we didn't. We're still having them look. Maybe it's some kind of rare agent, a hallucinogen that works in small doses. No one knows."

Hatcher doubted that. "What about Sherman?"

"What about him?"

"He was in that room. You saw him."

"Hatcher, I saw some bald guy on the floor holding his head, and I can barely remember even that. It could have been him, but Lieutenant Maloney says he doesn't think so. He personally reviewed the security tapes. There was nothing showing anyone who could be Sherman coming or going."

"I'm the one who put him in the fetal position. It was Sherman. Maloney was too busy trying to trip me up to listen. He needs to lose his hard-on for me and find the creep. That's where you'll get some answers."

"You're wrong about Maloney, Hatcher. He was the one

who insisted you be released. He said he believed you, and once Deborah St. James corroborated what you told him, he decided to let you go. But she said she didn't remember seeing anyone else in the room, either. We're hoping to talk to Sherman, but we don't have enough to issue a warrant."

A passing cloud blocked the sun. Hatcher watched its shadow fall over her. He popped the ejected round back into the clip and tossed it to her.

"There's more I want to know, but that'll do for now," he said.

The sound of the magazine slamming home and a round being chambered caused him to stop as he turned toward the door.

"Don't you ever do anything like that again," she said.

He looked over his shoulder, smiling. "Don't worry. Next time I'll do something totally different."

She stomped past him, pulling open the door and forcing him to take a step back. She paused as she started to go through. "Would you have really beaten me up to get my keys? Really have given this gun to some bangers? Are you that kind of guy?"

"What do you think?"

"I don't know what to think about you," she said. She studied him for a long moment before stepping inside.

When she was about ten paces in, he called her name. Still in the doorway, he reached into his pocket and tossed something at her. She leaned forward and caught it. A ring of keys. They jangled in her hand as she stared at them.

"And if I'm going to protect Deborah while you use her as bait," he said, "I expect you to buy me lunch first."

CHAPTER 10

❖

STARING OUT THE WINDOW OF DEBORAH'S APARTMENT, Hatcher scratched at the stubble on his chin as he watched the street below. Wright's car passed from sight after a few dozen yards, the view eventually blocked by trees along the sidewalk. It was an upscale part of town. He'd never spent much time in the city growing up, but affluence was easy to spot.

He scanned the avenue, taking in the parked cars. Compact types mostly, small and new, with a few hybrids thrown in. One black SUV parked a few stoops up. Back the opposite way on the other side of the street, a drywall van with a spattered aluminum ladder hanging on the side of it was wedged between a Camry and an Acura. A guy in a hat listening to an iPod was walking his dog toward it. A jogger passed him, probably heading to Central Park. No street people that Hatcher could see. One of the signs of money was the absence of people who had none.

Deborah's place was impeccably furnished, with a white oriental sofa and black tables. Four bright white walls surrounded a plush square of white carpeting. The several end tables and wall tables were like art stands, displaying one item each. A white phone on one, a white vase with a red rose on another. A white lamp on a third. Some kind of soft black lounge chair, S-shaped, like a tilted lightning bolt in the manner of an SS insignia sat alone at an angle on the far side of the main room, with a white throw pillow tossed on it. The woman chose to live in a world of black and white. He figured he wasn't in a position to knock it. Hatcher didn't know much about Manhattan real estate, but the apartment was large and he figured that meant pricey. All that white made it seem even larger. All that black even pricier.

The burial had not taken long. The cemetery was located little more than a mile from the funeral home, so the three-car procession only lasted a few minutes. It probably would have taken even less time to get there without the motorcycle cop running interference. A priest said some words about healing and God's children and being taken to His bosom, then they lowered the casket into the ground. Hatcher had found the scene a bit odd, since his mother wasn't Catholic. At least, he didn't think she was. He left the cemetery wondering if the funeral home arranged everything without much guidance on the religious end, or if his mother may have converted. Twelve years was a long time. He'd thought about how much can change during that kind of a stretch when he said good-bye to her, as she hugged him and sobbed against his chest, Carl eventually pulling her away and gently leading her toward their car. Hatcher'd had a number of new questions he wanted to ask her about Garrett, but some things would have to wait. Other questions were more pressing now, and they weren't the type his mother could answer.

Deborah emerged from the rear of the apartment. She had freshened up—which was the way she put it—and was wearing a change of clothes. Hatcher wasn't exactly sure what women did when they freshened up, but whatever she had decided to do worked. Good as she looked before, now she looked even better. The white cotton dress she wore clung to her curves loosely, like it was threatening to fall off at any moment. And those curves of hers just wouldn't quit. He was having trouble controlling the placement of his gaze. He tore his eyes away with great effort, thinking, there ought to be a law. He scratched that thought. He'd been plenty of places that had those laws. They weren't pleasant.

"Can I get you something to drink?"

"Water would be nice."

Deborah disappeared between a pair of swinging doors into the kitchen. Hatcher followed the tight movement of her rear as she went. When her ass disappeared his eyes wandered the room, settling on a framed black-and-white photo of the New York skyline hanging over her couch, taken from a rooftop. Along the bottom white border was an address and a date.

She came out a moment later with a tall glass and a bottle of Evian.

"From the tap would have been fine," he said. He gestured vaguely toward her leg. "What happened to the cane?"

She smiled, handed him the glass and bottle. "I can walk without it. It just hurts like a bastard, especially if I make it a point not to limp. But if you don't deal with pain, don't master it, a cane can become a crutch, don't you think?"

Hatcher nodded, unsure how she could be looking so healthy already. So healthy, and so damn delicious. They were standing close, facing each other, her eyes shining up into his. Every breath he took was inhaling her essence. He felt the swelling of an erection press against his trousers. He turned his attention to the wall.

"Did you take this?"

She shook her head. "It was a gift."

"You say that as if you don't like it."

"It's okay," she said, shrugging. "I keep it up for the man who gave it to me. Wouldn't want him to get suicidal."

Something like a silent laugh seemed to shape her expression for a fraction of a second, like she was enjoying an inside joke. It was gone before Hatcher could tell whether it had really been there, or was just something he imagined. A lot of her expressions seemed that way.

"I'm not sure what's supposed to happen now," she said. "Do we just sit around?"

It wasn't a bad question. Hatcher weighed how much of his take on things he should share. He decided not too much. There was something uncommon about this woman, more than her uncommonly good looks, more than her uncommonly attractive body, more than her uncommonly sensuous manner. Something he didn't understand. So he needed to be careful. No matter how aroused he became.

"I hope I'm not giving away some big surprise if I tell you this is all a trap," he said.

"What do you mean by that?"

"There's a van parked across the street, but I don't see any windows open in any buildings, don't see workers coming or going. Not that big a deal, but there's also an Expedition parked a few doors down, and it's the only vehicle among several that doesn't have bird crap on it. That would indicate it wasn't parked there overnight, like the others. But it's not shiny, so it hasn't been washed recently. I'm also guessing you're going to see a number of people walking dogs during the day, taking their time going up and down the street. Different people. But I'll bet if you look carefully, you'll see the same dog more than once."

"Sounds like the police. But didn't they say they couldn't spare the manpower? That's why you're here, isn't it? That's why I hired you. Which reminds me . . ."

She slid two fingers between her dress and a breast, removed a folded bill. She handed it to him.

"This is for you. A small advance. Since you said you were broke."

It was a Benjamin. Hatcher didn't want to take it, but knew he'd need it. He tucked it into his pocket. "Thank you."

He poured some of his water into the glass. "How much of this was your idea? Me playing bodyguard?"

"All of it. Or most of it, at least. Are you suggesting they manipulated me? Planted the thought in my head?"

The water tasted good. He'd been thirstier than he realized. "That, or something you said made a lightbulb go off and they ran with it."

"Interesting." She took a seat on the sofa, leaning sideways against the back of it, crossing one long leg over the other. She was wearing a pair of open-toed strapless shoes with wooden soles. She flicked them off with a wiggle of her foot and patted the cushion next to her. "What does your theory offer as to why?"

"They're trying to flush out whoever wants to kill you," he said, setting himself down next to her.

"That doesn't sound consistent with letting you guard me."

Hatcher shrugged. "It does if you look at it from their point of view. I'm expendable."

"Even if that were true, wouldn't you being here deter whoever is wanting to kill me?"

"Maybe. Or maybe they think it would look more suspicious if you were left naked . . . so to speak. They said they thought they might have a leak at the department."

She inclined her head, resting it on her hand, her elbow propped on the back of the sofa. "I don't understand."

Hatcher took another sip, then set the glass and bottle down on the slick black gloss of the coffee table. "If you're by yourself, whoever is out there may get leery and wait. Too easy. If you're with a cop, the person feeding them information may insist that the cop not be hurt. He—or she—might be afraid the resulting investigation would be more thorough. But if it's just some muscle you hired, that might be different. They may be counting on word getting out that that's the situation."

"Is that how you see yourself? Muscle?"

"It has nothing to do with how I see myself. That's just what I'm supposed to be at the moment."

"So why did you agree to this, if you're certain you're being sacrificed?"

Hatcher bent forward, resting his forearms across his legs and clasping his hands. He had to do it to avoid staring at her breasts. "Because I don't like being lied to. If I'm not going to get the straight story from them about what happened to Garrett, then I'll find out myself."

"You're a regular man of action, huh?"

"More like a guy who's let himself get jerked around one too many times."

"In that case, what do you propose we do?"

Hatcher realized she had just batted her eyes. He wasn't sure he had ever actually seen a woman do that before, but there it was. She pulled her leg up a bit, the smooth, glistening flesh of her thigh glowing in the afternoon light. Given her body language, the question she had asked was almost too much to bear. Was she inviting him to say something suggestive? Was she giving him a signal? He couldn't tell. Her face was too hard to read, her expressions too controlled. In some ways, she was obviously giving him signs. In others, it seemed there was no way to be sure, which made the obvious ones suspect.

"I need to figure out what's going on. I assume the police asked you a lot of questions about people who may have a motive to hurt you."

"Yes. Too many to think about."

"But you didn't tell them everything, did you?"

"What makes you say that?"

"Because another motivation for them doing it this way is that they don't trust you."

She regarded him, allowing the silence to draw out. Magnetic eyes, tugging at him. "You're right. There are some things I didn't tell them. Things I couldn't."

"I'm listening."

"I'm not sure I should say anything more. Not yet."

A hint of a smile played across her lips, but her brow was set with a serious aspect. The woman's expressions were a series of contradictions that Hatcher was finding impossible to get a handle on.

"And why is that?" he asked.

"For the same reasons I couldn't tell them. They wouldn't have believed me. And neither will you."

Hatcher rubbed his wrist. "I'll believe just about anything right now. As long as it's the truth."

Her fragrance was becoming intolerably overpowering. As if she sensed its effect, she pushed herself up and leaned toward him, almost close enough to brush his nose with hers. She ran her eyes over his face. He sensed his self-control was being tested. A pretty good test, he had to admit. Failure was looking like a rather attractive option.

"There is a group of women out there," she said, pulling back. "They are very beautiful and very dangerous. They want me dead."

"Why?"

She took a breath, hesitated. "Because of a man named Demetrius Valentine."

"Okay."

"I'm not comfortable saying anything more right now. It wouldn't be fair. The more I tell you, the more danger I put you in."

"I think it's pretty safe to say I'm in the line of fire now, considering I'm the guy pegged to take a bullet for you."

"There's more than that kind of danger in the world. Let me think about it for a while. I'm not sure how much I want you to know. Or how much you should."

Hatcher pondered that. Normally, he'd draw a line right then, tell her he wasn't going to let himself be played that way. But instead, he just took another sip of water and said, "Dangerous women, huh?"

"Yes. And beautiful, too."

"Most beautiful women are. Dangerous, that is."

"You seem rather dangerous yourself."

Hatcher let out an abbreviated chuckle, guzzled the rest

of his glass. "Me? I'm harmless. Nothing but a kitten, really."

"A very dangerous kitten, then." She pulled her knee up, sliding one leg along the other as she reached casually down to rub her foot.

Spec Ops guys, crude men they were, often compared the pent-up thrill of an anticipated firefight to sex. The way it got the blood pumping, the adrenaline surging. They thought the two things so linked, they had a custom of relieving the tension of one by achieving release through the other. A combat jack, it was called. Masturbating while in a firefight, when there was any kind of lull in the action. In some cases, when there wasn't much of a lull at all. Hatcher wasn't sure why he was thinking of that right now, but he was. Probably because he was going to need to do something similar, soon.

"These women, you called them a group. You didn't happen to have been part of this group at some time, would you?"

"All these questions. I told you I'd think about it. Show a little patience." She stretched her arms over her head, arching her back. Her breasts crested toward the ceiling. "I think I need to lie down. Don't you?"

Okay, Hatcher thought, that was definitely the green light. It took every ounce of willpower he had not to leap on top of her. But he knew that would be unwise. Self-control was the key to survival.

"Relax then, and get some sleep. Don't open the door for anyone but me. You'll be safe here. There are probably three cops watching the place. For the reasons I told you, you'll be safer without me."

"And what are you going to do?"

Hatcher stood, his fingers gravitating over to his wrist, still able to feel the dead grip of Garrett around the bones. "I'm going to find out why there was no one else at my brother's funeral."

"Stay away from beautiful women, Hatcher. The more beautiful, the farther you should stay away."

"Way ahead of you," he said. His eyes slid over her body. He tried to stop them, but self-control had its limits. *"Way, way* ahead of you."

FINDING GARRETT'S OFFICE WAS SURPRISINGLY EASY.

During one of Hatcher's initial operational briefings in Afghanistan, a spook advised that the first rule in gathering intelligence was to never underestimate the open source of information. Hatcher hadn't ever put much stock in that, his experience being that unless you got confirmation from a source in the know, you had no way of knowing what was true and what wasn't, but at the moment that rule had the attractive benefit of convenience. He had no car, only a hundred bucks and change in his pocket, and no local area knowledge. But he also knew you didn't get anywhere without starting somewhere. The second business he approached was a dry cleaner that let him use their Yellow Pages. That was about as open a source as there was.

So he began with what he knew. His mother had said Garrett described himself as a security consultant. He flipped through the S's among the reams of bound, spilling paper until he found headings starting with "security," saw a category for security consultants among the numerous ads for burglar alarms, window bars, and executive protection. A few dozen agencies were listed, names like Allied Security Network and Metro Investigations & Security. He studied the names carefully. No Garretts. No Hatchers. No Nolans. But somewhere near the middle of the pack, a one-line entry for GEN-Tech Consulting caught his eye. He read it several times, until the name tripped the right mental lever. The message he'd been given in the colonel's office popped suddenly into view. *Garrett E. Hatcher, aka Garrett E. Nolan, Deceased.*

Garrett E. Nolan. GEN.

He took a taxi to the address in the phone book. From what he could tell, no one had broken off the surveillance to follow him from the apartment, and he didn't notice anyone on the street paying attention when he got into the cab. But he was certain someone would have sent word that he left. He smiled at the thought. Whatever they were saying probably made for interesting radio traffic. Maloney and Wright would want to know where he was going. Want to know pretty badly, he supposed. Each perhaps for different reasons.

Different reasons. Something bothered him about that, but he couldn't get his mind to cough it up. He quit trying after a few intersections.

The building at the address for GEN-Tech was a crumbling midrise of gray stone blocks and ornate carved work. A pair of lion heads was arrayed above two large doors that looked like dark wood but were probably metal. The place smacked to Hatcher of something out of a gangster movie, the kind of building that would see big-wheeled cars with running boards pull up so a hood in the backseat could unload the magazine of a tommy gun at it, some guy on the stoop in a rakish fedora with a carnation pinned to his chalk-stripe suit doubling over from a bad case of lead poisoning. For-lease signs were visible behind the bare glass of a number of the windows in the surrounding buildings. The neighborhood had seen better days. Probably before the feds busted up the mob.

Hatcher entered the building and wandered until he found a floor directory. It looked like it hadn't been tended in years. Plastic white letters were pressed on black material behind scratched and cloudy plastic glass. Most of the letters were missing, but not the ones he needed to see. GEN-Tech was in suite 203. Hatcher circled around a Hispanic man with an iPod pushing a mop and bucket to some rhythm only he could hear, took the stairs to the second floor.

The door to GEN-Tech Consulting had a frosted window

with the company name stenciled on it. Much of the writing was scratched off. Hatcher stood in front of the door for a moment, waiting to see if anyone followed him into the hall, then tried the knob. It turned and the door swung gently inward a few inches.

With the door open a crack, Hatcher could hear the sounds of movement inside. The knock of a hand or arm against a desk, the scuffing of a shoe across the floor. He pushed slowly on the door and stepped into a vestibule. It was small and rectangular, with cheaply paneled walls holding a few framed Edward Hopper prints. A couch was nudged up against one wall, a couple of chairs against the other. There was a desk toward the rear. The desk had a phone and a blotter and too much dust for it to actually have seen a secretary any time in the past few months. Just next to it was the door to an interior office. The door was ajar. The sounds were coming from behind it.

Hatcher treaded lightly across the room and slowly opened the interior door. The office on the other side was a fairly spacious, square space. An oversized desk crowded the center, littered with file folders and stacks of papers. A man with white hair and glasses was seated behind it, bent over and leaning forward off the chair, rummaging through a drawer. He was older, age spots like faded coffee stains on his face. He looked vaguely familiar.

"Excuse me," Hatcher said.

The man's head popped up and he stared at Hatcher, blinking once, twice, three times. His mouth was open and stayed that way. He was wearing a shirt that read "Just Because You're Paranoid Doesn't Mean They're Not Out To Get You." Over the shirt, a pair of bright suspenders.

"You're the guy from the coffee shop," Hatcher said. "Fred. Or something like that."

Fred swallowed, but said nothing. His eyes swam like a pair of goldfish behind his thick horn-rimmed glasses.

"What are you doing here?" Hatcher asked.

"I'm, uh, looking for something," Fred said. He had obviously been caught in the act. The act of what, Hatcher wasn't quite sure. No one who considered themselves a security consultant would be likely to leave money in this kind of office, and there didn't seem to be anything in plain sight worth stealing.

"I guessed as much. Mind telling me what?"

Fred swallowed. The side of his mouth ticked up, trying to crack a smile, but barely made a dent. "Rather hard to explain."

"I'm a great listener." Hatcher stepped into the room.

"The . . . I . . ." Fred scratched his chin, took in a breath and puffed out his cheeks as he exhaled. "I made a promise to him."

"To who? Garrett?"

Fred nodded slowly, more a rocking gesture with his head than a regular nod, like he was trying to stop himself from doing it.

"What kind of a promise?"

The eyes were really swimming now, a pair of guppies frantically trying to avoid the net. "I'm not sure I'm supposed to say."

"Why didn't you tell me you knew Garrett earlier, when I was asking about him at the coffee shop?"

"I didn't know if he'd have wanted me to. His instructions were . . . I'm sorry. I really don't think I should say anything else."

"He's dead. I don't think he'd mind."

The look that squirmed around Fred's face was one Hatcher had seen before more times than he could remember. The look of someone conflicted, uncertain of the right thing to do.

"But that was what he made me promise," Fred said. "That I'd follow his instructions if anything happened to him."

Hatcher was about to tell him that since Garrett was his brother, he'd have wanted him to know, but stopped himself. Not because those things weren't true, but because they probably were. For some reason, that made him feel like a complete shit.

Fred looked like he was about to break the silence, got as far as parting his lips, but he froze at the sight of something over Hatcher's shoulder.

"Garrett?"

It was a woman's voice. Hatcher turned toward it, hearing her approach. "Garrett! Where have you be—"

She was a pretty brunette with hazel eyes and large lips. The lines of her face and jaw were pleasant, almost elegant, in a wholesome, girl-next-door way. Could probably stand to lose a few pounds. She wore dark blue stretch pants and a loose-fitting white blouse over a pair of reptile print shoes with peekaboo toes and kitten heels.

"Oh," she said. "I thought you were someone else."

Hatcher noticed the light in her eyes dim a bit. The fade of disappointment. "Who are you?"

"I'm sorry." Her gaze darted to Fred and back, eyes narrowing and flitting with confusion. She spun on her heels and headed back the way she came. "I made a mistake."

"Garrett's dead," Hatcher said.

The woman stopped. She didn't move for several seconds. Hatcher watched her carefully. Her stillness seemed unnatural, the kind that took effort, the kind people usually strove for when there was a storm of emotion roiling inside. She snapped her head and looked back over her shoulder, and he knew. The look on her face was genuine, something that couldn't be faked. Certainly not well enough to fool someone who'd seen the real thing as many times as he had. It was the look of absolute terror.

"No," she said, peering back into the interior office. Her moist eyes skipped to Fred, pleading. *"No."*

Hatcher lowered his gaze to the floor in front of her, taking in her shoes. It suddenly seemed impolite to stare. He'd expected the possibility she'd react to the information, but now he regretted unloading it on her that way.

"I just came from his funeral," Hatcher said.

"No," she repeated, shaking her head. "He can't be."

A sudden pallor overtook her face. Her eyes seemed to cloud, losing their focus. Hatcher lunged toward her, caught her just as she lost her balance. With some effort, he walked her back into the interior office. He could feel her weight sag in his arms as her legs came and went.

"Are you okay?"

"No," she said again. Her voice was weak, almost lyrical with sadness.

"What's your name?" Hatcher asked.

She seemed to have to think about it. "Susan."

Hatcher guided her to a chair, eased her into it. "I'm sorry you had to find out like that, Susan."

"It can't be true." She looked up at him. Her brow formed a triangle over her eyes. "Please tell me it's not true."

"I'm sorry."

Her attention dropped to her lap, where one hand wrung the other. Seconds seemed to tick slowly by. Hatcher took a knee next to her, placed a hand on her shoulder, found himself looking at her shoes again.

"You look like him," she said, lifting her face. "You must be Jacob."

"He told you about me?"

She nodded. "He said he had a brother." Her eyes welled up and her lips started to quiver. "Oh, God, please tell me he's not really dead."

"I wish I could, but I'm afraid it's true." Hatcher gave the side of her arm a gentle squeeze. "How did you know him? Were the two of you involved?"

"I . . . I have to go."

"I'm afraid you're not going anywhere," said a raspy female voice. "Not until you answer a few questions. Starting with that one."

Hatcher stood, spun to see Wright standing in the doorway. The redheaded cop from the interrogation room was standing next to her. Reynolds, the Clown guy.

"If I didn't know better, Detective, I'd swear you were following me," Hatcher said.

Wright pressed her lips together, almost puckering them. The set of her jaw seemed off, crooked, causing her right cheek to bunch into a dimple. Compared to before, it was like someone had peeled a layer of mask off, revealing more of the real her, showing a part that was a little sexy, a lot angry. Hatcher didn't know her that well, but he guessed this was a look any man in her life would see, and see often. He also had a hunch that no matter how many years a guy spent with her, he would never quite know where that look would lead.

"I think the other way around would be more accurate," she said.

Hatcher glanced at Reynolds. The guy held his eyes, but didn't seem too comfortable doing it. Wright was clearly in charge. He was carrying her water.

"You've been watching the building."

"Yes, and when I saw you go in, I knew you would be your subtle and discreet self and spook anyone else who showed up." Wright lowered her gaze to Susan. "Like I'm sure you did to our friend here."

Susan blinked, cleared her throat to cover a sniffle. "I was just leaving."

"I'd like to ask you a few questions first, if you don't mind."

The words sent a visible jolt through Susan. Hatcher could see the flash of anxiety in her eyes as they ricocheted between Wright and him. "Me? Why do you want to question me?"

"Just think of it as standard procedure. No big deal. We'd appreciate it if you told us what you were doing here." Wright glanced over at Fred, eyeing him with a polite wariness. "I'd also like to know who this gentleman is. But we'll start with you."

"I came to visit—"

"Me," said Fred, interrupting her. "I told her to meet me here." He smiled at Susan. "She's my niece."

Wright's cheeks seemed to bundle with coiled tension. Hatcher realized she was holding back a grin. "Your niece."

"Yes," Fred said. "My niece. Susan Warren."

"And what is your name, sir?"

He straightened his back, one hand rising to grab the strap of his suspenders. Senator Fred, hooking his lapel during a filibuster. "Frederick Jenrette."

"We just heard her say a moment ago that she was involved with Garrett Nolan, Mr. Jenrette," Wright said.

"No, you heard her being *asked* if she was involved with Mr. Nolan." Fred glanced at Hatcher, his face neutral. "She did not answer that question. Garrett was a client of mine. She knew him through me."

"Is that so?" she asked. "What kind of client?"

Fred gave a little shrug. "The occasional kind."

Now it was Hatcher's turn to suppress a grin. He had no idea what role this guy Fred played in all of this, but for an old man with a basketball-sized belly and a silver ponytail, he seemed to have a pair of balls you could go bowling with. The kind of guy you couldn't help but chuckle at. Hatcher guessed Wright felt the same way about him. Amused, hiding it beneath a thin veil of disdain.

"I meant, what kind of work do you do?"

There was a moment's pause before Fred answered, and Hatcher could tell he was considering a lie, but thought better of it. He'd seen that pause plenty of times. The length gave it away. If he were going to lie, he would have started to answer more quickly. Only people about to tell the truth feel comfortable enough to let others see them consider their words.

"I make custom electronic equipment. Both video and audio."

Wright bounced a look at Hatcher, a skeptical crease to her brow. "A surveillance tech."

"Something like that," Fred said.

"Make anything for him lately?" Wright asked. Her attention wandered to Susan.

"A digital audio transmitter," Fred said. "Cell phone frequency."

No pause this time, Hatcher noted. Still telling the truth, though. In for a penny, in for a pound.

"And what was that for?"

"I just make equipment. I don't ask questions." Fred smiled. It was a pleasant enough smile, but he was missing a canine and his gums were a shade of purple, almost black above some of his other teeth. Not a bad distraction, Hatcher mused. Good way to hide the fact he not only doesn't ask questions, but doesn't always answer them, either. Hatcher noted Fred hadn't actually said he didn't know.

"We're going to need you to come to the station and give a full statement, Mr. Jenrette."

"Certainly. Would tomorrow be good? I've a prior engagement shortly."

Wright looked Fred over like a butcher examining a side of beef. Her eyes narrowed as she addressed Susan without looking at her, her steely gaze remaining fixed on Fred. It was an act. Hatcher was certain of it. She was laying it on thick. "Ms. Warren, may I see your driver's license?"

Susan hesitated, then opened her purse and pulled out a wallet. She slid her license out and handed it to Wright, who peeled her eyes away from Fred just long enough to read it.

"What's your niece's middle name, *Uncle Frederick*?"

Fred acted like he had to think of it, but something told Hatcher he didn't. "Catherine."

"Date of birth?"

"September 14, 1975."

"Address?"

"Seventeen-twelve Spring Meadow Lane, Queens."

Wright stared at Fred for several more seconds, then returned the license to Susan.

"Susan was always sweet on Garrett," Fred said. A somber frown contorted the old man's mouth, and Hatcher wanted to tell him to knock it off, to not overdo it. "They met a couple of times. I work in this building. She would see him when she came by to visit me. I knew she wouldn't take it well. That's why I put off telling her."

"Is that true, Ms. Warren?"

Susan remained quiet for a long interval. "Yes."

Wright handed her back her license. As she did, Hatcher noticed something about the detective's eyes he hadn't caught before, a way she had of angling her brow that made them change appearance by degrees, like a pair of waxing or waning moons. He also noted she did nothing to accentuate those eyes, and wore very little makeup. She was either more attractive than she realized, or more attractive than she wanted anyone else to realize. He couldn't decide which.

"Okay, so Uncle Fred and Suzy knew Garrett Nolan-slash-Hatcher. That still doesn't explain what you're *doing* here, Mr. Jenrette."

"You can just call me Fred."

"In that case, what are you doing here, Fred?"

"I was hoping to retrieve my equipment. Equipment I had loaned to Garrett. I know it may sound selfish, but I need it back."

Wright glanced at Hatcher, nodding skeptically. "What kind of equipment are we talking about?"

"Digital recording devices. The same stuff I told you about."

"I thought you said you custom-made that for him."

"I did, but he didn't pay for it, and it was kind of expensive." Fred shrugged. "I need to recoup my costs."

Wright kept bobbing her chin ever so slightly. "Did he tell you what he needed it for?"

"No. I never inquire about such things."

Hatcher realized Fred was not a good liar, but he was doing a very good job of hiding the fact. Good liars were polished, smooth, casual. Fred was none of those things. That meant he was motivated. Anyone could lie well if the motivation was sufficient. If the stakes were high enough. All they had to do was keep their nerves in check.

"Well, Mr. Jenrette, I'm afraid you're out of luck." Wright tossed a look at Hatcher again. He knew that one, too. The look that always came right before a new piece of information was dropped, one that should have been dropped much earlier but had been held back. "I'm pretty sure the item you're looking for is badly damaged and is being retained as evidence anyway."

"Oh. I didn't know."

"Of course not. I mean, how could you, right? If you and your niece have no further business here, I would suggest you be on your way."

Fred nodded, glancing at Susan, then at Hatcher. He rounded the desk on Hatcher's side and placed a hand on his shoulder.

"Garrett was a good man," he said, staring into Hatcher's eyes. His chin began to shudder and twitch. "A very good man. I didn't know much about him, but he was always kind to me." His mouth tightened like he was fighting off a sob, and he suddenly leaned forward and hugged Hatcher, squeezing him and patting his back firmly. "I'm so sorry for your loss."

Hatcher could feel what he was doing, quickly formed a basic understanding of what was going on. Fred let go and motioned to Susan. "Come on, sweetie. We should get going."

There was an awkward pause before Susan stood. She caught Hatcher's eye as Fred placed a hand on her back and guided her toward the door. Her face was a jumble of sadness and confusion, each jostling for position. Confusion seemed to be winning for the moment.

Hatcher turned to Wright when they were gone. "That was all very entertaining, but would you mind explaining why you're following me?"

"You really are a piece of work." Wright shook her head in disbelief. "Jeez, Hatcher. Do I have to spell it out for you? We didn't follow you here. Hard as it may be to conceive, this isn't all about you. You crashed our party, not the other way around. We were staking the place out."

Hatcher thought of the janitor he passed in the lobby. Earbuds. He felt stupid for not pegging him. "Why?"

"This is going to be another hard one to swallow, but here it goes: I actually don't have to explain myself to you."

Hatcher looked over at Reynolds the Redhead. He tried not to look away, but wasted so much effort in holding Hatcher's stare he'd have saved more face if he had. "For someone whose force is stretched so thin, you sure have a lot of people available for surveillance. You must have called in your entire precinct."

Wright looked at him quizzically.

"Keeping an eye on this building and having all those guys over at the apartment . . ." Hatcher lifted a leg over the corner of the desk, half sitting, half leaning. "That's a lot of hats dedicated to a couple of cases."

"What guys over at the apartment?"

A twinge of something he didn't like crawled up the back of Hatcher's neck. "Where you dropped me off. You had a full surveillance going."

"Hatcher, we don't have anyone over there. Maloney told us not to bother, because we really don't have the manpower to spare. That's why he agreed to have you keep an eye on her. He said the threat was low at her apartment and that you'd probably be able to take care of anything that might happen anyway, given all your military training. Where is she, by the way?"

Her eyes were fixed on him, the muscles in her forehead slightly tightened, waiting for a response. He watched her, looking for some sign this was a game. Five seconds. Ten. Nothing.

"We have to get back there," he said, standing.

Wright's face was a portrait devoid of understanding.

Hatcher hooked her arm and took a step toward the door, shooting a look at the other detective to let him know this wasn't the time to man up.

"Right now," he continued. He started to hustle her out of the office. "I'll explain on the way. And if you've got a siren on your car, we need to use it."

CHAPTER 11

✦

"IF YOU'LL ONLY RELAX, COMPOSE YOURSELF A BIT, YOU might just survive this. I have to say, you're one of the lucky ones."

Valentine wasn't certain she'd heard him. Or if she had, whether it had registered. She was strapped facedown on the bed, limbs spread-eagle. A custom-made tilt cushion was wedged under her hips, pushing her ass up and out, presenting her. She was more cute than pretty, a strawberry blonde with freckles across her nose and cheeks. Loose, pale breasts pressed against the mattress beneath a set of lungs that wouldn't quit. The screams kept coming with hardly a pause to ventilate. Valentine hadn't ever heard anything quite like it, which surprised him. Loud and stinging in his ears. A looping shriek. It was giving him a headache.

Vocal cords, he thought, letting the words sink in. That kind of screaming wouldn't be good. He was going to have to do something about that when the time came. An idea surfaced, and he felt the satisfying click of a mental tumbler falling into place. *Vocal cords*. Yes. That would take care of two things. Three, the more he thought about it.

He gave a nod to Lucas, who stood like a sentry in the corner, holding a tranquilizer rifle across his body. Lucas smiled, nodded in response. The cage was set back some, farther from the bed, pushed into a custom recess in the wall designed for that purpose. Eager eyes watched from behind the bars, eyes almost glowing with a pent-up energy, a glint to the whites that was both animal and human, yet not quite either. Valentine unlocked the cage door, keeping the cattle prod at the ready. The Get was becoming more difficult to control each day. He'd drugged it the day before and put a radio collar around its neck, a high-tech piece of research equipment banned in the U.S. that was designed to administer a fifty-thousand-volt shock at the touch of a button, but he still wasn't sure it was enough. It was as if the Get could sense some ultimate moment approaching, the anticipation filling it with excitement and purpose. The thought pleased Valentine, even as he gripped the cattle prod tightly.

The woman screamed even more loudly at the sight of the cage door swinging out, something Valentine hadn't thought possible. The Get hesitated, then slid sideways through the opening, speeding up then shuffling to a sudden stop like an ape a foot away from her. It straightened its back and stood, the angle of its spine rivaling that of a man. It stared at the woman.

The regimen had been simple. Pornography in HD, several times a day. Allowing it to play with the bodies of the other women, explore them, experiment with them, after it finished consuming their hearts. It would sniff them, lick them, nip at them, embrace them, digitally penetrate them, then crawl back into its cage and masturbate. Valentine had given the Get a live woman once before. That test run hadn't turned out well. He was more hopeful this time, having exposed his creation to more explicit sexual imagery than most men would ever see in a lifetime. He was finding it hard to temper his optimism. After so many years, the goal was finally in sight. The winds of destiny filled his sails. So far, everything had fallen into place. He was confident this would be no different.

The Get stepped forward toward the bed and the woman let out her most piercing screech yet. Her facial muscles twisted and strained. Her tears dropped and puddled on the mattress.

"Y'know, Boss, I have a Nine Inch Nails CD out in the car. Might help set the mood."

Lucas's chuckle died in his throat as Valentine shut him down with a look. He glared at the large man for a pregnant moment, then shifted his attention back to the Get. Counting on more than one trial run, even thinking about one, was impractical. Only a few days were left, maybe even just one or two. There would only be one chance at getting this right when the time came, and he was not about to tolerate any distractions.

"I'm just saying," Lucas mumbled.

Its sense of smell seemed to be what the Get fell back on, what it relied on most of all. It sniffed the air, leaning its head toward the woman as it caught various scents. She was wearing a vanilla musk, a rather common type of perfume among the girls Lucas had procured. Fitting, too. They had all smelled like delicacies of some sort.

Things were definitely different this time, Valentine could tell. He noticed the presence of an understanding that hadn't been there before as it lowered its head and snuffled its snout against the small of her back, as it ran its nose down to the cleavage between the twin globes of her ass. She was sobbing now, yelping and choking as she tried to catch her breath. The Get nuzzled its face into her genitals, snorted, then climbed over her back and mounted her. His optimism notwithstanding, Valentine hadn't expected that. No hesitation, no tentativeness. No confusion. This time, the Get seemed to know exactly what it was doing.

The young woman gasped as the thing rammed itself

into her. She bucked and lurched as much as the restraints would allow, screaming again, yelling for it to get off of her. Whether it was driven by some primal instinct, some atavistic anger, or peculiar urges all its own, Valentine couldn't tell, but he watched in fascination as the Get threw its upper body forward and clamped its baboonlike jaws onto the back of her neck, biting right through the coils of hair. Her head snapped back, her eyes running with mascara, saucered and fixed, bulging in shock. She let out strangled grunts as the Get thrust against her repeatedly, jolting her. One of the thing's hands grabbed a clump of hair at the top of her head as it pumped harder and faster. Valentine heard a final gasp, a cracking, ripping sound. He watched, unblinking. The Get bit down harder, shaking its head, until its teeth tore through her neck and it pulled her head from her shoulders by her hair.

A fountain of blood spurted out and the Get covered it with its mouth, swaying its jaws euphorically as it drank, holding the young woman's head high, thrusting itself one final, violent time against her buttocks before rearing back and erupting in a feral wail of triumph.

"Holy shit!" Lucas said. His hands twitched, fingers fidgeting over the tranquilizer gun.

Valentine said nothing. He circled the bed slowly, carefully, watching as the bloodlust gradually drained from the Get's eyes. Its breathing began to grow more calm. Eventually it dropped the woman's head onto the bed and pulled out of her. Without the need for any prodding or encouragement, it climbed down and loped back into its cage. It reached back and pulled the cage door shut behind it, then receded into the shadows and curled onto the floor.

Blood was everywhere. Valentine took it all in, running his eyes over the scene. Sprays and splatters of arterial red dotted and slashed and pooled for a radius of several yards from the front of the woman's body. Her head lay on its side on the mattress, that same expanse of shock in her eyes, locked now in an eternal gaze.

"I can't believe it," Valentine said. He looked back over his shoulder at Lucas. "After all the planning, all the preparation. After all the *worrying* . . ." His eyes drifted back to the body. Blood was still dripping from the neck hole. "After everything, it turns out I couldn't have scripted it better myself."

He smiled broadly. "Absolutely, one hundred percent *perfect*."

HATCHER SAT ON THE WHITE SOFA, ELBOWS ON HIS knees, hands drawn to his face. One hand balled in a fist, the other cupping it. He bounced the edge of a knuckle lightly against his chin as he stared at the glass coffee table.

Wright flipped her phone shut, turned to Reynolds. "He wants you back at the precinct. He's sending a pair of uniforms over to watch the place in about an hour. I'm staying until they get here."

Reynolds nodded. Hatcher noticed he gave Wright a look behind her back. He caught Hatcher's eye and gave him a similar one, a cross between suspicious and irritated. Then he left.

Wright let out an audible breath. She tilted her head back and rubbed her hand across her eyes. She stared at the ceiling as she spoke. "Maloney made some calls. DEA was watching the street, had a tip about large quantities of crystal meth. Deal was supposed to go down this afternoon. That must've been what you saw."

Hatcher said nothing. There was nothing to say.

"Look, it's not your fault." She lowered her gaze and shrugged. "We shouldn't have left her with you in the first place. Our mistake."

The words hung in the air. Hatcher maintained eye contact but didn't respond.

"I didn't mean it that way. I meant, it wasn't fair to expect you to be her security." Wright took a seat next to him on the couch and placed a hand on his arm. Her touch was almost nonexistent, like she was afraid the weight of her fingers could cause a bruise. "If there really was a threat, there should have been a few cops watching the place, not one non-cop with no backup. We don't even know what happened, if anything even did. And you may not have been able to stop it anyway. You aren't even armed."

Hatcher rubbed his palms down his face and stood. "I don't feel guilty. So you can stop trying to keep me from blaming myself."

"You look like you feel guilty."

"Well, I don't. I feel frustrated. Angry. Somebody out there is fucking with me."

Wright shook her head, gave her eyes a roll. "I wish you could listen to yourself. That's pretty damn arrogant. This is all about you all of a sudden?"

"Yes."

"Would you mind explaining that to me?"

"Don't ask me how I know. It just is."

"So somebody snatched Deborah just to get at you?"

"No." Hatcher stared at a patch of carpet. "I don't know. What's important is that I figure out what's going on."

"I think it's best if you leave that to us."

He swiveled his head to meet her gaze. "Yeah, because you've been doing such a bang-up job so far."

"I mean it, Hatcher. You'd better not interfere with us on this."

"You're the ones who told me to protect her. I accepted the responsibility. I'm not walking away just because I screwed up."

"So what do you plan to do? Go around beating up people at random until you find someone who knows something? That seems to be what you're good at. You're not a detective, Hatcher."

Hatcher shrugged. "You don't need to be a weatherman to ask which way the wind blows."

"Don't be stupid," Wright said. "You wouldn't know where to begin."

Hatcher stared at her, locked eye to eye. Good for her. She was giving it right back to him, unblinking, refusing to give ground. He decided he liked that. And she was one damn sexy woman, he had to admit. Stubborn as all hell, but damn sexy. He circled the coffee table and walked toward the kitchen.

"Hey, wait a second." Wright followed him, then reached out and snagged his arm, turning him back to face her. "You'd better *not* know where to begin. Because if you do know something, and you're not telling me, things are going to get very difficult for you. Don't hold out on me, Hatcher."

"You guys are the ones who think you've got a mole in the department. Why should I tell you anything?"

"Because this is a *police matter*!" Wright tossed her hands in the air. "You can't try to storm the beaches and take the hill in this kind of situation. I don't care what the commercials say. You're not an Army of One."

"If you've got a mole in the department, I can't trust you. It could be you, for all I know."

She let out a short, disgusted breath. A you-can't-be-serious frown stretched her face as she stared into his eyes. Hatcher's expression didn't change.

"I'm not a mole," she said.

"Okay, suppose I did cross you off the list. Then how about Howdy Doody out there? You'll tell him, because he's not on your list. Thing about moles is, if you've got one, you can't assume you know who to exclude. The only safe play is to suspect everyone."

"Even me?"

Hatcher walked into the kitchen, got a bottled water from the refrigerator. She stood in the entryway and waited, watching him. He unscrewed the cap and tilted the bottle toward her before taking a drink. "Especially you."

"Thanks for the vote of confidence."

"You want my confidence? Help me find her. Just you. Nobody else gets involved." Hatcher took another swig of water. "Tell Phony Maloney I went to my mother's. Send Opie Taylor out to the filling station for some bait to make sure he doesn't follow me. Tell me everything you know, starting with that whole charade back at my brother's office."

"You've got some chutzpah, you know that? Even if it what you're proposing wasn't illegal, not to mention something certain to result in career death, why would I do all that for you? What could possibly be in it for me?"

Hatcher finished off the water, put the empty bottle on the counter. He walked past her to leave the kitchen, pausing in the entry to face her, their bodies almost touching. "Because you dig me, whether you want to admit it or not."

Tiny grunts of protest were all she could manage as she trailed him into the living room.

"Did I just hear you correctly? Dig you? What is this, *The Mod Squad*?"

Hatcher spun, stopping her short and peering down into her eyes. "In my line of work, we used to call that deflecting."

"You know, I used to think you were one of the most arrogant asses I'd ever met," she said, her teeth slightly clenched. "Now it's clear that you are—*bar none*—the single most arrogant ass of all time. Congratulations."

"Are you going to keep trying to laugh it off? Or admit it and help me?"

"I'm not *trying* to laugh anything off, I *am* laughing it off." She pressed up on her toes, bringing her glaring eyes closer. "And there's nothing to admit, and no I'm not going to—"

Her words disappeared into his mouth as Hatcher pressed his lips against her and wrapped his arm around her waist, yanking her body close. She broke the kiss off and slapped him across the face. He tugged her back and kissed her one more time. She slapped him again, harder.

The second slap really stung. He touched the side of his cheek, still holding her around the waist. She lifted her hand to slap him a third time and he caught it behind her shoulder. They both stood there in that position for several seconds, a mock tango pose, his arm tight around her, his hand fisted around her wrist. She began to squirm, trying to push him away. He constricted his arm around her more, pulled her in even closer. He leaned forward, slowly this time. She pulled her face back, arching her spine, almost in a dip. He managed to close the distance, brushed his lips against hers, staring steadily into her pupils.

"This is sexual assault," she said. Her raspy voice was barely above a whisper.

"So call in Deputy Pasty-Face and have me arrested," he said. He touched his lips against hers again briefly, retreated a few centimeters to watch her eyes as they switched focus between the two of his, back and forth.

"I can't do this," she said, her voice so low now it was barely audible.

He kissed her again, more urgently this time. He felt her kiss back, felt the flick of her tongue graze his as her lips parted. She shrugged her hand free from his grip and grabbed him by the hair, the other hand clawing against his back. She opened her mouth wider, devouring him, her tongue extending deep. Tasting, probing.

She seemed unnaturally light, weightless, as he grabbed the back of her thigh and stood straight, lifting her off the ground. She wrapped her ankles across the backs of his knees, never taking her mouth off him. He spun and stumbled forward a few steps until they bumped against the wall. He groped for the door latch nearby, still kissing her as he threw the deadbolt. It took him twenty seconds to cross the room like that, stiff-legged and unsteady, another five once he reached the bedroom until he reached the bed.

He fell forward onto the mattress with her beneath him. They bounced lightly against each other.

She sucked in a breath, like someone coming up for air. "This is a crime scene."

He kissed the side of her neck, sliding his lips from below

her ear to her shoulder and back again. "The bed is made. You already searched it. There's nothing in here to find."

"We shouldn't do this," she said. He unbuttoned her blouse and began to kiss the middle of her chest, kneading the sides of her breasts with his lips. He unclasped the front hooks and pushed them apart, let the cups fall to the sides.

"Do you want me to stop?"

"No." She swallowed, drew in a sudden breath as he tugged on her nipple with his teeth and began circling it with his tongue. "But we have to be quick."

He slid down until he was kneeling in front of her, running his hands up under her skirt and kissing her belly. She kicked off her shoes, ran her heels down his back. He curled his fingers around the silk bands of her thong near her hips and peeled them down. Her skirt bunched around her waist.

The well-manicured strip of light brown hair pointing toward her vagina was cottony, fragrant. The perfumed scent of it blended with the light odor of sweat and the moist, briny scent below it. He kissed his way lower, brushing his nose against her clit, inhaling her. He parted the outer lips between her legs and traced the contours of them with his tongue. She let out a moan as he licked her, gasped as he thrust his tongue deep. He felt her hands find the sides of his head. Her fingers burrowed into his hair.

"Still want this to be quick?" he asked.

"Take however long you want." Her panting, whispering voice was even raspier than normal. She pulled down on his head, pressing his face into her. "Just don't you dare stop. Not without finishing what you started."

WRIGHT FLIPPED THE PHONE SHUT AND FELL BACK NEXT to him on the bed.

"The uniforms have been delayed, thank God. Fortunately, Maloney didn't ask too many questions. I told him

I've been on the phone and asking you questions all this time."

"I heard you. I was right here."

She stuck out her lower lip, blew a few strands of hair away from her face. "I can't believe we just did that. I can't believe *I* just did that. Oh. My. *God*. I just can't believe it."

"If you're calling me unbelievable, I'll take that."

"I'm saying, I have no idea what came over me."

Hatcher yawned, stretched his arms. "I'm pretty sure it was me."

"You're not funny."

"Oh, come on. It wasn't so bad. You certainly seemed to enjoy it. I know I did."

"That's not the point. It was completely reckless. Astonishingly, foolishly reckless."

There wasn't much use in arguing the point. It was the truth. And he had to admit it bothered him a bit, too. In hindsight, acting out a letter to *Penthouse* was a bit surreal. And weird.

"If it makes you feel any better, it's not exactly something I planned. We just got swept up in the moment. It happens."

She sat up, started to button her blouse. "I don't even want to think about what I look like."

He leaned forward, ran his hand down her back. "You look great."

"Why do I think that means I look like a woman who just got fucked silly—while on duty no less—in the apartment of a possible missing person?"

"I told you that you dug me," he said, flopping backward onto the mattress. "You wouldn't listen."

"Okay, so maybe I was attracted to you. A little. Big deal. You're a good-looking guy. Believe it or not, I don't go around balling every guy I'm attracted to."

"I would hope not."

She turned away and finished buttoning her blouse.

Hatcher sensed her body grow quiet, could tell she was forming a question.

"How did you know?" she asked.

"Know what?"

She twisted back to look at him. "What did I do to give it away? I thought I was doing a good job of not sending you any signals."

"Remember when I took your gun?"

"Not something I'll be forgetting anytime soon. And I should hate you for that, by the way."

"I did it partly to test you."

She blinked a few times, thinking. "Test me?"

"Yes."

"I don't understand."

"I wanted to know if you were interested."

"And me punching you and threatening you and telling you that you were under arrest convinced you?"

"No, you not hurting me did. You could have tried to knee me in the groin, or gouge my eyes. You could have even simply left and called for the nearest patrol car to come assist. But you didn't want to hurt me, didn't want to get me in real trouble. You were just pissed."

"You're a strange guy, Hatcher."

Hatcher shrugged. "It worked, didn't it?"

"You know, Maloney put together a jacket on you." She leaned back on her arm. Her voice softened. "I read it. I didn't understand much of the military jargon, but I remember it said you were some kind of Special Forces interrogator."

"Something like that."

"And it said you were convicted of abusing a foreign national."

"That was the charge I was sentenced under, yes."

She rolled onto her stomach. "What happened? If you don't mind me asking."

"I don't mind you asking. I'm not sure I should answer."

"You don't have to tell me. I wasn't meaning to pry."

Hatcher let out a long breath. "I stuck a pistol in the mouth of an Iraqi interpreter and blew the back of his head off."

Wright swallowed. She watched him, examining his face. "You're serious."

"My jokes may not always be great, but they're usually funnier than that."

"Why would you do something like that?"

"I was having a bad day."

"Is that supposed to be one of those funny jokes?"

"No. I wasn't the only one having a bad day. That Iraqi and another were caught after an IED exploded near a barracks on one of our installations. It killed several GIs. They were both employed by the army, had access to the base. They were considered trustworthy. The other one had text messages in his phone that indicated another attack was imminent. But he wasn't talking. The sight of his comrade's brains in his lap loosened his jaws. I'd do it again if I had to do it over."

"Hatcher . . . that's *horrible*."

"No. Horrible was the sight of American soldiers with their limbs missing, good kids from Alabama and California and Kansas who were betrayed by people we're over there trying to help."

"And you think getting mad at that justifies cold-blooded murder? It doesn't matter whether he deserved it. What matters is the kind of person *you* are."

"I didn't do it because I was angry. I did it because American lives were at stake. And I didn't murder him. He was already dead."

A look of confusion contorted her face. "What do you mean?"

"He had a heart attack. Apparently some congenital defect."

"Are you saying you shot a dead man?"

"He was being interrogated separately. The EMTs hadn't

even arrived, but he was all gone. I could see what was happening, saw them being ridiculously gentle on the other guy, saw that he just knew he had absolutely nothing to fear. He had that mocking smile in his eyes, like we were powerless and the clock was ticking. I realized nobody there had the balls to do anything about it. As long as he had that look, he wasn't going to talk. So, I got rid of it. I dragged the dead guy into the room like he was still alive and did it before the other one could tell he wasn't. By the time I shoved the pistol I'd just taken from his cohort's mouth into his, he couldn't get the words out fast enough."

"I guess I should be glad to hear you're not a murderer. But still, that's brutal, Hatcher."

"The Iraqi government thought the same thing. They refused to believe the heart attack wasn't caused by torture. Torture was a big issue by then. Uncle Sugar couldn't afford to let it go."

"I'm surprised you only got twelve months."

"You shouldn't be."

"Why not?"

"Because they wanted to keep this quiet. But to do that, they had to offer a sacrifice, appease the locals. They knew if they leaned too hard on me, I'd be inclined to spill my guts about the role I played for our government, about what I was tasked to do over there."

"What was that?"

"Things far worse than what I was prosecuted for, that's for sure. It's the dirty little secret of war. We want to pretend torture doesn't work. We want to pretend we're too civilized to engage in it. Wrong on both counts. It does, and we're not."

"So they gave you a light sentence hoping to keep you quiet."

"Yes. That, and because they didn't want some inconvenient details to come out like the fact I wasn't even the one doing the interrogation. That I was summoned to observe through a two-way mirror. Or that they left a loaded pistol on the table a few feet from me. That three MPs and four field-grade officers watched me pick it up, check the clip, and walk by them into the interrogation room and drag the guy's body next door. Any one of them could have stopped me. No one said a word."

"Why not?"

"Because that was why I was brought in to observe. I don't think they knew I would do exactly what I did, but they did expect me to do something."

"I don't understand."

Hatcher waited a long moment before responding. "You know why I was selected for my prior specialty?"

She responded with a subtle shake of her head.

"The army gives everyone in SF these psychological profiles, a bunch of tests and questionnaires. At first, I thought it was because I scored so well. But that wasn't it."

The light in the room was fading, casting everything in a dim, silvery glow. Hatcher lay back on the bed and stared at the ceiling. He could feel Wright's eyes on him as he pondered his own words. He thought he may have already said too much, shared too much, but he kept going anyway.

"They knew from experience. It doesn't matter how just the cause, or how much the bad guy has it coming. How vital to the mission it is, or how many lives it saves. You can toss that all aside. What they wanted, what they needed, carried a steep price tag, and I was the type they could live with having to pay it, so long as they didn't have to themselves. They all knew the score. The rest of the people around you, your peers, they stop looking at you the same way. They keep their distance. They know it has to be done, but they can't relate to you anymore. I had no family to speak of. Hadn't seen my mother in years; my father in over a decade. No siblings, not that anyone knew of. Was unmarried, didn't even have a steady girlfriend. In their eyes, I could afford the price."

Wright put a hand on his chest, gave it a gentle press. Her lips parted, but she didn't say anything.

"That's why they picked me," he continued. "Same reason no one stopped me. It had to be done, and I was just the guy to do it. They needed someone they could live with damning." His eyes settled on hers for a moment, then he leaned his head back and stared at the ceiling again.

"I was damnable."

CHAPTER 12

✦

HATCHER WATCHED WRIGHT PULL AWAY FROM THE CURB, her car merging between two taxis. He stood there and waited until she was out of sight before he started to walk in the opposite direction. He took a left at the first corner, continued down the block a ways and crossed the street in the middle. On the far side, he walked back in the direction he'd come and stopped once he reached the corner. He scanned the area. No one seemed to have followed him. The sidewalk was almost empty, with no one headed his way. No cars had left their spaces. No shadows occupying driver's seats.

The sun was setting behind the horizon of rooftops. The shaded streets erupted with color as the western sky beyond glowed a yellow orange. Hatcher continued walking until he reached an avenue, the crosswalks busy with foot traffic. He rounded the corner, merging into the flow of people, and dug into his pocket. The cell phone that Fred had slid into his pants back at Garrett's office felt warm and solid in his hand. The small, square LCD on the front of it was blank and colorless. He flipped the phone open, once again surprised at how ridiculously small these things were getting.

The larger screen on the inside was dark and empty. It took him a moment to figure out how to turn it on, trying several buttons. A colorful design expanded and swirled into a logo before being replaced by a background picture of a well-lighted cityscape. Unlike the one on the wall in Deborah's apartment, this photo was slick and professional.

Now what? Hatcher pressed a few buttons, found a way to toggle through a menu. No contacts were listed. No voice mails. No photos. No text messages. He scrolled through another screen, found the call logs. Accessed an icon that said *outgoing*. Nothing. Tried *incoming*.

One phone number came up.

Hatcher started to commit it to memory, then thought to press the send button. The screen changed and the word *connecting* appeared, a looping set of ellipses beneath it.

He placed the phone to his ear and listened as the digital buzz indicated it was ringing on the other end.

"Hello?" The person who answered tried to disguise his voice, but still sounded to Hatcher a lot like Fred.

"You have an interesting way of making new acquaintances," Hatcher said.

"Who is this?"

"I think you know."

A scrape came through the tiny speaker, followed by a rustling noise. The sound of someone switching ears. "Are you by yourself?"

"Other than scores of people walking by on the street."

"Are you being followed?"

Hatcher scanned the nearby storefronts, used his peripheral vision to see if anyone stuck out. "No. But you are."

"What do you mean?"

"I mean, do you really think the NYPD would just let

you go so easily without asking more questions? And without getting better answers?"

Fred hesitated. "I was careful. I'm always careful."

"It doesn't matter. Where's Susan."

"She's here with me. She's terrified."

"I'm assuming you gave me this phone because there are things you want to tell me."

"Yes." A pause. "Where would you like to meet?"

"I'm going to come to you."

A longer pause. "You said I was followed. Will that be a problem?"

"You were, no doubt about it. But that's okay. Just tell me where you are. And stay put." Hatcher turned his attention again to the buildings across the street, reading every sign. Thinking there had to be someplace nearby he could find a pay phone. "I have an idea."

Hatcher listened to Fred supply him with the address and the nearest cross streets. He glanced over at the street signs and related his location, asked how far that was, then told him he'd be there in twenty minutes and flipped the phone shut.

A block away, Hatcher found a phone at a Laundromat. He used the change machine to get some quarters and dialed the Thirteenth Precinct. The desk sergeant connected him to the detective squad. He waited on hold for over a minute before Detective Wright picked up.

"I hope this isn't you calling already just to say hi. Needy guys are very annoying."

"Hasn't it been two days yet? I've had so many women lately I've lost track."

"Are you trying to get me fired? What do you want, Hatcher?"

That raspy voice. So damn sexy. He could still smell her on him, feel traces of her, like a rub-on lotion. Barely an hour ago, she was moaning and clawing his back and panting dirty encouragements into his ear. It was almost enough to make him feel guilty for what he was about to do.

Almost.

"Are you surveilling that old guy and the woman who were down at my brother's office?"

"No." He could hear her breathe into the phone. "I guess I'm supposed to ask why you want to know."

"Nah. It's not important. You're obviously not interested in them."

The line went silent for a moment. Hatcher thought he heard her huff. "Okay, fine. Why are you asking?"

"Because I thought you'd like to know I just saw them walk into a building not far from Deborah's apartment."

"That's . . . Are you sure?"

Hatcher smiled. He stared out the window at a couple holding hands across the street. "Yes. Positive."

"How positive?"

"Positive enough. Tell me something—if you're not keeping an eye on them, why are you so reluctant to believe me? And if you are, *surely* they couldn't have slipped your surveillance."

"You are a very annoying man, you know that, Hatcher?"

"So I've been told."

"Tell me the address. And you're really certain about this?"

"What kind of a relationship would this be if we started off lying to one another?"

He heard her grumble something unintelligible and ignored it. He repeated the address several times, then hung up and left the Laundromat. Outside, he stepped into the street and hailed a cab. The driver told him it would take about twenty minutes to get to the address Fred had given him.

It was obvious she was lying. That meant she had no right to expect the truth from him. Or did it? The question suddenly seemed important, but he decided not to dwell on it. He settled back into the seat and closed his eyes. In an op, you took sleep where and when you could get it. And he was starting to get the feeling this was the last chance he was going to have for the rest of the night.

THE TAXI DROPPED HATCHER OFF IN FRONT OF A DARK brick building with cascading fire escapes. The gloaming sky was fading to black, but he decided not to wait for nightfall. Hadn't even asked to be dropped off a block away. There was no sense in trying to be stealth in a zero-sum game. His play had either worked, or it hadn't.

He rubbed his eyes and pulled out the cell phone. He brought up the call log again, then pressed send. There was still only one number. It rang twice.

"Hello?"

"I'm here."

"At the door?"

"Yes."

Hatcher heard a buzz and moved to the entrance, keeping the phone at his ear. The door clicked open when he pulled and he made his way through the small lobby to a set of stairs that cornered at a landing.

"I'm inside."

"Third floor. Apartment E."

The third-floor hallway was narrow, with uninviting doors of almost identical painted metal staggered on each side. He scanned the tiny labels beneath each peephole until he found one marked *E*. The doorbell was a small square. It sounded cheap and efficient through the door when he pressed it.

The door opened and Fred gestured for him to come inside. Fred bolted the door behind him.

"It's not much, but it's home."

Fred's apartment looked more like Hollywood's idea of a command center than someone's residence. In the center of the living room, a giant pane of glass divided a billiard-sized table and stretched toward the ceiling. One half of the glass was a transparent outline of the United States, the other seemed to be a diagram of New York City. Tiny circles and squares and arrows were drawn on the glass in an array of colors indicating various points on the maps. The surface glimmered with reflections from electronic equipment that lined bookshelves along the walls, industrial-type units with display screens and dials. Most of them were turned on, circular panels casting a glare, some in digital green, others gray, shimmering with bars of light that circled like the fast-moving second hands of a clock. They left faint image trails as they made their circuits, ghostly specters that quickly faded. Hatcher could hear the squawking of a police band as monotone voices traded barely audible numeric codes. The staticky whir of a shortwave radio droned consistently in the background, like an alien wind.

"Cozy," Hatcher said.

Fred chuckled and circled the table, gesturing across the see-through maps for Hatcher to follow him. He passed another long, cafeteria-style table with fold-out metal legs. That table held an array of gadgets in various states of construction and deconstruction, with microchips and stripped wires and assorted computer input adaptors scattered among miniature screwdrivers and a precision soldering iron. Beyond that table was the entryway to the kitchen.

Hatcher followed Fred out of the room and saw Susan Warren sitting at a small dinette. She was huddled around an oversized cup of coffee, choking it with her hands. Her face came into view gradually as she raised her head. Her eyes were heavy and pink. Her mouth quivered into a weak smile. It was as sad an expression as Hatcher could ever remember seeing. And he'd seen some of the saddest.

Fred asked Hatcher if he would like a cup, and Hatcher nodded. Fred poured him some and set it on the table across from Susan, waving his hand for Hatcher to take a seat. The chair scraped lightly across the linoleum floor as Hatcher pulled it out, causing Susan to flinch.

Hatcher watched her for a moment, then said, "You were in love with him."

Susan said nothing. She dipped her chin and peered into her cup.

"How many months along are you?"

She'd been like a statue sitting there, but seemed somehow to become even more still as the words sunk in. Her eyes shot up in a delayed reaction.

"Your shoes," Hatcher said.

Susan rubbed away from the corners of her eyes with her palms. Processing what Hatcher had just said seemed to exhaust her. Fred stepped over and handed her a napkin. Her bottom lip trembled as she took it.

"How . . . ?" she said.

"You're wearing a loose blouse. Stretchy, casual slacks. Maternity clothes. Something didn't seem quite right about the look. Then I realized you hadn't gotten around to comfortable shoes yet. The heels are low, but they're too dressy for that outfit. I'm guessing you couldn't bring yourself to wear tennis shoes or sandals. Not yet."

"You got all that from my shoes?"

"That, and the fact you're showing. Well, almost showing."

Hatcher was lying, but felt justified. The shoes had been a minor point of curiosity that got him thinking. Something about them simply seemed out of place. But he knew even less about women's fashion than he did men's, and he didn't have more than a vague idea what maternity clothes looked like. It was her reaction to the news about Garrett's death that really triggered the thought. The look of someone suddenly alone in more ways than one. But he didn't see any use in being honest. Telling her that her emotions gave it away would just bring them back to the surface. Shoes were safer.

"I can't believe he's gone. I just can't."

"Can you tell me what he had going on? Why the police were watching his office?"

Susan glanced over to Fred, whose body jerked as if stirred from a standing sleep. He took a seat at the table, set down a steaming coffee mug of his own.

"Garrett was investigating a certain someone. Collecting evidence."

"My husband," Susan said. "There's no need to hold back now. He was investigating my husband."

"Why?"

Susan began to fidget with the napkin. Hatcher watched as she absently twisted it into a rope. "I came to Garrett a few months ago. I had a feeling my husband was hiding things from me. He started playing golf."

"Lots of guys play golf."

"Not Brian. All he was ever interested in was his stupid *Star Wars* stuff. Then, all of sudden, he was off golfing all the time."

"And you figured maybe he wasn't golfing at all."

"Things hadn't been good for quite a while. People were calling the house and hanging up. I decided I needed some information. He was very secretive about his business. I didn't really care if he had a girlfriend. I was planning a divorce."

"How did you and Garrett meet?"

"There was a woman where I get my hair done. I overheard her telling someone about how she caught her husband cheating and hiding money. We started talking, and she said her investigator was the best, that he saved her life and didn't even charge much. She gave me his number."

"Why didn't your lawyer hire someone?"

"I didn't have a lawyer. I didn't have access to that kind of money, not without asking my husband for it. And more important, once I did hire one I knew I would be starting something I might not be able to control. Like I said, I just wanted information first. Garrett was willing to let me pay him when I could."

Hatcher glanced at Fred, who merely shrugged. "You'll have to forgive me," Hatcher said. "But that doesn't make much sense. Lawyers deal with this kind of thing all the time."

"I was scared, okay? Too scared to go to a lawyer."

"Why?"

"Because I had this feeling something wasn't right. More than Brian just hiding money or seeing another woman. Sure enough, Garrett found out he had taken out a life insurance policy on me. A big one. I didn't even have a job. What did he need life insurance on me for?"

Hatcher scratched his chin, thinking. "Is that who Garrett was meeting when he was killed? Your husband?"

"Yes."

"Do you think your husband killed him? Or had him killed?"

"I'm not sure." Susan shook her head. "Garrett was much more street-smart than Brian. Much tougher. It's hard for me to imagine my husband taking him on. He's a wimp when it comes to stuff like that, guys like that."

"But you thought he was planning to kill you?"

"Garrett confirmed he was. That was what he was meeting Brian about. He was gathering proof. Enough to have him arrested."

"Proof? You mean he was wearing a wire? Working with the police?"

Fred straightened in his chair, gave a little cough. "He was wearing a wire, but he didn't get it from the police. He got it from me."

Hatcher stared at Fred, who broke eye contact and looked away. He could hear the guilt in the man's voice, the strain of believing he was somehow complicit in Garrett's death, either by having assisted Garrett with the wire or simply by not having stopped it from happening. Hatcher knew the man was a bit off, a crazy old guy living in a world of grassy knolls and tinfoil hats, but from that tone alone he also sensed that this was someone who rewarded friendship with extreme loyalty. Maybe because friends were so rare.

"But if the subject had already been brought up, why

wouldn't he get the police involved? Let them do the heavy lifting? Make the evidence more credible?" Hatcher watched Fred's eyes as they peeked through the thick lenses at him. They were unnaturally steady, holding a rigid gaze. Like he was waiting for Hatcher to catch on.

"Because," Hatcher continued, answering his own question. "He wasn't really gathering evidence to prosecute him. He was gathering evidence to blackmail him."

"He was planning on turning the information over to the police later," Susan said. "It wasn't blackmail. Not really. He just wanted leverage to make sure I got what I was entitled to, half of what he owned. It was my money that started that company. I inherited it. From my aunt."

Hatcher didn't respond. A picture was starting to take shape. Blurry, incomplete, but a picture nonetheless.

"He said it would make it impossible for him to hurt me, that it would make the divorce a slam-dunk and give me plenty of money. Then he and I, Garrett and I—then we could be together. Brian wouldn't be able to use the pregnancy against me."

"Where is your husband now?"

"I don't know. I've been staying at a hotel, waiting for Garrett to call. I knew something was wrong, but he made me promise I wouldn't go home until I heard from him. I didn't know what to do."

"How was he supposed to contact you?"

"TracFones," Fred said. "Susan got one."

"What's a TracFone?"

"A type of pay-as-you-go cell phone. You can buy them anonymously, prepay for minutes. It's how you called me. The phone I slipped you is one. Garrett bought a bunch of them. They're practically untraceable."

Hatcher nodded. Made sense. Garrett clearly had been a cautious man. Problem was, cautious men tended not to be killed by their marks. Hatcher was starting to wonder whether his brother had become an unrelated statistic, someone who'd simply been in the wrong place at the wrong time, trying to save the wrong woman. If he was really his brother.

"How did the police know about the murder-for-hire stuff?"

"The wire," Fred said. "I made him a state-of-the-art digital recording apparatus, sewn into the sleeve of his jacket. Microphones at the cuffs. Lens for streaming video in one of the buttons. Top-shelf stuff. They must have found it. I doubt they would be able to recover the video, based on the accident. But the audio's another story."

Hatcher sat staring at the table for a moment. Ironic, he thought. The police knew what was said, but they didn't know who said it. He knew who said it, but not what was said.

But something told him there was more to it than that.

"I think I need to take a cab over to Susan's house, have a word with our friend Mr. Warren. I'd sure like to know what's on that tape."

Fred's face brightened. "It just so happens I have a way you can."

CHAPTER 13

BRIAN WARREN STOOD IN THE DOORWAY TO HIS CLOSET, wondering how much to pack. Would two weeks be long enough? The police couldn't possibly have anything on him. He'd been very careful, never giving his real name, using only that untraceable phone Garrett had provided him. Now Garrett was dead, which was just as well, since that meant no one could find out what he'd been up to. So what if he'd been having lunch with him? They couldn't prove anything. Certainly not some murder plot.

But still. Susan had dropped out of sight. Nowhere to be found, no messages, no phone calls. The timing was too coincidental. She must have figured something out.

One month. He figured that ought to be enough to get a handle on where he stood. Most all of his business was with Asian laboratories. A business trip to visit his offshore contractors would be hard for the cops to use against him. Several countries, not too hard to string out for that long. Besides they'd have nothing. She'd have nothing. This was just precaution.

He pulled a rolling garment bag out of the closet, grabbed several pairs of pants by their hangers and laid them out on the bed. He tossed a dozen shirts on top of them. The checklist was short. Underwear, socks, a couple of belts. He could pick up anything he forgot to pack later, but he needed to take enough to make it look like a normal trip. Just in case.

Once he was safely out of the country, he could send for Jenna. Nobody knew about her. He was sure of it. Not Susan, not that scary client with all the bucks. No one. She was great at keeping things on the Q.T. And smart, like when it came to the insurance. Yes, this was looking like it could work out pretty well.

Of course, his client might not like it, but that guy was starting to give him the creeps. He didn't know what he was doing with all those genetic products they were smuggling in, and he didn't want to. He would have to call him after he got settled into a hotel in South Korea. Explain what happened. And if he didn't understand, well, fuck him.

He paused to blow his nose. He was stuffing his handkerchief into his pocket, his thoughts already starting to shift toward withdrawing several thousand in cash and getting an expedited visa, when he heard a knock at the door. *Rap, rap, rap.*

The police? No. Maybe. Shit. Calm down!

He paced the floor of his bedroom, a balled fist drawn up to his mouth. It could be anyone. Even if it was the police, so what? Ignore them. All that would mean was they identified him as having been at the diner. Big deal. So they had a few questions. Nothing to worry about. Unless they found some records that Garrett had kept. Shit.

Quit it. Hit men don't keep records like that.

Another knock, same set of three. Not too slow, not too fast. Patient, but determined.

They'll go away, he thought. They don't have a warrant; they don't know anything. Hell, it might not even be the cops. It could be a delivery boy, or a process server. Maybe

Susan filed for divorce. The more he thought about it, the more that made sense.

The seconds ticked by, accumulating and spilling over into a minute. There were no more knocks, and Brian finally let himself breathe. He even let out a chuckle as he started to put his clothes into the garment bag.

He bolted up at a noise from downstairs, freezing in place. It had been a muted thump. He stood still, slightly hunched over, listening. Nothing.

He reached for some more clothes and froze again as this time he definitely heard something. A clinking, like glass or china. The quiet afterward was interrupted by another soft bump, followed by some rattling.

Susan, he thought. It had to be. She was in the kitchen. Maybe she'd lost her keys. Brian realized he had come in through the back door, wondered if he'd neglected to lock it. Or maybe she had a spare hidden back there. The sense of relief started to give way to annoyance. She was the reason he was in this mess. He didn't want to have to deal with her. Bitch did nothing but cause him trouble.

Brian descended the stairs and crossed the living room, headed toward the kitchen. He stopped in the entryway and immediately pulled away, ducking behind the wall. It wasn't Susan in the kitchen. It was some guy, rummaging through the refrigerator. Pretty big son of a bitch, too, though it was hard to tell just how big the way he was hunched over, leaning with an arm over the door.

Goddamnit! Why wasn't there a gun in the house?

He owned one, a Ruger forty caliber. But Susan had freaked when he brought it home, threw a fit until he agreed to keep it at the office. And that's where it was. Sitting useless in a safe. That ditz messed up everything.

He needed a weapon, and if it wasn't going to be a gun, he had to find something else. The sound of food packages and drink containers being slid around gave him the courage to bolt across the entry and make his way toward the foyer. He glanced briefly at the front door, tempted to yank the knob and run. But his keys were on the bed, along with his wallet—*stupid!*—and he couldn't risk going back upstairs. He babied the closet door open, listening for noises from the kitchen. His golf bag was wedged in the corner, behind a heavy parka and his raincoat. He winced at the noise as he unzipped the bag's rainslicker, removed the nine iron. He slipped off the nylon headcover and stuffed it in his pocket. The club felt good in his hands as he hefted it. The head seemed heavy and meant to do damage. He realized he'd never actually swung it before. The club head was shaking as he held it out, prompting him to take several deep breaths.

The man was still at the refrigerator when Brian peeked around the corner, but now he had the freezer door open, his head hidden behind it. A plate with a large slice of chocolate cake was sitting on the island between the two of them. The man lifted a carton of ice cream and balanced it on the top of the door as Brian crept forward, but he never seemed to stop searching the contents of the freezer. Brian's hands were really trembling now, his legs felt unstable. He circled the island and started to raise the golf club, then hesitated as he drew within a few feet.

Damn, but he's really big. Bolting out the front door and just running until he was far away suddenly looked like a better idea.

The big man started to back away from the freezer, forcing Brian's hand. Suddenly fearing he was about to be seen, Brian cocked the golf club back over his head, clutching it with both hands.

Last chance, he told himself. *What do I do? Run away and take my chances? But what if he sees me? Chases after me? Or do I dive forward and bring the business end of this thing down like an axe?*

Brian made his decision, though not very decisively. Shaking and pale, he hoped he'd be able to live with it.

*   *   *

HATCHER SHOOK HIS HEAD. FOR PEOPLE WHO SEEMED to have a decent amount of money, the Warrens' refrigerator was rather bare. It occurred to him a bad marriage would probably result in lots of little things like that, minor deficiencies that added up to a miserable life. He wondered how long it had been since they had eaten together, imagined neither wanting to cook or grocery shop, each taking most of their meals on the run. There was some cake, some eggs, a few containers of yogurt, some juice. The cake looked good. Since no one seemed to be home, he thought about helping himself to a piece. It was a possibility.

He closed the refrigerator door and opened the parallel door to the freezer. Some ice cream, some bags of frozen vegetables, chicken breasts under plastic.

He shut that door and glanced around the kitchen again.

Where the hell was Susan's husband? The place seemed empty, with each footstep almost echoing in the large kitchen. He'd looked around, snooped a bit, but couldn't find anyone. It didn't make sense. A car matching what Susan had described was in the driveway and the front door had been unlocked. And a garment bag and clothes were on the bed upstairs.

More important, something didn't feel right. Years of combat had heightened his perception of foreign surroundings, honed his intuition. Sometimes survival simply meant listening to what your senses were telling you. And right now his senses were telling him to be wary. He felt alone and not alone at the same time. That was usually the vibe of an ambush.

Hatcher exited the kitchen and stepped into the living room, stopping to take in the surroundings more thoroughly this time. The house was old and big and had been renovated at no small expense. The living room was large, with a marble fireplace and a puffy sofa. Beyond it was an open set of double doors leading to a game room with a billiard table. The place was very upper middle class. It was also dark and lifeless and cold. Hatcher could almost feel the chill. Another by-product of a bad marriage. No heat generated from the master bedroom in this house.

Two things seemed obvious as Hatcher let his eyes wander: Brian Warren was a geek who made decent coin, and Susan did all the decorating. The rooms were tastefully furnished with a woman's touch. Earth-tone furniture and rich wood. Bowls filled with large ornate balls. A glass-top coffee table filled with river stones.

And an entire wall of the adjacent game room dedicated to *Star Wars* memorabilia. Tiny figures wielding lightsabers in a glass display case, a framed movie poster for *Revenge of the Jedi*, a life-size cardboard cutout of Darth Vader. A large chess table was set up in the corner with R2-D2s as pawns on one side, Stormtroopers on the other.

How did a woman like Susan end up with a guy like this? Hatcher wondered. It seemed a pretty safe bet that Brian Warren got beat up a lot as a kid.

This was getting him nowhere. Hatcher looked around for a few more minutes, then made his way to the front door. He stared at it, thinking.

There were six questions every interrogation attempted to answer. Who, what, when, where, how, and why. The most important one of them in Hatcher's mind was always *why*. If you could answer that one, finding answers to the rest instantly became much easier. You had a map of the terrain.

Why was the front door unlocked when he arrived?

If Susan's husband had left in a hurry, that might explain it. But why would his car be here? And the unfinished packing? Planning to run, but was he called away suddenly? Or maybe taken away? Hatcher shook that one off. He could have been kidnapped, but that was the kind of scenario that required more evidence before Hatcher was willing to consider it. The sound of hoofs tended to mean horses, not zebras.

Wrong question, he realized. Too specific to tackle at this point. It needed to be broader. Like, why are front doors *ever* left unlocked?

Hatcher continued to study the door, coaxing an answer out of it.

Because either the person leaving forgot, doesn't have a way to lock it, or doesn't care.

An unfinished packing job. A car in the driveway. Brian Warren didn't forget.

It suddenly seemed obvious. Somebody else had left through that door. Hatcher reassessed the possibility that maybe Brian Warren really had been kidnapped. Not a lot of evidence for it, but enough to play with, to see where it took him.

Assuming something like that, the next question was, what would a kidnapping leave behind?

Experience taught that being observant was mostly a matter of knowing where to look. Anyone could overlook anything if his eyes were focused in the wrong direction. On Ops, when trying to clear a building or tracking a hostile, he spent as much time as he could get away with looking down. It was a simple function of gravity. Everything that wasn't somehow stuck in or on a wall or ceiling invariably made its way to the floor. The odds were good if there was something to find, a trace of it could be found there. He could think of no reason the same logic didn't hold true here.

He found the nearest set of light switches, fiddled with them until he discovered the right one. The area lit up in a bright glow. He dropped his gaze to the floor and studied it. The foyer was tiled in off-white ceramic. Very clean. Not a spot on it.

Except in front of the door to the entryway closet.

Hatcher stooped down to get a closer look. No mistaking it. A small dot of something dark and red. He didn't need to touch it to know it was blood.

Standing, Hatcher placed his hand on the closet doorknob, hesitated a brief moment, then opened it.

The door swung outward and Hatcher sprang back as a man stumbled toward him, arms raised high, holding a golf club. The man didn't travel far before falling forward onto his face.

Hatcher knew who it was before he rolled the body over. By then, he also knew the man hadn't stumbled at all, rather the lifeless form had simply spilled forward, face-first. But Hatcher wasn't focusing on any of those points at the moment. His mind was running through all the things he was going to have to do in the next few minutes, and how he was going to go about doing them.

Hatcher stood and took one last look at the body before going through the mental checklist he'd just made, deciding where to begin, and it occurred to him whoever did this probably thought he was being funny. The head was facing the wrong way, twisted impossibly around, the mouth wedged wide open, the blade of a golf club shoved vertically between the teeth. Most significantly, the club itself hadn't been raised over his head, it just looked that way. It was protruding from the top the skull, embedded firmly, Brian Warren's hands clutching the shaft. The pathetic impression of a Jedi Knight by a guy who never quite stopped getting beat up.

CHAPTER 14

❖

"JESUS CHRIST, HATCHER! DO YOU HAVE ANY IDEA HOW
this looks?"

Hatcher yawned and wiped his face, the cuffs forcing
him to do it with both hands.

"I'm guessing not so good."

Wright let out a noise that sounded like a predator. Her
incisors were noticeably digging into her lower lip. She
seemed to be making fists with her eyelids.

"Just what the hell were you doing there?"

"I told you," Hatcher said. He shifted in his chair. "I
wanted to talk to Brian Warren."

"Yeah, *no shit*. What I mean is, *why* did you want to talk
to Brian Warren?"

"Because I had a feeling he was mixed up in this
somehow."

"Oh, you had a feeling, huh? That's just great. I'm not
even going to ask what you mean by *this*. You're about
two seconds away from a murder rap. Because you had a
feeling."

"Amy, you're not really going to sit there and tell me you think I killed him."

"It really doesn't matter what I think, Hatcher. Don't you get it? You were in the house, your brother was last seen with the man before he was killed. You admit your prints are all over the place. His blood is on your shirt. Motive, opportunity, physical evidence."

"I'm the one who called nine-one-one. What kind of murderer does that?"

"No one said you were very smart."

Hatcher glanced over at the two-way mirror on the wall of the interview room. Most laymen, and a good number of cops, believed it was there to allow others to observe the interrogation, but Hatcher knew that purpose had been long surpassed by technology. Cameras and audio equipment could provide better, more diversified monitoring far more surreptitiously. The real reason mirrors were still in use was because they wanted subjects to observe themselves during the interview. It was a tactic the military used liberally. Watching yourself lie is not the easiest thing to do.

He stared into his own reflection, thinking that watching yourself tell the truth wasn't always a cakewalk, either.

"Nobody's in there," Wright said.

"I know. You wouldn't be talking like this if anyone was."

"Maloney gave me five minutes alone with you. And he knows there's something between us, by the way. I can tell. Do you realize the position you've put me in, Hatcher? How could you do this to me? Tricking me like that? Getting me to pull men off a surveillance? Sneaking around and leaving dead bodies for me to answer for?"

There was no way to answer that question, since it wasn't really intended as a question at all. Posed by Amy Wright the woman, not Amy Wright the cop. He would have preferred to deal with the cop. At the moment, at least.

A few seconds of listening to the sound of her fingernails tapping against the table, then Hatcher said, "He's in love with you, you know."

"What?"

"Maloney. He's in love with you."

She glanced away, then fixed her gaze coldly on him. "Stop it."

"Stop what?"

"Whatever mind game you're trying to play."

"No, it's true. He tried to warn me off. I could see it in his eyes. That helpless, desperate look of a man in love. Willing to do anything to salvage it. I just thought you should know."

"That's ridiculous. And we're talking about you, Hatcher. Not him. *You*. I trusted you."

Hatcher let it go. She was lying, of course. She hadn't trusted him. If she had, he wouldn't have had to pull his little ruse. But she believed she had, regardless of her actions, and her belief was what mattered at the moment. Amy Wright the woman, not Amy Wright the cop.

"Don't you have anything to say for yourself?"

Before Hatcher could respond, someone knocked and the door to the room opened. Maloney stood in the doorway, one hand on the knob, the other holding a file folder.

"Amy."

Wright locked eyes with Hatcher one final time and sighed with obvious contempt. She marched out of the room doing her best impersonation of Amy Wright the cop.

Maloney let her pass without comment. He leaned back and glanced down the hall in her direction before turning his attention to Hatcher.

"She thinks you betrayed her," he said. He'd kept his voice low. He walked over to the table, dropped the file on it.

"I got that. Thanks."

Maloney sat. Reynolds appeared in the doorway, pausing before entering and closing the door behind him. Brimming with attitude today. Attitude, and something else Hatcher couldn't quite put his finger on. He stood in the corner, staring at Hatcher like he'd stolen the loser's lunch money.

"So, here we are again," Maloney said.

Hatcher scratched his chin, having to lift both hands. He was sporting a uniform stubble, his reflection reminding him of a vintage G.I. Joe doll. "Always a pleasure, Lieutenant."

"Reynolds, remove Mr. Hatcher's cuffs, if you would."

The younger detective made a face, but did as was asked. He eyeballed Hatcher the entire time. There was an edge to the way he was looking at him that made Hatcher take note. It seemed Freckles the Police Clown suddenly had a hard-on for him.

"I've told you all everything already," Hatcher said.

Maloney bounced his jaw a bit, almost nodding. "I know."

"Why don't I think that means you believe me?"

"What I believe is irrelevant. The evidence backs up enough of what you said."

Hatcher watched the detective in silence, waiting for him to say more.

"Blood evidence," Maloney continued. "The drop of blood on the floor wasn't a match for either you or the vic. But it was a match for what we pulled out of the trap in the kitchen sink. We haven't had time to run DNA analysis yet, of course, but the lab was able to type it and exclude the both of you."

"Someone else's blood in the house doesn't mean I didn't do it."

"Is that a confession?"

"Not the kind you mean."

"What kind is it, then?"

"It's me confessing that I know you have other evidence."

Maloney scrunched the side of his mouth, tilted his head, conceded the point with a flourish of his brow, then a shrug. "Cab driver says he picked you up in the city around when the ME's office puts the time of death. Maybe not airtight, but I don't want to waste energy on the wrong guy. Besides, it doesn't seem like your style, anyway."

He was lying, but Hatcher had expected as much. "Are you letting me go?"

"Not quite. There are still a few things I want to know."

Hatcher said nothing.

"Neighbors saw someone fitting your description leaving the house."

"Neighbors? At that time of night? Don't people in Long Island sleep?"

Maloney hitched his shoulders. "Guess some people can't. At least one person described you perfectly, said they saw you get into Brian Warren's car and leave. A car that was conspicuously devoid of fingerprints, I might add."

"Why would I do that?"

"That's what I want to know."

"Lieutenant, I'm the one who called you guys from the house. I was there at the scene when the first cops arrived."

"That's not a denial."

"Because there's nothing to deny. No neighbor is going to describe anyone perfectly at that time of night from the kind of distance away they'd have to have been. You're fishing."

Maloney glanced down at the file folder. "You're not as smart as you think you are, Hatcher."

"Why do I feel a threat coming on?"

"No threat," Maloney said, cracking a smile. "I just mean, you don't seem to know who your friends are."

"Maybe that's because everyone wants to ask me questions and nobody wants to give me answers. It was my brother who was killed, remember?"

The lieutenant tapped the file folder on the table. "Captain Gillis wants me to transfer you back to federal custody if I don't charge you."

"You and he becoming buddies now? That would be telling."

"I told him that you were a material witness, and that I needed you to remain in the jurisdiction. I also made it clear I'd put in requests as far up the chain as I had to."

"Exactly what are you trying to say, Maloney?"

"Nothing, only that you don't have to go back to Fort Sill yet, once you leave here. Not right away."

"That only matters if I'm allowed to leave here. Am I allowed?"

"Almost. But like I said, I have some questions I still need answered."

Hatcher watched Maloney's eyes, waiting. There was something about those eyes Hatcher found out of place. They were almost too steady. Like he was fearless. Fearlessness usually didn't go along with lying. But at the same time, part of those eyes seemed on edge, as if there was a collection of knowledge lurking behind them that he was having to work to hide.

"Do you think what happened to this guy Warren had anything to do with Deborah's disappearance?" Maloney asked.

The question surprised Hatcher, mostly because it was a really good one, lacking any pretense.

"I don't know. But I tend not to place much faith in coincidences."

Maloney stared at Hatcher for several breaths, then nodded. "Me, either. I'm assuming you believe this is all connected to your brother's death."

"Is that a question?"

"Yes."

"Of course, I do. Same as you."

Maloney looked as if he was starting to say something, then stopped himself. He glanced down and removed a business card that was paper-clipped to the inside flap of the folder. He slid it across the table toward Hatcher.

"Reynolds found this at the scene. It was on the floor of the closet. The Long Island boys missed it."

Hatcher picked up the card. It was slick, glossy. Centered on one side of it were two words, followed by what looked like an ambiguous address:

PLEASURE INCARNATE
FIVE BLOCKS EAST OF EDEN
MANHATTAN

In the top corner it read:

FOR DIRECTIONS OR
AN APPOINTMENT
ASK SAMARRA

Hatcher turned the card over. The entire back side was a partial black-and-white photograph of a woman's eyes, and hair that seemed platinum, almost like it was the one thing in color among the shades of gray.

"We can't find any trace of this place, who or what it is. I've had people check every business with the word 'Eden' in it and the surrounding ten blocks. They couldn't find a thing. Vice never heard of it. Do you have any idea what it is? Other than maybe an homage to Steinbeck?"

"No," Hatcher said.

He stared at the photo side, studying the details, thinking, *But I've seen those eyes.*

VALENTINE PLACED THE BOOK BACK IN ITS CASE AND gently closed the lid.

"I hope you're not thinking of sitting on my forty-thousand-dollar Italian leather sofa," he said, still facing the wall. "You put your bleeding head anywhere near it, and your day will deteriorate even more than you thought possible."

Sherman froze in a crouch, his ass hovering over the cushion. He was holding several layers of gauze against the back of his head behind his ear.

"Sorry, Boss," he said, wincing as he pulled himself erect. "I just need to get off my feet. I don't know how much more my head can take."

The lock on the case clicked into place and Valentine removed the key. "Fortunately, it probably won't be much more. You should consider yourself lucky. You weren't supposed to leave any evidence behind."

"I'm sorry, Boss. The fat fuck hit me with a golf club."

"As it turns out, he chose a body part you don't use much. Regardless, it seems to have worked out for the best. I believe I've figured out a way to turn it to my advantage. They have your blood. You didn't leave anything else for them to find, did you? Something I don't know about?"

"No, Boss. I wiped down everything I touched. Didn't bleed much, but I had to clean up somehow. Stop the flow. Before I started, you know, dripping."

"Our friend is going to find the Carnates. Our contact in the department tells me he was given the card."

Sherman pulled the gauze away from his head, grimacing, and looked at the pasty clump of blood and skin clinging to it. "You think he'll be able to?"

"Yes. Whatever he lacks in intellect, I suspect he makes up for in determination."

"All I know is, if I get another shot at him, he's not going to like it."

Valentine looked down at the book. "I wouldn't underestimate him if I were you. Remember what happened the last time you did."

"But, Boss, he caught me off guard. This is different."

"It most certainly is."

Sherman shook his head, wincing again. "It's almost as if you like the guy or something. I can't figure out what you got going on with him. He probably doesn't even know you exist."

"I know." Valentine placed his hand on the glass. A faint trace of a smile graced his lips. "Manipulating people close to you is one thing, but doing it from a distance, well, that's one of life's beautiful little pleasures, now, isn't it?"

*   *   *

THE SUN WAS ALREADY DOWN AGAIN BY THE TIME
Hatcher left the precinct. Wright had refused to speak to
him as he left, and the image of her turning away from him
in the hallway, the deafening tone of her body language,
lingered like a body blow. He tried to push the thought of
her out of his mind, but was finding it a tough task. He
lowered his head and walked, forcing himself to plan out
his next move.

He took the subway as far as was practical and then a taxi
the final few miles to get back to Long Island. It didn't seem
likely he was being followed, but cities had a way of making it hard to tell. During the trip, he tried to sift through
what he knew, but the more information he possessed, the
less everything seemed to make sense. Instead of forming
lines from dot to dot, the connections were multiplying in
ways that confused the picture even more. Why was Brian
Warren killed? What was his connection to all this? And how
did Garrett's death fit in?

The taxi dropped him off on Middle Island Boulevard, a
couple of blocks from the Hicksville post office. The street
gave him a good view of traffic in both directions as he
headed toward West John Street. After a few minutes, he
started to feel confident that no one had tagged along.

The walk to the post office was refreshing after having
spent so much time cooped up in the precinct, most of it
handcuffed. The evening air was cool and moist. He inhaled lungfuls of it, expanding his chest and letting it clear
his thoughts.

Hatcher walked into the post office and rang the buzzer
at the night window. He raised his hand to press it a second time when a postal clerk shuffled into view. He was a
middle-aged black man with white hair and a pair of half-
moon reading glasses hanging over his chest from a string
around his neck.

"Help you?"

"My name is Garrett Nolan. I believe you have a package
for me, mailed general delivery to this zip code."

The clerk rubbed the side of his face with his palm, long, knobby fingers stretched out. "General delivery?"

"Yes."

"Let me check."

The clerk disappeared. Hatcher's gaze wandered, sliding over the rows of post boxes, settling on the FBI's Ten Most Wanted poster. He read the names, studied the faces. Not a very nice-looking bunch of guys.

The clerk returned carrying a small box.

"Don't see people use general delivery very much. I'll need to see some ID."

"I don't have any. I told the person mailing it that I didn't. They said they'd note it on the box."

The clerk lifted his glasses from his chest and placed them on his nose. He held the box low and looked down at it from a steep angle. The words "No Identification Necessary" were written on the same side as the address, along the corner.

"Never saw that before."

"If I wasn't *me*, how would I know I was expecting a package?"

The clerk eyed him over his glasses for a moment, then shrugged. "I suppose I can just let you sign for it."

Hatcher scribbled a signature on a form attached to a clipboard and wished the man good night before leaving the post office. Once outside, he tore open the box and removed the cell phone Fred had given him and several hundred dollars in cash he had taken off of Brian Warren. He put the cash in his pocket, turned on the cell phone and called the only number stored in the phone's call log.

"Hello?"

"It's me."

"Did it work?"

"The fact I'm talking to you on this phone should give you a hint."

"Right."

"Did the police take you in?"

"No."

"How about Susan?"

"No. They came to the door and told her about her husband, questioned her for a long time."

"How'd she hold up?"

Fred paused before answering. "Well, considering. She cried, but I think they were mostly tears of relief. From what I could hear, she did okay."

"I'm assuming they're still watching."

"Yes. They're still right outside the building. I can see them from the window."

"Good. Are you sure they can't hear this?"

"Positive. This room is set up to disrupt any microwave or laser transmitters, and I have white noise machines tuned to frequencies that will wreak havoc with any parabolic mic."

Hatcher couldn't help but smile. Paranoia has its advantages.

"How's Susan doing now?"

"She's okay. She's resting. You have the money?"

"Yes. Thank her again for me."

"I will. But she knows the police would have taken it if you hadn't."

"Still, relieving a dead guy of cash isn't something I do. Often, that is. Are you handy with Internet research?"

"Is that some kind of joke?"

"Forget I asked. I need a favor. I'm trying to track down something called 'Pleasure Incarnate.' It's connected to all this somehow. It might be some kind of men's club or brothel. I doubt you'll find anything solid, but it's the address I'm interested in. I need to locate it. What I have doesn't make sense."

"What address do you have?"

"It's in some kind of code. 'Five blocks east of Eden.' Somewhere in Manhattan."

"That's it?"

"That's it. I could use a finger in the right direction. Do what you can."

"I'll get right on it."

Hatcher pressed the button to disconnect and looked the street over. Traffic was light, an occasional pair of head-lights approaching, taillights retreating. He checked the time on the phone. Almost nine. Hailing a cab back to the city might take a while. But whatever answers he was going to find, that's where he would have to start. Somewhere in Manhattan.

Five blocks east of Eden.

CHAPTER 15

HATCHER HAD THE REMAINS OF A DOUBLE CHEESEBURGER on his plate and was finishing his second cup of coffee when the phone rang. He dabbed his mouth with a napkin as he looked at the number on the screen.

"Anything?"

Fred cleared his throat, and Hatcher knew the answer. "Well, 'Pleasure Incarnate' doesn't exist, as far as the net is concerned. Not in Manhattan. I had to sift through a zillion uses of the phrase, but I did come across one reference, in some private chat room. It was archived less than twenty-four hours ago. Don't ask me how I got access. From what they were talking about, it might be the same place."

"Shed any light?"

"Only that it does seem to be some kind of brothel. But other than that, no. The poster was making an inquiry, got shut down pretty quickly by the moderator. I think I could track the hosts down, but it might take a while. From what I can tell, the moderator was local. Could probably find him in a day or two."

"I'm not sure I have that much time. Anything else? How about the address?"

"Nothing. All I learned was that there seem to be more Steinbeck clubs in Manhattan than there are Steinbeck books. Sorry."

Hatcher thanked him and broke the connection, dragged his hand down his face. He took the last sip from his coffee, fingered a French fry, then glanced down at the cell phone again and picked it up.

"Yes?"

"Why so many Steinbeck groups?"

"Huh?"

"You said there were more Steinbeck clubs than books. Why so many?"

"He was a major literary figure."

"I know who he was." Even though he could barely recall the two or three novels of his he'd rushed through in high school, one in college, Hatcher did remember his time learning Arabic in Monterey, California. Steinbeck country. "But I mean, why with this search? Why did his name come up?"

"*East of Eden*. It's one of his most famous works."

Through the ghost of his reflection in the window, Hatcher could see the activity on the busy Manhattan street. People walking everywhere he looked, engrossed in conversation, heading to various destinations, the nightlife of the most famous city in the world just getting started.

"Yeah, I know that much. But where did the story take place?"

"The story?"

"The book. Where was it set?"

A stretch of background noise filled the silence as he waited for Fred to answer. The clacking of a keyboard, the rustling and scraping of the phone brushing against something.

"I'm sorry," Fred said. "It's been a few years, so I had to check. According to this, California, mostly. A few scenes in New England."

"Any in New York?"

"I don't think so. Give me a moment." More clacks at the keyboard. "No, not according to Wikipedia. Why?"

"Because I'm trying to find the connection."

"What connection?"

"Between the book and the city."

"Oh. Well, I can think of one."

"I'm all ears."

"Something I happened to come across during the search. He wrote part of it while living here"

"Here?" Hatcher shifted in his chair, sitting up. "In Manhattan? I thought Steinbeck lived in California?"

"He did, but he also lived a while right here in New York. In a brownstone on East Fifty-second Street."

"You wouldn't happen to have the actual address to that, would you?"

"Would that make you happy?"

"Ecstatic."

"In that case, my friend, ecstasy is just a few keystrokes away."

DETECTIVE WRIGHT SAT AT HER DESK AND STARED AT AN open file, not seeing any of it. She felt literally beside herself, as if part of her was standing next to her chair, wanting desperately to pace. How could she have been so stupid? To let him have played her like that, to have . . . *given* herself to him that way—a practical *stranger*. A man still serving a prison sentence, no less. When had she become so reckless? The reminder of her sexual encounter with Hatcher was too unsettling. She scrambled for a handle on other thoughts to replace it, something—anything—to block it out. Nothing seemed to stick.

What had come over her? She had never experienced any urge like that before, like a sudden, burning thirst that had to be quenched. The feeling had swelled inside her and just wouldn't stop. It continued to build, pushing her beyond arousal, beyond desire. It had barely been relieved by her orgasms. Whatever it was, sex had never been quite that intense before. She'd come three times in those twenty or so minutes.

"Sergeant Wright?"

Wright looked up to see Reynolds standing in front of her desk. She sensed from his expression that he'd been standing there for several seconds. She broke eye contact, adjusting her sitting position as she reached for the nearest stack of papers.

"What is it, Reynolds?"

"Do you have a moment?"

"Why are you here at this hour? Don't you have a life?"

Reynolds took a seat next to her desk. "Can you keep something between the two of us?"

"That depends on what it is." She pretended to read the document in front of her. "You haven't done anything wrong, have you? If so, I don't want to know. I'm really not in the mood to play priest."

"No. Not that I'm about to tell you, anyway." He paused, smiling weakly. "This is about Jake Hatcher."

She leaned back in her chair. *God, why can't I escape that man?* "What about him?"

"You can't tell the lieutenant though, okay?"

That didn't sound good. Not good at all. But if he did have information about Hatcher, she wanted to know it. "Whatever. What is it?"

"I found a business card at the scene of the Warren murder. Maloney showed it to him."

"To Hatcher?"

"Yes."

"He showed Hatcher a card you found? So?"

"The card was for some kind of cabaret or something."

Reynolds pulled a folded piece of paper from his pocket and set it down on the desk. She picked it up and unfolded it. It was a photocopy of two images. One of a business card, the other a rectangular close-up of a woman's eyes.

The second image was the exact shape and size of the card.

"This picture is the back of it," Reynolds said, pointing. "It has some little riddle for an address. I think Maloney was trying to get him to go find it."

"Why do you think that?"

Reynolds shrugged. "Just a vibe I got. Look, you can't tell Maloney any of this."

"Yeah, you already said that. So why are you telling me?"

"Because if Maloney is setting Hatcher up, I figured you'd want to know about it. Maybe try to stop it."

"Oh, you did, huh?"

"Don't you?"

There was something sly about his expression, something suggestive in the way he raised his eyebrows, in the innocent yet knowing tone of voice he used. This was a side of Reynolds Wright had never seen. She wasn't certain what to make of it. She examined his face, started to sense things going on behind that expression she hadn't suspected before. Perhaps there was more to him than she had realized.

She picked up the photocopy and gave it a light wave. "Okay, so tell me what place this is."

Reynolds tilted his head from side to side, frowning. "Not quite sure beyond what I just said. Some kind of sexually oriented business, obviously. It must be an underground thing. Private club, maybe."

"And you think Hatcher's heading there?"

"I think that's what Maloney wants, yes."

"Why?"

Reynolds shrugged. "I don't know. But something strange is going on with him. Like yesterday, I overheard him on his cell phone when he didn't realize I was behind him. I think he was talking about Lucas Sherman. In fact, I'm sure of it."

"And that's strange because . . . ?"

"Because he sounded like he was giving someone assurances. Choosing his words carefully, if you know what I mean."

"What, exactly, are you saying?"

"To be honest, I don't quite know, but if you care about what happens to Hatcher, I think you may want to get a little proactive."

"Proactive?" Wright leaned back into her seat. "As in proactively doing what?"

"I pulled the number off Maloney's cell. I checked the times of his calls, found the one that matched the time I overheard that conversation. It's registered to Heart and Soul Imports, Ltd."

"Sounds like you've been busy finding ways to end your career."

Reynolds put his hands on her desk, leaning forward. "Guess who the registered agent is?"

"You're trying my patience, Reynolds."

"Stephen Solomon."

Wright said nothing. The name bounced around in her head as she tried to make sense of what she was being told, uncertain as to whether she should believe any of it. And if she were to, whether it really meant anything.

"And while there's no public record of the limited partners," Reynolds continued, "Heart and Soul Imports, Ltd., has a corporate general partner, with one director."

"Are you waiting for a drum roll?"

"That director is Demetrius Valentine."

Wright paused, considering what she'd just been told. "As in, the major philanthropist, high-society big-shot Demetrius Valentine?"

Reynolds nodded. "That's not all. I just found out that our Long Island vic, the dearly departed Mr. Warren, did business with Heart and Soul Imports. Found a file on his computer."

Wright said nothing. She stared past Reynolds, thinking.

"Now, don't you want to find out?"

"Find out what?"

"Why Maloney is talking to a billionaire about Lucas Sherman? Why he's calling a company linked to Sherman's high-priced mouthpiece? And why he's giving Hatcher information from a crime scene that may be connected and practically sending him out to investigate?"

"And how would you suggest I do all this finding out?"

"Well, I realize you've been doing this a lot longer than I have . . ." Reynolds reached into his pocket pulled out a stick of gum. He unwrapped it and popped it into his mouth, chewing it for a few seconds before he finished his thought. "But I was thinking we try something really clever, like we pay a visit to Mr. Valentine and ask him."

THE DANK SMELL OF THE EAST RIVER FILLED HATCHER'S nostrils as he stared across the water. Lights and reflections, shades of black and glistening surfaces. Shadowy stone and shimmering glass. New York was the only city he'd ever seen that looked like it was floating atop some gigantic barge. Several cities, actually, clustered together, connected by bridges. A metropolis rising out of the depths, water lapping at every edge.

He listened to the call ring, waiting for Fred to answer.

"Yes?"

"Unless you're supposed to swim there," Hatcher said, "we're missing something."

Two blocks east of the address on Fifty-first Street put him at the water's edge. The breeze off the water whistled between the side of his head and the phone, making it difficult to hear.

Fred made a noise like he was frustrated. Hatcher sensed he made noises like that a lot. "In that case, I'm not sure what to do. Did the card say anything else?"

"No."

"Anything at all?"

Hatcher pictured the print in his mind, though his thoughts kept slipping back to the photo. "Okay, one thing. It said to call someone named Samarra for an appointment."

"Did you say Samarra? Are you sure?"

"Yes. Why?"

"Hold on. Something else I ran across." Hatcher could make out a light rataplan of keystrokes. "Yes, here it is. Another author lived right near where Steinbeck did, a guy named John O'Hara. Wrote a book called *Appointment in Samarra*."

"Wait a second." Hatcher inclined his head, stared into the night sky. It was a blackish purple, devoid of stars. Rain was coming. "I know that story. Really short one. About some guy who saw Death and rode off to escape, not knowing he was running off to where Death had an appointment with him."

"If you say so. I just remembered seeing it on some site when I pulled up Steinbeck's address."

"Where did this guy O'Hara live?"

"All I saw was that he was staying at the Pickwick Arms Hotel when he wrote it. It was a few doors down from where Steinbeck had lived."

Hatcher pressed a hand to his face, shutting his eyes. That information confirmed the general location, but didn't seem to shed any light on what he was missing. *Five Blocks East of Eden*. He had to think, had to tease the answer out.

"What's the address for the Pickwick Arms?"

"Hold on . . . Hmm, it's not the Pickwick Arms anymore. It's now known as the Pod. Still a hotel, though."

"Unusual name for a hotel. Where is it?"

"Yes. Apparently the rooms are small. Like pods. From what I'm seeing here, it looks like it's supposed to be hip and trendy. And cheap. It's west of Second Avenue, about a block."

Hatcher looked out across the dark expanse of river. "But how do I get five blocks east of any of it?"

"I don't know. Sorry."

"Keep checking for me, if you would. I'm going to go back and take a look around."

Hatcher headed back down Fifty-first toward the numbers for Steinbeck's former residence. He crossed Second Avenue and found the hotel, thought about asking the desk clerk some questions, then realized it would be pointless. He ran the contents of the card over and over in his mind as he headed back toward the water again, passing Steinbeck's old building once more.

Five Blocks East of Eden.

He closed his eyes, tried visualize the card in detail, focusing on the writing. *For Directions Or An appointment Ask samarra.* He recalled noticing how some of the words hadn't been capitalized like the others, and now he knew why. Enemy networks in Afghanistan and Iraq had done similar things to call attention to key pieces of information. Misspellings, wrongs words, deliberately improper punctuation. He'd extracted enough information from captured combatants to know it was common.

The reference to *Appointment in Samarra* was an orienter, he was sure of it. It was meant to let the recipient know he was on the right track, to confirm the reference to *East of Eden*. If Fred's info was correct, Steinbeck and O'Hara had lived on the very street Hatcher was walking. That wasn't a coincidence.

Five Blocks East of Eden.

Crossing the East River put you in Brooklyn. The card said Manhattan. That was also an orienter. It was there to let the decrypter know to disregard that option and to stay on this side. Hatcher tried to recall what all the makeshift little field codes he'd come across had in common. The only thing he could think of was they always referred to something other than what they seemed to. Where was a good cryptoanalyst when you needed one?

Five Blocks East of Eden.

Hatcher continued walking east, studying the rows of buildings, brownstones, brick townhomes, cement slivers.

Serried structures of varying heights with adjacent walls, an occasional restaurant or store at ground level. This was a residential block, lined with trees and fenced-off flower gardens in front of some of the dwellings. It was quiet and upscale. Very expensive real estate, even for Manhattan.

At the corner of First Avenue, Hatcher leaned against a pole and shut his eyes again. It had to be nearby; there were too many clues. He was still missing something.

Five Blocks.

Blocks of what? Stone? Didn't make sense. Could blocks mean buildings? Maybe. He'd have to remember to go back and check the fifth building east. He was pretty sure it was a residence.

He jerked his eyes open and pushed off the pole. Five B? An address? He tossed the idea around. Maybe one of the residences? Or a slyly embedded clue, like someone named *Lock* in an apartment 5B? He would need to check every building east of the Steinbeck place, look for anything numbered 5B.

As he started to walk west, the idea lost some of its luster. Another thing these codes had in common, at least the ones he'd encountered, was that they pointed to things visible from a road or an alley. You never wanted someone knocking on the wrong person's door and creating suspicion with his questions. Or leaving a trail for others to reconstruct.

Hatcher scanned the buildings in each direction. What was visible from the street? Not all that much. Façades, windows, signs on the businesses. He glanced at the restaurant on the corner. It had an Italian name written in script along the side of the green awning extending from it. A dry cleaner was next to it. A few floors up, a sign in the window announced it was the Center for Kabbalic Studies.

Several paces up the street, Hatcher stopped and turned around. Center for Kabbalic Studies. He pictured the words from the business card one more time, saw them start to take a shape consistent with their meaning. CKS.

"Oh, you clever, clever bastards," he whispered.

CHAPTER 16

❖

THE MUTED SOUNDS OF THE CITY SEEMED DISTANT WITHIN
the confines of the car. Wright was feeling a bit cramped.
Uncomfortable. It was all she could do to sit still.

"Pretty tony neighborhood, huh?" Reynolds said.

Wright nodded. "It certainly is."

"Well, the rich ain't like you and me. They have more
money."

"Will Rogers," Wright said.

"Good one."

She glanced over at the younger detective. He was chewing another piece of gum, sitting back in the passenger's
seat, loose and composed, bantering like some old pro. His
red hair was pulled across his head in waves.

"What's gotten into you, Reynolds?"

"What do you mean?"

"You're just acting so much more *relaxed* than you usually do."

His mouth widened and curled at the edges. "Well, if you
want the truth . . . you might say I'm not a very trusting

person. And for some reason, I've never trusted Maloney at *all*. Not even a little. There was always something that didn't seem quite right. Now, just as I realized why, I also realized that you're not like him. I think I can actually trust you. So, I'm letting my hair down." He smiled broadly at her. "So to speak."

"That's very flattering, but let's not drag the lieutenant's name through the mud like that, okay? He may act like a jerk once in a while, and sometimes his passions get the better of him, but I don't think he's a bad guy. And no, I'm not going to tell him about anything you said. I just don't want you to think it's fine to bad-mouth him that way. Scandalous words can tarnish a reputation."

"Whatever you say, Detective. Want to go see if our man is in?"

Wright nodded and they got out of the car and crossed the street, heading toward Winslow Tower. It was a majestic building, standing tall among other majestic buildings in an area known for its stratospheric rent. As they reached the far sidewalk, Reynolds stuck an arm out across Wright's body, signaling her to stop. He nodded in the direction of a limousine with tinted windows emerging from the parking garage adjacent to the tower.

"Recognize that?" he asked.

Wright watched the car slowly turn away from them onto the street. "Should I?"

"It's the limo Lucas Sherman was driving when he was arrested the other night."

"How do you know?"

"I'm the one who inventoried the contents. I'm almost positive that's it." He snapped his fingers, nodding. "Yeah, I think that's the plate. In fact, I know it is."

Wright stood watching the taillights move away. "Okay, that's strange, I'll admit."

Reynolds swiveled his head, looking over to her. "Well?"

"Well what? Are you saying we should get back in the car and follow him? What about Valentine?"

"Don't you want to know where Sherman is going?"

She hesitated, throwing a glance at the back of the limousine as it pulled up to the traffic light at the corner, its brake lights coming on.

"We don't know that's him. Even if it's the same limo, we don't know who's driving it."

Reynolds made a face. He seemed about to respond when another vehicle, a rental do-it-yourself truck, came out of the garage and turned onto the street heading in the same direction, pausing just long enough for both of them to get a good look at the driver.

There was no mistaking the man behind the wheel in this one. Huge arms, bald head, and sideburns that curved into a mustache. He'd tossed a quick look down the street as he pulled out, but if he noticed them standing there, he didn't show it.

One more glance at Reynolds, then they both started a restrained jog back to the car.

"I told you this had something to do with Sherman."

Wright looked at him as they hurried, seeing the younger detective in a totally new light. She thought of the clown mask on his desk, how it seemed like he'd been wearing a mask of his own all this time, one that was finally being pulled off. He was starting to remind her of someone. Red hair, ruddy complexion, lots of attitude. David Caruso, maybe. "I don't know what to make of you, Reynolds. You've always just kept quiet, seemed kind of moody. Always waited for people to tell you what to do. Suddenly, you're out of your shell and cocky as hell."

"You like it?"

"I'm not sure yet. I'm still trying to understand it."

"Like I said, yesterday I didn't know who I could trust. Now that I'm past that, I can finally be myself around you, act like a cop." He jumped in the passenger seat as Wright rounded the car and got behind the wheel. "And let's face it, what good is being a cop if you don't let yourself enjoy the job, right?"

*   *   *

STANDING IN THE TINY ALCOVE NEXT TO THE DRY CLEANER,
Hatcher flipped the phone shut and put it in his pocket. The
directory on the wall had a list of names, each with a black
button next to it. The topmost entry simply read "CKS."

He counted down five slots, read the name listed for the
occupant. Any doubts he had about whether he had figured
it out were wiped away. John O'Hara.

Five Blocks East of Eden. Five—B—Lo—CKS. East
of Eden. Cute.

He pressed the button, feeling the vibration of the buzz
in his fingertip, and waited.

Almost a full minute later, a hollow-sounding voice,
feminine, came through a round piece of metal screwed
into the wall next to the directory.

"Who are you here to see?"

Hatcher took a breath, pausing. The tone of the voice was
neutral, but he could still tell its owner expected a certain
answer. "I'm here to see Samarra. About an appointment."

The response was immediate. "Where did you come
from?"

Hatcher had to think about how to answer that, and the si-
lence seemed like it started to stretch the moment it started.
No other option than to just take a stab. "Steinbeck's place.
West of here."

An audible click, and Hatcher realized the conversation
was terminated. Nothing happened for a couple of seconds,
then a buzz rattled through the speaker. It took Hatcher a
second to realize he was being let in. He pushed on the
door and stepped into the building.

The inside of the building smelled like a public restroom
after a cursory cleaning. The lobby was narrow, leading
back to a door marked "Stairs." Something about the layout seemed unusual, awkward, like a cluttered room where
a sofa or chair was missing.

He climbed the staircase to the third floor and exited the

stairwell. Instead of a hallway running the length of the building, he found himself in a small vestibule, facing an unmarked door. He knocked.

A mechanical-sounding hum, barely audible, then a click. The door swung gently inward.

The apartment was large and open, with islands of furniture. The walls were a shade of dove gray, but everything else was one of two colors. Whatever wasn't black, was red, and vice-versa. Black sofa, red carpet. Red love seat, black bearskin rug.

Red lipstick, black dress.

The woman wearing them boasted some exceptions to the scheme. Platinum hair. Eyes an evening shade of blue.

She was sitting on the red love seat, reclined to the side, legs tucked beneath her, a drink in her hand. Hatcher walked toward her to the middle of the living room, though he wasn't certain if that's what it was. The room was shaped like a horseshoe, wrapping around a large chunk of wall to his right. The wall seemed to take up a huge portion of the floor.

Hatcher glanced around, pretended he was admiring the décor.

The woman didn't move, other than to lift her glass. She eyed Hatcher without a word or gesture, waiting. Not a good sign, he realized. Patience like that was unsettling. Those capable of it were always the most dangerous. They waited for your mistakes, instead of making any of their own.

"Please, don't get up on my account."

The corner of the woman's mouth twitched slightly and she took a sip of her drink.

"What's your name?" she asked.

"Doe. My friends call me John."

The woman stuck the tip of her finger in her drink, stirring it. "How did you find us, Mr. Doe?"

"Some guy named Spitzer gave me your card. Are you Samarra?"

"More so than you're Mr. Doe." Samarra lifted her finger from her drink and placed it in her mouth, closed her lips over it in a pucker. She slid it out slowly. "I'll ask you again. How did you hear about us?"

"Deborah St. James."

Samarra nodded, pursing those red lips. "Are you armed, Mr. Doe?"

"Should I be?"

"Just answer the question."

"Only with my charm."

"I should warn you, it is not in your best interest to lie. The way to the PI is guarded by sentries. They are very good at divining whether someone is carrying a weapon. If they determine you are, you won't have the chance to explain. So you'd better tell me now."

"I already did."

"In that case, tell me why you're here."

"I was told Pleasure Incarnate was the one place I had to see for myself."

"And you say Deborah sent you?"

"In a manner of speaking."

The woman set her drink on an end table and stood. She closed the distance between them with graceful steps, coming close enough for her breasts to brush against his torso as she looked up at his face and started to circle his body, finally coming to a stop directly in front of him. She was tall, but not as tall as him. He peered down into her eyes, trying to get a read on her, finding nothing.

"One night. Ten thousand dollars. In cash."

She smelled like something delicious, a mix of vanilla and orange and cream. Her proximity caused his already stirring erection to grow stiff. It had to be showing.

His thoughts turned to how ridiculous his libido was becoming. First the hospital, then at Deborah's, now here. He hadn't popped standing boners like that since he was a teenager.

"Okay," Hatcher said.

The woman turned away abruptly. "You can pay when you get there."

"There? Where am I going?"

She crossed to Hatcher's right and opened a door in the large section of wall in the middle of the room. She stepped to the side and leaned back against the wall, arms behind her.

"Somewhere you'll never forget."

The door led to what looked like an unused closet. It was a small, square area, completely empty. No clothes, no shelves, no boxes. A small bulb in a round, plastic dome in the ceiling bathed the walls and floor in a bright yellow light. On the opposite side was another door.

Hatcher stood in the doorway, thinking.

"You did say you wanted to experience Pleasure Incarnate," Samarra said. "Didn't you?"

One more taste of those eyes, then Hatcher stepped into the room.

"By the way, Mr. Hatcher—my real name is Soliya. But you can still have your appointment in Samarra."

She shut the door as he turned back, his palms slapping against the cool metal a second too late. He reached for the knob, found nothing but a flat plate.

He felt a strange sensation in his head, subtle but unmistakable. He reached for the other door, grabbed the knob and yanked. The door opened with no resistance to reveal a concrete wall, flush against the doorway. The wall slid by, traveling upward.

He was in an elevator. Descending.

Something heavy thumped on the ceiling—*roof?*—of the room—*car?* Hatcher looked up. There was no hatch, no opening of any kind. Just a round, colorless piece of opaque plastic covering a bulb.

The room started dropping as if in a dive. It had traveled slowly at first, the movement barely perceptible. But now it was accelerating at what seemed like a ridiculous rate. The concrete was shooting past the door, launching skyward. The sensation of falling became acute. Hatcher could feel the blood gathering in his head, the veins swelling, becoming engorged.

His mind raced. There had to be something, some sort of control. He glanced up at the light, wondered if the fixture could be removed, maybe give him a way to climb out, realized there wouldn't be enough time. Couldn't be.

Time.

The room should have bottomed out already. The building was only a few stories tall. That could mean only one thing. He was traveling in to ground, dropping beneath the surface. Far beneath.

He started to reach for the light when his body suddenly became weighted down with g-force, pressed toward the floor. The elevator compartment was decelerating rapidly. The sudden change forced Hatcher to tense his legs and press himself into a corner, arms spread, trying to keep his balance.

Hatcher's attention shot to the doorway. The concrete wall briefly gave way to an opening. The opening immediately disappeared, replaced by a solid spread of earth.

The room jerked to a stop. Inertia slammed him against the floor. He pushed himself up gingerly and stood. The wall of dirt at the doorway looked hardened and thick. He stepped forward to touch it and heard a triplet of footfalls overhead. Clank, clank, clank, then nothing.

There had to be way out. He reached for the light fixture again, placing his hand over the plastic cover and twisting. The whole thing rotated. There was something strange about how it turned. He twisted it again, it turned again. He reached up with his other hand, stretching on tiptoes, pulled on the sides. The entire light popped off the ceiling and he found himself holding it. The ceiling was bare, no holes, no wiring. He looked at the back of the light. Four magnets on the bottom of it. In the middle, a removable panel covering a battery compartment.

He replaced it, felt it pop snug against the ceiling as the magnets took hold.

Before he was able to come up with any other ideas, he felt the tiny room shudder. Then the wall of dirt began to slide down. The cab was rising.

Within seconds, the dirt gave way to an open passage, and the room stopped again. The humming faded, and everything went quiet. The light from the elevator threw a triangle of pale white into a thicket of shadow, revealing a dark, empty space with a dirty tile floor. A buzzing, cracking noise broke the silence as a harsh, blue white light flickered on, brightening the immediate area outside the elevator.

Hatcher waited a moment, then stepped through the doorway. He found himself in some kind of utility room. Beneath a layer of dirt he could make out the faded remains of a black-and-white checkered floor. A small worktable stood against the opposite wall, with what looked like a calendar on the wall above it. It hung crooked and was so yellowed and worn, Hatcher couldn't even make out the year or the month. To the left, there was a passage leading into a blackened tunnel. Dim bulbs were visible overhead, stretching into the distance at large intervals, a small puddle of light on the ground beneath each one.

The door to the elevator-closet slammed shut behind him and the echo of it bounded down the tunnel. He glanced around the space. The fluorescent light was harsh and he found himself shading his eyes from it. With nowhere else to go, he headed toward the tunnel. He stepped into the darkness immediately beyond the doorway and stood there, waiting for his eyes to adjust. Visibility was limited. The first light was twenty yards or so away, the one beyond it just as far again, as was the one beyond that. Tiny oases of light, leading to God knew where. The distance between each bulb was submerged in shadow. He started to walk in the only direction available.

After a few steps, he stopped. He was between the residue of light from the elevator and the first pool of light in the tunnel, the area surrounding him dark with a blackness that seemed almost tangible, like ink. Tilting his head subtly, he dropped his eyes to avoid the light ahead, allowed his pupils to dilate fully.

Survival in combat sometimes hinged on unusual skills. In Hatcher's case, one of those skills had been the ability to focus on things without looking at them. It was a knack that proved vital on point, when avoiding death often hinged on not allowing the enemy to know you're aware of him, giving you the chance to take control. His mind zoomed in on the shades of black to his right, eyes low and forward. He took an audible breath, steeling himself. Then he shot his hand out in a burst to the side, his fingers locking around a wrist.

He pulled back several steps, yanking the body attached to it into the spill of light from the doorway.

"My! But aren't you a man of action."

It was a woman. She was black, with skin that beamed in the florescence and eyes that glistened like lacquered coal. Her smile revealed opposing rows of perfect teeth. She was wearing a white formfitting shirt and white capris.

She eased in close, walked two fingers up his chest and then tapped him gently on the chin. Her breath grazed his lips when she spoke. "I'm your escort."

Her proximity was making him uncomfortable. His erection was coming back with a vengeance, if he had ever lost it. He remembered the aching desire Deborah created, the instant arousal he'd experienced at the hospital. There was something about these women, about their scent, that was narcotic. It was like inhaling sex while your eyes drank in everything your body was screaming it wanted.

"I was expecting nicer accommodations," Hatcher said, letting go of her wrist.

The woman exhaled a subdued laugh. "Perhaps we were expecting a better-looking man. Call me Callista."

"What now, Callista?"

She reached behind her back, then held out one of her hands. A large silk handkerchief dangled from between two fingers.

"I need you to put this on," she said.

"I'm not sure it's my size."

"As a blindfold."

"And what if I object?"

Callista shrugged. "I'll leave it up to you, but I strongly suggest you wear it. The odds of you surviving the next leg of the journey will be significantly higher if you do. The last man who refused, well, everyone ends up wearing it. But if you want to risk it . . . you can't say I didn't warn you."

"I think I'll take my chances."

"Ohh, a real macho man." She turned away, shot a lingering glance over her shoulder. "Follow me, macho man. And do exactly as I say."

Hatcher watched her hourglass shape and perfect ass leave the wash of light and disappear ahead of him.

"You'll hear, perhaps even see, movement around you. Do not look. Keep your eyes straight ahead. Focus on the next light in the distance."

"Why?"

"Because if you make eye contact, even accidentally, they may attack."

"They? Who's they?"

"Not who. And whatever you do, don't you dare touch one of them. Sometimes, they may get close. If you don't make any sudden moves, or try to escape, they won't make physical contact, unless your eyes meet. And you probably wouldn't even know if that happens until it is too late. They can see in this like it was the middle of a bright, sunny day."

"And what happens if I touch one of them?"

Hatcher could hear the smile in her voice. "It will be the last thing you do."

The darkness enveloped him as he stepped forward. It seemed to have substance, a pressure, like a gas or liquid. Like something he could feel.

"What did you mean, 'not who'?"

Callista said nothing. Hatcher could make out her rough silhouette as she bobbed in and out of the way of the next patch of light a dozen yards or so ahead. He resisted the urge to glance to the sides, following her advice. The fact he knew he would be unable to see anything if he did made it easier.

Roughly halfway to the first cone of light, Hatcher sensed a presence next to him. It caused his skin to tingle and sent a slight jolt of electricity down his spine. Less than a yard away, he guessed, concealed in the blackness, either up against the wall or in a recess. He could feel the shifting warmth radiating from it as it moved silently, thought he could hear the low hiss of slow breathing. A feral, musky scent tickled his nostrils.

"Don't look," Callista said, her voice breaking the quiet. "And one more thing, as I'm sure Soliya told you, you'd better not be armed. They'll know."

"And just how would they manage that?"

"They read minds."

Hatcher bit back a laugh, but her tone and the silence that followed told him she didn't intend it as a joke.

"Still certain you don't want that blindfold?"

"Yes."

Callista stopped once she reached the first island of light. "You need to clear away any thoughts of aggression, right now."

"I'm not sure there'd be anything left."

"You're not taking me seriously. If something happens to you, Soliya will not be pleased."

"What do you want me to do? Think in French?"

"I don't think you understand the gravity of the situation. The Sedim you passed a moment ago let you go by only because her job is to block your route back, should there be trouble. I could feel her tensing, ready to attack. She's reacting to your aggressiveness."

"What the hell is a *Sedim*?"

Callista smiled and tipped her head as she pivoted on her heels and resumed leading him through the tunnel. Hatcher wasn't certain what to make of what she'd just said. He had passed a living creature in the shadows, that much he didn't doubt. Something large, standing upright—or almost upright. Probably a man. But the stuff about reading minds had to be nonsense. Complete bullshit. Yet the situation was too bizarre for him to simply dismiss things he normally wouldn't give a second thought. Even more disconcerting, she was talking as if whatever it was wasn't human but wasn't an animal, either. And, according to her, there were more of them.

The darkness folded over him once again as he left the circle of light. Within a few feet, he felt it, a presence next to him, the brush of air as it moved, the pulse of a breath on his skin.

He kept walking. Something grazed the back of his neck and he flinched.

"They're smelling you," Callista said, her voice emanating from the blackness in front of him. "It's the testosterone. You're very virile, if hopelessly stubborn. It intrigues them."

Hatcher said nothing. Callista emerged from the dark into the circle of light ahead. He joined her a few seconds later, a sense of relief spreading through his gut. Whatever it was playing hide-and-seek in the shadows, it was managing to give him the creeps.

"You'd think ten grand would get you an actual hallway to walk down," he said.

"You complain an awful lot for a Sagittarian. Keep moving."

The dark engulfed her again as she moved ahead. Hatcher took a few steps, stopped. He backed up into the light again. Callista's silhouetted head, bobbing with each step, froze.

"What is it?" she asked.

Hatcher didn't speak. He took in his surroundings, keeping his line of sight low just in case she'd been serious about not making eye contact.

Callista walked back toward him, pausing at the edge of the light. "You may as well tell me."

He realized the other one had addressed him by name, which was curious, but could have come from Deborah. But this one knew something else.

"How do you all know who I am? What my sign is?"

"I could say I guessed, but that wouldn't work, would it? Of course we all know about you, Mr. Hatcher. Word travels fast down here."

"You're not taking me to see Deborah, I gather."

"No."

He gestured into the distance with his chin. "This isn't where you take paying clients, is it?"

"You're just now figuring this out?"

"Then where, exactly, *are* you taking me?"

"You're a lucky man, Mr. Hatcher. I'm taking you to the actual PI. Not some pale facsimile. Pleasure Incarnate itself. A place you'll never forget. For the rest of your life."

The possibility, however remote, of putting an end to this and getting out of there flashed across Hatcher's mind, multiple overlapping scenarios of him dispatching Callista if she tried to interfere, knocking her out or breaking her neck or dragging her with him as protection, and it seemed no sooner had the thoughts appeared than two creatures lunged into the light. Each let out low, rumbling growls, hissing and snarling like wild beasts. Callista jumped forward between them and held a hand out to each side, blocking their path.

The first thing Hatcher noticed were the heads, which were too small for the necks but sat on jaws far too large for their skulls. Each creature was the size of a short, stocky man, with leathery gray skin, and long, muscular limbs. And breasts.

There was something batlike about their faces, small eyes set close together above sharp teeth. This was too much. Giant, muscular bats with tits.

They both growled, swaying. Straining at an unseen leash.

"I know what you're thinking," Callista said. "You're thinking perhaps it's best to take your chances now, see if you can fight your way out before things get worse. That would be quite foolish."

Hatcher looked at one of the Sedim. It started to spring forward as soon as he met its eyes. Callista's hand caught its shoulder, stopping it.

Hatcher focused on the woman, trying to control his heart rate. Every crisis involved an enemy, be it man, beast, or nature. Whatever these bizarre animals were, the rules still applied. And the first rule when confronting hostile forces was do not panic.

"Coming this far wasn't what I'd call the height of wisdom," he said, keeping his composure.

"Admit it, Mr. Hatcher. You're curious. You've never met women like us, never been so stimulated. Part of you is dying to know what lies ahead."

He glanced past her down the dark tunnel, keeping an indirect eye on the creatures. "It's the dying part that's throwing a wet blanket on the whole thing."

"But you're not afraid of dying, are you? It's failure that scares you."

"If failure was what scared me, I'd walk around one petrified son of a bitch."

"Not failure by other people's standards. Failure to accomplish whatever specific task you set out to do. It's your nature." She gestured with an impatient flick of her head. "Come. Do as I say. Time is wasting."

Hatcher took a breath, but didn't move. He tried to study

them—what she called the Sedim—from the edge of his vision. *Why do they react to eye contact?*

He mulled over what she'd said earlier. *They read minds.*

That begged the question. *So why do they react to eye contact?*

An answer was there, dancing in front of him. He could almost catch a glimpse of it.

"Mr. Hatcher, please."

Hatcher nodded, straightened himself. He stepped forward, passing cautiously between the two creatures as they moved slightly farther apart.

He was almost clear of them when he was certain. There was no room for error, but none for hesitation, either. He spun, throwing his foot out and catching the Sedim to his right across the side of the head with a heel kick.

The other creature leaped. Hatcher threw the hardest right he could, timing it like an inside fastball, and caught the thing flush on the jaw. It dropped to the ground.

Just as Hatcher had expected, the first creature, the one he had passed earlier, loped toward him, emerging from the darkness. Hatcher feinted to his right, leaning into the move, selling it with everything he could, committing to it, visualizing himself going that way. Then he planted his foot and cut left. The Sedim took one extra step before stopping, giving Hatcher an opening. He swung his fists down against its back, pushing the creature past him, and started to sprint.

He got ten feet before the other two were on him. Talons raked his skin. A hard, corded arm locked around his neck as he fell onto his forearms and his face smacked the ground. Snarls and grunts and hot breath pounded his ears. His throat was constricted, making it impossible to gasp at the sting of teeth digging like knives into his back. He swung an elbow, felt it connect. The teeth let go, then latched on again. He kicked and thrashed, feeling consciousness start to loosen and slip away as the arm tightened even more.

"Enough."

The word was immediately followed by some guttural commands, barked in a language Hatcher didn't understand. The back of his head bounced off the ground before he realized he had been released. He coughed and rolled onto his knees, rubbing at his neck, feeling the blood start to resume flow to his head.

That same voice, a woman's voice, spoke again. He realized it did not belong to his escort, and that he'd heard it before.

"At the risk of sounding like a cliché, you are either very brave or very stupid, Mr. Hatcher."

Hatcher swallowed, cleared his throat several times. "I've found the two tend to go hand in hand."

"It takes a wise man to realize that, so that gives me hope you are simply brave. That would be good, because the last thing I need right now is for you to be stupid."

Still massaging his throat, he turned his body toward the voice and got one foot beneath him to stand. He stopped as he saw Soliya step into the light.

Even in the bland, bleaching light shining down from the bulb above her, she had hair the color of a wheat field in a brilliant sunset, flowing in layers over her shoulders. The blue of her eyes reminded him of the ocean in space photos. She wore black boots and a black dress that formed two long triangles from her waist that traveled over each breast and met at a point behind her neck.

Her expression was completely neutral.

"Leave us, Callista."

Hatcher's escort glanced behind the other woman, as if spying something in the shadows, then looked at him and smiled. "I do hope we get to spend some more time together," she said, before turning and letting the darkness swallow her.

"Callista has never been known for her taste in men." The woman regarded Hatcher with a clinical gaze, like he was on a slide in a microscope. "You are confused. But your presence among us is no accident. I brought you down here for a reason."

"I came to find Deborah St. James." He coughed several times. "I have no idea who you even are."

"That is because you don't understand with whom or what you have become involved. Would it mean anything to you if I said I was a Carnate?"

"Before I could answer that, I'd need to know what the hell a Carnate was."

"Interesting choice of words. I do not wish to waste any more time, Mr. Hatcher. Come with me."

"And what if I don't want to?"

"I would tell you in that case I shall let the Sedim finish what they started, but I suspect that would simply harden your resolve. Please, Mr. Hatcher. Don't make this more difficult than it needs to be."

"If I go with you, will you take me to see Deborah?"

"I cannot do that, Mr. Hatcher."

"You wouldn't be going through all this trouble if you didn't need something from me. How about a show of good faith. Maybe proof that Deborah's alive."

"Your ignorance is astonishing. I would have thought someone with your . . . experience would be less easily manipulated. But as for a show of good faith, I anticipated a request of that sort."

Soliya stepped aside and gave a subtle gesture with her hand. A slight looking figure emerged from the darkness into the cone of light. At first, Hatcher thought it was a young girl, tall, but thin and prepubescent, sporting a head of lank black hair in a Prince Valiant cut. Then he realized it was a boy. Or male, at least, with shriveled genitals and soft, feminine features. The girlish boy was naked and pale. His skin seemed to give off a cobalt blue glow.

"I believe there's someone you've been wanting to speak with," Soliya said.

Hatcher looked at the frail figure, started to say something, but cut the words off as he saw the boy's skin shift beneath the aura, like a rubber sheath stretched tightly over a squirming body. Something pressed outward, a face, a chest and arms, straining against a film of liquid elasticity. A completely different visage was almost pressing through. Completely different, but almost as familiar as a reflection.

"Jacob Hatcher . . ." Soliya nodded vaguely toward the puerile body next to her. "Say hello to your brother, Garrett. He's traveled an awfully long way to be here. It's not like Hell is right around the corner."

CHAPTER 17

❖

WRIGHT WATCHED FROM HER CAR AS SHERMAN BACKED the truck up to the rear of Grace Church, parked it, and climbed down from the cab. The limo came to a stop a few yards away and a trim, distinguished-looking man whose face she immediately recognized stepped out and stood next to it, looking on. The man tossed Sherman a set of keys, then leaned back against the trunk of the car. Sherman walked behind the truck and out of view.

"That's Valentine," Reynolds said.

Wright pushed against the steering wheel, pressing herself back into the seat, thinking. They were across the street, two buildings away. The view was partially obstructed, but what she could see was suspicious enough. Truth was, anything involving Lucas Sherman was suspicious. The presence of Demetrius Valentine only made it more so. But suspicious in the real world and suspicious in court after lawyers got involved were two very different things.

"I think I read something about this," she said. "About him buying this church. He planned to renovate it, restore it. Said he was going to give it the diocese or something when he was through."

"Warms my heart. How much you want to bet they're up to no good?"

A sucker's bet, Wright thought, reaching for her purse. If Sherman was involved, they were up to no good. She didn't know what to make of Valentine.

"What are you doing?"

She riffled through her bag, pulled out a cell phone. "I'm calling Maloney. We need to get a real surveillance organized."

"And what if he says no?" His voice took on a smug, serious tone. "And he will say no."

"Is there something you want to tell me, Reynolds?"

"I'm just saying, if Maloney shuts us down, like I have a feeling he will, we'll never know what's going on. I told you, I don't trust him."

"Wait one giant second—when you said you didn't trust him, I thought you meant he might try to screw you over in the department, or something like that. Maybe he was holding back info. Are you seriously suggesting he's dirty? That he's on the take?"

"I'm not suggesting anything. I'm saying before we do anything else, we should find out more about what's going on, make it so no one can question whether we should move forward. Aren't you curious? I know I am."

"Okay, Supercop, what do you propose?"

He pointed through the windshield. "One of us circles around the other side of the church, sees if there's a way to peek inside. The other keeps an eye on our boys. We see if we can catch a glimpse of what they're up to in there. What they're unloading."

"Without a warrant?"

"This is a church, not his house. Where's his expectation of privacy?"

A misty rain started sprinkling over the windshield, blurring the various lights into starry shapes. "I don't know. Sherman is dangerous."

"I'm not scared of him." Reynolds pulled his arm back and patted his Glock. "All that muscle can't stop a bullet. We can silence our phones and text each other. Hopefully, I won't even have to go inside to get a look."

There was movement. The angle was bad, but Wright could see a large crate, about six feet by eight, being rolled off the back of the mover. Sherman was operating some kind of motorized hand truck. The sidewall of the cargo compartment blocked most of the view, with Wright only catching a glimpse as the crate crossed a loading ramp. It disappeared into the rear of the church, Sherman guiding it.

Reynolds hummed. A phony sound of surprise. "Well, Detective? Curious yet?"

"Okay. You win. But I'm the one who's going. You stay here. I'll look for a window. Text me if anything out of the ordinary happens. And no confrontations. Understand?"

"Completely."

"I sure as hell hope this doesn't bite us in the ass," Wright said.

"Aw, c'mon. You love this kind of thing. You have to. It's why people like us become cops, isn't it? It certainly isn't for the pay."

Wright said nothing. She wasn't sure she liked this new Reynolds. She realized she wasn't sure she'd liked the old one, either.

She got out of the car quickly. Reynolds slid over to take her place behind the wheel.

The light mist moistened her face as she hurried up the sidewalk. It took her a few steps before she was confident the church blocked any view Sherman or Valentine might have had. She slowed to a brisk walk and glanced back over her shoulder. Reynolds gave her a thumbs-up and she cut across the street.

An alley ran along the opposite side of the church, blocked by a wrought-iron fence set in several feet off the sidewalk. Wright stopped in front of the rope-twisted bars and tested the gate. Locked. She rattled it once, stared through the bars at the church windows. The big ones were stained glass. And high. The few that weren't twenty feet off the ground were tiny and opaque and very low. Basement windows. Trying to find a window to look through had been a stupid idea.

And Reynolds probably knew that. She stood there thinking about him for a few moments, then stepped back and glanced at the car. Reflections off the windshield made it impossible to see him, but she knew he could see her. It dawned on her that he never intended to just peek through a window, that it was just a pretext to put things in motion. She shook her head and scraped one index finger across the other in his direction. The little shit.

The rain started to fall a bit more heavily as she made her way to the front of the church. She climbed the stone stairs to a large pair of wooden doors set back in a portico. The handles to the doors were black iron, cold to the touch. She pressed a thumb latch. It didn't budge. She grabbed both handles and shook them.

Goddamnit.

She pounded the side of her fist against one of the doors and turned around.

Leaning back against the wood, she wondered why she was feeling so frustrated. But she knew the answer before she formed the question. It was because Reynolds was right. Sherman and Valentine were up to something, something definitely no good, and she wanted to know what.

The headlights of a passing car illuminated her as she circled back to the fence, stretching her shadow across the sidewalk, then snapping it back into darkness. She gave another look at the side of the building. A recessed side entryway was visible about halfway back, sunken, with a pair of rails descending down a short staircase.

There had to be a way to get back there.

Climbing the fence was not a realistic option. It was at least eight feet high, and she was in a skirt. And pumps. And not much of a climber.

The adjacent building was a general purpose structure, unmarked and dark. Probably belonged to the church at some point. She dismissed the idea. It would be locked, too, and even if it could get her behind the fence, there was no reason to believe the side entrance to the church wouldn't be.

An uncomfortable feeling swept over her as she realized she was wondering what Hatcher would do. That was ridiculous. Her brow tensed as she pushed the thought of him from her mind. The jerk. She couldn't care less what he would do. He was clueless. A clueless jerk.

Wright stood at the gate for a few more moments, staring through it, running mental traps. She had a habit of meticulously exploring all her options before reaching a decision. She wasn't about to give up and do nothing, not when Sherman was involved, so as she saw it there were only two choices. One was to try to get a warrant. That would take too long, another point she had to admit Reynolds had been right about. So really, there was only one. She would go back and get Reynolds, call for backup, and the two of them would go in and find out exactly what was going on. Let the lawyers fight it out.

Halfway across the street on her way to the car, she stopped and looked back. A sliver of pale yellow light knifed across the portico, falling from an opening between the doors.

She hesitated, then shot a glance over to Reynolds. She still couldn't see him through the windshield. The rain continued to thicken, drops audibly plopping off the sidewalk. Rivulets of water ran down her face and she wiped at her eyes. Trading looks between the car and the side of the church, she quickly cut across the street. The truck was still back behind the building, but no sign of Sherman or

Valentine as she made her way to the driver's-side door. That seemed a good thing at first, and she felt a bit of relief. But it didn't last long as she realized that meant she wasn't certain where they were.

The windows were streaked with water and the inside of the car was dark, but even with the rain making it so hard to see through the glass, she knew before she opened the door. The car was empty. Reynolds was gone.

Her eyes shot back to the front of the church. A glance up and down the street, one behind her, then back to the church again. Did he go inside? Was he the reason the door was cracked? How did he open it? How'd he get by her?

She stood in the opening between the driver's-side door and the car, getting drenched. *Think.* Maybe he hadn't seen her circle back to the side of the church to look through the fence the second time. Maybe he'd gone looking for her. Had she tried both handles at the entrance? Had she pressed down hard enough? Maybe he was in there, needing help.

Call for backup.

She glanced down into the car and stared at the radio beneath the dash. Backup for what? She had no idea where he'd gone.

Cell phone.

She retrieved her phone and punched in a quick text. She stopped just as she was about to send it. What if he was inside and hadn't set his phone to vibrate? He hadn't done it when she did. Not that she saw. That begged another question—why hadn't *he* texted *her* if he didn't know where she was?

The rain began to sheet. Wright shut the car door and darted toward the church, splashing through gathering puddles with short, rapid strides. She took the steps two at a time and paused only briefly at the front doors before pulling the open one wider and squeezing through as quietly as she could.

The change in surroundings was jolting. The damp and

wind and outside noise were all suddenly replaced by a hollow, almost sterile quiet, a solemn sense of space, of stillness. She moved further into the anteroom and peered down the aisle toward the distant altar. The church appeared empty, but the feeling in her bones told her otherwise. A church was one of those places that never felt empty, even when it was.

A small pool of water formed at her feet on the marble floor. She tried to shake off the excess before moving further. Without unholstering it, she placed a hand on the stock of her compact nine-mil. There was something about drawing a weapon in a church that didn't seem right.

She stepped forward into the nave, taking in her surroundings with a series of quick visual sweeps. Movement near the altar caught her eye, and she realized it had been more than just a feeling. She wasn't alone. She could make out a figure in a hooded robe, huddled down low, hunched over as if kneeling and bowing in prayer. She drew her pistol, held it low, arms extended, her left hand cupping her right, holding it steady.

Where the hell was Reynolds?

She tried to maintain area awareness as she moved closer to the person, keeping tension in her arms, her weapon in a ready position. As she drew within a few yards, she noticed a bouncing movement under the cloth, a rising, falling shudder. Whoever it was seemed to be sobbing. The slope of her back, the angle of her body, told her it was a woman.

"Police," she said, still moving closer, her voice low but clearly audible in the echoing quiet of the church. "I have to ask you to identify yourself. And to show me your hands."

The hood rose slowly, the face inside it obscured in shadow. Wright's fingers tightened around her weapon. The robed figure lifted its arms, and Wright saw delicate female hands, bound together with tie wraps. Wright reached forward and flipped the hood back, revealing the woman's face.

She drew back in surprise. The unmistakable double click of a hammer being cocked filled her ears. Before she could react, she felt the end of the barrel press against the back of her head. A hand closed around her upper arm like a vise, squeezing three fingertips into the nerve below her bicep so hard the entire side of her body seemed to go limp. By the time a squeaky whisper from behind told her to drop her weapon, it was already tumbling free.

Her gaze jumped to movement above her. A man leaned over the edge of an ornate pulpit protruding from an angled wall. The instant she recognized him, she felt a sharp, stabbing pain in her buttocks. She yelped and jerked her hips forward.

"Well, well, well. So glad you could join us, Detective," Valentine said, looking down at her. He flashed a broad smile, teeth sparkling like porcelain. "I was beginning to worry you wouldn't show."

HATCHER WATCHED THE SHAPE TWIST AND CONTORT BE-neath the glowing aura, the eyes of the host intermittently changing color. Changing *owner*. He wasn't certain whether he could trust his own eyes, and if he could, whether the form coming in and out of view was actually his brother.

"I . . . I'm glad I get to meet you, Jake," said a voice that didn't seem to quite come from the body.

Hatcher continued to stare, but didn't respond.

"Come now," Soliya said. "Don't you have anything to say to him? He's your flesh and blood. Or, was."

Hatcher turned his head toward her, his eyes lagging behind a bit as he peeled them off the spectacle pulsing in front of him. "This is some sort of trick."

Soliya's eyes danced. A short, bemused laugh escaped with her breath. "Feel free to test him. His memory will be limited, but it should be good enough to erase your doubts."

"I'm not falling for this."

"You're boring me, Mr. Hatcher. There's nothing to fall for. Talk to him."

A sickening air of fear and anxiety seemed to emanate from the boy. Hatcher could see it in the shifting expressions and undulating movements, could almost smell it, taste it. He was well acquainted with that mix of emotions.

"Why'd you get sent to Hell?" Hatcher asked, tossing the question out like he was making small talk.

"I don't know. They don't exactly tell you. Or maybe I just don't remember."

Hatcher glanced at Soliya, frowning.

"What's my—what's your mother's favorite animal?"

The boy's eyes seemed to close, though it was hard to tell through the bluish haze and stretched flesh. "My real mother, you mean? Our mother? Flamingos. She loves flamingos."

Okay, he thought. Score one. "What's it like? Hell?"

"I . . . I don't know."

Soliya spoke up. "Keep in mind he's been severely traumatized. Memories of actual life begin to fade immediately once the soul is in Hell's depths. What is retained is just enough to maximize emotional duress. Even after mere days, he would be completely incoherent, virtually insane once brought back. So the summoning is designed to block all that out. If he had any clear recollection of the torment now, you wouldn't even be able to converse with him."

"It's cold," the voice interjected, still eerily disembodied though appearing to come from the moving mouth of the figure. "A burning cold. I sort of remember that. And I remember it being so lonely. Like no one else exists. I just know I don't want to go back. Oh, *God*, I'd do anything not to go back."

Hatcher thought he could hear a sob in the voice. He turned to Soliya again. "This is ridiculous. I don't believe any of it."

Soliya wagged her chin. "You're not exactly asking him anything of substance."

The face pressed out again, a flash of light brown irises Hatcher had seen before. Every time he looked in the mirror.

Hatcher wasted no time striking the thought. This was absurd. *Just ask him something.*

"Do you remember how you died?"

"I remember being in traffic. There was a woman. I was trying to save her. Did I?"

"Yes."

A pause. "Guess it wasn't enough, huh?"

"Guess not."

"I did a lot of bad stuff in my day, Jake. Maybe, maybe I *do* know. Oh, God, yes, that's it. That stuff, I remember. I was a contractor. You know what I mean by that?"

"Like Blackwater?"

"Yeah. Just like that."

Hatcher nodded faintly. The so-called War on Terror had prompted new approaches to military operations, the extensive use of private security contractors being among them. They were well-paid mercenaries, tasked to do things the government didn't want the military being implicated in. Hatcher hated the whole notion of a War on Terror. You can't win a war with troops and weapons when the enemy is a concept. He hated the use of contractors, too. Not because they weren't good at what they did, but because they were. That led to bad strategy, winning battles while losing ground. Wars needed to be fought by soldiers, not mercenaries, and against enemies, not labels. Ideas don't die by bullets or bombs. They're defeated by will. You don't break your enemies' will by outsourcing.

He realized, though, that if any of this was real, you do apparently send those hired to do your dirty work to Hell.

"You're good," Hatcher said, turning to Soliya.

"Oh, I see. You still think this is some elaborate hoax. How predictably simpleminded of you. Regardless of whether you'd prefer to believe that, Mr. Hatcher, this is all very, very genuine."

"I wish it weren't, Jake," the maybe-Garrett said. "I can't tell you how much."

Hatcher started to move forward. He raised his hand, reaching toward the blue aura. "Let's just see about that."

"No."

Her voice was firm enough that Hatcher stopped. There was a quality to it that reached into his past, plucked at strings of experience, struck a jarring chord. It was that unnatural combination of urgency and calm. Like when someone was warning you your foot was about to trip a claymore. The experienced guys didn't raise their voices too much. Only enough to get you to pay attention. They didn't want you to jump at the sound.

"If you so much as touch him," she explained, "you'll share his fate."

"I don't understand."

"The damned are, for lack of a better description, un-clean. Once in Hell, a soul carries damnation like a plague. Touch him, and you'll be headed there when you die. No amount of repentance or faith or good works will change that."

"That's assuming I buy into any of this. Which I don't."

Garrett spoke up: "I'd listen to her, Bro. I don't know much about what's going on. I just know I'm completely fucked. I wouldn't want that for you."

To Soliya, Hatcher said, "Fine. Let's say I was to believe you. Why's he here? Why am I here? I think it's time you dropped the smoke and mirrors and told me what this is all about."

"He's here because I thought we might need to impress upon you the importance of the stakes. Those stakes are what this is all about."

"Stakes."

"Yes. Enormous ones."

"And what do these enormous stakes have to do with me?"

"That's an easy one, Mr. Hatcher." Her lips flattened and she gave him a sober, piercing look. "Everything."

CHAPTER 18

❖

WRIGHT BECAME VAGUELY AWARE SHE WAS BOUNCING.
Her eyes fluttered open. Bits and pieces of objects could be
seen through her hair as it swung across her face, the drier
strands puffed and fluttering. The side of her head and the
flat of her arms were slapping against a rounded surface.
At some point she realized it was a person's back. A man's
back. A very hard, very muscular back.

The bouncing stopped. Her head swooned as she felt herself flip, her upper body arcing backward, the world spinning in a circle, then changing directions as she slammed
down onto a mattress, rebounding off it slightly.

She was in a situation. She had to do something.

Her gun. She watched herself draw her weapon, roll off
the bed, double tap to center of mass. No time to waste.
Machinelike. The actions came without thought. Vault the
body, throw herself out the door, pistol at the ready. Down
the stairs two at a time, careful not to trip. Lose the shoes. Out
on the sidewalk now, pulling her badge, flagging down a car.

"It's so nice you're awake."

The voice pulled her back into herself. It was high, squeaky. She knew that voice, though she couldn't quite place it. She tried to lift her head. It lolled to the side, clusters of hair stuck stiff across her face. Where was she?

"Don't bother. You ain't going anywhere. I gave you a shot of flunitrazepam. I think that's how you say it. That's a fancy European name for roofies. They call it Darkene over there. Boss gets the stuff imported. In an alcohol solution, through a syringe, that junk is way powerful. You won't remember shit."

Her mind was swimming. The room was swaying, like she was on a ship. And why were her clothes damp? Was she at sea? On a boat? Maybe it was a sailboat, cruising the Hudson Bay.

"That's why it's a date rape drug, you know. Lots of drugs will make someone helpless. Combined with alcohol, this one also makes you forget. Odorless, tasteless. The perfect way to turn a glass of wine into a serious social lubricant."

The ceiling was squirming above her, the stucco swirling like liquid. What had she just been thinking? Something about shooting someone on a boat?

"Of course, I have little use for such stuff anymore."

That voice. She knew that voice. Kind of sweet, almost feminine. A cartoon voice. Mickey Mouse. Why was Mickey sitting on her bed?

"Do you know what you people did to me?"

Wait, this wasn't Mickey Mouse. She'd just imagined killing this person. Killing him, then getting out of there. He couldn't be Mickey Mouse. She wouldn't kill Mickey. M—I—C . . . K—E—Y . . .

"I had to take all kinds of testosterone just to get it up, that stupid drug treatment you all put me on. Doc says I overdid it, my body couldn't take the combination. Really fucked me up. Now I have to take all kinds of shit just to keep from growing tits and having my balls suck up into my crotch. Forget about getting wood. You fucking cops, you're somethin' else."

That's right, she was a cop. Of course. How silly of her. She had a gun, somewhere. Where was it again? All she had to do was find it. She wasn't sure why, but she knew she needed to. Maybe she would have to shoot someone. Maybe kill Mickey, after all. If he wasn't going to let her off this boat.

"Funny thing is, I still like girls. Still feel that tingly, eager feeling at the thought of a woman's body. I just have to get my kicks other ways now. Have to feed that need."

Wright felt the bed jiggle. She saw the blurry shape of a man standing next to it, one knee on the mattress. He was taking off his shirt. Wow. Mickey was one big mouse.

"I had pneumatic tubes installed. Little pumps stuck in my scrotum. Not quite the same as the real rex, can't get a nut or anything. But there's still that feeling of penetration, you know? That hard, slamming action. Gets my juices flowing for the other stuff."

Penetration. Oh, yes, she remembered that feeling. It had been fantastic. So spontaneous. So wickedly naughty. So wonderful. She hardly knew him, but the way he played her body. Hatcher, Hatcher, Hatcher. God, what a man.

"So what do you say, Lady Copper . . . Want to have some fun?"

Fun. Hmmm. What a fun word, *fun*. Fun sounded fun. But something felt weird. Wasn't she just thinking about shooting this guy? No, it must have been someone else. She'd never hurt Hatcher. Even if he did sound like Mickey Mouse.

THE TUNNEL SEEMED TO END AT THE LAST LIGHT, A WALL of blackness so thick it looked tangible. But Soliya walked up to it with a slight lean, as if she intended to keep going. The boyish figure, still glowing and undulating, stood nearby, looking anxious and confused.

"He is fading, if you haven't noticed," Soliya said. "We

need to keep moving. He'll be gone sooner if we stay this far away."

"You still haven't explained anything," Hatcher said.

"Come," she said.

Hatcher lost sight of her as she disappeared into the dense shadow. The boy followed, vanishing right after her, his glow snuffed out instantly. Hatcher paused at the threshold. The darkness that cloaked their way seemed somehow unnatural, liquid, like a pool of ink viewed from above.

He stuck his hand out, pierced the plane of it. Nothing.

Behind him, he heard a snarling grunt, harsh and low. Not very far away. A message, telling him to proceed. He let out a heavy breath and stepped forward.

A dank, fetid smell molested his nostrils. It took a moment for his eyes to adjust—a few extra seconds, given how they were watering—but he quickly sensed space around him. It was a cavern, vast and echoing. He blinked, testing his vision. It wasn't dark in the way the tunnel had been. There was a red incandescence gently illuminating his new surroundings, barely enough to see by. It seemed to cancel out the glow from Garrett's host, whom Hatcher could make out a few yards ahead.

As his eyesight grew more accustomed, he became aware of subtle movement. He glanced around. It wasn't easy to see at first, but if he focused on nothing in particular, it was hard not to notice. The distant walls of the cavern rippled and writhed.

Not the walls, he realized. Things on the walls. He looked back over his shoulder to the walls a few feet behind him, on either side of the opening he had passed through. Movement there, too, and these he could make out more clearly. They were like the creatures he encountered before, but even less humanlike. From what Hatcher could see, they looked like giant bats with small wings. They clung to the rocky sides of the cavern by the dozens. Hundreds, maybe. Bees in a hive.

"They are Sedim," Soliya said. She had stopped, blading her body to him and beckoning him to keep moving.

Hatcher said nothing.

"These are all juveniles. They lose their wings when they reach adulthood. They can't fly. But it does seem to allow them to leap from great heights."

The details were hard to make out, but Hatcher realized the floor of the cavern near the walls was littered with bones. Crescent-shaped ribs curving up from the ground, skulls piled like cannonballs. "That's a whole lot of demon chow for a herd like this. Purina must love you."

"Do you always try to mask your observations with wit? You're wondering how they are fed. An understandable question. They practically live on rats and table scraps. And, as you can see, each other, occasionally."

Hatcher's gaze wandered over the dark shapes. He imagined scores of eyes peering back at him. "Not to mention anyone who somehow manages to get this far without an escort."

"You catch on quickly," Soliya said, turning and starting to walk, but at a much slower pace, waiting for him to catch up. "Sometimes."

"I have my moments."

"Speaking of which, how did you know?"

"Know what?"

"That the Sedim couldn't really read minds? Of the people who've actually encountered them, you're quite possibly the first. They're usually quite convincing."

"Lucky guess."

"Skeptics like you don't believe in luck, Mr. Hatcher."

You're wrong about that, he thought. Hatcher had seen all manner of luck in his life, knew it played as much of a role in living or dying as anything else. More so, even. Dumb luck, blind luck, bad luck. He just didn't believe you could ever count on it. It was only something you could spot after the fact.

"The eyes," he said. "I knew there had to be a reason they

reacted to eye contact. I decided it was because they didn't want you watching them, watching you."

She started walking at a normal pace again. "Where were you planning to run? Or had you not thought things through that far?"

"That lighting near the elevator was way too bright. There had to be a reason. I was betting it was a firewall to keep the whatever-you-call-them from getting to the surface. The eyes again. It must hurt them."

"You've got some wits about you, Mr. Hatcher. I'll grant you that."

"Not enough to figure you out what the hell you are. What the hell any of you are."

She stopped walking. Reaching a demure hand toward his head, she rubbed her fingers over the side of his scalp, through his short hair. Her scent invaded his nostrils like a conquering horde. For a moment, he thought he was going to ejaculate in his pants.

"We're just women, Mr. Hatcher. Women who happen to be physically perfect in every way. Can't you tell a woman's touch?"

Hatcher took hold of her wrist and gently lowered her hand from his head. "Physically perfect?"

Soliya nodded. "Lacking in any cellular or genetic defects, precisely proportioned. Immune to all disease. Virtually impossible to kill."

"How is that possible?"

"You might call it hybrid vigor."

"What sort of hybrid?"

She started moving again, gestured for him to follow. "What do you know about demons, Mr. Hatcher?"

"I have a feeling less than I'm about to."

"Demons and angels are the same creatures, did you know that? Demons are merely the fallen ones, transformed—disfigured, some would say—by their separation from Heaven. They are brilliant, beautiful, dark, complex beings. Sworn enemies of mankind."

"I'm sure they're a hit wherever you take them."

"Ah, but there's the thing. They're relegated to Hell. Summoning a demon is very difficult. Spontaneous ascent is even more rare. A demon cannot remain corporeal for very long."

"You know what they say about fish and visitors."

"But as bitter rivals of Heaven," Soliya continued, ignoring him, "demons strive to wreak havoc among that most beloved creature of Creation: people."

"I'm going to guess this where you come in."

"In a manner of speaking. You may not know this, but demons and angels are capable of mating with humans. One in ten of the offspring are perfect human specimens in every way but one. They have no soul."

"Perfect human specimens. In other words, Carnates?"

"Yes."

"What about the other nine?"

She waved a hand, vaguely indicating the shadowy forms occupying the walls. "They are creatures like the ones you encountered earlier. Magnificent in their own way, but hardly humanlike."

"You're telling me you, and these other women . . . you're the product of this kind of crossbreeding?"

"Yes."

"So, you're basically demons. All of you."

"No. The hybrid offspring of demons. Transcendent. Like the ultimate slap in God's face. Human in every way. Perfect in every way."

"Except for the soul."

She nodded. "Except for the soul."

"In that case, what happens when you die?"

"We cease to exist. Fortunately for us, our biological perfection allows us to live for an average of seven generations."

"That's a lot of twenty-ninth birthdays."

"Not so many, when compared to the eternity afforded the rest of humanity. In the afterlife."

Hatcher let his gaze slide over her face, took in the flawless curves of her body. "What if I don't believe in demons, or angels, or Heaven, or Hell, or the immortality of the soul?"

"Yes, of course, the man too clever to believe in anything. Only a fool quarrels with a fact, Mr. Hatcher. But whether you believe or not has no bearing on the reality of their existence. This is not a philosophy class."

"As terribly intriguing as this is, I'm more inclined to think one of us is insane," Hatcher said.

"Clinging to skepticism is rather juvenile, under the circumstances. Face the evidence, Mr. Hatcher. Your dead brother's soul is present a few feet away, you've felt the teeth and claws of creatures that are the offspring of demons tear at your flesh. There is nothing rational about refusing to accept as true what you experience firsthand."

He had to admit she had a point. This had gone way beyond the possibility of an elaborate ruse. Still, just because he'd witnessed some rather bizarre and inexplicable things, it didn't mean everything he was being told was true. In fact, he thought it made the questioning of it all even more important.

The path they were following seemed to end, the red glow giving way to another black wall. Garrett, or what was supposed to be him, walked at an anxious pace, heading into the darkness without looking back. Soliya appeared about to follow, then stopped and turned. At the periphery of the shadow, throngs of clinging creatures vied for position, dim forms nudging and nipping at each other, like giant wall rats.

"I hope you're not foolish enough to try anything," she said. "Or anything *else*, I should say."

"I still don't see where I fit in," Hatcher said.

A blink of a smile creased her cheeks, then she stepped forward and disappeared. Hatcher moved closer, peered into the tarry divide, half expecting someone or something to reach out and grab him, seeing nothing. The scraping, shuffling sound of movement behind him grew louder. He resisted the urge to look. He was on his own. It stood to reason some of the creatures surrounding him now considered him fair game.

He hesitated, then took a step and pierced the darkness, waiting for it to wash over him, and just as quickly found himself squinting and shading his eyes at the sudden light. An almost panoramic scene stretched before him, colorful images of glistening water and ornate foliage. Beautiful women in flowing garb. Mirthful conversation and laughter bubbled its way up in soft echoes and every breath carried the scent of spring water and wildflowers, spiked with the unmistakable tang of food and drink and sex. He knew immediately this place was like nowhere he'd been. An understanding quickly settled in. Only one word seemed to describe its organizing theme, its unifying purpose.

Pleasure.

CHAPTER 19

❈

WRIGHT HEARD THE SONG RING OUT, LIKE A CLOCK RADIO
trying to wake her up. She knew that song. "Dirty Deeds
Done Dirt Cheap." She smiled. Who knew Mickey Mouse
liked AC/DC?

Did Hatcher? He had to. All men liked AC/DC. All real
men, at least. And Hatcher was definitely a real man.

The music ended abruptly, and Mickey said something.
Was he speaking to her? No, she decided, though she wasn't
sure why. He was the only one she could hear. Maybe he
was talking to Hatcher.

Her panties were down around her knees. Mickey had
been helping her get undressed. She reached down and
pulled them up, unbunching them. Thong panties. Why
had she worn them? Oh, that's right. Because of *him*. She
realized she was giggling. How naughty she had been. Was
going to be.

But, where was he? Hadn't Hatcher been there a moment ago? Weren't they about to get it on, just like before?
He must have had to leave. Maybe Mickey knew where he

went. Maybe he could tell her when he'd be back. After he got done talking to himself.

Mickey said something, and she heard a beep. Phone call! Of course! The idea popped into her head, just like that. Mickey had been on the phone.

"Looks like the fun is going to have to wait," he said.

Wait, she thought. Yes, wait. Another idea just popped in there. Wait, wait, wait. That's not Mickey. It's just Mickey's voice.

"That psycho son of a bitch has got some kind of ESP or something, I swear. But don't worry, we'll still be having that fun later."

Wright smiled and hummed, losing her train of thought for a moment. Fun. Fun was good. She and Hatcher were going to have so much fun. But Hatcher was gone, and she certainly wasn't going to have fun with *him*. What was that thought that just flashed? This man, his name. Lucas?

No, couldn't be. She closed her eyes and rolled onto her side. Lucas was the name of a bad guy. This was a giant mouse named Mickey. She repeated that to herself as she drifted off. Trying to think was too tiring. She needed to rest now. Mickey must know where Hatcher went. He told her they were going to have fun later, that must have been what he meant.

Then she'd be part of the club. She'd heard him say so.

"WELCOME TO PLEASURE INCARNATE."

Hatcher rubbed his eyes, clenching them shut. He was standing on a ledge, high above an enormous open space. Above, he saw what looked like blue sky, with puffy white clouds punctuating the vista in bursts of floating cotton. The light was intense, tinged with that brilliance of late afternoon sunshine that artificial light can never seem to match. But he knew it couldn't be real, any of it. It was the middle of the night, probably three or four a.m., and he was dozens, if not hundreds, of feet underground.

But it sure as hell looked real.

The area was gargantuan, a gaping expanse of circular space, with Doric columns rimming the perimeter, redolent of a Roman coliseum. Discrete points of activity were everywhere, tiny groupings of people, knots of women as far as he could see, standing in tight clusters or lounging in conversation, pairs and trios sampling trays of food and wine. A number were openly engaged in sexual activity of various sorts, seeming unabashed and casual about it.

"Are you just going to stand there?" Soliya asked.

To his left, a set of stairs descended from the ledge, carved from the wall of earth. Soliya was almost halfway down, turned partly back to face him, straddling two steps.

He descended the stairs, taking in everything he could. The flattening angle caused his view to contract with each step.

As he left the final step, he spied a pair of cream-skinned blondes a few yards away. Centerfold quality, nubile and lean, flicking their tongues over each other's bodies, rubbing and penetrating each other's vaginas, wearing the bunched remains of togas around their waists but nothing else as they kissed and writhed on a daybed surrounded by ferns and enormous flowers of blue and purple and yellow. They glanced over at him, one, then the other, and smiled. The one on top held out a finger toward him and curled it back.

Soliya reached over and stroked his chin, gently turning his head. "Normally, I would suggest you take up any invitations to mingle and enjoy yourself. But I'm afraid we haven't much time."

Hatcher started to respond, but then stopped himself. He raised his eyes and took in the sky. He knew it wasn't real, that it couldn't be. It didn't even look real. Not because it looked fake, but because it looked more real than any sky he'd ever seen, or remembered ever seeing—more deeply hued, more halcyon, more perfectly clouded. The sky in a dream. A fairy-tale sky. An illusion of sky.

"It's amazing what you can buy," Soliya said. "If you have enough money. I saw one of these in a mall in Las Vegas a decade ago. An almost perfect simulation. I decided we needed one. Only ten times better. Come."

Something about what she said didn't seem right, but before he could form a thought around it, the blue glow of what he was starting to think of as his brother caught his eye. The effeminate boy, skin stretching and straining, was standing next to a woman who was hunched over a large bowl on a pedestal. The woman was an alabaster-skinned brunette. Like all the women he'd seen, she looked fit, somewhere in her late twenties or early thirties, and very, almost ridiculously, attractive. Soliya headed toward them.

The woman raised her eyes from the bowl and gave a barely perceptible shake of her head before dropping her gaze.

"You need to say your good-byes," Soliya said, coming to a stop near the boy.

Garrett's face pressed through, a look of panic contorting its shape. "Already? I feel like I have a much better hold now, being close like this."

"I know how difficult this is, but you can't stay any longer."

"But it's . . . I've only been here . . ."

"Why does he have to go back now?" Hatcher asked. As soon as he spoke the words, he felt as if he were being co-opted. Fooled into being an accomplice to his own deception.

"Because Willow can't last much longer." She gestured to the brunette. The woman was staring into the bowl. She did not look up again. She seemed to sway slightly, a sapling in a breeze. "The connection can only be maintained for so long. One has already made the ultimate sacrifice for you to have this chance. I won't allow for another."

No one said anything else for a long moment. The silence became awkward.

"Can you bring him back later?" Hatcher asked.

"No. I'm afraid it's just not possible."

Hatcher's gaze darted to Garrett. He still wasn't sure what to believe, but the panic in those eyes was real. That much he knew.

"I guess I should be grateful I had a chance to meet you," Garrett said. His voice was strained, someone putting up a front.

Hatcher nodded grimly, unable to find words. What do you say to the damned? Take care? Good luck?

He finally settled on, "I'm sorry."

Garrett managed a weak smile. Through the bulging and undulating skin, it looked like a clown's grimace.

"Me, too."

Hatcher felt like he needed to extend a hand, maybe give a hug, something—but Soliya stuck an arm out across his chest.

The woman at the bowl twitched, jerking her head back, gasping a breath.

And then the boy's skin snapped back into place. The glow disappeared instantly. The air was filled with an abrupt sense of change, like a room having its power cut off, or a car stalling. Something Hatcher hadn't realized was even present, a feeling of energy, a hum in his spine, was suddenly missing.

The boy flopped forward onto the ground without so much as an arm out to break his fall. That kind of collapse only meant one thing. Soliya's words now struck him. The ultimate sacrifice.

Jesus.

He'd been wrong, and he knew it. A flood of questions raced through his mind, questions he wanted to ask his putative brother, starting with how and why he had grabbed him from his casket, if that even was him doing it. Questions that now would never be answered.

Garrett was gone, and though he wasn't certain why, Hatcher suddenly felt very alone.

"Now, Mr. Hatcher," Soliya said. "Before anyone else is sent to their final reward, let me tell you about Deborah."

VALENTINE SET THE HANDSET OF HIS PHONE DOWN INTO its cradle, relishing his good fortune. Despite Sherman making an occasional mistake, and despite having to get harsh with his well-paid cop for going off script, things were falling into place perfectly. Truly, this was fate unfolding, coming to a head. The feeling was beyond exhilarating. It was pure adrenaline.

So much planning, time measured in years, money measured in small-nation GDPs. So much energy, so much focus. It seemed like every waking moment of his adult life, and a good number of sleeping ones, had been consumed by this goal. Fueled by it. And what a goal it was. He knew few could even conceive of the scale on which he was plotting. Even fewer would believe anything like it was remotely possible.

And no one—no one—could possibly hope to achieve such a thing. It was beyond rational thought.

But he was about to pull it off. He could sense it in his bones, taste it in the air. Momentum was with him. Events seemed driven by the inertia of inevitability, like he was riding a wave of destiny.

And, of course, there was the book—the book knew. The book didn't lie.

His biggest enemy now, he realized, was complacency. Destiny was will manifested through effort. People could be controlled, manipulated, but someone had to be pulling the strings, making the right decisions, keeping the object in mind, relentlessly working toward a vision. If there was one thing the book had taught him, it was that destiny was a blueprint, not a preordainment. Mistakes could still be made. Outcomes could still change. Keeping his eye on the prize was critical, as was not letting up. Not even a little. He would not fall prey to traps laid by fate's fickle fingers.

He would redouble his efforts in light of his success. Nothing would be left to chance.

He left his study and took his private elevator to the subfloor of his penthouse. The Clinic. This was where the real work took place, where the tools of his obsession were put to use. His laboratory equipment, including some of the finest gene-splicing technology available, was set up in a clean room more sterile than any Silicon Valley production line. His computer array, rivaling the processing power of a NASA control station, took up almost half the floor. His surgical lab was suitable for performing everything from exploratory operations to heart transplants.

Almost nine figures invested in this floor. Two PhDs imported on temporary work visas from India at a cost of several more million. Finding them was almost as expensive. They had to be the kind that no one would miss. Staff without knowledge had been pink-slipped almost a year ago. People more intimately involved in the work had been silenced permanently by Lucas. He was never one to place stock in faith. Two men could keep a secret if one of them was dead.

And now it was all paying off.

The process was simple in concept, but incredibly complex in execution. Human DNA, extracted from bone marrow, was injected into the pineal gland of the subject fetus. A form of gene therapy was applied as the fetus developed, and specific DNA markers were incorporated into the chromosomes. Such genetic recombination was crucial, as this unprecedented achievement—a true interspecies chimera—had to have specific traits. Foremost among them was the ability to reproduce.

And to be a male. That was key.

Daunting as the challenge was, the problem was further complicated by the fact human DNA did not recombine with the particular host species as it needed to. It was as if a defense mechanism was encoded in the genetic material, preventing the very thing he was trying to accomplish. He had come to think of it as Heaven's firewall, and modeled himself a determined hacker. He attacked the problem assiduously, refusing to be deterred. The answer came gradually, through trial and error, facilitated by some intuitive guesswork, and refined through large-scale bio-testing in Asia. The key was in isolating the problem codes. Different coding produced different results, derailing at different points in the process. It was only when he utilized swine and simian strings at certain markers that he was able to smash the barrier. He realized afterward that he hadn't actually believed he could accomplish it, not until he finally did. A true chimera. Part human, part animal, part Sedim.

Mostly Sedim. The spawn of a demon, unlike any other. A sexually functional male. A male capable of reproduction with a human female.

Valentine walked the hall with purposeful strides. Each floor of the building was large enough to house a good-size law firm, but Valentine had designed this one with the functionality of a research facility. He passed various special-purpose rooms on his left, the computer room on his right, traveling the wide hallway that bisected the floor in each direction. The corridor ended at a stainless-steel, double-wide door. It sported an external set of dual, offset actuating rods with corresponding bores. Few banks had vaults guarded by a locking mechanism as advanced.

A retina scanner protruded from the wall next to the door. Valentine leaned into it, staring as a beam passed over his right eye. A light above the console flashed green, coinciding with a soft beep. A deep hum rose, followed by the heavy groan of metal disengaging.

The area beyond the door was like a small prison dayroom, with small cells on each end. The wall opposite the entrance was solid Plexiglas. Valentine liked this room. It was so corporate, so functional, like an executive lounge. A very comfortable place to observe test subjects. Or captives.

On the other side of the Plexiglas wall, in a bare room, bodies of Sedim lay on the floor.

"Are they all dead?" Valentine asked. He circled the large conference table in the middle of the room, peering through the partition, hunting for movement.

Deborah did not look up. She was sitting on the table, more or less in the middle of it, wearing only a lacy set of bra and panties, propped up on one arm behind her. One of her legs had a creamy lather on it, and she was pulling a razor up her shin, over her bent knee.

"All but three," she said. "And they won't last another few hours."

Valentine nodded. He watched the bodies, studying their inanimate faces. Bony, ridged brows, exposed nostrils in the manner of bats, primate musculature. It was hard to believe they were genetically almost the same creature as the one sitting on his table a few feet away, tending to her buttery skin.

"It's happening tonight," he said.

"Are you sure?"

"Yes."

Deborah dipped the razor in a small bowl of water next to her, shook it until it stopped dripping. She eyed Valentine for a long moment. "Are you ready?"

"Oh, yes. Just make sure you are. We will need a substantial show of force. He's no idiot. Speaking of idiots, how's our friendly detective?"

"Smitten, of course." She lowered her eyes back to her leg. "You'd think he'd never had sex in his life."

"Just make sure he sticks with the game plan."

"I wouldn't worry."

"That's why you're not me."

Deborah ignored the remark, stroking the razor along the inside of her calf.

"He's down there now," Valentine said, leaning against the glass. "Learning all about you. Just as I said he'd be."

"Such a waste. He's a man I might actually have enjoyed bedding."

"Pity for you." Valentine gestured toward one of the cells with his chin. "How's our young lady of the cloth?"

"Quiet as a church mouse."

"Let's hope she stays that way." He turned his attention to the Sedim, watching for signs of life. "Only hours to go."

Deborah crossed her wrists over her knee, rested her chin on the back of her hand. "You're awfully confident about Hatcher. How do you know he'll show?"

Valentine drummed his fingertips against the glass, staring at the bodies. Two of them were moving now, one twitching occasionally, the other clawing pointlessly, as if trying to drag itself somewhere.

"Do you recall the parable about the scorpion and the frog?"

Deborah took in a breath, exhaled with a sigh. "Vaguely."

Seven generations, Valentine thought, smiling. Carnates were highly intelligent, and learned quickly, but invariably lacked intellectual curiosity. Few in his experience ever read anything more substantial than a billboard. They mimicked refinement, erudition, but internalized little. For centuries, people have wondered what immortality would be like, but Valentine figured he had a good idea, acquainted now with a race that lived seven times longer than normal humans. Seven generations was close enough for him to know what that kind of longevity breeds. Laziness. When every one of you has seven lifetimes to accomplish everything, no one accomplishes anything.

"A scorpion was trapped on a riverbank," Valentine said. "He called to the frog, asking to be given a ride on the frog's back, across the river. Oh no, says the frog, if I let you on my back, you'll sting me and I'll die. Now, why would I do that, says the scorpion. If I sting you, then I'll die, too. The frog thinks about it and decides the scorpion's logic makes sense, so he paddles over and allows the scorpion to climb on his back. Not even halfway across the water, the scorpion stings him."

Behind the glass, one of the Sedim twitched, rising off the floor, then collapsing.

Valentine glanced in the direction of the movement. "Why did you do that? the frog asks. Now we're both going to die. I can't help it, says the scorpion. It's my nature."

A half-amused smirk appeared to tease the side of Deborah's mouth. "So you're saying Hatcher is like the scorpion, huh? That's how you know?"

"No. I'm saying Hatcher is the frog. Always wanting to believe there's someone worth saving. Even when it means sacrificing himself."

Valentine stepped closer to the glass, spied the Sedim that had shot up, concluded it had been a death throe. It hadn't moved since. "Himself and, as it turns out, everyone else."

HATCHER STARED AT THE BODY WITH THE TINY PENIS AND little-girl breasts. Had the boy known he was going to die? Had he not cared?

"His kind are natural conduits," Soliya said. "But they cannot survive the ordeal.

"You killed him."

"The situation is desperate. You wouldn't believe us without proof."

"I still don't believe you."

"Why? Because I'm saying that Deborah is not who you think she is? Believe it. If there's one thing I can assure you to be true, it's that."

Hatcher's eyes were still on the boy's body. *His kind.* There had been something off about him, about the way he seemed unconnected to his surroundings. Mildly autistic, maybe. But who knew what kind of mindfuck they'd put him through.

"If this is some kind of hoax, you really are one twisted bitch."

"It's no hoax. That was really him. That was really Garrett."

"Even if I were to accept that, I'm still not convinced he is—*was*—my brother."

"Yes, you are. The blood bond between brothers is powerful. It often transcends time and distance. It can be sensed."

Hatcher said nothing. The woman from the water bowl seemed to have recovered. She was joined by another, a tawny, exotic type, Mediterranean of some sort, who led her away, dabbing at her nose with a cloth, soaking up the blood. Hatcher watched them walk off. They passed behind other gaggles of women and disappeared from view.

"Time, as I said before, is crucial, Mr. Hatcher. We need to proceed."

"Proceed with what?"

"The reason you're here."

"Why don't you start by telling me, then we'll both know."

Soliya walked over to a nearby bench. It was large, with white leather cushions. She lowered herself elegantly onto it. "You're here because of Demetrius Valentine."

"You said that." Hatcher mulled the name, remembered Susan had mentioned it. But that was all. "Is that supposed to mean something to me?"

"It should. But I'm not surprised it doesn't. Something tells me you don't pay attention to such things. Mr. Valentine is a very wealthy, very powerful man. One of the richest men in the country, if not the world."

"Okay. So, he's got more money than God. What does he have to do with me?"

"Funny you should mention God. Valentine lost his parents at an early age. He was raised by an aunt who was devoutly religious. His parents, especially his father, had been atheists. Notorious, outspoken atheists. After they were killed in an automobile accident, his aunt told him his parents had gone to Hell, would never let him forget it. She tried to give him a religious education. The religious part didn't take, but the teachings did. He became obsessed with the notion of his parents being tormented in Hell, devoting every moment of free time he had to finding a way to bring them back. The wealthier he became, the more determined he got."

"You sound like you know him pretty well."

Soliya shrugged. "Well enough. Valentine sought us out years ago. He was intriguing. A man of means with an intensity, a tenacity, like few I've ever seen. Resourceful enough to find out things about us, about who we were. He wanted to learn about summoning the souls of the damned."

"I'm guessing things didn't turn out too well between you."

"After the initial suspicion wore off, the relationship was mutually beneficial. He had resources we needed. We provided him insight no book ever could. It was a marriage of convenience."

"But?"

"But what he wanted was out of the question. He was very secretive about his goals at first. When he finally revealed them, we attempted to reason with him, to tell him it simply couldn't be done. But he refused to accept that as an answer. He would not rest, so long as they were in Hell."

Hatcher turned to look back at the boy. His body was gone. There was no sign it had ever even been there.

"So you're saying this guy Valentine got it in his head that he could bring his parents back?" He waved a hand toward the water bowl. "Why didn't you just do it for him? You keep insisting this little dog-and-pony show you put on was real."

"Summoning a newly damned soul is one thing. Permanently retrieving a soul long banished to Hell is another. After a few weeks, damnation's hold is too great. Even now, a soul such as your brother's can only be retrieved for a matter of hours. He knew most of this long before he found us. He wanted more than to talk to his departed parents. Much more. He wanted revenge."

"Against whom?"

Soliya held his gaze for a long moment, unblinking. She swept her arm out with a flourish. "Everyone."

VALENTINE UNLOCKED THE CELL DOOR AND LET IT SWING shut behind him. The cell was a ten-by-ten square, walls and floors of reinforced concrete, painted a medium gray. There was a metal toilet in one corner, a steel shelf large enough for a twin mattress bolted to one wall.

The young woman was sitting on the floor against the back of the cell, her wrists manacled, hanging by a chain secured to the wall just above her head, forming an upside-down V. Her legs were angled to the side, one beneath the other. She wore a habit, but without a veil. Her long blonde hair spilled over her shoulders.

Valentine knelt next to her and smoothed several stray strands of blonde from her face. A number of them peeled off her cheek, stuck in the moisture from her dried tears.

"If I were to tell you I really don't wish to hurt you, would you believe me?"

The woman was not looking at him, but turned her head away even further.

"You think I'm evil. That's understandable. But what is evil, really? Killing? Causing death? When acts of God kill thousands, do we call Him evil? No, we say He works in mysterious ways. But what we're really saying is, when you have enough power, you can do what you want."

A few sniffles, then a sob. She closed her eyes tightly, buried her face against her sleeve.

"Someone like you is filled with love for God, but has He really ever earned it? We call someone who is devout *God-fearing*. If God is so wonderful, why should anyone fear Him? He makes people love Him, through threats and intimidation. If you don't, He sentences you to eternal hell-fire. That's not love. That's terrorism. That's egomania."

She swallowed. Her voice cracked a bit when she spoke. "You're wrong."

"Ah, found your tongue, have we? I'm afraid I'm not, my dear." Valentine pulled back, allowing her some space. "But give me your best pitch."

"God loves everyone," she said, giving him a sideways glance, almost peeking from behind her arm. "People don't go to Hell because He wants them to; they go to Hell because they refuse to accept His Grace."

"Oh, is that so? And what of people who live and die without ever being shown the Gospels? What about aboriginal tribesmen and native islanders who never heard the name Jesus Christ? What about people raised in other religions. Does he love them, too? Or to Hell with them, so to speak?"

"That is why we must spread the Word. So their blood will not be on our hands."

"But the ones you don't reach, just tough luck for them, huh?"

The woman said nothing.

Valentine stroked her cheek, hooking a finger beneath her jaw and coaxing her chin out from behind her arm. "Don't worry, my child. I'm going to change all that. I'm going to level the playing field."

He propped the point of her chin between his thumb and the first knuckle of his forefinger, like he was holding a teacup, prodding her until she looked at him. Tears welled over as she blinked, dropping to the cloth of her habit.

"You have an illness," she said softly. "You're a lost soul. I pray for you. I pray for your salvation."

"That's quite touching. Unfortunately, I can't return the favor."

"Your hatred has consumed you."

"What does that even mean? Consumed me? I find such banalities insulting. That would be like me telling you religion is a myth. Please, Sister, come up with some original material."

"It means, it has destroyed everything else about you, like a fire."

Valentine's features hardened. "You see, that's where you're wrong. The other parts of me were destroyed already. The hatred merely moved in to take their place."

"What do you want with me?"

"That, my dear, is exactly the kind of question you should be asking." He reached into his pocket, removed a linen handkerchief. He dabbed at her cheeks with it. "You are pure, virginal. Holy. You are the perfect sacrifice."

"Killing me will not bring you peace. Or power. Satan does not reward his followers in the hereafter. That is the Great Lie."

"But I don't want peace. And I fully expect to go to Hell, as things stand now."

"What do you want, then? Why are you doing this?"

"What do I want? I want God to reboot, that's what."

Valentine stood, folded the handkerchief, and placed it back into his pocket. "And you, my dear, are going to help me crash His system."

EVERY WOMAN HATCHER GLIMPSED SEEMED TO MAKE EYE contact with him as he passed. Many were engaged in sexual acts with one another, and those who weren't gave off a vibe like they recently had, or were about to.

"Are you gals always this . . . congenial with one another?"

Soliya glanced over her shoulder. "Certain times of the year are observed by tradition. Right now, we are in the midst of the Liberalia, the Great Bacchanalian Festival."

His gaze wandered. A redhead lifted her eyes to meet his as she tongued the clit of a tanned and firm woman with raven black hair. He wasn't certain which one was more attractive.

"And you celebrate with orgies?"

"We're sexual creatures, Mr. Hatcher. We celebrate our sexuality. Don't you?"

The chamber was enormous. Soliya made her way through a maze of debauchery, gatherings of beautiful women pleasuring each other on pillowed furniture, laughing over glasses of wine, showering, naked and joyful, beneath a rocky waterfall. On a far wall, between two majestic columns, a black space like a tunnel entrance came into view. Hatcher trailed a few steps behind. Just as before, she stepped into a darkness that seemed to swallow her. He hesitated only briefly before following, figuring there was no sense in worrying about her intentions now. If she'd wanted to kill him, she could have just left him for those things.

The darkness gave way to a bluish glow. He couldn't see clearly at first, but gradually a much smaller chamber came into view, roughly the size of a high school gymnasium. In the center was a large wheel-shaped stone, laid on its side. Three women lounged around it on small mounds of cushions and pillows, studying Hatcher intently. Gorgeous women, he noted.

"Is this him?" one of them asked, slowly rising to her feet. A honey blonde. She wore the same kind of white togalike dress most of the others did. She held a cylinder in her hand, low and at an angle, brandishing it in a way that told Hatcher it was likely a weapon.

Soliya approached the stone platform. "Yes."

Hatcher's vision continued to adjust. As he drew closer, what lay atop the stone gradually came into view. He stopped a few feet away. This one was most definitely a weapon, a small sword of some kind.

Soliya swept a hand. "This is the Dagger of Cain."

"Cain?" Hatcher took another step, keeping an eye on the other women, who were obviously keeping an eye on him. "As in, am-I-my-brother's-keeper Cain?"

"Yes."

Hatcher leaned forward and studied the object, examined its lines, its roughly forged metal. Weapons, he knew. He straightened his back and shook his head. "Sorry to break this to you, but this was made long after biblical times."

"You're sharp, Mr. Hatcher. But I didn't say it was the dagger used by Cain. Cain didn't even use a dagger, truth be told. This was, as you noted, crafted long after his time. It is called the Dagger of Cain for another reason."

"What reason is that?"

Ignoring the question, Soliya stepped toward a stone outcropping, walking a tight line with the hip sway of a swimsuit model. One of the other women moved swiftly to place a cushion beneath her as she lowered herself onto it. Only after she sat did Hatcher realize it was chair—a throne, almost—carved from the rock.

She crossed her legs and eyed Hatcher for a several seconds before speaking. "There are some things you need to understand."

"Oh, you think?"

"You are being manipulated, Mr. Hatcher. You have been since you stepped foot in New York."

His gaze drifted back to the women, brushing over them one at a time. Two blondes and a brunette, each with skin he could almost taste. "Tell me something I don't know."

"This is no time to be flip. A number conspire against you."

"Well, if there's a point to get to, I'm ready for it whenever you are."

"Deborah was—is—one of us."

"I'm shocked."

"She left us—an intolerable act in itself, I must say—and has been assisting Valentine."

"If you're trying to break it to me that you tried to kill her at the hospital, I already figured that out."

"Then I'm sure it occurred to you that the hospital wasn't the first time."

Hatcher let her words sink in. "That's how Garrett died. You killed him. Trying to kill her."

"He couldn't help himself," she said, interlacing her fingers and forming a steeple. "He was like you. He had to try to save the day."

"The guy he was trying to stop, he was already dead."

Soliya nodded.

"How the heck does that work?"

Her lips pushed out in a pout and her cheeks sunk slightly inward. Hatcher realized these women had two kinds of looks. Sexy and sexier.

"Our connection to the other side affords us certain abilities. Making contact with what you know as Hell is one of them. Animating the recently deceased is another."

Protect her. A subtle shift in understanding rearranged his thoughts. Deborah had done that, from the bathroom. Used him. Probably had used Garrett somehow, too.

"She'd been following him," Soliya added.

"Why?"

"At some level, you must know."

Hatcher said nothing. His attention shifted back to the dagger on the platform.

"You're here because we need your help." Soliya said. "We need you to stop Valentine."

"Stop him from doing what?"

"From upsetting the balance between salvation and damnation, from summoning Belial, the Lord of the Underworld."

"And just how would he manage that?"

"Have you ever heard of the Book of Thoth?"

"The book of *what*?"

"Thoth. A god of ancient Egyptian myth. Actually, he's the most powerful demon in Hell, a demon we know as Belial."

"I was waiting for the movie."

"Followers of the occult know the name well. Pop devil

worshippers and Satanists have invoked him promiscu-
ously through the years. The original book, however, was
lost to history, many millennia ago."

"Are we ever going to get around to that point I was asking about?"

"Few have ever known its contents. It is a work of enchantment so powerful, it was believed the gods punished
anyone who laid eyes on it, and cursed their issue for generations to come."

"Enchantment? You mean, like, magic?"

"Yes, but not the kind you're thinking. It contains the
secret to controlling the earth and the skies. The keys to
Heaven and Hell."

"And you think Valentine found a first edition somewhere."

"Don't be so dismissive, Mr. Hatcher. You don't understand what this means. The Book of Thoth is not merely
something dangerous. It is hard to comprehend what one
who possesses it may be capable of."

"And where do I fit in to all of this?"

Soliya gestured to one of the other women. The woman
stepped over to the dagger and folded the leather over it.
She then carried it to Soliya and handed it to her.

"Valentine is attempting the unthinkable, to use the Book
of Thoth to rip Heaven from its moorings and fulfill the
prophecy of Belial."

"I have no idea what that means."

"It means, Valentine has promised Deborah something,
something big. Perhaps to be made a demon. One may pre-
sume Belial will be grateful to be unleashed."

"Why would she want that?"

"She's a seventh g. This is the last leg of her life. After
this, there is nothing. It is something we must all come to
grips with. Deborah never did."

She raised the bundle in her hands. "You wish to know
why this is called the Dagger of Cain? Because it is destined that the one who wields it shall slay his brother. We

have guarded it for centuries, protected it from harm. Kept anyone from breaking the purity of its purpose. The Prophecy of the Carnates says that our time will end once Belial has ascended. This life, long by your standards though it may be, is all we have. That is why the dagger was made. That is why we protect it."

"And my role in all of this?"

"You are the one who is fated to wield it, Mr. Hatcher. You are the one spoken of in the prophecies. It all depends on you."

"Lady, you are several slices short of a loaf. I may not understand everything, but I certainly know I'm not some chosen one. I ain't Moses. Or some character from *The Matrix*."

"And what makes you so sure of that, Mr. Hatcher?"

"The whole idea is ludicrous. I don't believe in that kind of stuff. And even if I did, you obviously haven't thought this through. I can't be your guy."

"Why not?"

"Because you said the person who wields this thing is destined to kill his brother. Last I checked, I don't even have a brother. And if I did, well, you already took care of that, didn't you?"

The puff of a tiny laugh seemed to escape her nostrils. "You disappoint me, Mr. Hatcher. I took you to be more astute. Just because Garrett is dead does not mean you are not destined to kill your brother."

"You're starting to sound like a sphinx. What are you saying?"

"I am saying, one brother is dead, yes. Another still lives."

"Another what? Brother?"

"Yes."

"I don't have another brother. I'm not even a hundred percent certain I had one to begin with."

"Oh, you did. And you do."

"Who is this other brother, then?"

"I can't believe you haven't guessed yet. The man I've been talking about, Mr. Hatcher . . ." Soliya tossed the dagger to him. He wasn't expecting it but managed to get a hand firmly on it, feeling the blade through the leather.

She waited several seconds before finishing the thought. "Demetrius Valentine. He's your brother."

CHAPTER 20

◆

IT WAS STILL DARK WHEN HATCHER STEPPED ONTO THE
sidewalk, self-consciously wedging the dagger between his
arm and ribs. The long piece of metal was heavy and awkward. The thick binding around it seemed almost as old as
the blade itself. Or almost as old it was supposed to be.

He felt like he was crashing, the foggy remnants of a
drug that was wearing off. The weight of the dagger tucked
at his side was tugging at his mind, forcing him to wonder
what the hell he was doing. Was he actually carrying some
legendary weapon? Entertaining the possibility of using
it? To fulfill a prophecy? Jesus, he thought. I need help.
His grasp on reality felt strained, and the dagger wasn't
the only thing. He was having trouble believing most of
what he'd just witnessed. Some sort of supernatural *Maxim*
party.

The cool of the night chilled his nostrils and he breathed
deeply, as if trying to exhale what air lingered in his lungs
from where he'd been. The feeling of a crash made him
think. Had he been drugged? He doubted it. In some ways

it felt a bit like it, in other ways it didn't. More like he had inhaled fumes that gave him a mild buzz. It took several blocks for his head to feel clear, even if his thoughts were jumbled, coming too many at a time.

Why hadn't he just said no? He knew the answer. Because those gals were literally irresistible, and even now he had an erection that could bead water. The extent of his self-control was to not throw himself on top of any of them.

And the other reason was because he wanted to know what the hell was really going on.

The streets were quiet, but not quite empty; the splashy sound of tires lightly spraying water occasionally came and went. It was the time of the night that was really early morning, too early for business, too late for recreation, when most cities would be completely devoid of life. Hatcher realized New York was different. It wasn't that it never slept, it was that it always kept moving a little even when it did, as if its existence depended on it, like a shark.

But even in a city like Manhattan, Hatcher figured a guy walking by himself at that hour was suspicious, probably up to no good. Especially when there were two of them, one across the street, one a block behind him. Shadowing him.

Hatcher turned at the cross street, then cut diagonally to the other sidewalk and waited at a bus stop. The one who'd been across the other street followed unsteadily after him, almost getting grazed by a taxi before stumbling forward. His clothes were ragged, a threadbare navy peacoat over several shirts and a dark pair of pants that seemed stained with even darker patches of moisture and specks of gray paint. He wore a cheap yacht cap, dingy white over a scuffed black brim with a little gold anchor on the front, and black gloves with no fingers. He looked homeless and drunk, the thick neck of a bottle sticking partially out of one of the side pockets of his coat.

The one who'd been tagging directly behind Hatcher arrived at the corner and stopped. He was a large black man, wearing a gray hoodie and matching sweatpants, the hood of his sweatshirt lipped back and bunched up behind his neck. He stared in Hatcher's direction, but didn't move.

The guy dressed like a bum stopped once he reached the corner, just like the other one. A pair of bookends, one on each side.

Weird, Hatcher thought. They weren't trying to be inconspicuous, weren't pretending not to notice him. He walked back across the street toward the homeless sailor. Just out of curiosity, to see what the man would do.

The answer was, nothing. The man just stood there, looking blankly at Hatcher as he walked by. On the other corner, the guy in the hoodie waited until Hatcher turned and resumed his prior course before starting to follow again. After a dozen yards or so, Hatcher looked back and saw homeless guy had fallen in a few yards behind. Hoodie and homeless, both looking right at him, staggering a bit.

They weren't planning to rob him or kill him. At least, Hatcher didn't think so. If they were going to make a move, they would have done it back there. They were just tailing him.

Hatcher walked a few more blocks, checking randomly to see if they were still there, then pulled the cell phone from his pocket. Having a tail had managed to stop his mind from swimming, and that was a good thing. If you didn't master your thoughts, they'd run amok, drown out your ability to reason, to problem-solve. That kind of lack of focus cost many men their lives. He'd seen it happen. But tail or no, he had a lot of questions to answer, and if Soliya was to be believed, time was a factor.

Deciding whom to call first proved unexpectedly difficult. He knew he needed to check in with Fred, see if anything had happened in the past few hours. But he really wanted to speak to his mother. A few days ago, he knew he was an only child. Now, he was being told he had two brothers, one dead, one living. He looked at the time on the phone. Four forty-five a.m. He had no compunction about waking his mother up, but Carl would probably answer and refuse to put her on the phone. Waiting a few hours was impractical. He had a feeling there wasn't much time.

The phone made the decision for him. It chimed out a sharp ring. He glanced at the number and flipped it open.

"Hello."

"Hatcher? It's Fred."

"I was just about to call you."

"Yes, I'm sorry. I know you wanted me to wait to hear from you, but this is important. I've been trying to reach you for a while. Where are you?"

"I'm a few blocks from Hugh Hefner's place in the twilight zone."

"What?"

"I'll explain later. I'm not far from where I was before." He twisted his shoulders to glance at the two men. They were standing a block back, swaying a bit from side to side, watching him. "And I seem to have attracted some company."

"You mean, you're being followed?"

"Yes, and they're not trying to pretend otherwise."

"Are you in danger? Can you talk?"

"I'm fine." He turned away from the men. "I'd like you to look up something else for me, find out what you can about women who call themselves 'Carnates.'"

"I, uh, okay, but, Hatcher, there's something I need to tell you."

"You sound like something's wrong."

There was a hiss through the line; Hatcher realized it was a heavy sigh. "Well, like I said, I've been trying to reach you. I got a call—"

"Does this have something to do with Am—with Detective Wright?"

"Well, not . . . there is that, yes. Lieutenant Maloney has been looking for you about her, too. He said she's missing."

"Missing? As in, she's disappeared?"

"He said she's not answering her cell phone, not on the radio, and not at home. He was quite anxious to speak to you. There's that, and—"

"And he thinks I'm responsible?"

"Well, I'm not sure about that, but he said they can't find her, her or a Detective Reynolds. I think he was the one with her earlier, at Garrett's office. That Lieutenant Maloney fellow sounded agitated. I don't think he believed me when I said I didn't know where you were. I was surprised he didn't threaten to arrest me. He left a number."

Hatcher listened intently, committing the number to memory. "Okay, I'll try her myself, and if I have no luck I guess I'll give Maloney a call."

"There's something else, something more important. I—I was trying to tell you . . . the reason Maloney called wasn't just about Wright. Hatcher, your father . . ."

"What about him?"

"There's been some kind of complication. Maloney said you need to get to the hospital as soon as possible. He said there wasn't much time."

Hatcher said nothing. More thoughts started to bubble up, another layer of noise in the system. But before he could entertain any of them, a long black sedan screeched to stop near the curb. It looked very familiar. Two women piled out. They were trim, extremely attractive, and each sported a black cylinder in her right hand. Hatcher had seen cylinders like them earlier and suddenly realized what they were. Almost simultaneously, the woman snapped their wrists, the rods shooting out to full length. Telescoping batons. The shafts made whipping noises as the women slashed the air with them, the slicing sounds of a freshly cut switch.

"I'll have to get back to you," Hatcher said, flipping the phone shut.

*   *   *

STEPHEN SOLOMON GROPED FOR THE PHONE NEXT TO HIS
bed with a heavy hand. He picked it up in time to cut off the
third ring. He glanced at the blue digits on the nightstand
clock. Somewhere in his mind he thought, *You've got to be
fucking kidding.*

He answered in a dazed voice, almost slurring.

"Stephen! Good morning!"

Solomon looked at the clock again. Who the hell considers this "morning"?

"What's that, Stephen? I couldn't quite make it out."

He rubbed at his eyes. "I said, do you have any idea what
time it is?"

"I certainly do. Time for you to start earning your ridiculous monthly retainer."

"What is it?" He felt his wife stir next to him, mumbling
about him being too loud. He turned away and lowered his
voice to just above a whisper. "Did you get arrested?"

"No, Stephen."

"Sherman, then? He knows he doesn't have to answer
questions."

*"No. Nothing like that. There's something I want you to
do for me."*

"Can't it wait until morning?" He ran a hand through his
hair, blinked at the glowing numbers on the clock. "Later
in the morning, I mean?"

*"Absolutely it can. And it shall. But I need to explain it
to you now."*

Solomon listened, the side of his head sinking down into
his pillow. He perked up after a few seconds, eyes popping
wide.

"Why the hell are you telling me this?" he asked. He shot a
look back at his wife and dropped his voice several decibels.
"Have you lost your mind? You know I can't knowingly be a
party to anything illegal. There are rules, ethics."

*"Please, Stephen. You're a lawyer. Your idea of an ethical dilemma is deciding whether to bill a client for the time
you spend screwing his wife."*

"This is beyond the pale. I'm hanging up now. We can talk tomorrow—later, I mean. I'll just pretend we didn't have this conversation."

"Speaking of wives, by the way, how's yours? What do you suppose her reaction would be to knowledge of your multiple trysts with a certain irresistible female? Did you find the guest bedroom at my place comfortable? It certainly looked like you did. Hard to tell on video though. It doesn't capture quite the same detail as film, the subtle facial gestures. Maybe I'm just old-fashioned. I'm sure the divorce lawyer she hires won't be so picky when he's taking every dime you have. Or do you think he'll be generous out of professional courtesy?"

Solomon sucked in a breath. That woke him up. The fucker had taped him? He slid his legs off the bed, eased his weight onto the floor. His wife rolled away, tugging her pillow down. Treading softly, he slipped out of the bedroom into the hallway.

"Okay, goddammit, what do you want?"

"I want you to hold on to something at your office and give it to someone when they show up."

"That's it?"

"Yes. And no matter what happens, you mustn't tell him anything about me. Absolutely nothing. Not about me, not about my whereabouts, nothing."

"Demetrius, you're my client. I couldn't tell anyone anything even if I wanted to."

"Glad you feel that way, Stephen. Nice we're on the same page. Then again, you made a solemn vow before God to your wife, so your word isn't exactly bankable."

Solomon scratched at the back of his head. He turned and leaned back, peeked into his bedroom. "Jesus, did you really videotape me?"

"Fail to do exactly what I've told you, and you'll be sure to find out."

The lawyer said nothing. He thought Valentine had hung up, then he heard him add: *"If you live that long."*

*   *   *

HATCHER EASED THE PHONE INTO HIS POCKET, KEEPING his eyes on the two women. One was a stunning redhead, the other a sultry brunette. He'd seen them before, in the hospital. These were the women dressed as nurses. Women like that were hard to forget.

He tossed a look back up the sidewalk. The two men were heading his way, moving at the same slow, deliberate pace. He chastised himself for not catching on sooner. That's what they'd been up to, keeping him in sight until these two could arrive.

One of the women, the redhead, stepped forward. She held the retractable baton like she knew how to use it.

"You're him," she said. "You're the one."

"That's very flattering, but I think we should slow down. You don't even know if I'm good in bed."

"You're not going to see Valentine."

"Are you asking me? Or telling me?"

The woman didn't answer. Hatcher was about to ask her another question when she darted forward and flicked the baton across the side of his face. The move was surprisingly quick, catching him off guard. He stumbled sideways, then crashed back against the metal grating of a storefront. He pulled his hand from his cheek. A long, thin patch of blood started to drip from his palm.

"Ow!" he said. The pain made him grimace. He sucked air through his teeth. "That kind of hurt."

The other woman moved quickly to his right, sealing off that flank. Without a word, she slashed her baton across the back of his leg. His body stiffened as his thigh seemed to ignite. Searing jolts exploded up the side of his torso, nerves screaming in protest. The leather-bound dagger dropped to the sidewalk with a muffled clang as he fell to a knee. He clutched the end of his hamstring. His pant leg was shredded. Blood oozed through his fingers.

"Son of a *bitch*! Will you cut that out?"

It was clear those batons were lethal, some kind of juiced-up version of the old cobra sticks. They were hitting him with probing blows, testing his defenses. The next one would likely be a coup de grace of some sort. The neck or temple, maybe. This was what his team used to call a Reaper Moment. He forced himself to think, to disregard the pain. They weren't being distracted by his banter, they didn't seem interested in talking. If their minds weren't accessible, he'd have to deal with their weapons. He needed a paradigm for it, a defensive principle to latch on to.

But first, he needed to avoid the next strike. To do that, he had to figure out how to see it coming. They were not telegraphing their moves, not in any way he could read. But both strikes had been delivered right after he spoke. He guessed that wasn't a coincidence. They probably assumed he'd be expecting a verbal response. Striking while he was talking was too predictable, something he could anticipate. These women knew combat psychology better than most soldiers.

Going for the dagger was out. It was too far and they were too quick. And it was too obvious.

He held up a hand, taking a gamble. "Why don't you just tell me what you want?"

Before either was able to react, he lunged forward, battling through the pain in his leg, and threw himself at the redhead. He lowered his shoulder into her abdomen and drove her back across the sidewalk. He yanked on her legs and rammed her into the side of the black sedan. He heard the back of her head smash the passenger window.

The woman let out a yelp. Her hands shot to the sides of her skull. Hatcher took note. Soliya had said they were almost impossible to kill. But apparently they could be hurt.

Three moves, and quick. He knew every effective technique consists of three parts, and that each has a corresponding action. Balance, control, execution. With her weight back against the car, he pulled her arm across his chest and threw his own over it, pinning it against body. He grabbed hold of her wrist and spun, pulling on it, forcing her body to arc around his. Simple geometry. The circle she traveled had to be much faster than his, since he was turning in place. She slammed against the car, face-first this time, and he maintained control of her arm, barring it at the elbow.

She had absorbed a hard impact, one that he felt vibrate through her bones. He was surprised she hadn't dropped her baton, but didn't have time to dwell on it.

Behind him, he knew the other woman would be ready to attack. Using the car, he braced himself, readying a side kick. Properly executed, a side kick could be devastating. It was actually a misnomer, since a perfect side kick was more to the rear than the side, a natural angle that allowed the full thrust of the quadriceps to power it. He was situated perfectly for one, as he'd hoped to be. He glanced over his shoulder, weight shifted, muscles loaded, set to fire out.

The brunette hadn't moved. She stood in a battle-ready type stance, broken down, like a defensive back. Watching. Before he had a chance to ask himself why, he felt the redhead push off the car. His weight moved back more than a body width, despite pressing against her as hard as his muscles would allow. *Goddamn, this is one hell of a strong chick.*

Then she put a foot against the car door and flipped backward, her lower body arcing over his head.

Against his chest, he felt the pop of her shoulder as it dislocated. Her knee smashed into the side of his head, dazing him. He backpedaled, trying to maintain his grip on her arm. A jumble of sensations bounced through his skull and he had to fight to keep his balance. He was unable to follow her movements as she flipped again, forward this time, and there was no way to react in time when in almost the same move she speared one leg behind his and another across his chest. She twisted, her weight supported by his body, and Hatcher crashed onto the sidewalk, the back of his head knocking the cement.

Pain shot into his eyes, hot, battering waves of it, bringing dark flashes as he squeezed them shut and the muscles of his face clenched into knots. He gripped the back of his skull with both hands, realizing too late he had let go of her arm to do so.

He managed to open his eyes to a squint and saw her push her shoulder back into its socket.

Combat had taught him many things, not the least of which was that the brain is the most important weapon. Without a functioning one, everything else in the arsenal was useless. He scrambled to get his working again, trying to focus, to shake off the dizziness and the knifing ache. His instincts told him he had seconds before a kill strike. A binary situation. Act or die.

The sound of a baton slashing whistled nearby. He flinched, instinctively covering up. Nothing. He glanced up at the redhead and saw she was looking past him. More noises from behind. Moving as little as possible, he angled his body so he could see what was going on, not wanting to take his eyes completely off of the redhead with her so close.

He looked just in time to see the brunette rip her baton across the throat of the large black man who'd been following him. It split the flesh of his neck wide. Blood began to drip down his sweatshirt. The gash was deep enough to open an artery, which meant the guy was as good as buried. Hatcher eased his feet beneath him, still trying to clear his head, still blinking, watching the man bleed. The redhead seemed to have lost some interest in him.

As strange as things were, he realized something even stranger was happening.

Sweatshirt guy wasn't reacting. He wasn't grabbing at his throat, wasn't dropping to the ground. He wasn't even bleeding that much. The only thing he was doing was keeping his eyes trained on the brunette.

Then he launched his body at her, pouncing, surprisingly quick for a big man. The brunette seemed agile enough to avoid him, but she lowered another blow across his skull instead. It sliced a huge wound spanning the side of his head and face. In hindsight, Hatcher realized it was a tactical blunder, because the man kept coming. He managed to grab a fistful of hair and wrap an arm around her waist, before dropping like an anvil and rolling on top of her.

Hatcher strained to unscramble his thoughts. This didn't make any sense. Was this guy trying to protect him?

The redhead suddenly turned to him. Hatcher pushed himself up against the car, knees bent, trying to find the energy to dive at her. Before he could, she cocked her arm to the side, baton bending in the direction of the move, and took a step toward him, whipping the baton diagonally, a hard, thrashing blow to the side of the neck. He ducked, a moment too late.

Only the strike never reached him. It took Hatcher a few beats to realize that another body had insinuated itself between him and the woman, absorbing the sharp snap of the baton. The slash of it ripped off an ear and part of his cheek. The redhead followed up with a wheelhouse kick to the side of the man's head, knocking him face-first to the concrete.

It was the derelict sailor guy. Without a noticeable pause, sailor guy got back to his feet and turned to face the redhead, his back to Hatcher. Hatcher could see his ear dangling by a sliver of skin, bobbing around his shoulder. The woman delivered another lash with the baton. A splatter of blood exploded from the man's face and his yachting cap fell to the sidewalk.

Like the other one, homeless sailor guy didn't seem to react. Didn't make any noises, didn't throw his hands to his face. He just moved to place himself firmly between the redhead and Hatcher.

The man smelled horrible. His open coat swung when he moved. Sticking out of the side pocket of his coat was the neck of a bottle. Hatcher's eyes fixed on it. A weapon. He grabbed hold of it and tugged it free. Vodka, it looked like. Almost empty.

The woman delivered another roundhouse kick to the man's head, knocking him to the side. Hatcher sprang forward as soon as the opening appeared and landed a solid blow with the meat of the bottle against the side of her head.

Her head snapped to the side, but slowly righted itself. She launched another baton strike at his knee, but Hatcher saw this one coming and blocked it with the bottle. The glass exploded on impact.

The redhead's hands bounced to her ears, and she let out another yelp, this one more like a scream. She opened her eyes and stared at Hatcher, who was still holding the dripping remnants of the broken bottle.

Stepping back, she held Hatcher's gaze until the last second, then shot a look down at the brunette, who was struggling beneath the massive girth of the guy in the sweatshirt. The man pushed himself off her, pinning her down with a forearm across her chest. One of his shins was across her leg. She was kneeing him to the head viciously with her other leg, but he didn't seem to care. Or notice.

There was something in his hand. Elbow buried against the brunette's throat, the big man raised it above his head. Hatcher realized it was the dagger. The man was holding it by the base of the blade instead of the handle, with only a few inches protruding from his fist. The cloth it had been wrapped in lay in a bundle on the sidewalk not far away.

The redhead threw out a hand. "No!"

Sweatshirt plunged the dagger straight down into the brunette's stomach, tearing open a wound. Then he dropped the dagger and looked like he was about to thrust his hand inside of it. Probably would have, if the redhead hadn't delivered a semi-airborne foot stomp to the side of his head, knocking him off balance. The brunette managed to roll free and stand. She was clutching her stomach in a way

Hatcher had seen before, several times. Someone trying to hold his guts in.

The redhead bent down to pick up the dagger, but the big guy had already rolled back and slapped a huge, black paw over it, just as homeless guy jumped on her back. She shrugged him off and kicked him in the chest, sending him sprawling, then turned back and raised her baton, ready to take sweatshirt's head off. Hatcher took an unsteady step, taking his weight off the car, his shoes crunching over bits of glass. He lost his balance a bit and put a hand back on the window.

Baton cocked, the redhead stopped and shot a look over her shoulder. The whine of a siren grew in the distance. Her eyes left Hatcher and made a circuit, taking in the scene. Homeless guy was getting back to his feet a few yards away. Sweatshirt had pulled the dagger in close. She glanced at the brunette. The woman was still doubled over, but had a surprisingly game look in her eye. The redhead finally looked back at Hatcher.

She stood like that for a pregnant moment, exchanging looks with the brunette. The siren was closer now. Throwing one final stare Hatcher's way, the redhead took off running, smashing a shoulder through homeless guy and sending him to the pavement again. The brunette immediately followed, almost as fast even with one hand still pressed against her abdomen. Hatcher watched them dart around a corner.

The siren sounded very close as they disappeared from view, but quickly started to fade after that. It seemed to pass one or two streets over.

Hatcher managed to stand and, with some effort, keep his balance. He surveyed the area, then walked over and pried the large man's fingers from the dagger pinned to his chest and rewrapped it in the cloth. Sweatshirt and homeless guy lay on the sidewalk, motionless.

Hatcher didn't bother to check them. The men were

dead. He'd known it long before the fight had ended. It hadn't been too hard to figure out.

Multiple blows to the head, kicks to the face and chest, and neither of them had blinked once. Not even homeless sailor guy, who still had a shard of glass sticking out of his eyeball from his first nosedive into the pavement.

CHAPTER 21

IT TOOK HATCHER SEVERAL MINUTES TO CONVINCE HOS-
pital personnel at the front desk—first the receptionist, then
a pair of passing physicians—that he did not need to go to
the emergency room. He was just there to see his father.

As he caught his reflection off the shiny steel doors of
the elevator, he was surprised they didn't take him to the
ER by force. His face was bruised and cut, the shoulder
of his shirt torn and bloody, his pants ripped with a wet,
sticky-looking wound gaping through the tear. A bright red
welt stood out on the side of his arm like a brand. On top of
all that, he needed a shower and shave. Badly.

No wonder hailing a cab had been so difficult.

It had been almost half an hour since his encounter with
the two women, and as the adrenaline dissipated he started
to feel the effects. He winced with each step, his leg feeling
like something had taken a bite out of it. His arm burned.
Raising it might as well have involved a ninety-pound
dumbbell. His cheeks felt like they had been sandpapered
raw and covered with oatmeal.

At least the dagger was reasonably well concealed, he thought. He'd managed to cram the handle down his sock, up to the hilt. The blade almost reached to his knee. He cut a slender piece of the cloth it had come in and used it to secure the blade to his calf, knotting it tightly. The dagger still wobbled a lot, and the blade and hilt edges made his pant leg protrude in odd ways when he moved, but as long as he was careful he figured it would do for now.

He pulled out his cell phone. No signal. He still had to call Fred, but had been too rapt in thought trying to sort though what he knew to bring himself to do it in the cab.

The elevator doors opened on the fourth floor. He stepped into the hallway and paused. A question burst into his head, disrupting his thoughts like a slap. Would he be here if he didn't need some answers? He tried to remember whether he had thought about his father's condition at all on the way over, or whether he had simply imagined how he would go about asking him if he really did have another brother. This one named Valentine.

He couldn't be sure.

Remembering the general layout of the floors, Hatcher veered to his left down the main corridor and found the nurses' station. Several women in scrubs were behind the counter, chatting. He identified himself and noticed the sound of his name put a damper on the conversation. One nurse stood, a sober expression on her face, and asked him to follow her.

The nurse led him to a small waiting room. Hatcher saw his mother there, crying. Carl had his arm over her and patted her back.

"I came as soon as I could," Hatcher said.

Hatcher's mother raised her head. Her gaze, wet and red, seemed to reach out when she saw him. She stood and held her arms up to receive him. He gave her an awkward hug.

"Is it bad? Is he in surgery?" They seemed like natural questions to ask.

His mother pulled away and looked at his face. Her

heavily veined eyes skipped back and forth. Her lips trembled. She suddenly seemed much older than she did a few days ago.

"Jacob, *oh, Jacob* . . . They just told us, not a few minutes ago. Your father's—"

Her face tightened and tears spilled down her cheeks. She didn't finish the sentence. She didn't have to. Hatcher understood.

The room was hospital-quiet for a moment, the kind of silence you don't find anywhere else. His mother's sobs were the only sound other than the subtle ambience from the hall, the faint footfalls, the barely audible roll of a distant cart. Hatcher saw Carl eyeballing him as he patted his mother's back, realized he had been trying to console her the same way a moment earlier. Carl was standing a few feet away, hands in his pockets, staring accusingly. This had to be awkward for him, Hatcher thought. Watching his wife become emotional over the death of her first husband. Driving her to the hospital, staying for hours, probably going sleepless, probably having to be at work in a few hours. He seemed to be supportive of her, which Hatcher grudgingly appreciated. It was possible that in his own way, Carl wasn't such a bad guy.

Hatcher shot him back a look intended to let him know he was not in any mood to be fucked with anyway.

A few minutes later, Hatcher's mother began to relate what the doctors had said, about the infection, the circulatory problems, the damaged organs, the weakened immune system. Hatcher listened, guilt festering in his abdomen. He'd hardly known his father, hadn't developed any special kinship for him. They had never spent time together, and now they never would. He wasn't certain what he was feeling.

"Mom," Hatcher said. "There's something I have to ask you."

Hatcher took a breath. He had questions he needed answered, and he'd just been informed the only other person who could give them was dead. Soliya had impressed upon him how time was a factor. He wasn't sure how much of that he should believe, but he wasn't sure how much he could afford to dismiss outright, either.

"What is it, Jacob?"

His eyes crept over her shoulder to Carl. He gently steered his mother toward the far wall, near the doorway.

"Did you have another son?"

"I told you about Garrett."

"No, mom, I mean, another one. Besides Garrett. Do I have another brother?"

The unfocused, searching look of confusion shone in her eyes. I'm a complete jerk, Hatcher thought. Asking a woman who just lost a son, or someone who thinks she lost a son, a question like that. He tried to think of an appropriate apology.

Before he could, he saw that look give way to another. Her features slackened, her eyes set. The hyper-focused stare of shame. Whatever was going through her mind, it mortified her.

"Tell me," Hatcher said.

"What's going on?" Carl was on his feet, bulling forward. "Are you upsetting her?"

"Stay out of this." Hatcher leaned in close, pressing his gaze tight. "Tell me."

Carl grabbed Hatcher by the arm, squeezing it. "Get away from her! Who the hell do you think you are?"

It hurt just enough. His arm was just sore enough, the wound just fresh enough, that the jolt of pain was more than he was willing to tolerate. Hatcher spun around, clamping a hand on Carl's throat, and almost lifted him off the floor as he rammed him into the wall.

"You know, I've had just about enough of you." He pinched his hand tighter, kept pinching until he saw all the bravado drain from the man's face. "Pathetic cocksuckers like you make me sick. You think being some dickhead makes you tough? Huh?"

"Jacob!"

"Do you? Answer me, you potbellied loser. Where's all that lip now?"

"Jacob! *Please!*"

So much hate. It bubbled up like molten lava, hotter for the depths it had occupied for so long. This lame excuse for a man who appeared in his life unbidden, who immediately started fucking with what little Hatcher the teenager had, his independence, his space, his brooding peace. And what the hell was he? A nothing. An ignorant jerk.

"Jacob! I'll tell you! I'll tell you!"

When a person is in actual fear for his or her life, facial muscles contract and peel back, exposing the eyes completely, maximizing perception. It's a primal, atavistic look, one that cavemen surely had when attacked by a vicious predator. Hatcher saw that look in Carl's eyes, a look he had seen many times, a look he had intentionally induced many times. It took him a moment to realize that not only was the man genuinely afraid of dying, but that his fear was completely rational. Hatcher was choking him to death.

Hatcher dropped his hand from Carl's neck and stepped back. Carl coughed violently. He bent forward and grasped at his throat, looking like he might vomit. His face was changing from a shade of purple to more of a pinkish hue. The dark veins in his forehead and neck were fading. Hatcher's mother put her arm around him, crying again, asking him tenderly if he was going to be okay, and if she should get a doctor.

That was bad, Hatcher thought. Jesus, that was bad. Stupid, stupid, stupid. He could not ever let that happen again. Ever.

As the coughing subsided, Carl raised his eyes. He glared at Hatcher, but it lacked conviction. If he was expecting an apology—or even if he wasn't, for that matter—Hatcher wasn't about to give him one. He didn't feel sorry for what he'd done, didn't feel remorse. Just anger. At himself. He'd lost control. That was inexcusable.

Besides, Hatcher thought, his mother was doing all the apologizing for him. Karen Woodard kissed her husband's cheek and hugged him over and over, sobbing a tune of "I'm sorrys."

His mother's words finally registered. "You said you were going to tell me."

She wiped at her eyes. Carl snarled, cleared his throat, but deferred to his wife as she patted his shoulders and told him it was okay.

"Do you want to step into the hall?" Hatcher asked.

"No." She wiped at her nose, leaving one hand on her husband's back. "I have no secrets from Carl."

"But you do from me," Hatcher said. "You lied."

"No, not really. I never wanted to keep anything from you."

"You omitted a rather large fact. You led me to believe Garrett and I were your only sons."

"I didn't lie."

"So I don't have another brother?"

The pressure seemed to be visible as it built inside her. Her body trembled and she glanced in various directions, as if the right answer might be floating around the room.

"I'm not sure."

"How can you not be sure whether you had another son?"

"I didn't. But your father may have."

The implication settled in slowly, and as it did Hatcher began to feel stupid. The obvious possibility hadn't even occurred to him.

"Did he ever mention something like that to you?"

"No. I never spoke to your father after I told him I was pregnant."

"What are you talking about? You were married to him for years."

"Jacob, I never wanted you to know this, but . . . Phillip wasn't your father."

At that moment, almost everything Hatcher thought he

understood about his life ceased to exist. His father wasn't his father. Things that had made sense suddenly didn't, and things that didn't suddenly started to.

"Who was, then?"

"You have to understand, Jacob. Your father—I mean, Phillip—I never told you this, but he came back from the war sterile. He said it was from a 'jungle fever,' but I always assumed he'd picked up some venereal disease. That's why he married me when he found out about Garrett. Because he knew that would be his only chance at a son. When we were unable to find him, he—we drifted apart, Jacob."

"Who, Mom?"

"I felt so alone, so starved for affection. Your father— Phillip—he wasn't a bad man, he was dealing with so many issues from the war, so much stress. And I was so hurt by how distant he became."

"Who was it?"

"I started waitressing nights, to make extra money. There was a man who came in, handsome, very intelligent. He asked me to keep him company. He talked about all kinds of things I didn't understand. But he made me feel important. Told me how beautiful I was. Said I asked very intelligent questions."

"His name, Mom."

"Myles. Myles Valentine."

Now it was Carl's turn to comfort her. He wrapped his arm around her, smoothed her hair back. Rested his head against hers.

To Hatcher, he said, "Happy now? Just leave. Leave her alone. If you weren't her son, I'd make sure you got what was coming to you."

Hatcher said nothing. There was nothing left to say. Soliya wasn't lying. This guy Valentine was his brother. His half brother. It looked like Garrett had been his half brother, too. What else had Soliya said? Something about Valentine's parents having been killed. The father he never knew was now dead. The father he did, but not very well, was now dead, too. And belief in some sort of prophecy was driving a series of events that still seemed unreal. His mind seemed to be buckling, a gummed-up machine ready to throw a piston. There was simply too much new information for all of it to be processed.

The disturbing sound of his mother weeping, punctuated by Carl's whispers of consolation, was too much too take. Hatcher left the waiting room and ventured into the hallway. He leaned back against a wall, pressed the heel of his palm against his forehead. He needed to think.

"There you are."

Hatcher snapped a glance toward the voice. Lieutenant Maloney was approaching. He looked stressed. His eyes sagged, bags starting to form under them. His clothes were wrinkled. Something was eating at him. Badly.

"I've been looking for you."

"So I heard."

"What happened to you?"

"I got mugged." He took a breath and leaned his head back against the wall. "Never a cop around when you need one."

Maloney eyeballed him for several seconds. "If there weren't other considerations, I'd throw you in a cell and let you rot. I have half a mind to as it is."

"I won't argue with the half-a-mind part."

"Don't fuck with me, Hatcher. Cut the bullshit right now. Have you seen Detective Wright? Yes or no."

"No. Not since I left the police station."

The words seemed to deflate him. He mopped his face. Maloney was obviously nervous, shaken. Hatcher could tell he was trying to hide it, but doing a poor job.

"Do you think something's happened to her?"

Maloney shook his head. "I'm not sure. I just didn't expect . . . She went off with Reynolds somewhere. Now they're both incommunicado."

"There's more to it than that," Hatcher said after a pause.

"What do you mean?"

"I mean, you're not telling me everything."

Maloney stood quietly for several audible breaths, thinking. He started to speak once, twice, until finally seeming to settle on the right choice of words. "Reynolds has been acting strange lately."

"Strange how?"

"It's not really any of your business, Hatcher. I'm just worried, that's all."

"And you think maybe he's the reason you can't reach Wright?"

"I think I don't want you to fuck around and get anyone killed. Other people may think you can be relied on to do this or that, but I think you're a loose cannon."

Hatcher gave a gesture of exasperation. "Just what do you think I'm going to do?"

"I don't know, and I don't want to know. I just think that you know how to go about finding her. Whatever you do, just don't put anyone at risk."

The sagging lines of his face matched the hint of desperation in his tone. The man was feeling impotent, scared, and the logical explanation was that he was in love, in love and afraid of losing her. All his warnings were simply his way of letting Hatcher know he was turning him loose to find her.

"Where do you think they may have been heading?"

"I don't know for sure, but I think it had something to do with Lucas Sherman. Reynolds was asking me questions, like he wanted to know what I knew."

"You think Reynolds is dirty?"

Maloney said nothing. Before long, the silence was interrupted by the tweeting of a cell phone. It took a moment for Hatcher to realize it was his. The ringtone seemed different than what he'd heard before, two short jingles, like dinner bells. He retrieved the phone and glanced at the front panel. It told him he was receiving a PIX message.

"That reminds me," Maloney said. "Give me your cell number. I need to be able to reach you."

Damn it. Hatcher told him the number. There was no sense in holding it back now, since he couldn't pretend he didn't have one.

Just as he finished reciting it, the phone rang again, this time with the tone Hatcher remembered. He recognized the number of the incoming call.

Hatcher looked at Maloney and shook his head. "It's not Wright."

"I'll be in touch," Maloney said, gesturing for Hatcher to take the call. He narrowed his gaze before leaving. "Don't put her in danger."

Hatcher watched Maloney walk away, dodging an orderly and disappearing around a corner. He flipped the phone open and answered. But it wasn't Fred's voice on the other end, as he'd expected.

"Hatcher! *Oh my God!* You have to come back here! *Right away!*"

"Susan?"

"Please, get over here *now*!"

"What's wrong?"

"It's Fred! I think he's *dead*! Oh, dear God! Hurry!"

"I'm on my way."

Hatcher slapped a hand to his forehead and squeezed his temples. Jesus, had he gotten the poor old bastard killed? Just what the hell was going on?

He heard a beep as he started for the elevator and glanced down at the phone. The screen told him the PIX message had finished downloading. He pressed a button corresponding to the word *open* and a photograph with a caption filled the screen. It was a picture of Wright, sitting on the floor behind a coffee table, leaning against a black sofa.

The caption read, *If you want her to live, be at the offices of Stephen Solomon, Attorney at Law. Commerce Plaza, Manhattan. 5:30 p.m. sharp. Not sooner, not later. Show this message to or tell anyone about it, she dies.*

Just as he finished reading it, another text message came in.

And bring the dagger.
Brother.

CHAPTER 22

✦

LUCAS SHERMAN WIPED THE SWEAT FROM HIS BROW ON the back of his heavy work glove. The pause prompted him to remove his safety glasses and rub his eyes, first with the gloves, then without them.

"Boss, I don't mean to complain, but I gotta get some sleep."

Valentine turned from the stained glass and surveyed the interior of the church from the chancel. "You're an atheist, Lucas. You'll sleep when you're dead. Why would you want to now?"

With an audible sigh, Sherman slid the thick clear plastic stems of the glasses back over his ears. He slipped the gloves back on, his gaze aimed near his feet.

"There's not that much left for you to do," Valentine added. "You can rest for a while after you finish that section. In fact, I'll insist you do."

Sherman leaned against the push bar of the groove cutter and glanced around. "The priests are gonna freak when they see this."

"This isn't a Catholic church, Lucas. No priests. And, for the time being, I'm the leaseholder. I can do what I want."

"But isn't that chick a nun?" He jerked his thumb to a far corner. The young blonde woman in her habit was crouched in a cage barely large enough to fit her. "I thought nuns were Catholic."

"She is. This church isn't."

Sherman half shrugged, half nodded. His eyes wandered back to the hard floor. His lips silently mouthed the word *Whatever*.

"It's called being ecumenical, Lucas. It is not important you understand. I have my reasons."

"I'm sure you do, Boss."

"The faster you get back to work, the sooner you get to rest."

The groove cutter came alive, vibrating violently. The business end of it sent shards and chunks of marble flying as he pushed it, spitting them in every direction.

Why was he always doing that? Sherman wondered. He'd never told Valentine he was an atheist. Never even thought of himself that way. He just didn't think there was a Heaven or Hell. God, he wasn't sure about. The devil? Who knew? And who cared? But he definitely believed in freaks and monsters. He'd seen plenty in his time. Hell, in a way, he was one of them.

The machine rattled his arms, numbing them. Desecrating a church might be fun another time, but not this way. This was work.

The outline he was following curved sharply. He disengaged the blade and repositioned the cutter to begin a new groove perpendicular to the one he just finished. This one had to form a half circle. What a pain in the ass. Valentine and his fucked-up rules. *No guns*. What kind of a fruit doesn't let his muscle carry a gun?

Sherman lifted his eyes as he pushed on the bar. There she was, cuffed, bound, and gagged. He would be glad when this was all finished, because then he'd be able to take care of the cop. Valentine hadn't spelled it out yet, but he knew the cop would be a loose end. Sherman supposed he was, also, but that didn't bother him.

Valentine needed him for stuff like this. Who else was there? Deborah? Those other freaky women? Talk about weird. Even if they did have some creepy-ass abilities, he doubted Valentine could trust them.

Plus, those charms of theirs didn't work on him. One of the many wonderful benefits of that treatment the state administered.

There was no one else, he concluded. So for now, he was safe. All he had to do was go about his business, and then, when the time was right, he'd take that skinny shit's money—he had to have a safe he kept in that penthouse with a few hundred grand stashed away—and beat him to death. Maybe feed *his* heart to that fucked-up creature he made.

Until then, he'd just keep working. Working and, assuming the fucker ever let him, sleeping.

IT TOOK HATCHER ALMOST TWENTY MINUTES TO GET TO Fred's apartment building. He took the steps two and three at a time and arrived at the unit slightly winded. The door was a sliver ajar. He pushed it open with a slow hand.

Susan was sitting on a chair, her face contorted in a painful sob. She was looking down at Fred's body.

The thing about the dead that stuck out to Hatcher was that they never looked peaceful. Not before the mortician got a hold of them. He'd seen his fair share, rifle wounds, stab wounds, shrapnel wounds, wet work. One thing they had in common is how they seemed frozen in the act of dying, a pantomime of that final moment of resignation. Their bodies were always in uncomfortable-looking positions, even when lying flat on their back. Nobody lies on the floor like a dead person does, not using an arm for a pillow, not lying on one side. The dead he'd come across hadn't simply drifted off; they'd vacated bodies that looked like they had been fighting to stay alive. In his mind, death equated to eternal discomfort. A restless state, endured in perpetuity.

Perhaps those who died in bed—people who passed by nonviolent means—were different. But he couldn't recall ever seeing someone who'd died that way. Not even his father, he realized.

Fred was no exception. He looked like someone who'd just taken a bad fall, wrenched his back, and couldn't get up. His spine was slightly arched, his head bent to one side. His eyes seemed unfocused, with one slanting slightly inward. One arm was resting across his belly, the other palm up on the floor.

An oval puddle of blood spread out across the tile from beneath his head. His neck was cut from one side to the other, just above his Adam's apple.

"He called and asked me to come back, said there was something he wanted to give me. I was glad he did. I wanted to thank him. In person. I thought maybe I could give him some money, for helping me." Susan paused to sob. "Something to show my gratitude."

Hatcher knelt next to the body. He briefly contemplated checking for a pulse, but realized it would be futile.

"Did you see anything? Hear anything?"

"No." She started crying more forcefully as she spoke. Her words came out like poignant lyrics to a sad song. "The door was unlocked . . . I just opened it and found him like this."

"Police?"

Tears dropped to the floor as she shook her head. "I started to, then I remembered how he told me that if anything were to happen, that I was to get in touch with you. He made sure I had your number."

His number. Somebody else seemed to have it, too. Hatcher stared at the dull eyes that already seemed to be cloudy. *Sorry, pal,* he thought. *I'm the one to blame. You just picked the wrong guy to help out.*

"I didn't know what else to do," she added. "Also . . ."

"What?"

"I—I think the police may have had something to do with this."

Hatcher stood, looking into her eyes, willing her to look back at him. "Why do you say that?"

"Because when he called me he told me Detective Reynolds was on his way up, but that he'd be gone by the time I got here. He sounded very nervous. Like he was trying to keep calm about it."

Reynolds.

"I asked him which one was Reynolds, if he was one of the ones at Garrett's office, and he said no. But I think he was wrong, I think he was there. The one with the red hair."

Amy. Maloney had been right to be worried. She and Reynolds had gone off together, and now they were both unaccounted for. But Wright was the one he knew was being held. Reynolds had to be involved. The little apple-pie-looking creep.

"I was scared," Susan said. "So I called you."

"It's okay," Hatcher said. "You did the right thing. When he called, did he say what he wanted to give you?"

"No. This seems like it's all my fault."

"That's just survivor guilt, Susan. This had nothing to do with you." Hatcher wished he could believe that about himself. This actually was his fault, he had no doubt. "Can you think of anything else he told you?"

"Nothing. He just told me to come back, that he had something to show me."

Nodding again, Hatcher surveyed the room. No obvious signs of a struggle. And there was no shortage of things that could break. The room looked like an air traffic control tower, so many computer monitors and electronic display screens around. One monitor on a corner desk caught his eye. A UFO was bouncing off the edges of the black screen, crisscrossing it in diagonals. A screen saver. Hatcher found a keyboard tray where a drawer normally would be. The moving image disappeared when he tapped the space bar, replaced by icons and a wallpaper that took a few seconds to populate the screen. The wallpaper was a photo of a tree and a fence with a slope of grass. A street was in the foreground. There was something familiar about the scene. It took him a moment, but Hatcher realized it was a picture from Dallas. The grassy knoll.

He slid the mouse and clicked on the Internet icon. The front page of a website called TrustNoOne appeared. A clearinghouse for conspiracy theories, from the looks of it. Hatcher clicked on the drop arrow next to the web address box. Nothing. Hatcher realized he shouldn't be surprised. He imagined paranoiacs like Fred didn't leave web trails.

"What are you looking for?" Susan asked.

"I don't know. Anything." He straightened up and swept the room again. As he did, the sight of her standing next to Fred's corpse hit him.

Had he been entertaining the notion Susan may have killed Fred, or been in league with whomever did, the way she stood there would have struck it from his mind once and for all. No one was that good an actress. She looked a wreck. Not physically, like he was sure he did, but emotionally. Her shoulders weaved as she shifted her weight from one foot to the other. She was biting at the back of her thumbnail, her other arm wrapped around her torso, hugging herself. The press of her arm against her loose blouse showed her pregnancy. His dead brother's child. He found it ironic that after finding out Garrett may have been at most a half sibling, he finally started to think of him as a brother.

His thoughts formed a silent but sharp rebuke, and he reminded himself that not everyone was as numb about these kinds of things as he was. What kind of a guy lets a traumatized woman stand there staring at a bloody body? A pregnant woman, no less. One who was practically a relation.

"You should go," he said. "You don't need to stay here. Like I said before, get out of town. Take a taxi, go far. Philly, maybe. Take a train from there. Pay in cash. Do you have plenty of cash?"

"Yes. How long should I stay gone?"

"Until it's safe."

"When will that be?"

Maybe never. "Soon, I hope."

"Will you call me? When it's safe?"

"Yes."

"Where should I go?"

"Anywhere." Flashes of concern peppered his thoughts, worries about cell phones being tracked, credit cards, ATM withdrawals. No, he thought. This wasn't a movie. A rich guy, some spooky chicks, a bad cop, some muscle, but not some enormous government conspiracy. And even if it were, the government should be so competent. He knew better.

But still.

"Go somewhere out of the way. Use cash whenever possible. And buy one of those TracFones Garrett was using. Check your voice mail from it. I'll leave a message and a number if it's safe. Use your head."

Hatcher paused, contemplating his own words. Cell phones. He glanced at the body, then moved toward it. Taking a knee, he patted Fred down. He reached into the dead man's front pants pocket and removed a phone.

"What is it?"

He opened the phone and pushed the send button. A list of numbers appeared. The last call was an outgoing number. Susan's, he gathered. Twenty-two minutes prior to that was an incoming call. He didn't recognize the number, but he guessed it was Reynolds's. Sloppy of him. He may have been a cop, but he wasn't a pro. He hadn't thought things through. Hatcher struggled to assess the implications of that. Why wouldn't a cop think of that?

"Hatcher?"

"Nothing," he said. He slid the phone into his pocket. "Just checking his calls."

Because it seemed like the thing to do, he walked her down to the street and waited with her while she hailed a cab. Dawn was breaking. The streets were still empty, but shadows were being infiltrated by the blue gray glow of morning.

The first cab they saw pulled right over. Susan kissed him on the cheek and hugged him tightly as he held the rear door open. His brother had good taste. She really was beautiful.

"You're not a Carnate, are you?"

"A what?"

"Never mind."

"Are you going to be okay?" she asked.

"I'll be fine."

She held his gaze for several beats. "Why don't you come with me? With Brian gone, there's plenty of money. I can hire lawyers, cash in everything. You can protect me." She placed a hand on her belly and lowered her eyes. "Protect us."

"That's a tempting offer. But I just can't."

"I didn't mean to imply . . . I wasn't saying you and me, you know—"

"I know." Under different circumstances, it would have been comical. He hadn't shaved in days. His clothes were filthy and in tatters. Dirt and dried blood lined the creases of his skin. She was soft and clean and smelled like some kind of succulent flower. He didn't even want to think what he smelled like.

But what she said hadn't surprised him. He was her only tie to Garrett. She would do anything to hold on to a piece of him. Girlfriends of fallen soldiers often became involved with returning members of their unit. Or brothers.

"It's just, this baby is your niece or nephew. That makes us family."

"I suppose it does."

She tried to smile, but her eyes were sorrowful, seemed to push down on the corners of her mouth. Sighing, she slid into the cab. "Don't get yourself killed . . . Jacob."

He shut the door and slapped the roof of the taxi a couple of times. When it was almost out of sight he said, "Nobody lives forever."

The hushed words had barely passed his lips when he thought of Wright. He moved quickly back toward the building. One innocent person was already dead because of him, one person who had trusted him, who had tried to help him. He wasn't about to let it become two.

DESPITE NOT REALLY EXPECTING TO FIND ANYTHING, WITHIN a few minutes Hatcher discovered something Fred left for him. His primary reason for returning had been to wipe everything he'd touched. After a short debate on his way up the staircase, he'd decided he still didn't completely trust Maloney, so calling him was out. Given that, he also decided he didn't need to be connected to the scene of a homicide. Zero residual presence seemed to be in order. The obvious problem would be fingerprints.

As he was finishing up, relatively certain he had retraced his steps accurately, a whirring, rumbling noise caught his attention. It was coming from a cabinet beneath the computer. Inside was a printer. It had quieted down, sat there dormant, a single green light signaling its readiness. He assumed what he'd heard was an automated adjustment, the realigning of print heads.

On top of the printer, where the printed pages eject, was the research Fred had done for him. He saw the name Valentine on some of the pages, the word Carnate on at least one other. He folded the thin stack and shoved it as far into his pocket as it would go, then finished wiping down everything he had touched. He paused over Fred's body before leaving, heard himself whisper the words "I'm sorry," then moved cautiously but hastily down the staircase and out of the building, trying to beat the early risers.

He hailed a cab a few blocks later, something he once again found much more challenging without Susan next to him. Getting a cab from the hospital had been easy—even if the driver had given him the fish eye—because they were lined up near one entrance. But now it was just him waving an arm, and the drivers were being discriminating. He didn't blame them, but that didn't stop him from cursing more than a few who'd shut off their duty lights and drove past.

With some time to kill until his appointment with Stephen Solomon, Attorney at Law, he needed a place he could think. This posed a slight dilemma. He pulled out his cell phone, had to double-check to make sure it was his and not Fred's, and retrieved the picture message of Wright. He was pretty certain it was taken at Deborah's apartment, given what he could see. He was also pretty certain whoever sent it expected he would know that. Going there would be a sucker's play.

His best guess was, he was being tested. To see whether he would follow directions. Whether he would do as he was told. That made the decision easier. He told the driver to take him to the New York Public Library.

But that begged the question. Who really did send the picture? The easy answer was Valentine, but he wondered whether he could be sure. Anyone could sign a text message and say they were whoever they wanted to be. The Carnates—one of them, at least—told him Demetrius Valentine was up to something sinister and that Valentine was his brother. Half of that had more or less been confirmed, but how could he be sure the Carnates weren't lying about the other part? They were so hard to read, their faces like masks, their bodily control almost unnatural. For all he knew, they could be setting Valentine up.

No. Something told him that wasn't the case. He recalled seeing Solomon the day he met Wright at the precinct—the lawyer who got Sherman off. The Carnates said Valentine was behind the string of missing prostitutes. Wright had said he was a high-priced mouthpiece. That fit with Valentine. It also explained how Sherman could afford him.

Valentine and Sherman. It did fit.

And Valentine was looking like he really was his brother. Hatcher was still having a problem with that one.

Then there was Deborah. If Soliya had been telling the truth, Deborah was also involved. That would mean the picture of Wright being taken at her place made sense. Sort of. Deborah knew Hatcher had been there. Unless someone was simply trying to make him think these things.

Simple, he told himself. Keep it simple. The simple answers were usually the correct ones. And the simple answer—if anything about this could be considered simple anymore—was that Valentine was behind it and Deborah was working with him.

And Reynolds.

Hatcher wasn't sure what to make of Reynolds. Maloney seemed to imply he was dirty, but was he ready to trust Maloney? No, he decided. But he did trust Susan, and she'd said Fred told her Reynolds was on his way. Of course, he knew he had no real reason to trust Susan, but experience had taught him you can't accomplish anything if you trust no one. If he was going to be that way, he might as well take the next step and question whether Wright herself might be involved, playing the role of captive for his benefit. There was a fine line between being distrustful and walking around with tinfoil headwear.

The taxi dropped Hatcher off on Fifth Avenue near Fortieth. He found a nearby shop serving breakfast sandwiches and ordered two. He inhaled them in just a few bites, washed them down with a large glass of orange juice. Then he made his way back to the library.

Feeling the food and OJ churning agreeably in his stomach, he hurried up the enormous staircase. Two lions guarded the steps, famous landmarks that reminded him of his childhood. He'd learned about them once on a field trip. The pair were nicknamed Patience and Fortitude by the wife of some long-ago mayor. He figured he could sure use some of both, but he doubted they were sharing.

Near the entrance, he remembered he was still carrying a large dagger strapped to his calf. He slowed down and stiffened his gait, trying to keep the pants leg from bulging. A pair of security guards gave him dirty looks as he passed, but no one stopped him.

The interior smelled like must and furniture polish and scents he couldn't quite place. It reminded Hatcher of an old house, where smoke had staked claims on the upholstery, and aging wood created a pleasant background scent of decay.

The library was enormous, and proud of it. Sprawling marble floors and vaulted ceilings, elaborate stonework and ornate bay windows. Majestic staircases curving to unseen destinations. A castle for books, conceived when the written word was king.

Hatcher made his way to the main reading room and took a seat at one of the myriad large wooden tables serried in rows that appeared to extend for at least a couple of city blocks. Sinking into the chair, he felt small, relatively impotent. He couldn't think of a feeling more appropriate for the situation.

He unfolded the printouts he'd taken from Fred's apartment and started to read. It quickly became obvious that Demetrius Valentine wasn't just rich, he was *uber* rich. An article from the *Wall Street Journal* recounted how he'd developed an Internet meta-search engine, how he sold it for millions, how he demanded and got tens of thousands of stock options as part of the deal, and how he cashed those out during the height of the dot-com bubble before turning around and shorting industry stocks in a bold prediction of the coming bust. Mr. Valentine was purported to be a billionaire, perhaps a multibillionaire.

The piece also described him as a private man who gave

a lot of money to charities, especially churches. The writer referred to him as "the orphan of two high-profile atheists, who seemed to be atoning for the perceived sins of his parents."

Parents, Hatcher thought. One of them, Hatcher's father. A high-profile atheist. He wasn't sure what to make of that.

Two more articles on Valentine were in the stack, one that focused on an unprecedented act of charity involving Grace Trinity Church. Leasing the aging main church for two years while he gave it a full renovation, its first in a half century, and paying enough on the lease for the church to rent temporary space with enough left over to establish a large scholarship fund for orphans.

Saint Valentine.

Hatcher had to scan one other page almost to the bottom until he found Valentine's name. Under a subtitle "Valentine's Day-Job Massacre," a tiny snippet of business gossip dated more than three years earlier mentioned that "word on Wall Street" was that Valentine's dumping of a particular stock was not an isolated incident, and that after returning from an extended sabbatical in Africa he started liquidating most of his holdings and fired his entire staff.

Okay, Hatcher thought. The man is very wealthy, very generous, and possibly very weird. If he were to believe a certain Carnate, also quite deranged and homicidal. But he still knew next to nothing about him. Nothing that seemed helpful, at least.

The last page he came to was from a website dedicated to demonology. Hatcher hadn't even realized there was such a thing. But there it was, apparently an entire website devoted to the discipline. The page had a black background with Gothic-looking title and text fonts. A banner ad for a horror movie ran across the top. Fred had obviously printed it out because the page contained a brief description of Carnates:

A Carnate is the female offspring of a demon and a human woman. Not much is known about these creatures. There is no mention of them in the recognized books of the Bible. A few legends trace them to Solomon, who was rumored to have enslaved demons through magic. Some demonologists have speculated that Solomon wanted to produce a race of demons that could walk the earth to guard his mines. One ancient source described Solomon as having been so enchanted by these females that he married every one he'd been responsible for creating as they came of age. Carnates are said to be sexually irresistible and, compared to people, virtually immortal. They have been vaguely linked to other types of demons, such as Sedim and Djinn, and descriptions of those beings may be references to the same creature, and vice versa. Most of the scant information there is about Carnates comes from the transcripts of a heresy trial involving an alleged Carnate presided over by Pope Benedict I. The transcripts remain sealed by the Vatican, but the diary of one priest who claimed to have read them said the accused gave testimony that Solomon had placed a curse on them for treachery, a curse that would last until the gates of Hell swallow all of humanity, though the priest did not specify precisely what that curse was. Being obsessively fond of material wealth, Carnates apparently conspired to relieve Solomon of much of his treasure, greatly angering him.

Below this description was a minimalist sketch of a shapely woman in veils. Below that were three citations to source material.

Hatcher read the paragraphs several times, unable to decide whether they provided anything useful. Assuming demons even existed—an assumption he was still resisting—determining the accuracy of the information seemed impossible. Any fool could post something on the Internet, and every fool would believe it. He supposed he could check the sources listed, but that didn't seem to be the best use of his time, and he doubted it would yield anything more believable. Or verifiable. Despite what he had seen below ground, he wasn't yet ready to accept ostensible myth as fact. Carnates seemed to exist, and additional background on them would be nice—especially if Deborah had indeed set him up—but his concern at the moment was Wright. All indications were that Valentine had her, and that Valentine may be pursuing some personal agenda directed at him. Right now, his gut told him he needed to find out more about Valentine. And about Valentine's father. If for no other reason than he might have been his own father, too.

After that, he decided he could use any time he had left to do more research about Carnates. There were still hours left until 5:30.

His phone chirped as he folded the pages and stood. It took him a second to figure out which phone it was.

Hatcher answered. It was Maloney.

"Where are you?"

Hatcher glanced around. Angry eyes peered over glasses, their owners hunched over books. "Catching up on some reading."

"You need to get down to the precinct. Now."

"Why?"

"Because you're wanted for questioning. You're a suspect, about one misstep away from being a subject. It was all I could do to keep them from issuing a material witness warrant."

Fred's body, Hatcher thought. Somebody saw him leave, or he missed something when he cleaned up.

"I didn't kill him."

"Them," Maloney said.

"What?"

"We have two bodies. And an anonymous tip named you. Said you killed two men in a street fight. Said you were cut and injured during the scuffle."

"I can't come down there right now, Lieutenant."

"Goddamnit, Hatcher. You can, and you will. I'm not asking. Maybe I can still straighten this out if you let me help. I'm trying to convince them you're not a flight risk. But if a warrant gets issued, I'll be hunting you down myself. Just for making me look bad."

"You don't understand, I have to be somewhere a little later. Really have to be somewhere, I mean."

"Then the faster you get your ass over here, the better."

Hatcher found a large clock on a far wall. He still had time. He wasn't sure whether he could trust Maloney, but he also wasn't sure he had a choice.

"Okay," he said.

"And Hatcher . . . try not to leave any dead bodies along the way, for Christ's sake."

CHAPTER 23

❖

CONSCIOUSNESS RETURNED TO WRIGHT IN STAGES, accelerated by the pain in her back and shoulders as she moved. She was in complete darkness, and felt the shackles biting into her wrists before she realized a black hood had been placed over her head.

Her neck revolted as she tried to straighten up, so stiff she wondered if she'd ever stand holding her head normally again. It hurt enough she cried out.

Only, she didn't.

A tight numbness constricted her throat. It felt swollen, heavy. She could breathe, but not easily. And her groan had made no sound.

There was no air, no light, only her hot breath flushing over her face. The blackness was smothering her, strangling her, drowning her.

Oh, dear God, I'm buried! Buried alive! Left to rot beneath the earth in a hole where I'll never be found, an unmarked grave, probably in Jersey—oh, Jesus, no!

Her heart was pulsing in a rapid drum roll. She could feel herself slip into a panic.

Calm down! Catch your breath! You're not in a coffin! You're sitting up! Your arms are cuffed above you! There are sounds nearby! Listen . . .

It took minutes for her to get her breathing under control. Several times she wanted to gag on her own saliva but couldn't, felt and heard it gurgle with each breath. She concentrated on slowing down her respiration, counted backward from a hundred more than once. Latched on to the tiniest noise, homing in on it, pretending she could follow it, picture it.

Someone else was near. She realized she could hear his breathing as hers began to slow. This is a good thing, she told herself. You're not alone. You haven't been buried alive or walled up or abandoned in a bomb shelter.

His breathing. It had to be a he, she decided. The breaths seemed deep, aggressive even. She wasn't sure how reliable that conclusion was, or whether one could even detect what she was imagining, but the sound smacked of a man. A large man.

Sherman.

Fragments of memory began to align themselves into an imperfect recollection. She'd been at a church with Reynolds. She remembered not finding him at the car, going inside. Valentine had been there.

The missing nun. She'd seen the woman, huddled over in a cloak of some kind. Then what? A dreamy patchwork of images floated by. She was floating, like on a boat. But it didn't seem like a boat now. Had Hatcher been there? It seemed like he had, but everything kept going back to Sherman.

She'd come to briefly in an apartment—Deborah's apartment, she realized. Sherman had been there. But everything was so blurred, so distant. Like she was remembering a dream about a dream.

And now she was here, wherever here was.

Reynolds!

Now she remembered. That son of a bitch! He'd sent her out to the church, then disappeared. Sent her out, and set her up.

So, whose breaths was she hearing? Sherman's? Reynolds's? Someone else's? She realized there was no way to tell. She was certain she'd know if it was either of the first two as soon as he said word one. Reynolds, because she knew what he sounded like. Sherman because even one squeaky syllable would give it away with that little-boy-kicked-in-the-nuts voice of his. But whoever this guy was, he had yet to speak.

What she did know was that someone definitely was there. She could hear him moving in place, shifting weight. Feet or knees or ass scraping and shuffling against the floor every few moments.

She waited, silently, until she couldn't stand it any longer. She opened her mouth to call out.

Nothing. No words, no sounds. Her throat felt dead. She tried again.

Not a peep. The only noise was the faint rustle of breaths.

She shook her hands, rattling the chains of her shackles. They clanged off the hard stone wall behind her.

Things went dead quiet. Seconds passed, then the breathing resumed.

Again with the chains. Harder this time.

Nothing. The responding silence lasted barely a couple of beats, just a brief interruption in the pattern. Breath, pause. Breath, pause. Low, rumbling hisses of air. An occasional snuffle.

A thought popped like a bubble in her head. *He's asleep.*

Trying to regain control of her own breathing, she diverted her attention to her shackles, ignoring the continued acceleration of her pulse, the fluttering in her chest, the surging jolts of anxiety squeezing her lungs and stomach. The shackles, she told herself. Concentrate on the shackles.

Too tight to slip her wrists out of them. Too high to allow her to reach her head from where they were. She curled her wrist over and down, tried to push herself higher, bring her head toward her hand. The damn hood had to go.

Something heavy was around her waist. She could feel it pulling down at her hips, anchoring her to the floor. If she could just push up six inches or so, stretch her spine, extend those fingers just . . . a . . . tiny . . . bit . . . more.

Her middle finger flicked the protruding edge of the cloth. She pressed harder, clenching her jaw, accepting the pain as the thick, flat metal cuff dug into her skin and cut off circulation. Her fingertips were tingling; her entire hand grew cold. But the tip of her finger now fluttered back and forth against the material at will. All she needed was to get that index finger a bit lower, or that hood just a smidge higher, clip that cloth between the two, then let her body sink down and pull her hand back.

Closer now. The pain in her wrist was excruciating, a hot, knifing burn, her fingers all pins and needles, her palm icy. The ligaments in the back of her hand were screaming in agony.

Just a few more—

Got it.

She worked the fold of cloth up between her fingers, sliding it slowly, careful to keep hold. Within seconds, she was able to curl her fingers toward her palm, pulling cloth with it. She managed to get several digits hooked into the cloth and balled her hand tightly. She pulled her head down, yanked her wrist up as far as it would go.

The hood slid up, then off as she bent her head to the side. She shook out her hair, blew strands away from the front of her face. She squinted, blinking. A figure was there, a few feet away. In a cage. Looking at her.

She screamed without making a sound, her mouth stretched, jaw agape, face twisted—a scream in every way except the lack of noise—as the thing lunged forward toward her. It slammed against the bars, teeth bared in a feral snarl, snout pressed through, a gurgling growl exploding the silence. Arms, incredibly, impossibly long arms reaching for her, insectile fingers grasping, slashing just inches away. She pulled herself back against the wall, head turned to the side, frantically trying to get her legs more fully beneath her. As far from its reach as possible. Far from those teeth and claws and wild hair.

And those eyes. Those eyes locked on her, manic and hungry, lustful and intelligent. Human eyes. Inhuman eyes. Merciless eyes. Eyes that seemed to know exactly what they were seeing.

She trembled in fierce waves as she watched it withdraw its arms and sit back in its cage. She could see more of it now, the body coming more into view. It settled into a semi-lotus position, one knee up. A dark, fleshy penis stood tall and unwavering. It rested a hand on it, stroking it gently every few seconds.

Those eyes were still locked in a coveting stare, but its expression had shifted, causing her heart to palpitate as adrenaline pumped through it.

Rows of canine teeth fully exposed, head dipped slightly forward, it let out a long, deep breath, almost a sigh. She recoiled, not wanting to believe what she was seeing.

It was smiling at her.

HATCHER SAT IN THE SQUAD ROOM AND WAITED, STARING at the clock on the wall. Time, he decided, was nothing if not relative.

He'd shown up at the precinct less than a half hour after he'd gotten off the phone. Maloney had marched him straight to the room he was in, gotten him a beverage, and told him to sit tight after asking him a few questions. That was hours ago. Hatcher had passed the time staring at Wright's and Reynolds's desks. Maloney had stuck his head in every fifteen or twenty minutes, would ask a few more questions, then leave again. It was already three thirty. He couldn't wait much longer.

What a difference a day makes, he thought. Maloney was much more cordial this time around, leaving Hatcher to himself unsupervised. No cuffs, no threats. The only time he even sounded like a cop was when he kept reminding Hatcher not to leave.

He had to go back to the library, then get to Solomon's office by five thirty. He figured he needed at least forty minutes to be safe, but he would like at least a little time to do some research before he went. That was looking less and less likely.

Of course, not being restrained or babysat, he could just get up and leave. If challenged in the hall, he could merely say he was looking for the restroom. He decided he'd give it another fifteen minutes, then do just that. If Maloney wanted to issue a warrant, so be it.

Hours earlier, Hatcher had snooped around. He checked Wright's desk first, then Reynolds's. He had no doubt Maloney expected him to and figured being left alone like that was a form of permission. But if Maloney'd also expected him to find something that shed any light, he hadn't.

One thing was different, he noticed. The clown mask was missing from Reynolds's desk. He wasn't certain what the significance of that was. Maybe the guy knew he wasn't coming back. Wanted his trophy.

Hatcher stood and walked over to the window near Wright's desk. He looked down at her computer monitor, studied his reflection off the dark screen. He'd looked better, that was for sure. But he'd definitely looked worse, too. He wondered if maybe he was being tested again, if Maloney had someone watching him through a camera. It didn't matter. Whoever it was would have died of boredom long ago.

At least sitting in that room had given him time to think. So many things now seemed to make sense, so many others that he'd taken for granted no longer did. The way his father—or stepfather, was it?—had always seemed distant. Now he realized why. Raising a son who wasn't his, the product of an adulterous affair, was probably too much. Hatcher was already starting to think differently about him. Given the circumstances, he'd actually been sort of decent to him. He'd clearly blamed Hatcher's mother, not Hatcher himself.

It also explained why he'd become so chummy with Garrett. His real son.

But what about Valentine? Hatcher still didn't know what to make of him, junior or senior. His father had been some sort of professor, an evolutionary biologist, and outspoken atheist. Hatcher had never been much for going to church, but like most soldiers he didn't consider himself an atheist, either. And in light of what he'd seen over the past few days, he really wasn't sure what to believe.

The serious question was, how did he fit into all this? What was Valentine's game? If the Carnates were right, his half brother was a serial killer with some kind of Hell fetish. And now he had Wright. He didn't even want to think about Deborah and what role she was playing. It made his head hurt.

The door to the squad room opened and Maloney entered. He dipped his chin in greeting and grabbed the nearest chair. He didn't seem to care that Hatcher was behind Wright's desk.

"I got my counterpart over at the One-Seventh to back off," he said. "I told them you didn't do it, that you're a cooperating witness helping me out. They're willing to wait to talk to you, not issue any warrants or treat you as a subject."

"Why does it smell like you're about to stick your hairy 'but' in my face?"

"A pair of deputy U.S. marshals just stopped by my office. They said they had a transport order for you, were supposed to put you on a JPATS flight."

"Gillis," Hatcher said.

Maloney bobbed his head in agreement. "Your boy must have shot out a request as soon as he found out you'd been detained."

"And conveniently forgot to let them know I was cleared and released."

"Guess he figured it was worth a shot."

Hatcher's gaze shot over to the clock. "What did you tell them?"

"That you weren't in my custody. That you had been picked up for questioning and were released. We didn't have enough evidence to hold you."

"Gee, thanks."

"Grow up. If I'd started popping off about you being innocent it would have only made them suspicious."

"So, I can go?"

"In a minute, yeah. But there's something I need to say. I know you've been holding out on me. I know you know something about what happened to Amy. Don't even try to bullshit me. I just know."

Hatcher said nothing.

"I doubt there's anything I can do to persuade you to tell me, but you'd better understand this. Do not do anything to put her in harm's way, *capisce*? Whatever you're doing, whatever you're up to, don't take any risks with her life. Or so help me, you'll regret it."

Hatcher started to say something, but stopped himself. This was unexpected and a bit confusing.

"I'm going to let you walk out of here, but you need to promise me that when you find out where she is, you tell me. Okay? That's my price for letting you go do your thing."

"You think Reynolds is behind her disappearance," Hatcher said. "Don't you?"

"I think wherever she is, Kid Clown isn't far away." Maloney stood, placed his hand on the doorknob, and paused. "Wait a few seconds, then head toward the back of the station. I'll let you out a side exit. Wouldn't want anyone who's looking to take you back into custody see you leave."

Maloney opened the door and glanced in each direction down the hall. "As you may have already noticed, we cops are nothing if not committed," he added with a wry chuckle. "Especially to our lies."

THEY WERE ALL STILL THERE. THE DAGGER, FRED'S CELL phone, the printouts—all where Hatcher had left them, hidden behind dusty binders on the top shelf of some obscure stacks of periodicals in a poorly lit corner of the library's third floor. He'd doubted anyone would be likely to pull any of the bound collections of *Popular Mechanics* from the 1960s in the time he was gone. Judging by the layer of dust, it had been quite a while since the last person had.

With almost ninety minutes available, he spent the better part of the next hour trying to research Valentine and his father. He found very little, other than a few more newspaper pieces about Valentine's charitable contributions and business dealings. Valentine Sr. had a few articles published in peer-review journals in the sixties and seventies, esoteric works about various evolutionary proofs observed in waterfowl and insects that Hatcher was not inclined to read. But he was able to find the man's obituary. Myles Valentine had died with his wife Roberta in a car accident in 1976. It described him as a high-profile intellectual and "activist" for secular causes. Tenured professor at Princeton, member of the National Science Board. A rising academic star. The obit said he and his wife were survived by a son, Demetrius, eight.

He picked up the pages Fred had printed, found the one containing the info on Carnates. He checked the time on the cell phone. Forty minutes. That gave him fifteen or so more before he needed to leave. There were three sources listed. He found two of them on the library computer system.

The first book was titled *The Slaves of Solomon*. The

index referenced a three-page section next to Carnates. The pages were part of a discussion of Jinn and mentioned that Carnates were possibly the female offspring of those creatures and demons. It described them as very beautiful and mentioned that there were tales of Solomon marrying them. Apparently, Jinn weren't human, but were humanlike.

The second book was old, a rare 1950s reprint of an eighteenth-century text. The *Encyclopedia Infernale*. It didn't contain much about Carnates. The only mention of them was under the entry for Belial, who was reputed to be their sire. It mentioned they were "very humanlike" and "of great beauty," living for "a generous number of years." One passage, however, did catch his eye.

> Carnates, being the issue of a fallen angel of hostility, are similar to their relations the Sedim; it is presumed they have inherited the infirmities of same, though perhaps to a less vexing degree as their blood is not whole; iron blessed most hallow, the scream of a virgin pure, and the shattering of glass which carries the ring of God's judgment, all may cause distress to their senses.

Glancing first to each side, he bent down and untied the dagger from his calf and slid it out of his sock. He hefted it, ran a thumb along the blade. *Iron blessed most hallow*.

He placed the dagger back into his sock beneath his pant leg and laced it against his calf. He left the books on the table and stuffed the printed pages and the cell phone into his pocket. It was time to go.

THE BUILDING AT THE COMMERCE PLAZA ADDRESS WAS a tower of glass and metal that would have been impressive had it not been wedged between larger towers of even shinier glass and sleeker metal.

There was a minor exodus of people as Hatcher arrived, a thin stream of white- and pink-collar workers filing out of elevators and heading toward the subway. He waited outside the revolving doors for a few minutes before entering. Loitering around the lobby might draw unnecessary attention, but he didn't want to show up early.

The floors were waxy green and the trim was black. Hatcher hadn't been in many high-rise urban office buildings, but he could still sense the look was dated. The architecture, the décor, all of it smacked of the 1980s, peppered with self-conscious nods to modernity that now seem forced and heavy-handed, a look redolent of pastels and synthesizers. A security guard with a buzz cut in a navy blazer and dark blue tie sat behind a circular counter between the banks of elevators, watching an array of monitors while he chatted on a telephone. Hatcher stopped at the touch screen monitor in front of the counter. The guard gave him the once over, but continued his conversation.

According to the directory, the Law Offices of Stephen Solomon were located on the fourteenth floor, suite 1403. Hatcher exited the elevator and checked the time on his cell phone: 5:27. The suite was not hard to find, located at the end of a corridor to one side of the elevator bank. Two large glass doors with frosted insets partially blocking visibility stood at an angle to the hall. The lawyer's name was etched through the frosting starting on one door and ending on the other.

Hatcher paused, looking around. An artificial tree in a large wicker pot stood in a corner of the hallway, near an exit stairway. He walked over and inspected it, then checked the ceiling for security cameras. Seeing none, he removed the dagger from beneath his pant leg and hid it behind the tree. It wasn't completely concealed, but from the entry to Solomon's offices it wasn't visible. Hopefully, he wouldn't be there very long.

Inside, a slender blonde sat behind a hutch in an L-shaped reception station near a glass door with a push bar across the middle of it. She looked up as Hatcher approached, flashing a plastic smile.

"Can I help you?"

"I'm here to see Mr. Solomon."

A black man in a button-down shirt with an open collar and khaki slacks entered the reception area from the elevator bank.

"Last run of the day," he said. He waved a file folder as he walked past and headed toward the back. The woman reached beneath her desk and the door behind her buzzed with a click. The man pushed on the bar and disappeared behind it.

The woman turned her attention back to Hatcher. "Do you have an appointment?"

Good question, he thought. *Depends on how you look at it.* "Yes."

The woman picked up a telephone handset and pressed a button. "Name?"

"Hatcher."

"Oh, I have something for you." She replaced the handset and reached into a corner of her desk for a large envelope. After checking the front, she handed it to him over the narrow counter of the hutch.

The envelope felt flimsy, flat, like it was empty. The name "Hatcher" was written in pen on the face of it.

Hatcher tore the envelope and removed a single sheet of paper. The paper bore a short message in ink:

Leave the dagger with Penelope. Someone will contact you later.

He lifted his eyes from the page. "That's all?"

"Yes," the woman tilted her head. "Was there supposed to be something else?"

"I want to see Mr. Solomon."

The woman's brow furrowed. "I'm sorry, sir. Mr. Solomon is currently out of the office. He'll be back tomorrow."

"Try again. You were picking up the phone to call him when you asked me my name."

She slid an appointment book closer, avoiding his gaze. "Would you like to reschedule?"

"No. I'd like you to tell him I'm out here, and that my patience is wearing thin. Almost as thin as the ice he's skating on."

"I'll be happy to give him a message for you," she said, paying undue attention to the calendar.

The door opened and the man who'd just entered exited, carrying a thicker looking file. The door started to close slowly behind him

"Not necessary," Hatcher said. "I'll just tell him myself." He slipped past the station and got a hand on the door before it shut.

"Sir! You can't go back there!"

Ignoring her, Hatcher opened the door and walked into a hallway that ran perpendicular to it. The space taken up by Solomon's firm was relatively compact. A large conference room was separated from the corridor by a glass wall. To the right beyond it was a supply room and what looked like a tiny kitchen. Hatcher walked to his left. A few empty cubicles lined the interior, opposite a pair of empty offices. The hall terminated at a large corner office with double doors. He checked the nameplate and shoved the door open.

Solomon was standing behind a large desk, leaning slightly forward over a phone. His charcoal gray suit looked sharp against his white shirt and bright yellow tie. He looked up at Hatcher and pressed a button.

"It's okay, Penelope. Don't bother. He's here now. Just call it a day."

The voice that came over the speaker was loud and tinny. "Are you sure?"

"Yes. I'll see you tomorrow. Everything's under control."

Hatcher stepped into the office. It was triangular, with a view of neighboring skyscrapers through floor-to-ceiling windows, a vista of silvery reflections and glistening steel, the shadows cast by the setting sun hinting at a labyrinth of passageways between them. There was a couch and a small table with chairs in one corner

The lawyer held up a finger and pressed another button on the phone. "He's here," he said. He kept the finger up as he reached over to flat CD player mounted on a stand. Jazz flooded the room in hi-fi stereo. Hatcher thought he recognized it. Prominent horns. Chuck Mangione, maybe.

Solomon straightened and raised his brows, turned up his palms with a *what now?* shrug.

"I want answers." Hatcher gestured toward him with his chin. "You're going to give them to me."

"I'm afraid I don't have any," Solomon said. "Even if I did, the information would probably be privileged. I wouldn't be able to disclose it if I wanted to."

"Oh, you'll want to. Trust me on that."

"There's no need for threats. I was told you were coming and to have you leave a certain dagger. That's all I can say."

"Where's he got Amy?"

"Who?"

"Detective Wright?"

Solomon hitched a shoulder. "Can't say I know what you're talking about. Honest."

"In that case, where do I find Valentine?"

Solomon hesitated, shot a glance over Hatcher's shoulder toward the door. Before Hatcher could react to it, a pair of massive arms wrapped around his chest, pinning his arms to his side. Arms like enormous steel cables, tightening, squeezing his ribs, lifting him off the ground. Constricting him.

Hatcher flung his head back, trying to drive it into his attacker's face. Nothing there to hit. Whoever it was had his head pulled back, probably turned away. Ready for him. He could tell his assailant was much bigger than he was, bigger and freakishly strong.

Sherman.

Breathing was becoming difficult. The man seemed to know what he was capable of. Those arms were literally squeezing the life out of him, tightening relentlessly.

Hatcher flailed, clawing at the hand that was clamped over the other in a fist. He swung his legs, mule-kicking, tried to scrape a heel down Sherman's shin, tried to catch a knee. Nothing. He had no leverage, and Sherman was in a stance that made it difficult to connect a kick. The few he managed to land were glancing strikes that didn't seem to make a dent.

Tighter, tighter, tighter. Hatcher focused on expanding his chest cavity, pressing his arms outward with all his might. It seemed to slow down the constriction but was exhausting. He couldn't believe it was even possible, that someone could be so strong. He was able to breathe a little, which was good, but the realization hit that suffocating him wasn't what Sherman had in mind. He was trying to crush his rib cage.

Sherman's fists wouldn't budge as Hatcher dug his fingers into them, unable to even pry a finger loose. He could feel things start to pop near his breastbone. The desk, he thought. He swung a foot toward it. Too far. There had to be something else.

His eyes felt like they were going to pop out. His head seemed to swell, vessels all engorged with blood. Every breath was now a struggle. It was only a matter of time before his chest really did cave in. *Chair.* He raised a foot toward one of the chairs in front of the desk, managed to catch a toe on the armrest. Did his best to draw Sherman's attention to it.

Sure enough, Sherman swung him away from it.

One more time. Hatcher flung his foot out, pointed his toe at the chair. Sherman yanked him away farther, until he faced the opposite direction.

The move brought Hatcher closer to the sofa. He kicked his foot out toward the armrest. Sherman twisted him away from it.

Now they were facing away from the desk.

Hatcher drove his feet back wildly kicking in bicycle motions with all he could muster. Sherman moved backward a few steps, trying to keep his balance. This was his chance. If he could just—

—get him—

—to turn—

—around.

Hatcher reached his foot out for the chair again, tiny bursts of light going off in his head, veins throbbing in his temples. He hooked his foot around the backrest and toppled it in front of them. Just as he'd hoped, Sherman swung him away from it. An overreaction. They were facing the desk.

Before Sherman could move again, Hatcher set both feet against the edge of the desk and thrust his legs out as hard as he could. Sherman stumbled back, tripping over the chair, and landed hard on his back.

Goddamn, if this son of a bitch isn't strong. Hatcher couldn't believe it. Two hundred and change landing right on top of the man as he fell straight back, and his grip didn't release. Hatcher's head was swimming from lack of oxygen. He imagined his face a crimson purple color, since that was how it felt. Sherman was still squeezing. But now he was on the floor, and Hatcher realized he couldn't move his face back anymore. With a desperate snap of his neck muscles, Hatcher fired his head to the rear, catching Sherman in the cheek, around the eye orbit. Again, then again. The grip seemed to loosen slightly. He managed to get two fingers wedged beneath Sherman's little finger and pull out with both hands. Another vicious crack to Sherman's face, and the grip finally slipped.

Bending Sherman's finger back as mercilessly as he could, Hatcher ripped himself from the bear hug and gulped air. Sherman held a palm over his nose, favoring his right cheek, and tried to get up. Hatcher threw himself on top of him, riding what remained of his adrenaline surge, heart cannonading painfully in his chest, lungs burning as he drew desperate breaths. With all his weight, he slammed a forearm down across Sherman's face. Then another, then another. Then a bladed palm strike to the throat, then another forearm, mostly elbow, to the head, sinking into it with his full body weight. He reared back for one more, barely able to lift his arm, but let up. Sherman was out.

His muscles were trembling, his legs wobbling as he stood. He felt completely drained of energy, gasping, unable to inhale enough air. He dropped onto the sofa and sprawled against the cushions, tried to fill and empty his lungs as rapidly as he could.

"I hope you don't think you're leaving," Hatcher said, not bothering to open his eyes.

Solomon stopped in mid-stride. He was halfway to the door. "This has nothing to do with me."

"Only a lawyer would have the gall to say that in his own office." Hatcher pulled himself up, stayed perched on the sofa's edge. He lowered his eyes to Sherman. "While standing over his unconscious client."

"The police are on their way."

"No, they're not."

Solomon swallowed, cleared his throat. "I called them while the two of you were fighting."

"No, you didn't," Hatcher said, rotating his shoulder and stretching his chest. "The last thing you want is to answer questions about why I was here, why Sherman and I fought. Or what you know about a missing cop."

Solomon's eyes widened, brows clenching. "I don't know anything about a missing cop."

"Where's Valentine?"

"Right now? I have no idea."

Hatcher pushed himself off the couch. He twisted his head until his neck audibly cracked. He fixed his gaze on the lawyer and moved toward him.

"Whoa!" Solomon held his palms out, a surrender gesture. "I really don't know where he is. Or anything about a missing cop." Solomon dropped his gaze to the floor where Sherman groaned, stirring, and pointed. "But I'm pretty sure he does."

CHAPTER 24

❖

IT TOOK THREE ROLLS OF STRAPPING TAPE, A DOZEN large FedEx boxes, a telescoping camera tripod, and the string from Sherman's shoelaces for Hatcher to be able to use Solomon's brass letter opener they way he wanted to. The large set of scales, held by a blindfolded Lady Justice, her foot on a serpent, weren't ideal for what he had in mind, but they'd do.

Solomon's crystal basketball, commemorating his role in a conference tournament championship some twenty-two years earlier, would be a casualty, but oh, well.

"Please be careful," Solomon said. "That's rather special to me."

Hatcher set the ball down on the desk and glanced at the lawyer. Tied up with telephone cord to a chair in the corner, knowing by now that the guy who tied him up wasn't messing around, yet still voicing concerns over a piece of glass rather than anything that was about to happen to his client. Hatcher wasn't sure whether it was admirable or pathetic. He decided maybe it was just lawyerly.

Using his cell phone, Hatcher checked the time. He'd given himself twenty minutes. The rigging had taken almost fifteen, most of it scavenging for the materials in the supply room.

Binding Sherman facedown on the coffee table had taken the better part of two rolls of tape. Hatcher double-checked to make sure none was coming loose. Multiple wraps over the back and under the table held down Sherman's upper body, while a similar number kept his legs secure. Both legs were bent at the knees, feet pulled up toward has back, and the ankles were bound tightly together and held in place with strips that were fastened in a dozen layers around his wrists also, palms facing out. The trickiest part was his head. Hatcher had used almost as much tape securing it, the chin jutting out over the edge of the table, length after length of tape running from the legs over the back of his neck and skull to keep it in place. To keep him from turning it, Hatcher had bent a coat hanger and taped it to Sherman's back, positioning each end of it so they dug into the depressions behind his earlobe. He looped more tape over the back of his head so that the bend in the wire at each lobe was tightly secured to a table leg.

That was one beat-up looking head, too. Hatcher wondered how one scalp could have so many lacerations. Some of them had started to bleed again.

A mirror Hatcher pulled from the wall in the washroom was set beneath Sherman's face at an angle, so he could see it if he moved his eyes to the side.

Hatcher looked over to Solomon. "Are your bindings too tight?"

"No," Solomon said, clearing his throat. "Thank you."

Hatcher inspected Sherman's wrappings, then moved toward Solomon. The lawyer had been reasonably helpful in letting him know what materials would be available and where to find them.

He looked Solomon square in the eye. "Trust me, this is for your own good."

He punched Soloman hard across the jaw. Flexed his hand, then drew back and punched him again. Solomon's eyes rolled into the back of his head, the surprised look evaporating off his face. His body slumped down, supported only by his bindings. His mouth was bleeding and his cheek and jaw had already started to puff. Whether it would be enough to convince whomever he needed to that he didn't cooperate was hard to say, but Hatcher figured it was better than nothing.

Hatcher left Solomon and returned to Sherman. He leaned forward and pinched the big man's nose shut. A couple of seconds later, Sherman's head shuddered and his eyes blinked open. Hatcher ripped the strip of packing tape from his mouth. Sherman let out a loud grunt and sucked in air, panting.

"Let's get past the preliminaries." Hatcher crouched down, looking at Sherman's eyes in the mirror. "This is where I say you're going to tell me what I want to know, and you say something like 'fuck you' or just about as original and then spit at me and maybe tell me all the things you're going to do to me when you get free."

Before Sherman could respond, Hatcher moved to the side of the table, grabbed a firm hold of Sherman's little finger, and broke it. It made a loud snapping noise.

"Ah! For fuck's sake!" His voice squeaked loudly, like a rat under a boot. "What the fuck? Jesus!"

"Let me explain to you how torture works. It's not about pain. It's not about mutilation. It's about the anticipation of pain. The anticipation of mutilation. Or worse. The biggest obstacle in the beginning of a session is overcoming the belief that the interrogator is bluffing. You need to know I'm not bluffing."

Sherman let out a sound that sounded like a tiny dog growling. He shook his body, rattling the table slightly. "Break all my fingers, you fuck. I'm not telling you shit."

Hatcher nodded. "I didn't exactly expect you to be what we call pain-responsive."

The big man struggled beneath the tape, huffed a few times, but said nothing.

"If you look in the mirror, you'll notice there's a track," Hatcher said.

He picked up the statue of Lady Justice and placed it in front of Sherman's head. The letter opener was fastened to one end of the scales, the tip pointed upward at a slight outward angle. The weight of it tipped that side of the scale down. He adjusted the position so that the sharp end of the opener was pointing toward Sherman's right eye.

"What the fuck are you doing?"

"Tell me where Wright is and tell me what Valentine is up to."

"I don't know anything. I'll give you Valentine's address and you can ask him, jack-off. Let me go."

Hatcher held up the crystal basketball so it was visible in the mirror. "This weighs about fifteen pounds. Dropped from the height of the desk, it will pack a lot more force than that."

"I told you, I don't know anything."

Smiling down at the mirror, Hatcher scratched his cheek and sighed.

"This is called a rat trap," he said, moving behind the desk. "Kind of like a mouse trap. There's no specific design. The idea is, you set in motion something on one end that results in something happening at the other."

Sherman's body shook and the table trembled. But he hardly moved. An elephant wouldn't have been able to move. "Let me out of this!"

"You use a rat trap to make sure the subject understands that once set in motion, your role is done. When I drop this ball, it starts rolling down the track and toward the edge of the desk, then it drops off the edge and hits the near end of the scale, which drives the other end of the scale up, stabbing that letter opener into your eye. I barbed the tip of the opener so that it will stick and pop your eye out when it's removed."

Hatcher lifted the glass basketball to the top of the hutch behind Solomon's desk, perching it atop a stack of four books from the shelves below that he'd placed near the corner. Next to it was a stack of three, then two, then one lone book laid spine out, set back a bit, its cover propped open with some paper, with more books stacked on the other side of it to hold it in place. The cover was angled like a ramp that fed to a V-shaped gutter of FedEx boxes taped together and bound to the extended legs of the tripod for support. The boxes ended at the edge of the desk a few feet from Sherman's head.

"Let me know if you don't have a good view. I'll adjust the mirror."

Sherman squealed something unintelligible, followed it up with some curses and threats. Hatcher waited. He only had one shot once he let it go, and he had to make it count.

The noises Sherman made died down into grunting breaths and Hatcher looked at his eyes in the mirror. He gave the ball a gentle push. It turned slowly off the first stack of books, dropped heavily onto the second and almost came to a stop after it dropped onto the third. It teetered on the edge before dropping onto the tilted cover and rolling off of it onto the makeshift track. The boxes sagged a bit, but didn't collapse. The ball picked up speed, making a loud crunching, scraping noise on the cardboard as it bowled along.

"Okay! Okay! He's at some Episcopalian Church on Ninety-ninth! Grace something or other! He's got the cop with him!"

Hatcher lunged forward and got a hand on the ball, stopping it a couple of feet before the edge of the desk.

"Is she hurt?"

Sherman exhaled, panted like a sprinter after a dash. "No." He hesitated. "Little banged up, maybe. That's all."

"Why does he want the dagger?"

"The dagger?"

"Yes, the dagger. The one I was told to leave at the front desk. Why does he want it?"

"I don't know anything about any fucking dagger."

"Then why did he want me to bring it here?"

"Because when you're *here*, you're not *there*."

Hatcher let those words float though his mind. "How much time do I have?"

"For what?"

"To stop whatever he has going down."

"All he told me to do was to make sure you didn't get there."

"Tell me what he's up to."

"Who knows? He's fucking crazy, man. He talks about punishing God and raising some demon." Sherman swallowed, still trying to catch his breath. "I don't even listen half the time. I just take his money."

"And kill women for him."

"That's his gig, man. I just find 'em for him. He's got some fucking freak he made, some genetics shit. He calls it the 'Get of Damnation.' He feeds it those gals' hearts. You believe that? It was all him."

Hatcher looked out the window. The blue of the sky was fading. Lights from the buildings were taking on a new brightness. "Why?"

"Why? 'Cause he's *fucking crazy*. Says it has to be trained. So the demon won't be confused or some shit. I'm telling you, he's whacked. He's holding a fucking nun captive."

A nun? Memories of the missing nun Wright had told him about bubbled to the surface.

"Why Wright?"

"Huh?"

"The cop, Detective Wright—why did he take her?"

"I don't know, he doesn't tell me all that shit. Just said she was part of the plan. Heard him talking about it on the phone with that cop he's got in his pocket. He didn't seem to know about it till the last minute, either."

"What cop?"

"I don't know, some detective. I think he works with that chick."

Reynolds. He wanted to ask Sherman more about that, but he knew he didn't have time.

"What about Deborah?"

"What about her? That's one psycho bitch."

"Is she a part of this?"

"*Duh*. Her and her Carnate friends. Freaks, man. All of them."

"Why were you trying to kill her at the hospital then?"

"Kill her? I was there to *protect* her. Valentine knew some of those other freaky bitches would make a move on her."

There were so many more things he wanted to know, so many more questions, but daylight was all but gone. He didn't have the luxury.

"And Wright's there, now. At the church? Alive?"

"Yes, Sir Lancelot. Valentine insisted she be there."

"How much muscle does he have, other than you?"

"Just some of those bitches, man. They can be ruthless."

"Weapons?"

"Hates 'em! Would freak if anyone brought a gun in there."

"Why?"

"Who the hell knows? I told you, that son of a bitch is crazy, just plain loony tunes."

Hatcher nodded. The shadows slanting across the room told him the information he had would have to do. He took his hand off the ball and let it continue down the track. He saw Sherman's eyelids spread wide in the mirror.

"Hey! What the fuck! I told you everything! *Hey! Wait! No—!*"

The ball slipped of the end of the desk at a full roll and plummeted straight down. It shattered as it hit the floor, a few inches short of the statue.

"Oops," Hatcher said. He pulled out his cell phone and

checked the time. "One of these days I'm going to learn
how to build a better one of these."

MALONEY ANSWERED ON THE THIRD RING.

"Hatcher?"

The taxi swerved into the next lane, causing Hatcher
to drop his hand and catch himself against the door. He'd
offered the driver a hundred bucks if he'd get him to the
church as fast as possible. The guy made a wisecrack
about being dressed funny for a wedding, but he obviously
wanted the money. If he was observing any traffic laws,
Hatcher had yet to notice.

He raised the phone to his ear. "I'm here."

"What's going on? Where are you?"

"I need to know I can trust you."

A pause. "To do what?"

"I'm heading to an Episcopalian church on Ninety-ninth.
I think it's called Grace. You know it?"

"Yes. Grace Trinity. It's closed."

"I think Wright is there. I'll be there in fifteen minutes."

Another pause, longer this time. "I'll meet you out in
front."

"Be discreet," Hatcher said. "And come alone. At least
until we can see what we're dealing with. She might get
hurt if there are sirens or cars pulling up all over the place.
This isn't your normal hostage situation. There's a lot you
don't know. I'm trusting you, against my instincts. Have
the cavalry ready to go, though."

"I'll be alone."

Hatcher shut the phone and adjusted the dagger. The
edge of the hilt was rubbing a sore spot on his calf. He
realized he should have switched legs. But right now, he
couldn't afford to worry about that. There were too many
other things to think about.

Nothing made sense, and he couldn't shake the feeling

that he was missing something, something right in front of him.

He had the driver drop him off at the corner and he made his way back along the opposite sidewalk. The church facade was Old World, with Gothic trim over weathered stone. Tall panes of stained glass towered above wrought-iron gates. Slender spires speared heavenward from behind medieval arches. Small gargoyles crouched atop the structure's corners, mouths open.

A sign noted services had been relocated for renovation.

Hatcher kept walking, reversed course at the corner, passed again going the other way. He kept that up for several minutes until he spotted a car parallel park one block over. A man got out and headed his way. He saw right away it was Maloney.

The detective nodded grimly as he approached. "Been here long?"

"Few minutes." Hatcher looked at the skyline. Darkness was spreading like a stain of ink.

"I've got several units on standby. So, Rambo, what did you have in mind?"

Hatcher turned his head toward the church. "I was thinking I'd have a look around. Inside."

"And I suppose I should let you lead, since you're the only one who seems to have any idea what's supposed to be going on in there."

"I have no real idea what's going on in there. But there's only one way to find out. If there's trouble, you call in the troops."

"Sounds simple enough to me," the lieutenant said, as if considering a suggested place for lunch.

"You think I'm full of shit, don't you?"

Maloney twisted his mouth into a warped frown. "I'm here, aren't I?"

Hatcher said nothing. He watched Maloney watch him for a moment, then crossed the street and angled toward the church.

An alley with a driveway next to the church led through a patch of shadow to some kind of back lot. A single lamp-post threw off a cone of light.

"I'm just going to use the front door," Hatcher said, pausing at the alley.

Maloney gave a noncommital nod. "Because no one would be expecting it?"

"That, and because in a church, it should provide the most visibility. I have a feeling that if anything is happening in there, it's happening at the altar. We might be able to see it right away. And if my information is wrong, we'd have a lot less explaining to do. I don't want to scare some clergyman into a coronary."

"Okay by me."

Hatcher didn't tell him the real reason—that going in the front afforded him the most opportunity to keep some space between him and Maloney, to keep him in his sights as much as possible. He still didn't trust the man. An altercation ending in a gunshot after being caught breaking into the rear of a church seemed like a good setup. A little paranoid, maybe, but he figured that low-grade paranoia had kept him alive this long. You always dance with the one that brung you.

"Give me ten minutes. If you haven't heard from me, call in some of your troops. If I find something, I'll either come get you, or reach you on your cell. Clear?"

Maloney patted the side pocket of his coat. Hatcher could see something compact move when he tapped it, realized it was his phone. "Five by five."

The action on the door handle was heavy. The door opened with a subtle creak as Hatcher tugged on it, spilling a dim yellow glow onto the stone platform of the entrance.

After glancing one final time at Maloney, Hatcher entered.

The inside of the church was cool. Hatcher pulled the door shut, heard the latch quietly catch behind him.

Looking into the nave, he could tell right away something

was off. The center aisle ended in abrupt shadow halfway into the church, with soft light illuminating the pews up until that point. The stained glass populating the upper perimeter twinkled with the glow of outside streetlights.

He walked the aisle slowly, stopping after a few yards, listening. There were sounds he could make out, subtle rustling noises and bumps. He tried to see into the shadow, to what lay inside and beyond it, but couldn't make out more than a few indistinct shapes. He looked to each side. Passages and walkways beneath arcade columns were draped in darkness.

This is a trap.

He turned and started back toward the entrance, then paused. He stared through the anteroom, watching the huge set of double doors. Maloney. Why had he been so agreeable to him going in alone?

Another tentative step, and something hard scraped under his shoe. He stooped to pick it up. A chunk of marble flooring, flat and smooth on one side. He stood, heard the sounds of the street rush in, then the shutting of the door as he looked up. Maloney was standing in the anteroom. Hatcher watched as the detective drew his revolver and pointed it at him.

Son of a bitch. I knew it. I knew it, and for some reason I called him anyway. Why the hell did I do that? How could I be so stupid?

Hatcher tensed his legs, prepared to dive, slide behind one of the pews, use the concealment to move out of the light. But then he became aware of footfalls behind him, growing louder. He whipped his body to the side, blading himself to Maloney, and shot a look back up the aisle.

A man with a clown's head was charging toward him, arms high and flailing, enormous bright gloves holding long blades that lashed the air. Hatcher had seen that clown face before, the creepy, elongated eyes, large and maniacal as they sagged to each side, the insane, demonic grin, orange tufts of hair sticking out from each temple and one protruding from the top. The clown mask at the precinct.

Reynolds's trophy.

Three deafening shots rang out in quick succession, a double tap, then a third. The clown's body jolted as it continued stumbling forward, two tiny explosions erupting in its chest. The mask snapped back violently on the third shot, and the man fell forward onto his clown face. The outstretched blades clanked off the floor barely a yard away from Hatcher's feet, still in the man's hands.

The church had gone unnaturally quiet with the first shot. Hatcher's ears felt plugged, submerged, and everything he could hear was distant and muffled. Numbness quickly gave way to ringing. He looked at Maloney, who was still holding his gun out. A wisp of smoke curled up from the end of the barrel.

Hatcher gave a visual sweep of the area, shooting looks in every direction. Nothing seemed to be moving. No other attackers stormed out of the shadows.

He glanced one more time at Maloney, then moved to the body and took a knee alongside it. He removed the mask. Red hair. Freckles. One blue, unfocused eye, the other eye socket a pulpy, raw wound, oozing blood and other viscous fluids onto the floor. His hands were covered by red hockey gloves with a large machete attached to each, the gloves and blades secured to his forearms with buckled leather straps in some kind of homemade rig.

"It's Reynolds," Hatcher said, barely able to hear his own voice through the ringing in his ears.

Maloney said nothing. He swallowed and nodded uncertainly.

Hatcher pressed around his neck for a pulse, not expecting to find any. The front of Reynolds's throat felt swollen. He was about to turn the body over to inspect it when he caught movement out of the corner of his eye.

There were shapes in the shadows down the aisle. They were getting closer.

He heard Maloney say something through the cotton in his ears, and realized Maloney had been calling out for at least a few seconds.

As he turned, he spied more movement to each side, shadows within shadows, weaving, bobbing, walking.

"Go!" Hatcher yelled, pointing toward the front door as he broke into a run. "Get out of here!"

Maloney seemed rooted to the spot. Before Hatcher could reach him, something dropped in front of him. It slammed against the floor and even through the ringing Hatcher could hear the sickening sound of bones cracking. He stumbled to a stop. The creature pushed itself to its feet uneasily. Hatcher realized it must have leaped from a balcony. It looked at him with black eyes and the upturned snout of a bat.

Sedim.

They started to emerge from the darkness in all directions. Four behind him, two from each side. The one in front of him moved toward him with a wobbly gait.

Hatcher lowered his weight, coiling his leg muscles. The creature reached out for him. Catching hold of its arm, he spun into it, jamming the lower part of his back against its midsection and jerking his body down as he pulled. The Sedim flipped over him and crashed into one of the pews.

He turned back in time to see Maloney being dragged away by two more, heading into the shadows behind a stone arcade. He vaulted several rows of pews as he heard two more shots ring out, these muted somewhat by the walls, their reports echoing. He sprinted to the edge of the shadow, where two Sedim lunged out of the dark, tackling him.

Kicking and punching, he managed to rip himself from their grip and get to his feet. He took a few steps back, then barreled through the pair as they stood, knocking them to the floor. He sprinted into the blackness, barely able to see the walls. There was a door to the side. He pulled on it, but it didn't budge. He called out to Maloney. No response. He called out again. Nothing.

Think.

Darkness surrounded him. Placing his back against the door, he pulled out a cell phone—not caring which one— and dialed 911. Nothing. He looked at the glowing display. No signal.

Shoving the phone back in his pocket, he headed back the way he came. In the light, the two Sedim he'd bowled over were still sprawled on the floor. Strange, he thought.

The front door was not very far. He bolted out into the light, hurtling the bodies of the Sedim. Six Sedim were in the aisle, near Reynolds's body, another two were on the far side, straight across from him. None seemed to be moving very fast. Without breaking stride, he rounded the corner into the anteroom, bounded into the set of front doors with a slap. He pulled on each of them, together and one at a time, thumbing the latch repeatedly.

Shit.

He turned. The Sedim were close now, almost to the threshold. There was no avoiding them. He took a breath and threw himself forward.

The only plan he had was to get through them, to try to find an exit on the other side of the church. He crashed into the first one, knocking it backward. Another latched on to his arm. He kicked that one in the chest, sending it flying into a row of pews.

They're weak, he realized. Not like in the tunnel. *Maybe being aboveground saps their strength.*

He let them come. Eight more in all. A hail of punches and kicks and throws. A few got up, but were easily dispatched the second time around. Within a couple of minutes, the aisle was scattered with scaly, inhuman corpses, totally lifeless.

His shadow suddenly appeared over the bodies. The center of the church erupted in light. He turned toward the altar.

Scaffolding had been erected along the sides near the pulpits. A portion of one pulpit had been removed where it connected to one of the platforms. The front pews had been moved to the side, clearing a large area. An enormous symbol was engraved in the marble of the floor, something that resembled a huge cross whose bottom half turned into an upside-down question mark, the curling three-quarter circle of it like a fish hook. To either side of it, a few yards back, walls of thick cloth mirrored each other, curtains screening off the view of whatever was behind them.

On the scaffolding, opposing rows of women stood over bowls set atop pedestals. Beautiful women. Deborah was on one side of the pulpit. Soliya on the other.

A man stood in the pulpit. An aristocratic air marked his demeanor. Across his face an expression of mild amusement danced in the light.

"My, you certainly are a bull in a china shop. I believe you've met my charming friends," Valentine said.

Hatcher recognized several of the other women from the tunnels. Callista winked.

Dozens of Carnates. And Valentine, looking very much like the photos Hatcher had seen. All of them standing triumphantly, expectantly. All of them watching him.

"Jacob Hatcher," Valentine continued. "We finally meet. My *brutha from anutha mutha.*"

Hatcher looked directly at Deborah. She stared back like he was a complete stranger, no more familar than a passing pedestrian in a crosswalk, able to hold his gaze without any trace of shame, her expression coldly inscrutable. He did detect the tiniest hint of satisfaction, though, a hint that he sensed had nothing to do with him.

"Where's Wright?" Hatcher asked.

"Ah, yes. Our knight in shining armor, come to save the lovely damsel." Valentine leaned down, reaching beneath the wall of the pulpit, and started to drag something onto the scaffolding walkway. It was Wright, wrists cuffed in front of her, ankles bound together with tie wraps. He was pulling her by her hair, forcing her to scoot with him on her knees, moving like a rabbit. She looked frightened and angry and tired and helpless.

When she saw Hatcher she opened her mouth, but nothing came out.

"What do you want?" Hatcher said.

Valentine stopped near a large cable suspended above him. An industrial hook dangled from the end. He placed his fingers over the curl, eyes on Hatcher, and let it take some of his weight, like a subway commuter.

"Think of this as . . . a game show. I'm going to give you a choice. You can have the lovely Detective Wright, or what's behind curtain number one."

Hatcher glanced at the curtains, let his eyes roam over the Carnates, embodiments of pure sex all, then returned his gaze to Valentine.

"And the catch?"

"Such cynicism! Think of it as a challenge. Aren't you curious as to what's hidden from view? I'm disappointed."

Without waiting for a response, Valentine nodded to one of the Carnates. She reached down and picked up a slender cord. When she tugged on it, the walls below her to Hatcher's left lost their support and split apart, falling forward at perpendicular angles. Behind them was a woman, naked, chained obscenely on a platform over a wedge of cushioning. She appeared to be fighting back sobs, though she made no noise. She looked at Hatcher with eyes that seemed to pity him and implore him at the same time. Scared eyes, but sophisticated for someone so young. Someone hardly more than a girl.

There was movement on the scaffolding, and Hatcher saw Valentine lean behind Wright. She resisted him at first, but then he pressed his fingertips behind her ears and yanked her to her feet. With her ankles bound, she had no means to fight him as he forced her arms up and slipped the tip of the hook under the chain between the cuffs. The hook started to rise, pulling Wright's arms high, and soon she was being winched into the air.

She kicked out at Valentine as she left the platform, a dolphin move with both feet. Valentine leaned to the side, easily avoiding it, grinning.

Hatcher followed the cable with his eyes. High above, he could make out a catwalk of some sort in the shadows. A featureless shape moving in the darkness. Another Carnate, he realized, operating a power winch.

"So, Brother—save the woman you love, or save the innocent maiden, a true child of God."

"Save them," Hatcher said. His eyes jumped from Wright, to the naked girl, then back again. "From what?"

Valentine smiled. "What a terrific question." He nodded in the direction of the other enclosure. One of the Carnates on that side pulled on a cord, sending the walls of it tipping outward and falling to the floor.

"Behold!" Valentine continued. "The Get of Damnation!"

Visible behind where the walls had stood was a roughly eight-by-eight cage, with bars at least an inch in diameter. Inside the cage was an animal. Hatcher assumed it was a primate of some sort. It was the size of gorilla, but more angular, less hirsute. It had the elongated snout of a baboon and long hair hanging from its head. Its flapped ears looked like they belonged on a farm animal. The eyes appeared almost human. Almost.

It clasped two enormous hands on the front bars of the cage and let out a sound that sent a jolt through Hatcher's chest. Those almost-human eyes grew wide at the sight of the girl, but quickly shot over to Hatcher and leveled on him. It sat back on its haunches and slightly bared its teeth. Its gaze remained fixed.

The side of the cage that faced the young woman suddenly rose about an inch off the ground, then stopped. The movement drew Hatcher's attention to an inconspicuous mechanism on the top corner, a square box with a thick-toothed gear on the side of it. The teeth bit into grooves connected to one of the vertical bars that extended higher than the others.

"Since I am nothing if not a good sport, there is one other option." Valentine held up a tiny electronic device. "This controls the gate. You have approximately three minutes before the bars rise high enough for the Get to escape his confines. If you could somehow reach me and retrieve this in time, perhaps you won't have to make the choice."

Hatcher ran his eyes down the scaffolding, then glanced at the cage. The little box let out a whir and the gate moved up a small distance, doubling its height. The creature shot an arm through the opening, already trying to squeeze through.

Wright hung a few yards away, her body swaying as she bucked and swung her legs. He could get to her, lift her high enough for her to get the cuffs over the tip of the hook, but it would take too long. If he carried her away, the other woman would fall prey to whatever that thing in the cage was. If he tried to undo the tie wraps first, that thing may be out and attacking before he was done.

Not much of a choice, as he saw it. Without wasting another moment, he broke into a sprint directly at the scaffolding. The Get snarled as he passed by, raking its fingers through the air, it's impossibly long arm coming much closer than Hatcher had expected.

No slowing, no stutter step. Hatcher leaped in mid-stride and grabbed hold of the metal cross supports of the scaffold, swinging his legs up and hooking them so he could press up and grab a higher set. Muscles still aching from his run-in with the Carnates on the street, ribs still making him wince from the squeeze Sherman had put on them, it took him almost a full minute to reach the top. He expected to be met there, his putative sibling kicking at him as he pulled himself up and onto the platform. But Valentine kept his distance.

"Not bad. But you've only got a minute and a half.

Ninety seconds." Valentine took the device, which at this closer distance looked to Hatcher like the remote control to some child's toy, and shoved it deep into his front pocket.

"And the problem is," Valentine continued, "you'll have to kill me to get it. And you just don't have that in you. *Brother.*"

The hell I don't. Hatcher dropped to a knee and pulled up his pant leg, yanking the dagger free from his calf. He took two forceful steps forward.

"Last chance," Hatcher said. "Give me it, or I take it from your corpse. You don't know me, Valentine. You don't know what I'm capable of."

"Oh, but I do."

Hatcher lunged forward, grabbed Valentine's shirt, pressed the point of the dagger to his throat. He moved his hand to reach into Valentine's pocket, but Valentine grabbed his wrist.

"Do it," Valentine said. He pressed his flesh against the blade, causing an indentation near his Adam's apple. "*I dare you.* Complete the Prophecy of the Carnates. You must kill your brother. It is preordained. Do it. If you're man enough. *If you have the balls.*"

There was no fear in his eyes, no concern. Other than maintaining a surprisingly strong grip on Hatcher's wrist, there was no real resistance. Hatcher shot a look past Valentine's head. The Carnates remained where they were. He glanced back over his own shoulder. Deborah was still in the same place. All were watching intently, but none of them had moved.

A tiny droplet of blood appeared on Valentine's neck at the tip of the dagger. Hatcher felt the urge to drive the blade home, tightened his grip around the handle.

Something in his head clicked. Valentine wasn't armed. Why? Why play this kind of game, why not just pull a gun? Why didn't any of them have guns?

This whole thing has been a setup.

"No." He pushed Valentine away.

"What? But you must! Surely you don't put any stock in some silly prophecy, do you? A worldly man like you?"

"I'm not going to let myself be tricked into doing what you led me here to do." He swept his chin toward Soliya. "What they led me here to do. I'm not going to murder you, you sick bastard."

Valentine dropped his gaze toward the cage. "Then you'll watch both these women die."

The box on the cage hummed, and the cage door clicked up another notch. That was just enough. The creature slithered under the bottom bar and rolled to its feet. It seemed to aim its body at the naked form of the woman as it rose, ready to spring.

"The hell I will."

Hatcher vaulted the side rail of the scaffolding, aiming directly for the animal's back. It was a fifteen-foot drop. The Get looked up and roared, moving just enough so that Hatcher's feet glanced off its shoulder and arm, knocking the thing off balance but doing little damage. Hatcher dropped the dagger and took the brunt of the impact with the floor off his own shoulder, tucking his head and managing to roll away.

The dagger lay on the marble surface between him and the Get. For a moment, neither moved. The creature watched him with eyes that were both wild and comprehending. Both its expression and posture were entirely feral. It was almost humanlike in its shape, with the elongated limbs of a primate. But now it was in a four-point stance, baring oversized canines. An enraged ape. A rabid baboon.

Feinting first, Hatcher dove at the dagger. The creature leaped high, arms above its head, legs coiled beneath it, jaws cocked wide. It roared midway through its leap.

In one continuous motion, Hatcher grabbed the dagger and rolled, thrusting it straight up. It plunged firmly into the animal's chest, dead center, the Get's own weight burying the blade deep.

A short burst of vibration buzzed through Hatcher's hand

as the hilt of the dagger slammed against the thing's breastbone. He felt the internal workings of some mechanism in his palm, a click of disengagement, the releasing of a spring.

The Get yanked itself back, stumbling. It looked down at its chest. A small portion of the end of the blade protruded, like a flattened tube. Blood spurted out as if from a hose, landing on the marble floor with a splat. It formed a small pool as it poured out and flowed into the grooves of the symbol that had been engraved into it.

Hatcher dropped his eyes to his hand. The handle was still there. A thinner blade protruded from the hilt. Around its base, he could see the prongs of a mechanical catch. A spring-loaded dagger, designed to release an outer blade. A weapon designed to exsanguinate its victim. A weapon that, judging by what he was witnessing, did its job very well.

Each beat of the creature's heart sent another gush through the hollow blade until after a few seconds there was nothing but a trickle. The Get stood motionless, seemed to try to move, but instead dropped face-first. It landed on the floor with the dead slap of deli meat.

Dropping his hands to his knees and resting his weight on them, Hatcher tried to make up for lost breathing. His body was enervated, his legs shaky, his arms sacks of wet cement. He sucked in several lungfuls of air and forced himself to straighten up. He looked at Valentine. At first Hatcher thought the man was stunned, too shocked to react. But a distinct feeling of unease started to worm its way through his gut.

There was no look of dejection, no crestfallen eyes or slouching shoulders. Valentine was staring intently, the expression on his face hard to read, but one that Hatcher could only describe as brimming with anticipation. His gaze remained fixed on the body of the Get.

Hatcher looked at each of the Carnates. They watched without expression, but their eyes seemed wide, the mouths and cheeks of a few twitching with the hint of a smile. Almost simultaneously, they produced tiny knives in their right hands and cut the wrists of their left. They then submerged their wrists in the bowls before them and closed their eyes.

Wright's eyes were saucered as she hung from the cable, frozen in a look of dread beneath a tense, pleading brow. Her lips quivered. She held Hatcher's gaze and shook her head slowly.

"Did I mention that one of my triple majors was in psychology, Brother?"

Two ropes dropped from the catwalk above. A pair of Carnates descended onto the scaffolding near Valentine. A redhead and a brunette, both of whom he recognized immediately. The brunette was slightly favoring her abdomen.

"You may not have realized it, but Carnates are not only irresistible, they are world-class actresses. They followed my script masterfully. First, working that hapless sap Warren into pondering the killing of his wife, then directing his worried spouse to your half brother, who played the role of tragic hero on cue."

Valentine's tone taunted and teased. The unease was now acute anxiety. Oh, shit, he thought. *What the hell did I just do?*

"It all came down to you, Jake. There was only one man in the world who could do it, one man who could enable me to complete the most extreme of summonings from the Book of Thoth. One who had my own blood. One whose psychological profile I deconstructed and reconstructed over and over and over, one man I studied until I knew him better than he knew himself. College curriculum, high school courses, base assignments. Just literate enough to know Steinbeck, to recognize a few allusions."

The blood that filled the groove of the symbol began to pop and bubble, quickly roiling into a boil. A putrid smell wafted over Hatcher, almost making him gag.

"Throw in a useful idiot like Sherman—a sap who had

no idea what was really happening but would give you what I wanted him to when he cracked—throw some money and sex a corrupt detective's way, and everything I needed was in place.

"And you. Bravo! You played your part to perfection," Valentine said. *"Perfection!"*

Hatcher raised his eyes to Valentine's, then back to the Get. The floor beneath the creature trembled. Cracks spread out from the carved symbol.

"In the beginning, God created the Heavens and the Earth. No one ever stops to think about that, do they, Jake? No mention of creating Hell. Our concept of Heaven, you see, was created for this experiment we call Earth, both at the same time. Hell is eternal, but Heaven is not."

The creature's body began to twitch.

"You did what no other could. You killed your brother, *our* brother, a brother neither man nor beast, an abomination born of the blood of its one, slain by the blood of its other."

Movement. Just the limbs at first, but within seconds the chest spasmed and the eyes shot open. The Get jerked up to its knees, springing like a marionette. Once on its feet, it started to grow.

"The tens upon tens of millions of dollars I've spent, the countless hours over years and years . . ."

Its arms swelled, its chest stretched as if something were inflating it. The creature became enormous right in front of Hatcher's eyes. Its head seemed to add bone layers as it expanded. The eyes turned a dark shade of cherry black, like motor oil mixed with arterial spray.

"I have actually done it! *You* have actually done it! We have smote the Get of Damnation, *and have raised the Prince of Hell.* Have risen the one who will not rise!"

The thing inhaled a deep breath, flexing its chest and spreading its shoulders, then it roared with a fury that scalded Hatcher's ears.

"I will give those boys in uniform some credit. Their

psych profile of you was *spot-on*. I had to tweak it, of course, since I knew some things they didn't. But they were quite thorough. And for someone not functioning in the private sector, the GI I found with access to your records was quite the businessman. He shook me down for a substantial sum of money."

Hatcher watched the Get as it tried to orient itself. It looked in several directions, taking in its surroundings. There was no question it had grown in front of Hatcher's eyes since he'd stabbed it, larger now that it had been, taller, wider. Like something was inside of it, wearing a formfitting costume several sizes too small, the material stretched to its breaking point. Two bumps bulged from its skull over its brows, cranial protrusions that looked almost like horns.

The Get seemed confused. It scanned the church with a wary, predatory gaze. Its eyes finally settled on the naked woman. Her head was turned, set to look back over her shoulder at it, but her eyes were tightly shut. Her lips were moving, as if she were mouthing a silent prayer.

"Let them go," Hatcher said. "You've got what you wanted."

"Let them go? Now why would I do a thing like that? Brother of mine, you don't seem to understand the point of the exercise."

Hatcher's mind raced, scrambling for an idea. There had to be something he could do, but his options seemed severely limited. The Get was enormous. It would be like attacking a grizzly. He looked down at the knife in his hand. The thinner, shorter blade looked impossibly small.

"That cost me a pretty penny, you know. A medieval spring-loaded dagger, the genuine article. Of course, the pedigree was pure cock and bull. The Dagger of Cain. Ha! How gullible, how easily manipulated, you were."

The Get was staring at the woman now. Eyes wide like some insane animal. Its body seemed to shudder.

"His brain, you see—it's not quite capable of channeling Belial's *mind*. Not right away. That's why I had to imprint it, to condition it. Allow for instinct to take over, so he would know what to do. What he would know himself to do if he could process a rational thought."

Its breathing was heavier now. Hatcher noticed its penis begin to rise, the shaft extending, swelling erect.

"Don't even think about it, Jake. It's too late. Once Belial consummates the ritual, once he defiles the innocent one, the child of God, once he who cannot be risen has done the unspeakable, I will have achieved what no other dared ever even think of. I will have brought to pass the events foretold in the Book of Thoth.

"I, Demetrius Valentine, will have ended the covenant of Creation. *I will have brought down Heaven.*"

The Get seemed to have whipped itself into a frenzy staring at the woman, her legs spread and genitals exposed in an obscene pose. It moved toward her with a deliberate stride.

There were no options, Hatcher realized. This was the grenade in the foxhole, and someone had to throw himself on it. He bolted toward the Get in a dead sprint, angling to intercept. He lowered his shoulder and exploded with his legs as he reached it.

The thing stumbled sideways a couple of steps but didn't go down. Using the knife handle like a roll of coins, Hatcher threw the hardest punch he could muster directly across its chin. He slashed the knife toward the side of its neck as he yanked his fist back, but the thing wasn't as stunned as he'd counted on. It caught his arm solidly at the wrist. Too fast, too strong. Its grip was crushing. It shook its head and roared again, an angry, earsplitting, atavistic sound, as it thrust its other hand under his jaw. Hatcher felt his neck stretch, felt himself jerked into the air. The Get snapped him back and forth a few times, then lifted him high over its head. The fingers pressing into his flesh and muscle seemed like they were going to pinch his head clean off. He was certain his skull was about to explode, but before that could happen the thing threw him into the first remaining rows of pews. The section he hit crashed into the one behind it, the wood cracking and splintering. Hatcher bounced off of it and landed facedown on the marble floor.

Hatcher's chest felt caved in. His head was a foreign object, only loosely attached to his neck. He couldn't breathe, could barely move. The Get lunged toward him with long, menacing steps. It stopped a few feet away and screamed, a visceral, primal shriek. An echo from the birth of Creation, resonating from Hell.

The Get watched Hatcher lie there for a few seconds before it turned back and refocused on the woman.

"I suppose it would have only been fair to warn you ahead of time, but by touching him like that, you've damned yourself for all eternity. This is the crown prince of demons. So much as a brush against him, against this magnificent corporeal vessel I created, renders a person unclean. Unclean, with no hope of Salvation. Sorry, *Brother*.

"Of course, it doesn't really matter, because once Belial has fulfilled the final step, there will be no more Heaven. You see, there is no Prophecy of the Carnates, Jake. Never was. That was just something tossed into cyberspace to back up our story. There was only the ritual of the Book of Thoth. A ritual kept secret for thousands of years, hidden by cloaks of magic. Broken down and brought to pass, by *me*. By *you*."

Hot stabs of pain shot through Hatcher's chest as he forced air into his lungs. His limbs were heavy and stiff, packed with wet cement that was starting to dry. Searing pangs shot through his back as he tried to push himself up. He raised his head, willed his eyes to flutter open.

The panes of a large stained-glass window glowed dimly in the darkness on the side of the church. A depiction of Christ, head rounded with halo, tilted down and to the side, his arms extended outward. Surrounded by apostles.

"I know I've never been much to you," Hatcher said, his voice barely louder than his breath. "But I sure could use a hand about now."

Christ continued to stare, his gaze the same mix of compassion and apathy.

"Figures." Hatcher managed to roll off his stomach onto his back. Something dug into the bone of his spine. He reached behind him with great effort and removed it.

The knife. His hand ached as he let go of the heavy handle, letting it slide to the floor. Hatcher dropped his head back and breathed. A gun would be nicer. If only the damn thing had a glass jaw.

Hatcher tilted his head. The Get was circling the woman warily now, sniffing at her. It touched its penis as if it were uncertain it had one as it circled back behind her. Her eyes were squeezed shut, and she was mouthing something over and over again, silently. He was amazed she didn't scream.

I'm sorry.

Above the Get, Hatcher saw Soliya, observing intently. All the Carnates were rapt, their eyes fixed, their bodies tense with expectation. Wright still hung from the cable, kicking her legs, trying to swing. He shot a glance over to the young woman again, then back at Wright. Why doesn't she make any sounds, either?

Hatcher turned his attention to the stained-glass window one more time as a nascent thought squirmed, trying to emerge.

The image of Christ remained impassive as Hatcher took it in.

He remembered the Carnate on the street, remembered how she winced.

Carnates, being the issue of a fallen angel of hostility . . . it is presumed they have inherited the infirmities of same, though perhaps to a less vexing degree, as their blood is not whole; iron blessed most hallow, the scream of a virgin pure, and the shattering of glass which carries the ring of God's judgment, all may cause distress to their senses.

The Get dropped over the woman's back onto its long arms, a push-up position, snuffling at her hair, hovering over her.

Taking a firm grip of the knife, Hatcher forced himself to his feet. What was it Sherman had said? *He would freak if someone ever brought a gun in there.* He looked at Christ one more time and cocked his arm. *Don't you be a tease, damn it.*

Please.

He threw the piece of metal like a tomahawk. It tumbled end over end high into the air. He'd aimed right at the head of Christ. Watched it flip, flip, flip through space toward Him, rising in a triumphant arc, then curving down. It wasn't going to reach.

No . . .

The object started to fall in a lazy lob. Hatcher held his breath. It was going to be short, it wasn't going to reach, it wasn't—the glass shattered with a loud crash. The knife had smashed through the bottom of the window, near Christ's feet.

The Get seized up, bouncing back onto both legs. Its hands shot to its ears and it let out a long howl. Its head was thrown back, twisting and shaking atop its neck.

A few more panes of glass adjacent to the one smashed dropped from the window and shattered on the floor, causing the Get to screech in agony even more loudly. A crack raced up the window, winding its way through the image of Christ. It stopped abruptly before reaching His head.

Almost simultaneously the Carnates' hands shot to their ears and their bodies seemed to sag. Most stepped back from their bowls, blood dripping from their wrists. The expressions Hatcher could make out seemed contorted in anguish.

He scanned the scaffolding, eyes skipping from one Carnate to another, looking for Valentine. He couldn't find him.

There was no time to worry about him. The creature looked vulnerable, but Hatcher had no idea how long that would last. Already it seemed to be catching its breath, shaking off the effects. Hatcher's gaze jumped to the broken pew next to him. He needed a weapon. If he could find a large enough section of wood, he hoped that might be something he could use.

Then his head erupted.

Something jarred his skull from behind, setting it on fire, a dull, muted, flame of pain flashing over his thoughts. He placed his hand on the back his head and felt a scalding thrash, a crack of arm bone. He dropped to his knees, recoiling. He fell forward and instinctively rolled out of the way. The tip of the weapon bashed against marble.

Valentine was standing over him. Eyes red, jaws clenched.

"Do you have any idea how much time and money I spent? I devoted my life to this!"

He slashed the baton toward Hatcher's face. Hatcher was able to block it with his forearm. It left a singeing, stinging gash, and his arm threatened to fall limp.

"I will *not* let the bastard son of a whore ruin this, my one chance at changing everything!"

The end of the baton whipped down again. Hatcher took it more toward the elbow this time. He bit down on his tongue as the pain shot up his arm and through his head.

"I'm going to see this through. Nothing—*nothing*—will stop me."

Pushing with his legs, Hatcher started sliding away, trying to keep as much distance between the baton and his head as he could. He glanced over at the stained-glass window. The cracking had stopped. No more panes looked ready to fall.

He glanced the other way and saw the Get standing erect again, breathing heavily, still shaking its head.

Valentine stepped forward and drew the baton back.

"Just tell me why," Hatcher said, pulling himself up to a knee. He needed to buy time. Time to think. Time to recover some energy.

"Why?" Valentine lowered the baton, but only slightly. "Do you know who my father was? Who *our* father was? A brilliant, brilliant man. How dare God decide he should spend all of eternity burning in Hell, simply because he didn't *believe*? What kind of hubris is that? What kind of almighty being is so petty? So jealous? We're supposed to worship *that*?"

The baton fired downward, glancing off of Hatcher's shoulder as he twisted out of the way. Hatcher grunted, clutched at it.

"I spent every waking hour of every waking day of my life searching for a solution to a problem no one ever dared tackle. How do I save my parents from the lake of fire? The answer was simple. *Damn everyone else*. Then God will either have to give up on the ones He loves so dearly, the devoted followers who praise Him and feed His ego, or He'll have to undo all of it. Once Heaven is done, He'll have to allow the gates of Hell to open. He will have to start over. A new covenant. A new Heaven. A second chance."

"But what if you're wrong? What if there is no second chance? What if it just means everyone goes to Hell?"

Valentine sneered. "Then so be it. If my parents must burn in hellfire for all eternity, so must everyone else."

This was going to hurt. Hatcher watched Valentine raise the baton again, saw his arm cock, then threw his hand into its path, catching the whippy end in his palm and clenching it tightly.

An agonizing sizzle lanced through his hand and up his arm, but he held fast. With an abrupt tug, he got Valentine to take an extra step forward, then threw one of his legs in front of Valentine's shin and scissored him off his feet. He brought the baton down with a crack across the bridge of Valentine's nose. A small burst of blood, then Valentine's face disappeared behind his hands. He screamed into his palms.

Hatcher managed to stand on wobbly legs just as the Get was starting to move toward the young woman again.

He looked down at the baton. He wouldn't be able to intercept the thing before it reached her, and wasn't certain if something so small would do any good, anyway. He shot his gaze over to the stained glass window where he had thrown the knife, saw the cracks that had spidered through it.

His thumb found a notch. With a click, he snapped the telescoping rod of the baton back into the handle. He reared back and hurled it as hard as he could. This time, the dense metal tube smashed through the center of the window.

The sound caused the Get to seize up just as he reached the woman. Its back arched and it grabbed the sides of its skull. Pieces of the window started to fall rapidly, crinkling and cracking and shattering with a splash as they hit the hard floor below.

The Get seemed to be in a tortured state. It spun around, frantic, holding its head like a carnival mask that wouldn't come off, madness bulging through its eyes.

Definitely vulnerable now, Hatcher thought. But obviously still dangerous, maybe even more so than before. Hatcher's eyes raced around the room, searching for something he could use. Anything.

Another chunk of glass broke free, shattering against the floor. Hatcher feared it was the last, but resisted the urge to look.

His gaze stopped on the body further down the aisle. Reynolds.

He bolted toward it, dropping to a knee at the nearest arm. The long machete blade was attached to a large leather hockey glove by some kind of adhesive. The glove was secured tightly to Reynolds's arm by an array of leather straps and buckles. Hatcher fumbled them undone and removed the glove. He slid it on and ran toward the Get.

The creature was flailing wildly now, a spinning, twisting, thrashing dervish of primal insanity. Hatcher looked for an opening, a chance to get one solid strike, a blow that would count. As he started to circle it, he glanced at

Wright. She was bucking her body, mouthing soundless words, eyes bulging.

A warning.

Before he could spin to look, his head snapped back and he catapulted forward.

He stumbled toward Wright, falling onto his hands and knees, the machete clanging as he went down. Valentine landed on Hatcher's back, driving his face against the floor, and started to pummel the back of his head.

"You won't stop me! You won't stop this! *This. Will. Happen!*"

The blows wracked his skull. Hatcher's body felt like it was about to give out. His head was being pinched in a vice, a corkscrew twisting through his brain. He tried to get up, but Valentine kept hitting. Hard, blunt shots, thrown without any apparent regard for the bones in his hand. Hatcher crumbled forward again, trying to fend off what he could. Wright was above him. He could feel her looking down at him. A hollow nausea churned through his gut. Failure.

From someplace that seemed far away, Hatcher heard another tiny explosion of glass against the floor. Heard the Get howl yet again, an insane, strangling bellow.

Valentine stood, sucking breaths. He seemed punched out, raw and bloody knuckles like hamburger meat over fractured bones. Hatcher started to crawl, ended up rolling to one side, onto his back.

"I didn't follow my own warnings," Valentine said. "I underestimated you. That won't happen aga—"

Valentine stumbled sideways, trying to catch his balance. Through blurry eyes, Hatcher was able to see just enough to make it out. Wright had fired out with her bound feet, thrusting her legs enough to send her swinging backward. Enough to send Valentine staggering from the kick.

Bent over, Valentine caught his balance as he came within a few feet of the Get. He slowly straightened his back. The Get's wild eyes bore into him.

A word started to come out of Valentine's mouth, but

before it escaped his lips, the Get shot forward, stabbing claws into Valentine's chest with one hand, grabbing a fist-ful of hair with the other. The thing clamped its massive jaws across Valentine's throat and tore the hair off the man's head, taking Valentine's scalp off with it. Valentine's body collapsed to the floor. His skull dropped after it, a glisten-ing net of red tissue surrounding white teeth and eyes. His face and his heart remained in the Get's clutches.

The thing flung both across the church and let out another screeching yell as the brittle shattering of a small piece of glass echoed. The heart bounced and rolled. Valentine's face lay crumbled and eyeless, staring hollow at the ceiling like a discarded mask.

Hatcher assumed the last piece of glass that fell was it, that the rest would stay put. His head was pounding and he was having difficulty thinking straight, but knew his options were limited. There were plenty more windows he could try to break, but he would have to find things to throw, and he wasn't sure how much longer he could last. To walk would be grueling. He could tell at least two ribs were broken. His shoulder was certainly separated, and his head felt about to split open from the pressure building inside.

He looked up at Wright. She blinked at him, her expression almost apologetic as she swung gently, her arms relaxing but obviously exhausted. She'd stopped trying to free herself from the hook. The message came through clear enough. No matter what, he had to finish it. There was no one else.

Wincing, he pushed himself to his feet and adjusted the glove. His ribs hurt too much to stand erect, so he hunched a bit. The Get was standing over the blood-filled symbol on the floor, clutching at its hair, giving occasional shakes of its head.

Just one opening, Hatcher thought. Just give me one.

He stepped forward, each breath stabbing at his rib cage. His legs were shaking, but he felt a tiny surge of strength, enough to keep him moving. Enough for one last play of scrimmage.

The Get saw him, snapped into an aggressive pose, baring its teeth and roaring, even as its eyes struggled to stay in focus, its head not fully clear.

C'mon. Just give me something, anything.

Beyond the Get, Hatcher noticed the stained-glass window. About the top fourth of it was still there, an uneven diagonal line zigzagging from right to left down through Christ's neck. If only he could throw something else at it, dislodge a few more of the panes. Then he realized there were plenty of windows like it all around him. It didn't matter. Unless he was willing to heave Valentine's heart, there was nothing handy to throw, and he knew even that wouldn't work. The glove and machete were awkward, but they were all he had.

The sound of something crinkling, a faint spreading noise made him stop to listen. He could barely hear anything through the Get's snarling. The thing seemed ready to lunge.

Then he saw the remaining panes of stained glass drop from the window, falling as one section. Christ's face, encased in halo, flashed as the glass rotated. It exploded against the floor with the crash of something bursting into innumerable tiny fragments, shards launching in all directions.

The screech from the Get tore into Hatcher's ears. The creature snapped erect, every muscle straining as if an electric shock was coursing through its system. Its arms were flung out from its sides, its back arched, head thrown to the rear. Its body seemed to start vibrating, and as it did the lines of its form became blurred. Another figure expanded outward from it, a magnified shadow, the enlarged shape of it taking on different features. The head was the vague imprint of a horse, with knobby horns on its skull and eyes that were more like portals to an endless void. It dwarfed the Get as it mimicked its pose, enveloping it, a transparent cloud the putrid color of a bloody stool. The shape of two dark wings fanned out behind it.

A stench invaded Hatcher's nasal passages like an angry swarm and he almost heaved. Something inside clicked, a battle instinct, and without hesitating he bounded forward. He pulled the machete across his body, swung it back to the other side as hard as he could. The blade sliced through the Get's neck. The thing's head fell off and rolled to a stop near Valentine's heart.

The shadowy form surrounding the Get remained, its dark specter of a head now above a decapitated body. The insane rage on its face grew and those views of the void seemed to focus on Hatcher. Before the look could stick, the shape was sucked down into the Get's body with a force that caused the church to rumble. What was left of the Get stood there for a pregnant moment, a headless body uncertain what to do. Then it dropped to the floor.

Hatcher collapsed to his knees. The glove and machete slid from his fingers. His upper body slumped until his face was almost on the floor.

Some murmurs from behind him, urgent whispers. He smelled the smoke as he turned to see Wright trying to say something, tiny sounds coming from her throat. She was gesturing with her head to a corner of the church. The guttering glow of flames was visible from the recesses.

He lifted her legs so she could clear the hook with her cuffs. He set her gently on the floor, then retrieved the machete to cut the tie wraps around her ankles.

The fire was spreading rapidly, already climbing the walls. He realized there was a sharp odor in the air. Kerosene, maybe.

Wright took the machete and scampered to the young woman while Hatcher tried to keep from passing out. The woman seemed slightly dazed. Wright led her gently but hurriedly toward Hatcher. She didn't even try to cover her breasts.

With surprising strength, Wright grabbed Hatcher's wrist and tugged him toward a back corner of the church. He looked up as she gave him a push. The Carnates were all gone.

A corridor led straight back, branching out into smaller hallways. There was a large wooden door at the end. It was locked. A double-sided deadbolt. Hatcher leaned back against the door and tried to find some as yet untapped reserve of energy. He closed his eyes, then heard the smash of breaking glass. Wright was standing in front of a mounted case housing an axe nearby. She dropped the small, dense hammer chained to the side of it and pulled the axe from its clips. She gestured for Hatcher to move, then lifted it with her cuffed hands and took a swing at the door. The blade bounced off, taking a large splinter of wood with it.

Hatcher put a hand on her arms as she hefted the ax a second time. He took it from her, sucked in a smoke-tinged breath, and chopped at the door. It took him five swings to knock off enough wood to loosen the deadbolt. They pushed the door open and stumbled into the back parking lot.

They ended up on the pavement, mostly because Wright fell trying to keep Hatcher on his feet. He rolled onto his back, felt her next to him. She whispered into his ear, *"We made it."*

This is nice, he thought, as he drifted off. Even the darkness of sleep couldn't remove the naked form of the young nun from his sight, hovering over him like an angel.

CHAPTER 25

THE EMTS INSISTED ON GIVING HIM OXYGEN, SO HATCHER sat on the rear step to one of the ambulances holding a clear rubber mask over his nose and mouth to keep them from pestering him. The first few puffs perked him up a bit, but he still just wanted to lie down and get some sleep. The back of an ambulance wasn't what he had in mind.

Wright approached, returning from one of her multiple forays past the blockades out on the street. She had refused to be taken to the hospital, telling the techs in her gradually improving whisper that she was needed here. She wasn't, but Hatcher figured she needed to believe she was.

She stopped as the gurney carrying the young nun passed and gestured for the EMTs to pause. She took a moment to stroke the woman's long blonde hair. The woman didn't react. Her head was turned toward Hatcher. She stared, unblinking. Wright left her and sat next to him and placed a hand on his.

Hatcher watched the EMTs load the gurney into the back of another ambulance. The legs retracted as they lifted it as if it were designed to fly. The nun was still looking in Hatcher's direction as she disappeared into the rear of the vehicle. A glint on her cheek suggested she was crying. At some level, he knew it was for him.

The ambulance pulled away. The space it left was quickly filled by police and firefighters, milling around like ants.

The church was smoldering. The stone frame was intact, but the stained glass had melted and popped, and thick black smoke was piping out of every opening. According to what Hatcher had overheard, the insides were gutted. Firefighters were forced into containment mode from the time they arrived. He and Wright watched together in silence as the hoses shot powerful streams through the windows, trying to douse the last bits of flame.

"How's your throat?" Hatcher asked. They had yet to address the most disturbing aspects of what they'd witnessed. He wondered if they ever would. Or if she had even seen it the same way he had. If Valentine was just another nutcase to her, and nothing more to it.

"I'll be fine."

"I thought about what you'd said. He probably injected your vocal cords with botulinum toxin. BOTOX. It's not an uncommon way to paralyze the voice box. You need to see a doctor. You don't want to risk any damage."

"How would you know something like that?"

Hatcher said nothing. Removing someone's ability to cry out, taking away their ability to scream or even communicate, can scare the hell out of them. Combine that with some pain, and many subjects panic, suddenly become willing to write a memoir with the first thing they're handed. He hadn't done it. But he'd learned about it, heard about it. The Egyptians came to mind.

Wright reacted to something and hopped off the back of the ambulance. A man made his way toward them, crossing between the barriers and nodding to the uniforms milling around the perimeter. It was Maloney.

There was a scrape on his cheek, smears of soot on his

face. Wright ran to him and gave him a hug as he drew close.

"I didn't think you made it," Hatcher said.

Maloney shrugged. "I got lucky. Shot both of those crazy things, managed to shut myself in a room and lock the door as some of their friends showed up."

"Did you call for backup? They sure took their sweet time."

Maloney shook his head. "Cell phones wouldn't work. Some kind of jammer."

Wright said something to him that Hatcher couldn't hear. He nodded but seemed distracted.

To Hatcher he said, "Did you ever find Deborah?"

"She was in there. She was part of it. I think they're long gone."

"Where?"

"I don't know."

Maloney went quiet. A small, dark-haired man in a windbreaker with a badge hanging from a chain around his neck walked up and introduced himself as Detective Garcia. He spoke with Maloney for a few moments, wrote something in a notebook, then left.

"I told him you both would finish giving statements tomorrow. You don't need to be dealing with this crap after what you've been through. Right now, I've got to go make sure they've been listening to what I've said. You two should go get some sleep."

"Thanks."

Wright sat down next to Hatcher as Maloney walked off.

"He can't be too happy to see you with me," Hatcher said.

"Not that again." Wright rolled her eyes. "Sheesh. I told you, there's nothing between us."

"I didn't say there was. I'm just saying, he wishes there were. I'm pretty sure he loves you."

"Hatcher, we dated a few times. It was a while ago. He

hasn't so much as asked me out since. Don't you think a gal would know when guy is in love with her? Quit being paranoid and just let it go."

The words sunk in as she laid her head against his shoulder. After a moment, she patted his leg. She said she'd be back and hopped off again.

Paranoid. Maybe she was right. He thought about how he'd suspected everyone. He thought about Deborah luring Garrett to his death. What an actress she was. He thought about Susan, how Garrett must have fallen for her, how Valentine used that to get at him, just like he used Wright. What a man will do for a woman.

Then it hit him. Garrett. Himself. It started as a thought, spread as a feeling of realization. *Carnates are not only irresistible, they are world-class actresses.* The implications made the acid in his stomach churn.

Options started to flash through his mind almost immediately. None of them was appealing.

Oh, boy. He watched Wright slip past the barrier, thinking about how much he'd been looking forward to them having something together, to trying to make it work. The feeling of loss was already setting in. He put the mask to his face and breathed, mumbling into it.

"This absolutely sucks."

CHAPTER 26

MALONEY PACED ALONG THE EDGE OF THE ROOFTOP, checking his watch every few moments. The breeze pulled on his artificial hair as he paused to look around before reversing course and starting over. It was almost three a.m.

He stopped and patted at the pocket to his coat, reached in, and removed a cell phone. A quizzical glance at the screen, then he flipped it open.

"Hello?"

"Hello," Hatcher said.

Maloney spun around, dropping the phone from his ear. "Jesus! Hatcher? What the hell are you doing here?"

Hatcher walked over to the concrete ledge, took a spot right next to Maloney. He leaned over it, looking out across water. The lights of the city twinkled like some magical island. It was a hell of a view.

"She's not coming," he said.

"Who"—the words seemed to stick in Maloney's throat and he coughed lightly—"who isn't coming?"

"I'm the one who sent you the text message."

Maloney didn't move. He stared at Hatcher for several seconds. "That could be considered interfering with a police investigation. Why would you do something like that?"

"Because . . ." Hatcher turned, unloaded with a right. It was a short, compact punch, but it landed squarely on Maloney's solar plexus. The detective grunted and hunched forward. "It was the one way to be sure. And to get you to come alone."

Hatcher reached a hand inside his coat, slid it around his belt until he found the revolver. He unsnapped the strap with his thumb and yanked it free from its holster, reared into a wind-up and threw it as far as he could. It flashed in the lights then disappeared. He imagined he heard a plunking sound from far below, but couldn't be sure.

"Are you crazy?" Maloney's face was set in a grimace. He clutched his stomach and leaned against the concrete border.

"No. Apparently I'm just easy to manipulate."

Maloney took a second to catch his breath, gradually easing himself more upright.

"Look," he said. "I know you've had a rough few days. I'm sure I didn't help much. You haven't slept, probably haven't eaten—"

"I slept plenty. Had a big meal earlier, too."

Maloney's palm patted the air, his long, lithe fingers making it a feminine gesture. "You're pissed. I don't blame you. You don't want to go back to prison." He paused, wincing as he sucked in a labored breath and let it blow out. "As far as I'm concerned, this is just between a coupla soldiers here. Whatever was eating at you, you got your poke in." Another grimace. "I'm willing to overlook it, pretend it didn't happen."

"I'm not."

"You better think about what you're saying, Hatcher. I can make things very, very difficult for you. Think about it. When are the marshals coming to pick you up?"

"Six a.m."

"I'm the one who set it up so you could just meet them, remember? Gave you an extra day for your statements and to wrap things up. I even made calls on your behalf, made sure everyone knew you weren't involved."

"Were you in love with her? Is that why? Or, in the end, was it the money?"

"Hatcher—"

"This view is from the photo on her wall. My message said meet me at 'our place.' I'd prefer it if you didn't insult my intelligence by trying to tap-dance your way out of it."

"I don't know what you think this proves."

"That call you just got"—Hatcher pulled a phone from his pocket, held it up—"I made it. Want to know how I got that number?"

Maloney said nothing.

"It was on Fred's call log. You remember him? The poor old schmuck whose throat you slit?"

A ship's horn blared across the river, faint in the distance. Maloney held Hatcher's gaze unsteadily, his focus jumping from one eye to the other.

"I learned a thing or two about TracFones," Hatcher continued. "Virtually untraceable. Provide you with anonymity, old-fashioned analog stealth in a digital world. But I realized to get the benefit you end up having to carry two phones, because it only works if no one knows the number. No one, except maybe your lover. And the rich psycho you let buy you."

Maloney turned to peer out over the water, eyes drifting over the cityscape. His face was suddenly drawn.

"It was you. You were the leak. Pretty clever. Limit everyone's access to what was going on, cover your tracks by pretending to be concerned about a mole. So, tell me. Why'd you do it?"

For several moments, Maloney didn't speak. He just stared into the night, seemingly transfixed by the lights of the city flashing in clusters off the water.

"I grew up not far from here, you know," Maloney said. "This was like my secret spot as a teenager. I used to come up here to just sit, do nothing. Take a magazine or a book and just get away from everything."

Hatcher listened, waited.

Maloney glanced down, lowered his voice. "Ever been in love?" he asked softly.

"She isn't in love with you, Maloney. She never was."

"It didn't matter. Just being with her, it was more than I ever thought I could get out of life. More than I ever had before, more than I ever dreamed of having."

"She was using you."

"That's what people do, isn't it? Use each other?"

"You let them kill those women, were going to let that thing do whatever it was going to do to that nun. A young girl. Christ, Maloney."

"It didn't start out like that. Deborah was . . . troubled. I found her here, ready to jump. I could tell."

Hatcher wagged his jaw slowly from side to side. "It was all a setup. Women like her, they have a way of getting to you."

"Carnates. I know." He angled his body to face Hatcher. "Jesus, it's not like I just decided to become a dirty cop, you know. It started out as a favor here and there. Little things. Nothing to lose sleep over. And she was always so appreciative. The sex—the sex afterward was incredible. Indescribable. I just couldn't say no. Then gradually the favors started getting more serious. I was scared of losing her. And, yeah, sure, soon money started coming. Money I could use to retire. She and I were going to be together. She promised. I couldn't help but believe her. Still can't."

"She was supposed to have sex with me, wasn't she? Wrap me around her finger the same way. That was the original plan, wasn't it?"

Maloney rotated back to face the skyline.

"But you threw a fit, didn't you? Made them change tacks. Got her to rub some of that seduction on Amy and me. Set it up so we would sleep together instead. Have Deborah disappear like she did, get Amy and me together in her apartment. Sexed her place up with pheromones or something. You dragged Amy into this, almost got her killed, just so you didn't have to think of Deborah touching another man."

Maloney stared across the water, shrugged meekly. "I wasn't going to let anything happen to Amy," he said, shaking his head.

"Which is why you had to set up Reynolds. Had to make it look like he was in on it. He wasn't attacking, he was just running, waving his arms. An injection of BOTOX in his voice box made sure he wouldn't be able to cry out or give anything away. The stories about him and the clown mask gave you a cover. You could kill him in front of me, in front of me and in front of Amy. I probably wasn't supposed to live, but that way there wasn't any chance that I could tell her anything different before I bought it. But you had to promise you'd be careful with your shots, didn't you? Valentine hated the thought of guns, stray shots or ricochets hitting the stained glass, maybe stressing out the Get or cluing me in on its weakness. And when things didn't go as planned, when I did figure that out, you started the fire. You were supposed to do that anyway, when it was finished, weren't you? To destroy as much evidence as possible."

"If I told you I was sorry, it wouldn't make a difference. The fact is, it's over. You can't prove any of it. And Valentine is dead. Whatever sick stuff he was up to died with him."

"You're wrong. I *can* prove it."

"And how's that?"

"I've been recording everything you said. Another wonder of modern cell phone technology."

Maloney's expression sagged. He blinked a few times, then seemed to buck up, almost relieved. He leaned in toward Hatcher, lowered his voice to a whisper. "What I just said won't be enough. Too ambiguous. The most you can do is be a pain in my ass. And since you're a convict, going back to prison in a few hours, you won't even be too much of that. Leave it alone, Hatcher. The smart play would be to not even try."

"It's not just what you said. It would be the call history on the cell phone you have that I could take off your battered body. The recording will get it started. Then the million little things you did will make the proof."

"I said—" Maloney paused, lowering his voice again. "I said I was sorry. It may not be much, but that's all I can do. You're a tough nut, I'll give you that. But you're venturing into my world now."

"You're right."

The words seemed to catch Maloney by surprise. His face shifted into a skeptical look, but a glint of hope flashed in his eyes.

"I already thought it through," Hatcher continued. "The only one I could trust giving this to would be Amy. She would start investigating. Maybe confront you, maybe not. But a guy like you, a dirty cop who's trying to cover his tracks, he'd be very alert. Constantly watching everyone around him. You'd figure out what she was up to. Then you'd kill her."

Maloney's eyebrows jumped. He started to object, but Hatcher cut him off.

"Oh, you'd agonize over it, or tell yourself you did. You wouldn't like it. You'd console yourself with the thought you really had no choice. But the decision has already been made. It was made the first time you looked the other way after realizing Valentine was killing hookers. The fact is, you were going to end up killing her anyway. She's too smart. It was only a matter of time before you decided she was a loose end."

A storm of emotions—anger, anxiety, fear, shame— seemed to roil behind Maloney's expression. Then just as quickly they were gone and his face was slack. He stood there in silence, shoulders drooping, the thunderheads dissipating into wisps of misty gray.

"You can say whatever you want," Hatcher said. "I turned off the phone."

"I suppose this is where you tell me you're going to keep the recording as insurance. That you'll find a way to use it if anything happens to Amy."

"No. That would just mean you'd be scheming to figure out how to kill me first. I decided the only way to protect Amy, the only way to set things right, was a suicide."

Maloney blinked, his head flicking back a bit. "You're going to kill yourself?"

"Not mine. Yours."

Maloney started to take a step away, but Hatcher was on him before he could react. He led with a solid palm strike to the cheek, snapping Maloney's head and connecting with the nerve that runs down the face. The detective's body shuddered, his eyes went blank, and he appeared stunned, almost paralyzed. Hatcher knew it would only last for a second, but that was all he needed. He grabbed Maloney by the collar of his coat, thrust his other arm between his legs, and heaved him over the ledge. Slender fingers raked his arms and shoulders, desperate attempts at clutching something, anything. Maloney tried to scream, but his voice seemed to catch and he only managed a weak *no!* His body shrank into the distance, almost like he was moving in slow motion. The wet, cracking thud, sudden and then gone, reached Hatcher's ears a second after Maloney hit the ground.

Hatcher pulled back from the rooftop's edge and sucked in a heavy breath.

Damn good thing I'm already going to Hell.

EPILOGUE

❖

THE STATIONERY WAS SMALL, WITH HIS MOTHER'S NAME across the top and a pink flamingo perched on one leg in the corner. Hatcher finished reading the handwritten letter just as he heard the mechanical moan of the cell-block door being opened and the clip of footfalls off the concrete.

He placed the letter back into its envelope and put it in the folder with the others. His mother had written him twice already. So had Amy. Two letters, two unopened envelopes. It was only a matter of days before Susan sent one. He wasn't sure whether he was going to open hers.

Gillis stopped in front of his cell and stared through the bars. He stood long enough to get Hatcher's attention before moving over a step and allowing an MP to unlock the cell door. The bars slid to the side. Another MP came into view leading Tyler Culp into the cell. The MP uncuffed Tyler's hands and backpedaled a couple of steps to allow the door to close. Tyler looked at Hatcher and tried to give what Hatcher assumed was intended as a menacing glare. He ended up looking more like a pale, constipated ape.

"Now, I won't be tolerating any trouble from you men," Gillis said. "No more fights. Understood?"

Tyler bared his teeth in a simpleton's grin. "Yes, sir."

Hatcher said nothing. He let his eyes drift over to Gillis. It was all a show. For the guards. Gillis the Innocent.

"And Hatcher, Colonel Owens told me to tell you he'd have his decision on a terminal furlough in a couple of weeks."

Right, Hatcher thought. Fat chance, especially after Gillis had been in his ear about it so much. He knew that's where Culp had been, giving a statement to Owens. Telling him everything Gillis had coached him to say.

"In the meantime, don't you start getting it in your head you're a short-timer. You've got six weeks, until the commander says otherwise. It's unclear what exactly you got involved in while you were gone, but it doesn't matter how many friends in the New York Police Department you made. You'll get no special consideration. The colonel and I are on the same page on that."

"Congratulations," Hatcher said.

Gillis gave a short speech about insubordination and letting it slide for the last time, then patted himself on the back for his leniency before leaving the cell block. Hatcher hadn't paid attention.

Tyler climbed into the bunk beneath Hatcher, gave a poke through the mattress. "So, I been meaning to ask you—did you get laid while you were out? Man, it seems like forever."

A good line popped into Hatcher's head, but he let it go.

"What was I talking about before? Oh yeah, praying mantises. You know, the females eat the males after they fuck? Bite their heads off, like I was telling you. Sometimes, they do it *while* they're fucking. The males go on living for a spell, continue what they're doing, not even knowing they're dead yet. Can you believe that?"

Yeah, Hatcher thought. I sure can.

"You know, you better start responding to me. Know

why? I've got permission to turn your life into a living hell, that's why."

Hatcher let out a short huff of a laugh. "It'll be good practice."

"What?"

"Nothing."

Tyler started rambling again about insects and animal sex habits, comparing women he'd been with to various members of the animal kingdom. Hatcher tuned him out, thinking about Amy. Tried to tell himself what they'd had was artificial. A chemical form of entrapment. No different than if they'd been drugged. He realized some of that might even be true.

He rolled onto his side, grunting a vague response to something Tyler said about females being deadlier than males. One thing he was certain was true was that Amy Wright was a cop and a good person. There was the rub. If he were to pick up where he left off with her, he would have to lie, a humongous whopper of a monster lie. She couldn't know, not ever. It didn't matter that he did it for her more than for himself. Telling her meant putting her in an untenable position, forcing her to choose, to compromise herself or else turn him in. But not telling her meant carrying around a huge secret, poisoning the relationship from the starting gun. Killing a cop—her boss, no less—wasn't some small detail. She would sense there was something large looming over them like a dark, swollen cloud, probably drag the truth out of him eventually. Sooner or later, all masks get removed. Then she would have to live with her choice. He couldn't do that to her. One of them was already going to Hell.

"Hey!" Hatcher said. He raised his voice far above his cellmate's drone. *"Hey!"*

Below him, Tyler cut himself off. Hatcher heard the mattress springs below creak.

"What?"

Hatcher flopped onto his back again and stared at the

ceiling. It felt like an absolute barrier pushing down on him, a divide with nothing beyond it. Nothing for him, at least. As if whatever future he had was on this side of it. The way the ground used to feel.

"If you're going to keep talking about sex," he said, closing his eyes. He thought of Garrett. Wondered if any of this meant that he'd see him again someday. If that was how any of it worked. "Tell me more about those ghost brides."

#1 *NEW YORK TIMES* BESTSELLING AUTHOR

DEAN KOONTZ

ALL NEW EDITIONS

WITH NEW AFTERWORDS BY THE AUTHOR

PHANTOMS	COLD FIRE
STRANGERS	HIDEAWAY
WATCHERS	DRAGON TEARS
LIGHTNING	MR. MURDER
MIDNIGHT	DARKFALL
THE BAD PLACE	TWILIGHT EYES

NOW AVAILABLE

penguin.com

M153AS1007

Don't miss the page-turning
suspense, intriguing characters,
and unstoppable action that keep
readers coming back for more from
these bestselling authors...

Tom Clancy
Robin Cook
Patricia Cornwell
Clive Cussler
Dean Koontz
J.D. Robb
John Sandford

**Your favorite thrillers
and suspense novels
come from Berkley.**

penguin.com

M14G0907